ABANDONED SHIPS, HIJACKED MINDS

Settler Chronicles Book 3

JEANNETTE BEDARD

Chapter One

Ignoring the knot churning in her gut, Margo gripped the shuttle's controls tighter and tried to focus—the three-dimensional world of flying was more disorientating than she'd expected. She glanced over her left shoulder and out the cockpit's side window. The planet's two suns sat high in the sky. Far beneath, the rubble-strewn surface of Thesan, grey as always, stretched to the horizon. She shifted her gaze out the forward window and saw more of the same landscape. The colony must be behind the shuttle.

Her hands started to shudder from the strain. *How do pilots make flying one of these contraptions look effortless?* Relaxing her grip on the w-shaped controls as much as she dared, she banked the shuttle to the left until their settlement came into view. The surfaces of the greenhouses reflected light from the suns overhead—a glittering effect that obscured the thick ring of the original spaceship, *Settler III*.

"Time to try a landing," said Max from the seat beside her.

He sounded calm for someone who'd spent the last week teaching beginners how to fly. Only the translucent sheen of moisture on his forehead betrayed any unease about her flying ability. She'd be surprised if Max had yet celebrated his nine-teenth birthday, but his mom, Ash Jones, had taught him both the necessary patience to teach beginners and essential flying skills.

"Where do you want me to put the shuttle down?" Margo returned her gaze to the landscape below. Extending out on opposite sides of the colony's original ring were two newly constructed long, thin greenhouses. Gan had described them as 'spokes on Settler's wheel' and the name had stuck. The nearest spoke was her greenhouse, where she nurtured banana plants and all manner of insects. She wished she was there instead of learning to fly a shuttle. Flying spaceships wasn't what she'd signed up for when she joined this mission.

"See the circle to the west of the colony's main entrance?"

"Yeah, I see it." The not-subtle flashing lights circling Max's practice landing pad made it impossible to miss—even in the bright sunlight. *Of course that's where I should land.* She edged the shuttle's nose down on a path for the circle.

"Lower the landing gear," said Max in a neutral tone.

Margo flipped a switch and the shuttle's landing gear extended beneath them. She held her breath until she heard the click that told her the skids were fully extended. On the dash before her, a green light blinked. The landing gear was down.

On the shuttle training schedule, Abigail was next. The head of terraforming's abrasive personality likely tested Max's patience more than Margo's lack of flying skills. She suppressed a chuckle as she checked her altitude. The thought of Abigail taking direction from a teenager seemed as ludicrous and sure to fail as the tentative friendship that she and Abigail had forged—yet the other woman had excelled at flying under Max's guidance.

An acrid scent pulled her attention from the landing pad. She sniffed, trying to get a handle on what it was. Twisting in her seat, she looked back into the aft section of the shuttle and saw a wisp of smoke snaking out of the port access panel. She blinked and the smoke vanished.

"What the…"

With a jerk, Margo struggled to level off the shuttle. She overcompensated, pointing the shuttle up towards the sky. Trying to keep her motions smooth in the midst of her rising panic, she brought the nose parallel to the horizon.

"Focus on your landing," coached Max.

"But something is burning!" Margo faced forward again as the knot in her gut tightened. "Smoke is coming out of the port access panel."

Max turned and glanced back. "I don't see anything," he said, checking the diagnostics screen in front of him. "The shuttle's fine. I'll take over."

"No, I got this." Margo swallowed. She couldn't smell smoke anymore. *Did I imagine it?*

Angling the nose down, she banked right to line up with the landing pad a second time. On the ground, their two shadows, one from each sun, moved in tandem with the shuttle, growing as they descended until the outlines merged. Over the undulating terrain, the combined shadows looked like a butterfly in flight—but the shuttle's utilitarian design was not remotely butterfly-like. Her chest tightened as her breathing sped up. *Why in the hell am I seeing butterflies everywhere I look?*

Max was talking, but she couldn't process his words; instead, her entire focus was on the shuttle's twin shadows. Watching the butterfly form made her insides churn. *Get a grip Murphy!*

She took a deep breath, then another, before her heart rate started to slow. Max wanted her to land and she wanted to prove she could do it. With a glance, she saw more sweat beading on Max's brow, making his dark skin look slick. Even after more than a dozen lessons, she hadn't grasped the basics.

Pushing her distracting thoughts away, she assessed the distance to the landing pad. The ground was coming up fast, and Max's hands hovered over the other set of controls ready to take over if she botched it. Taking a deep breath, Margo mentally went through the landing checklist Max had drilled into his students that week.

Keep the shuttle level. She feathered the controls until the horizon once again lined up with the artificial horizon on the heads-up display. Check. *Slow down.* She checked her speed, then decelerated some more. Check. The landing pad loomed dead ahead. She was perfectly lined up for a smooth landing.

"Okay, you're looking good," said Max. Margo detected more than a hint of tension in his voice. "Keep focused on where you want to put the shuttle down."

Fixing her gaze on the centre of the landing pad, she clenched her jaw. *I can do this.*

In a cascade of flashing wings, the landscape vanished behind a kaleidoscope of shimmering butterflies rising from the ground. She yanked the controls back, once again nosing the shuttle towards the sky. But the butterflies moved with her, clustering into a loose formation and heading towards them. It wasn't the first time hordes of these insects had come for her.

Not real, not real, not real.

"What are you doing?" Max's cool demeanour was gone. To Margo, his words didn't register.

The silver butterflies glinted in the intense light of the twin suns as they advanced on the shuttle. They moved with purpose—like they were on a vendetta. Their behaviour made no sense to Margo's lepidopterist mind—butterflies weren't evil and weren't anyone's worst nightmares—yet she knew they were coming for her. Her heart rate raced as she jammed the controls to the left to avoid the approaching swarm. The shuttle lurched sideways.

"I've taken control." Max's voice was higher pitched than normal as he levelled the shuttle.

"They're going to catch us!" exclaimed Margo, working her controls. Nothing happened.

"I locked you out," said Max, his voice calm again. "You're

freaking out again, Margo. For no reason. We're the only ones out here."

"But…" Margo's words trailed off as she dropped her hands and stared out the cockpit window. The plateau and white sky were empty. She gave her head a shake, but the view didn't change. Nothing outside looked remotely butterfly-like.

Her mind raced as she tried to figure out why anytime she did anything remotely stressful, butterflies appeared. *Am I losing my mind?*

"I'm okay now," she said, feigning confidence.

"Good." Max banked starboard then levelled out. Under his expert control the shuttle moved smoothly.

"Let me try again," Margo suggested, before glancing at her hands. They were shaking. *What the hell is wrong with me?*

"No, we're done." Max guided the shuttle past the training landing site and headed for the colony.

"How about we try again after lunch?" Perhaps if she spent some time before then focusing on calming her breathing, she could avoid any butterfly hallucinations.

"Look, I don't want to do this…" He paused and licked his lips.

In that moment, Margo remembered how young he was.

"I'm grounding you until Dr. Dogan clears you. Today wasn't the first time you did something weird."

"But the colony needs more pilots."

"And we only have the one shuttle," he said. "We can't afford to lose it."

"Crap," Margo muttered. She'd been avoiding talking with Paul Dogan since his arrival with the other insurgents-turned-refugees from the destroyed lunar base. *Had they arrived only a month ago?* It seemed like they'd been at the colony for much longer.

Max glance her way. "What?"

Crap! She'd talked out loud, now Max would think she was even crazier. "Nothing."

Margo intertwined her fingers and held her hands against her chest as Max angled the shuttle down. His motions were smooth, a sharp contrast to her own erratic attempts at flying. *Maybe I should give up on this pilot thing.* Even if she stopped hallucinating butterflies, she couldn't match his control over the craft— and likely never would. Swallowing back her disappointment, she watched the two-story colony loom ahead, the walls bleached white by the intense sunlight.

Too large for their hangar, the Insurgent's ship, the *Staffelwalze*, was parked just to the right of the twin hangar doors. More accurately, it was Ash Jones' ship, as she was the one who put her heart and soul into keeping it flying.

Once the ferry of diplomats travelling in style, it had long ago been decommissioned. For years it sat in a salvage yard until pressed into service once again. Its grey, chipped exterior clearly showed its age. The *Staffelwalze* wasn't the pretty ship it once was, but it was airtight and reliable.

As Margo attempted to distract herself by studying the ship, Max radioed the colony's Control Room. A moment later a hangar door opened on the side of the structure. As the door slid upwards and out of view, the dark interior was revealed. Without hesitation, Max flew the shuttle past his mother's ship and into the hangar, his landing perfect. As soon as they stopped, he began going through his post-flight checklist.

Margo unbuckled and stood, drawing a deep breath to say something. *Should I apologize?* She hesitated, but wasn't able to come up with appropriate words. Max didn't look up from the displays, so she turned aft and walked past the two benches that lined the interior walls of the shuttle. At the rear, the small vehicle-sized ramp remained closed.

Her eyes lingered on the cabinets left of the ramp as memories surfaced of two friends she'd lost—one perished in this very hangar on the day of their arrival, another died while flying this shuttle's twin the day she'd discovered their colony's saboteur. Biting her lip, she waited until the outside hangar door had closed and breathable air had circulated in before she opened the side door. The memories of everyone who'd died since departing Earth would continue to haunt her.

Margo descended the three steps to the hangar floor and strode away from the shuttle. Perhaps it was time to admit flying wasn't for her—her ability to focus was gone. She might even be losing her mind. Max was right, the colony couldn't risk letting an unfocused pilot control their only shuttle

Leaving the hangar bay, she turned right into the corridor that looped around the colony. She barely noticed the coloured stripe on the Loop's white wall, indicating the sector she was in, now red for operations. As she walked on autopilot towards her greenhouse as her mind raced with worry.

Her hallucinations started four months ago after she'd projected her consciousness to another solar system—the technique was only experimental and she'd projected for a much longer time than recommended. Paul Dogan, the brains behind consciousness projection, now resided on the colony meaning she could go to him for help. But, she doubted his chemical cocktails would fix her head and was too afraid to even try. In the corners of her peripheral vision, butterflies started forming anew.

"Stupid, bloody hallucinations just let me be!" She stopped and leaned against the purple strip of the domestic quarter and took a deep breath. "Get a grip, Murphy."

With a hand against the butterfly-shaped birthmark on the side of her neck, she took a second deep breath and tipped her head back until it made contact with the wall. Before that first projection, her husband Gary made her promise never to do it —a promise she broke. Squeezing her eyes closed, she thought about the apology she owed him.

Gary Holbrook was one of the original doctors—along with his twin brother—and the man she'd married to get on the mission to colonize Thesan. They'd been mismatched from the start and hadn't gotten along, but then they'd worked together to solve the mystery of the colony's saboteur. She'd even felt hints that a romantic relationship between them would be possible—but she'd blown any chance of that when she broke her promise. Since then he'd barely spoken to her.

"Hey," said Abigail.

Moving off the wall, she turned to see Abigail come out the Hub's doors just up ahead. Margo faked a casual smile at the woman whose dark skin had almost as many freckles as her pale skin.

Abigail's big hair and vivid magenta scarf paled next to her bold personality. Like Gary, Margo and Abigail hadn't hit it off in the first months of their colonization of Thesan, but Margo had come to realize the other woman's gruff exterior was a front. Abigail had turned out to be a solid friend.

"Hey," Margo said.

"Wanna come with me? Gan's latest brew is ready, and he's invited us for a taste test."

"It's not even noon." Margo tried to keep her tone light in a hope to avoid questions she wasn't ready to answer.

"So what?" Abigail shrugged.

"Aren't you scheduled for a flying lesson?"

"Max cancelled. You must've scared the kid." Abigail put a hand on her hip and stared at Margo. "Come on, Gan's still is set up in Engineering."

"I might come by later," said Margo.

"I doubt it." Abigail eyed Margo as if she were a lost cause. "You're going to go off and practice being a recluse."

"It's been that kind of day." Margo rubbed the side of her neck. For some reason, her butterfly-shaped birthmark itched.

"I'm heading back to the Centre Module in the morning," said Abigail. The Centre Module was a terraforming module about 10 kilometres away from their main colony. "Hannah's itching for me to return."

"I hear you've planted cold-hardy rye in the valley there."

"Yeah, the first shoots are just emerging from the soil."

"If I don't see you before you go, say hi to Hannah for me," said Margo.

"Remember, you promised to come out next week and check on the work in the caves." Abigail cocked her head.

A group of them had stumbled across the cave network while exploring the valley where the Centre Module of their spaceship had landed. Not only were the caves useful for additional storage, there were a seriously lucky find given the threat Nigel Maximillian West and The Conglomerate, which he controlled, had made against their home. Nigel had vowed to come for them and, when he did, Margo felt certain he'd annihilate each and every one of the colonists, as well as the refugees who'd recently joined them.

An image of Nigel's boyish features laughing at her surfaced in her mind. *I'll be back,* he'd said before vanishing. She shook her head, banishing his image. Then she realized she was just standing there staring at Abigail.

"Hello?" Abigail didn't hide her concern. "Thesan to Margo," she added, snapping her fingers.

"Right, the caves. Sorry. Don't worry, we'll still get to go spelunking." Margo's smile didn't feel sincere. For a moment, she entertained the idea of telling Abigail about her hallucinations. It would be nice to confide in someone, but Abigail was on a mission to taste Gan's home-brew.

"You'd better show up." Abigail called over her shoulder as she headed down the Loop towards engineering.

Once Abigail was out of sight, Margo continued in the direction she'd been going before. As she passed the main entrance to sickbay, the door slid open.

Please don't be Gary, please don't be Gary.

A lanky black man stepped through. It was Abeo, their medic, and he nearly walked into her. He put his a hand on her arm as he stepped around her. "Margo, did you get the message about the meeting?" he asked.

"What meeting?"

"Lucas called a meeting in the Control Room. Your name is on the list," he said. "We're going to be late."

Margo took a deep breath. "Dirty circuits! What is Lucas going on about now?"

"No idea," Abeo said as he started walking towards the Control Room.

Margo fell into step beside him, annoyed that her plan to go to her greenhouse and sulk had been thwarted.

Chapter Two

Gary dodged left as Neil swung a fist at his skull. Lunging forward, Gary tried to catch his twin with a hook, but Neil danced out of range. Gloved fists up, the two circled each other searching for opportunities to strike.

"Have you been to Margo's greenhouse?" Neil ducked under Gary's next punch.

"No," said Gary as he moved back.

Although he tried not to glance beyond the clear walls of the gym, Gary couldn't help it. In between dodging his twin's fisted gloves, he kept sneaking peeks towards the large courtyard that served as the nerve centre for their domestic existence. Surrounded by apartments, the space was thick with lush plants, including a greenwall by the main entrance. But the verdant greens didn't interest him; instead, he hoped to see a flash of iridescent blue. Margo's contraband butterflies had once occupied the space, but it had been almost four months since he'd seen one. He missed them. He also missed the butterflies' keeper.

Gary barely managed to block Neil's next punch. *Focus!*

"You sure hold a grudge," said Neil, sidestepping out of Gary's reach.

"A grudge?" Gary dropped his fists for a moment and rolled his shoulders. He asked the question despite knowing exactly what Neil was talking about. Every covert attempt Neil made to dig into Gary's love life—or lack of—left him with heightened tension in his shoulders. Sparring with his twin was supposed to lessen his stress, not increase it.

"Against Margo." Neil pushed his sandy blond hair out of his eyes with the back of his gloved hand. Then he circled around as Gary raised his guard.

"That's not true..." he knew his objection lacked sincerity.

"Bullshit," said Neil, attacking with a right jab and a left hook.

Barely in time, Gary danced out of reach.

After his failed strike, Neil backed away and dropped his arms. "There was a moment in time the two of you were practically inseparable."

Gary stopped moving and stared at his twin. Neil never let things go. "We were working together on something."

"You were working on something and Margo was working on something. Yet the two of you were together more than apart," said Neil.

"You're exaggerating." Gary raised his fists and shuffled back and forth on his feet, taunting his twin to attack.

Neil stepped forward without raising his hands, giving Gary an opportunity. He took it, landing an uppercut to Neil's chin. Gary dropped his fists and watched Neil stagger back a few paces before working his jaw back and forth.

"There was a spark between the two of you. I saw it. So did Amanda," said Neil. Amanda was Neil's pregnant wife, in charge of the colony's kitchen and one of the kindest people Gary had ever met. "And then you stomped on it with your grudge."

"I warned her not to do something, and she turned around

and did it," stated Gary, remembering the sinking feeling in his gut when he'd tried to bring Margo back from wherever her mind had gone. Her unconscious form had looked so helpless. He'd felt less than useless when he couldn't help her.

"You mean when she tried the experimental consciousness projection," said Neil.

"I told her about the risks." Gary stared down at the gloves enveloping his hands. For the millionth time, he tried to think of a way things could've gone differently. *Why didn't she heed my warning?*

"You wanted her to be safe."

"I thought I lost her once, and I didn't want to lose her again," snapped Gary. But now he'd said too much. He hadn't come here to open up to his meddling twin, no matter how much Neil wanted him to. He used his teeth to loosen the laces of his gloves, then yanked them off. "We're done."

He stormed out of the gym before his brother could say another word. *There was never anything between Margo and I. She's just a grubby entomologist who refuses to clean under her nails.* Gary wished that observation made him think less of Margo, the way it had when they'd first met. But now his mental slur against his wife rang hollow.

Outside the gym, he stopped and took a deep breath of moist air from the Hub's garden. As he exhaled, his whole body slumped forward and his gaze fell to his shoes.

He was deceiving himself. Margo was the most fascinating person on their colony—even with all the new arrivals. *How can I mend things now, after so much time has passed? Do I want to mend things?* Their rift was her fault—she'd broken her promise. Even she would admit that. *How can I trust her not to break a promise again?* He'd been-there-done-that with his first wife and he didn't want to have that kind of relationship with Margo. So, instead, he simply froze her out. But after four months...

He let out another long exhale. *I'm being a fool.*

"Gary!"

At the sound of his name, Gary glanced up. An urge to hide washed over him, but it was too late. Paul Dogan's eyes were already fixed on him as he raced over. The Insurgent doctor's mass of white hair and custom of wearing a lab coat made him look like a mad scientist—which wasn't far off the mark.

Letting out a sigh, Gary turned towards his colleague. He hoped Paul wouldn't go on and on and on again about his work, that was unpleasant in itself. But the fact that Paul's work revolved around consciousness projection, the very thing that nearly took Margo's life, made having to listen to the brilliant but boring man intolerable. Worst of all, Paul showed no remorse for the compromised health of his subjects as a result of his research—the man even wanted to continue the work.

Gary's jaw started to cramp and he realized he'd been gritting his teeth. Forcing himself to relax and appear casual, he half turned towards the Hub's exit.

"I'm on my way to grab a quick lunch," said Gary, seeking to pre-emptively escape. He started walking towards the dining room.

"I'll join you." Paul fell into step beside him. Gary exhaled sharply, but didn't say a word. "I need to discuss the colony's latest internal air quality readings."

"What about them?" asked Gary. Paul stuck his nose into every aspect of their small community, regardless of whether it was his business.

"There are some trace gases." As they walked, Paul pulled out his scroll and opened it up, displaying detailed readings from inside the colony.

Seeing no polite way to escape, Gary stopped beside him and looked at the screen. *Why am I being so polite?* For a moment, he pictured himself turning and walking away, only to have the image replaced by a memory of his mother's endless lectures about how he needed to be responsible.

"None of these are of any concern," said Gary, after scanning through the list of constituents. And none of these were Paul's business. Or Gary's, for that matter.

"True, but we don't need these gases. They offer no benefit. We should hunt down the sources and eliminate them."

"Sure," said Gary. "Why don't you go ahead and do that." What he wanted to say was *why bother?* Why waste valuable resources hunting them down and eliminating trace gasses that posed no risk? But Paul took Gary's neutral response for agreement and support, or so it seemed.

"Great. Now I need you to come with me and justify this work to Lucas. He wasn't willing to consider it when I spoke to him this morning."

"Why do you need Lucas' permission?"

"I'll need engineering support. When I asked Kat, Kate, Ka…" His voice trailed off as he struggled to remember the head of engineering's name.

"Her name's Kasume," Gary responded, resuming walking, Paul practically jogging at his side.

"Right, Katsume. Anyway, she said no. I need Lucas to order her to help me."

Gary rubbed the back of his neck. He could feel a headache coming on. "Why don't you just monitor these gases over time and see if they change?"

"It's not my job to do so. It's our leader's job to assign resources so that these sorts of details are benchmarked and tracked. Your leader isn't anywhere near as thorough as Iago."

Iago Ocon, leader of the recently arrived group of former insurgents held their unshakable respect. A former cop forced into hiding, Iago had gained fame by leading protests against The Conglomerate back on Earth—his final campaign unforgettable since it cost him his left arm. He'd leveraged his misfortune though. The replacement prosthetic, more statement than a masquerade for a missing limb, seemed to enhance his aura rather than detract from it, and people took note of everything the man said.

Gary didn't know Iago well, but it was clear the man was decisive. He didn't strike Gary as the sort to put up with too much of Paul's meddling. Perhaps Iago gave Paul free reign just to keep him out of his hair, or lack of since Iago was bald.

"And there's something else I wanted to ask you," said Paul.

Gary stopped to face the other man, and raised an eyebrow.

"I need you to talk to Margo."

Why does everyone want me to talk to Margo? Gary continued to stare at the other man, keeping his expression bland.

"Please talk her into letting me question her. Her consciousness projection was longer than any other. She might be experiencing multiple side effects."

"You'll have to ask her yourself," said Gary.

"She refuses to talk with me."

"That *is* her prerogative." Gary started walking again. "I'm getting something to eat." Paul moved quickly to keep up with Gary's long strides and the two of them entered the dining room together.

The scent of garlic and thyme tickled his nose as Gary gazed at the lunch buffet—he really was hungry. A potato and kale soup bubbled in a slow cooker beside bean cakes and salad —all the result of their gardening efforts. The food on their colony in this remote outpost of the galaxy seemed to be getting better every day.

Paul deflated at seeing the meal offerings. "Is all we're going to get around here peasant food?"

"Looks good to me," said Gary, taking a bowl and filling it with soup. Others started filing into the dining room behind them. "You can't have been engaging in fine dining hiding out on the moon."

"No, it was mostly hard rations there." Paul continued to stare suspiciously at the vegetarian fare.

In that moment, Gary realized he hated Paul. The man found fault everywhere and, frankly, Gary was sick of it. Amanda, Gary's sister-in-law, worked hard to ensure there was decent food on their table—even now while in the second trimester of her pregnancy. And the gardening efforts behind getting food into the kitchen and in their bellies consumed a great deal of the colonists' time. Plus, the fact that there was now a steady supply of home-grown food meant their colony had a good chance of succeeding—even with the additional mouths of the newcomers.

"I'm sure Amanda can find some hard rations for you." Gary scanned the dining hall, searching for a table with only one unoccupied chair, but the place wasn't busy enough yet.

"I'm going to go talk with Iago about the food." Paul turned and left.

Tension drained from Gary as he watched the scientist leave. The colony was feeling smaller and smaller with Paul around.

Gary slumped into a chair at an unoccupied table along the windows and looked into the interior greenhouse. The original colony was comprised of a ring-shaped space ship that had traveled from Earth—or, more accurately, been a sling-shot through space—to land on their destination, the planet Thesan with its two suns. Since landing less than a year before, the colonists had, as intended, covered the interior of the ring with a massive dome, creating a farm-sized greenhouse in the hollow centre.

In the four months since what would hopefully be their last major power outage, the greenhouse garden had blossomed. The willow grove around the pump house already obscured the structure while the pond boasted a thriving shoreline ecosystem, including a flock of contraband ducks. Crops ranging from potatoes to beans to amaranth to edible flowers, and even an extensive collection of herbs, now filled the space, creating an oasis reminiscent of an Earth-based farm.

Margo's bee hives drew his attention—A colony of bees within the colony of humans. He watched the chaotic flight patterns of the pollinators as he sipped his soup. The sight of the bees brought his thoughts back to Margo. He'd been avoiding her, and he couldn't do that forever. Their colony was simply too small. He needed to go visit her greenhouse.

But, as he finished his soup, he still didn't know the answer to the question he'd been asking himself for weeks. *What do I say to her?*

Chapter Three

The Control Room buzzed with activity when Margo followed Abeo in. Stopping at the door, she cocked her head to one side. A menacing vibe filled the space.

People were gathered in a number of small clusters—former insurgents stuck with former insurgents and colonists stayed with other colonists. The hum of hushed conversation seemed furtive, as though the occupants of the room were trading secrets she wasn't privy to.

A shiver skittered up her spine as she wondered again what this meeting was about. If nothing else, it was a distraction from the flawed inner workings of her mind. As a distraction was welcome, she began to study her environment through a scientific lens.

As the brain of their colony, the Control Room consisted of a series of three platforms, each two steps below the one above. Margo stood on the top level at the entrance to the room, which was open and uncluttered to allow a large number of people to gather. The middle platform, contained workstations in a semicircle facing away from the entrance and towards the large screens mounted high on the far wall. On the bottom level a transparent wall separated the servers from the rest of the room.

Lucas Ordaz stood on the middle platform, his jet black hair in need of a cut and his dark eyes fixed on the data displayed on the largest of the wall-mounted screens. Bad luck made Lucas their colony's third Commander in as many months.

From Margo's position a level above him, he seemed shorter than he actually was—and a little less handsome than he'd been when they'd arrived. Their fearless leader's nose hadn't healed straight after the second time it had been broken, or, more precisely, after he'd removed himself from medical intervention. But, the crookedness tempered his boyish look, and gave him a much-needed boost of authority.

He'd had a rough ride at first. But over the last few months, he proved himself capable. When he'd asked Margo to be the colony's Chief of Security based on her previous military career, she reluctantly—no, foolishly—accepted. Seeing her hovering at the door, Lucas gave Margo a half smile.

Turning, Lucas bent over the console occupied by Vince, the teenage hacker who'd arrived with the insurgents. He sat characteristically hunched in front of his terminal with the hood of his jacket pulled over his purple hair. As he listened to Lucas' instructions, he nodded and his fingers raced over the touch screens.

Vince's technical skills extended to robotics and the elegant prosthetic arm worn by Iago was a fine example of his skill. Stepping further into the room, Margo glanced around for the insurgent leader, but was relieved to note his conspicuous absence.

"This is bat-shit crazy," muttered Abigail from where she leaned against the wall.

Margo looked over. Abigail stood next to Gan and Iva, the generously proportioned woman's stature making Gan and Iva look downright petite. Despite her cropped hair and boyish clothing, Iva looked utterly feminine while the grease stains on

Gan's clothing suggested he'd just stepped out of the machine shop—which was likely true. Lanky and tall, Abeo stood on Gan's other side. Other than Lucas, the five of them were the only ones from the original *Settler III* mission.

Margo leaned against the wall beside Abigail. "What's going on?" she asked.

"Rumour is our dumb-ass leader wants to send us off on a dumb-ass rescue mission." Abigail crossed her arms across her chest. "As to why he called a last minute meeting, I'm baffled."

When scientists discovered the wormhole connecting Earth's solar system to Thesan's, they'd mistakenly concluded it provided a link to three different solar systems depending where Earth was in its orbit around the sun. They contracted The Conglomerate to explore all three systems with robotic probes. After a thorough exploration, The Conglomerate realized the wormhole only went to a single system—but they kept that information to themselves while publicly confirming the original scientist's hypothesis.

Five years before, Earth's Colonizing Counsel sent the first of three colony ships through the wormhole, followed soon after by the second, and then the third, the one that had taken Margo and the others to Thesan on *Settler III*. They'd only recently learned that all three colonizing missions had, in fact, gone to different planets in the same solar system as Thesan. Ever since learning this, Lucas continuously tried to contact the others.

"Did we finally hear back from one of the other colonies?" Margo knew Lucas held hope others were out there.

"No. That's why it's a dumb-ass idea," said Abigail.

The ongoing silence from the other colonies was worrisome. Margo wanted to make contact with them as bad as Lucas did. For a moment, she let her mind wander to what it would be like to be on one of those two colonies that failed—a fate that could have been theirs if their saboteur had succeeded.

A schematic of their solar system flashed up onto the main display screen. The periodic wormhole which all three *Settler* missions traveled through was clearly marked along with their twin stars and neighbouring planets.

"Just because there hasn't been a word out of either of them, doesn't mean they're not there," said Margo.

"Blind luck is the sole reason we survived. If the other colonies had even half the troubles we've had, they're likely all dead."

Margo turned to look at Abigail. "We need to know for sure, don't we? There could be someone out there to save."

"Then it's up to the Colonizing Counsel to look for them. They're the ones who sent them. They're responsible. Not us."

"But there hasn't been a comms window since we found out the other two colonies are in our system," said Margo. An open wormhole was needed for Earth-Thesan communications. To further their control, The Conglomerate led everyone to believe that the wormhole opened once every five months when, in reality, it could be opened at any time.

"The Conglomerate knows we're on to them. They're not going to open the wormhole and risk us telling their secrets."

"They might. They need to maintain the lie that the wormhole opens at regular intervals," said Margo. "People on Earth would protest if they knew the properties of the wormhole operation were a sham."

"Like The Conglomerate gives a shit about protesters," scoffed Abigail, her gaze drawn to the remaining screens as they came to life. "I vote *we* request the Colonizing Counsel to force The Conglomerate to give us control of that wormhole."

Margo stared up at the solar system image. Abigail was right —it was not in the best interest of The Conglomerate to open the wormhole and allow Thesan to communicate with Earth. Her gaze fell on Iago as he marched into the room and stopped at the top of the first platform.

Iago put his fists, one mechanical and the other flesh, on his hips. Even though he'd yet to speak, everyone shifted their attention him. As he turned, he made eye contact with everyone one-by-one. When his gaze met Margo's, he winked.

Margo curled her lip in disgust. She'd turned down his advances, repeatedly, but he wouldn't take no for an answer. It wasn't that Iago wasn't attractive—his exceptional looks would've fit in amongst the ancient Nubian kings—and he oozed sex appeal. The problem was, over inflated confidence turned Margo off. He assumed she would welcome his advances and just couldn't accept her disinterest.

"Good. Everyone is here." Iago's deep, musical voice resonated throughout the room. He stepped down to the middle platform, stopping next to Lucas, seeming to enjoy towering over the short-statured colony leader. With a grand gesture with his prosthetic arm towards the main monitor, he said, "We're going to go save your fellow colonists. Lucas will explain the plan."

Lucas grimaced. Even from across the room, Margo could tell it annoyed him to have his meeting hijacked by Iago.

"For those of you who are new, I'll start at the beginning," said Lucas in a patient tone, so different from Iago's arrogance. "In closer orbit than Thesan are three planets. Closest to us is a cold Neptune planet, massive and gaseous, not a candidate for a colony. But Geb, its moon, has a solid surface. That's where *Settler II* went." As Lucas spoke, Vince highlighted the relevant locations on the screen. "Nak, the next world in, is opaque to our sensors. But we know it has a solid surface. That was *Settler I's* destination. I've been…"

"Okay, now we have the background." Iago cut Lucas off. Lucas pressed his lips together, but said nothing. "Ash, what's the state of the *Staffelwalze?*"

Ash Jones stood off to the side with her son and co-pilot, Max. Her closely cropped, black hair and her solid stature gave her an air of competence. When Margo had projected her consciousness into Ash's body, she was awed by the other woman's raw physical strength.

Margo let her eyes roam over the others in the room as Ash explained the navigation issues. Yuko, the mean-spirited insurgent astrophysicist who was Iago's devoted side-kick stood, as usual, near Iago. At the workstation next to where Yuko stood, Vince had looked up from his display. The awkward programmer seemed to be trying to catch Max's attention, but Max's focus remained on his mother.

"Considering the current planetary alignments," Ash explained, "the next two days are our best window for starting this journey. With a small crew, no more than ten and our upgraded ion drives, a four-week loop would take us by both colony sites and back home again."

"I'll lead the mission. We leave tomorrow," said Iago, his deep voice booming in the room.

Lucas rubbed his hand over his face, then looked over at Margo. He shrugged.

Margo knew, as did everyone on Thesan, that Iago was making a play for the position of colony commander. He might be charismatic, but the man lacked subtlety. But when the time came for the Thesan colony to vote for their leader and assuming everyone who came with Iago voted for him, Lucas would be out—the 36 insurgents outnumbered the 29 colonists.

"From my group, Ash, Max and Yuko will go," said Iago.

Yuko perked up at her name, replacing her normally sour expression with a smug smile.

"I want Gan along as engineer. With his recent work on the ion drives, he's an asset to any off-world mission." Iago's arrogant tone nullifying the compliment to Gan.

Margo heard Gan sigh. She suspected he wouldn't be keen to go, considering how morning sickness had hit his wife, Lily— her pregnancy was only slightly less advanced than Amanda's.

"And I want Margo." He looked right at her, his eyes lingering too long.

Despising the double entendre in his choice of words, Margo glared at him. She abhorred the thought of being confined in close quarters with Iago. It was bad enough evading his advances in the relatively spacious colony; it would be exhausting on the tiny *Staffelwalze*. "Why would an entomologist be required on an exploratory rescue mission?"

"You are head of security," Iago responded.

"All the more reason to remain on Thesan," said Margo.

"I want you to go." Lucas took a step towards her. "You have a wide range of skills that might be needed—I don't know what you guys might face out there."

With a sigh, Margo nodded.

Everyone's attention shifted back to Iago as he pointed to Abeo. "You will act as our medic."

"Take Abigail, too. She's familiar with the life-support systems on the *Settler* ships and can provide back up for Gan," said Lucas. "Plus Iva should go. She's knows the *Settler* computer systems inside and out. You don't know what you'll find out there."

"Nine crew, plus you and Max." Iago looked at Ash. "Does that satisfy your definition of 'a small crew'?"

"We can accommodate that number," Ash replied, her face betraying no emotion.

"Good. Arrange the supplies we'll need," said Iago to Ash, then he turned to address the group. "We will find these people." As though his saying it made it true, Iago strode out of the room. Everyone remained silent as they watched him go.

Gan turned to Margo, Abigail, Iva and Abeo. "Lily will hate this," he said in a low voice as the others circled around. "But, Iago's right, I'm the only expert on ion drives around. I wouldn't feel right staying behind when I should be tending those engines."

"As I said before, this will be a clusterfuck!" Abigail's nostrils flared as she spoke. "I've gotta call Hannah. And don't you dare let them leave without me." She charged out of the room, plowing through the insurgents filing out of the room. Margo almost smiled, Abigail was playing tough, but clearly she wanted to go.

With a nod to Gan, Margo and Iva, Abeo followed Abigail.

"We're all pissed about being volun-told for this." Iva looked over to where Yuko worked on a console and frowned. "Being stuck in a confined space with her will drive me nuts."

"We just got this place working right," said Gan. "I don't want to leave. We've been trying to make contact with them for months and haven't heard a word. And a part of me doesn't want to know what terrible thing might've happened to the other colonies."

"Me neither," said Iva.

"Someone needs to find out what happened to those people, even if all we find is ghost ships. It might as well be us," said Margo. Inwardly, she wished that the 'someone' didn't include her—she'd much rather stay and tend to her greenhouse. "At the very least, it'll give the people back on Earth closure."

"I'd better go tell Lily," said Gan in a disappointed tone. "I'm going to have to think of a way to make this up to her."

"I should pack," said Iva.

"See you on board," said Margo as the other two left. She looked up at the main screen, now displaying Ash's course. First up was the mini Neptune's moon. It was going to be a long trip.

Chapter Four

With a mug of steaming coffee in hand, Gary walked into sickbay after finishing his lunch. The waiting room always calmed him—as it was designed to do. The ceiling glowed softly, casting a diffuse warm light over everything. The curved, off-white walls created a cozy, amoeba-shaped space lined with inviting benches. Moss green cushions the same shade as the floor added to the soothing ambience of the room.

Radiating out from the waiting area were a series of examination rooms, storerooms and offices. Gary passed the door leading out to the Hub as he went straight through to his office, leaving the door open, and set the coffee down on his desk. Taking a seat, he opened up his scroll to look at the schedule for the afternoon.

A half-hour later, Abeo stuck his head in the door. "Julien's here for his appointment. I've put him in examination room one."

"Thanks," said Gary.

The eleven-year old boy hadn't come to Thesan on the colonizing mission, but had been brought by his mother three months later when she'd been banished from The Conglomerate ship orbiting the planet. Since her death, the boy was cared for mostly by Amanda and Neil. Up until a month ago when the insurgents arrived, he'd been the only child on the colony, but now he had Dr. Dogan's two children as playmates.

Abandoning the dregs of his coffee, Gary picked up his scroll and went to see the boy. When he entered the examination room, Julien sat on the table behaving as though he was right at home, which, based on his ongoing need for medical intervention, was likely true.

Despite Gary's medical background, the boy was the only full albino he'd ever met. Julien's pigment-less skin put him at an extreme risk of sun burns if he'd stayed on Earth. But, it was the genetic modifications that was the cause of most of the boy's problems, from his distorted eyesight, to his once regular seizures. The Conglomerate scientists had tinkered with his DNA to give Julien the ability to manipulate an ancient, dangerous artifact that they themselves could not touch. Now, he could not only touch the artifact without going insane, he could view possible futures and he'd brought the artifact with him—a secret Julien had shared only with Gary.

"At least here, I won't be stepping outside," Julien said with a smile.

"Still reading minds then." Gary returned the boy's smile even though Julien's uncanny ability unnerved him. "Lay back and I'll scan you."

Julien lay down on the table, leaving his goggles on. He was small for his age, and looked even smaller laying on the adult-size examination table.

"Knock, knock." Julien had an unending supply of knock-knock jokes.

"Who's there?" Gary turned to the console and flipped a switch to start a general scan. The scanning bar descended from the ceiling and began to sweep over the boy from head to toe.

"Boo," Julien said, staying still without being instructed.

"Boo who?" The scanner finished and retracted back into the ceiling.

"What? Are you hurt?" Julien laughed at his own joke. Now that the scan was complete, he knew he was allowed to move and turned towards Gary. "You didn't think that one was funny."

"True," said Gary. He transferred the results of the scan to his scroll and started reading the results. "I've heard it before."

"I guess I need to work on my material." Julien sighed. "She won't make it back unless you go too."

Gary shifted his gaze from the scroll to the boy. This wasn't the first time Julien had casually delivered an ambiguous prediction. Gary had no idea what the boy was prophesying about this time. Julien's latest predictions tended to be accurately timing when fresh baked goods were available (which was always good to know) but his earlier prophecies were serious, including his mother's death.

"Who won't make it back from where?" Gary asked.

Julien's prismed goggles caught the overhead light as he moved his head slightly. Even though Gary couldn't see the boy's eyes, he knew Julien was staring back.

"Margo."

Gary froze momentarily, then decided to change the topic. The boy wasn't always right. "Dr. Dogan's therapy seems to be working." He pointed to the scan results on his scroll.

Julien had changed dramatically in the month since Paul's arrival. Originally, the boy had been sickly and suffered regular seizures. Now, alabaster skin aside, he looked healthy. He'd even grown a centimetre since his last scan.

"How have you been feeling?"

"I like having others to play with," Julien said with a lopsided grin. "I run and run after them, all over the colony. I never could've kept up with other kids before."

Gary smiled at him. "That's great. The best thing you can do is keep running."

"You're not going to do more tests?" He sat up, swinging his legs of the table and facing Gary.

"I think you already know the answer to that one."

"So I can go?"

When Gary nodded, Julien jumped down from the examination table and bolted from the room. Then he stuck his head back in.

"I'll touch the cube again and see if there's anything that can help you," the boy said.

Gary tilted his head and pursed his lips. "What are you talking about?"

"For your trip."

"What trip?" asked Gary, looking down at his scroll. The boy tended to be confusing when he talked about possible futures.

"You're going to go with her. She'll never ask, but she needs your help," said Julien.

"Who?" Gary looked up, but the boy was gone.

Gary realized Julien must be talking about Margo again. *Is Margo taking a trip to the Centre Module? And is the boy trying to play Cupid and get us back together?*

With a sigh, Gary added a few notes to Julien's medical file. No matter what Julien might be wishing for when it came to Gary and Margo's relationship, Gary knew it was wasted effort to salvage any hope on that score.

An hour later with sickbay empty of patients, Gary sat slouched on one of the waiting room benches across from Neil, who was lounging Roman style. Gary had his scroll out, and they were discussing their medical cases when Abeo returned from the meeting Lucas had called in the Control Room. The medic looked sullen as he flopped his lanky frame down on an empty bench.

"Is there a problem?" asked Gary, rolling up his scroll.

Abeo sighed. "Iago ordered me to join their mission to investigate what happened to the other colonies."

"So the rumours are true," said Neil, sitting up.

"We aren't so busy here that we can't spare you. And they'll need someone with medical experience along," said Gary.

"I suppose, but we'll be gone at least a month. It's just that Omolola and I want to start working on…" Abeo's voice trailed off to nothing.

Neil grinned. "You're wanting to follow in Amanda and my footsteps and start a family."

"I hear the *Staffelwalze* has a reasonable medbay," said Gary. So far, he hadn't had a reason to set foot on the antiquated vessel.

"It does now, thanks to our printers. And I helped set it up," said Abeo, regaining his composure. "It's sufficient—but not state-of-the-art."

Neil leaned forward. "Who's all going?"

"Iago will lead the mission, with Ash and Max as pilot and co-pilot. Iago wants Yuko along, of course, because she never questions his orders. Gan, Iva, Abigail and Margo are all also going. And then me as the medic."

"That's the trip Margo's going on?" muttered Gary. Julien's prophecy suddenly made sense. Gary stood and walked out of sickbay, ignoring Neil questioning where he was off to in such a hurry.

Gary was half-way to the Control Room when he realized what he intended to do—volunteer to take Abeo's place. And it wasn't just because Julien had said he needed to go, although the kid's prophecies and predictions were worth taking seriously. But Margo would be gone a month, if not longer. He wouldn't be able to live with himself if something happened to her and he wasn't there to help.

He found Lucas alone in the Control Room sitting at the main console on the middle platform

When Gary entered, Lucas turned. "Hey. Is there something going on?"

"I want to take Abeo's place." Gary stopped at the top of the stairs.

"Is he unfit for this mission?" asked Lucas.

"He doesn't want to go, and he should stay here with Omolola," said Gary. "It just…" He almost told Lucas about Julien's prophecy. "With Dr. Dogan here, we have three doctors. Thesan doesn't need three. And maybe the mission itself doesn't merit a doctor, either. But who knows what we'll find at the colony sites?"

Lucas raised an eyebrow. "I assume you heard Margo's going."

Gary put a hand on his hip and tried to appear nonchalant. "Yes. So?"

Lucas stood and climbed up to the top level beside Gary. "My guess is that you're worried about Margo. Fair enough considering you two are married."

"True," said Gary in a flat tone.

Lucas nodded. "Let Abeo know you're taking his place," he said before returning to his console.

Gary paused for a moment, staring at the back of Lucas' head. *What am I getting myself into?*

Chapter Five

Even though she wanted to be alone after the meeting, a rumbling stomach sent Margo to the dining room instead of her greenhouse. When she arrived, all the chairs were atop the tables and the floor glistened from a recent mopping. Lunch was long over.

Beside the door to the kitchen was a long counter where food was put out for meals. It was clean and empty—except for a slow cooker. After retrieving a bowl from the shelf above, Margo removed the lid from the pot. A spicy aroma wafted up with the steam—Amanda's corn chowder flavoured with fresh basil and cilantro. Salivating in anticipation, she filled her bowl.

Cupping her bowl of chowder with both hands, she strolled out into the central greenhouse. Taking a seat on the ground, she relaxed back against the outside wall of the dining room—a wall that once had been an exterior wall of their donut-shaped spaceship. As she ate, she glanced around the greenhouse. It didn't have the same welcoming vibe as hers, but it was still a nice place to be.

Gan and Lily walked hand in hand by the duck pond. Lily's small baby bump was easily visible on her slight frame. The two of them were engrossed in conversation and didn't appear to notice her. Watching them felt like an intrusion, so she shifted her gaze to the kitchen garden and the bees buzzing through Amanda's herbs.

After setting her empty bowl down, she leaned her head back against the wall and let her mind drift to the upcoming mission. She wished there was another option to investigate the silent colonies that didn't involve leaving her greenhouse or traveling under the leadership of Iago.

Maybe they could delay the mission and give Gan time to make an autonomous craft that could investigate for them. Or they could send a message to the Colonizing Counsel asking for help, like Abigail had suggested—but, they would have to wait until the wormhole was open and whether the Counsel could help or not was another matter.

The manufactured breeze brought an unpleasant whiff from the duck pen, dragging her back to the present and the realization that investigating in person was the right thing to do. Collecting her dishes, Margo got up and returned to the dining room.

Realizing she wouldn't have the benefit of Amanda's cooking, she said to herself, "If I must go, I can at least ensure we aren't on a four-week hard rations diet."

As Margo entered the kitchen, Amanda looked up from her scroll and smiled. She sat perched on a stool at the worktable. Her baby bump, significantly bigger than Lily's, made her position seem precarious. Her black hair looked glossier than usual and her dark skin was more vibrant—being pregnant agreed with her.

"Hi. Are you here to check up on the food supplies for your trip?" asked Amanda.

Margo smiled and pulled up a second stool. "I thought I could give you a hand."

"Iva and Max have requested six months of hard rations," said Amanda.

"Six months? For a one-month mission?"

"I agree. Overkill. But you know Lucas. He's nothing if not cautious." Amanda noticed Margo's grumpy look. "But, you won't want to dig into the hard rations unless you absolutely have to."

"You read my mind," said Margo with a smile. She'd eaten more than her share of hard rations back in her army days. Even in they encountered an apocalypse, she wasn't certain she could stomach them. *Maybe if I were starving. Maybe… probably not.*

"I'm putting together a basic meal plan that will work with the *Staffelwalze*'s small galley. Really, just frozen dinners and a few other things. There won't be much variety, I'm afraid." Amanda sighed. "Could you help me box up some ingredients? My feet are killing me."

"Of course. What do you need?" Margo stood.

"Let's start with some carrots. They're in a bin to the right of the door in the cold room. And onions."

When Margo went into the cold room, her jaw dropped. The space was filled almost to capacity with fresh vegetables. Bins and burlap sacks overflowed with produce, from root vegetables like potatoes and turnips, to vine ripened vegetables like squash and tomatoes, to ears of corn and mounds of Brussel sprouts. Dried bunches of bean plants and amaranth hung from the ceiling, awaiting threshing. This, Margo knew, was only one of their many food storage spaces. *Are they all this full?*

"I had no idea we'd been this successful with our crops," she called back to Amanda.

"Food keeps coming in," said Amanda. "We've started packaging up some of it for long term storage. Hell, with all the Brussel sprouts we've harvested the last couple of days, we could eat nothing else for weeks."

"Please don't. Brussel sprouts may be the only thing worse than hard rations," said Margo as she continued looking around. The bins of vegetables were right where Amanda had said. She stacked the onion bin on top of the carrots and picked them both up. Back in the kitchen, she put them on the worktable.

"They're already cleaned. All we need to do is chop them into rounds."

Working in tandem, they chopped the vegetables. Margo liked that Amanda didn't need to fill the silence, and she felt the welcome relief of her body relaxing. The anxiety around her imminent trip receded into the background. Even her fear of Nigel making good on his threat to come for her waned.

"Why don't you join me and Neil in our quarters for dinner tonight?" said Amanda, breaking the silence. "It'll be a family affair as Gary's coming, and I'm making his favourite lentil stew."

Margo's hands paused as she stared down at her knife and the pile of orange circles. She liked Neil and Amanda. Now that Julien lived with them, she'd even come to appreciate the boy's humour and had a few knock-knock jokes ready. But dinner with Gary? That could be awkward. She hadn't spoken to him in months and knew he was still mad at her.

"Julien's been asking about your bananas. If any are ready, you could bring them along."

"No bananas yet," she said, resuming her chopping. Her mind scrambled to come up with a reasonable excuse to refuse Amanda's invitation. "But the plants are doing well, so it won't be long."

"Are you and Gary still not speaking?" Amanda asked without glancing up from her work.

"Has Gary said anything?"

"No, you're the one topic he consistently avoids," answered Amanda. "I suspect he actually wants to get back together with you. But since he's a hard-headed putz holding a grudge, he likely has no idea how to make that happen."

"We were never *together*," Margo stated in a vehement tone, venting her frustration on the pile of carrots in front of her.

"Well, *try again*, then," Amanda conceded.

Chop! *Gary is holding a grudge all right!* Chop! *He is definitely a hard-headed putz!* Chop! *I broke my promise for good reason!* Chop!

Margo paused and put the knife down, taking a moment to inhale slowly. If she wasn't careful, she'd chop a finger off and that would force her to see him. She thought again about her complicated relationship with Gary. She'd never apologized to him for breaking her promise. *But why should I? He must know I had good reasons.* And, admittedly, she was as hard-headed as him. She'd been hiding in her greenhouse for the last month.

She comforted herself with the knowledge that at least while she was off searching for lost colonists, she could take the time to figure out how to deal with him. Knife poised over a final carrot, she paused and wondered why she suddenly felt dejected.

"That'll do," said Amanda as she scooped the carrot rounds into a big bowl.

"Thanks for the dinner invitation, Amanda, but I still have a lot to do to get ready," said Margo.

"Perhaps when you get back," said Amanda.

They both turned when Julien marched into the kitchen. The boy headed straight for Margo as though on a mission. His prismed goggles caught the light, refracting rainbows around the space.

"Margo," he stated in a tone too serious for a child.

"Hi Julien. What's up?"

"Can we talk?" asked the boy. Margo glanced at Amanda and lifted an eyebrow. Amanda shrugged in response.

"Okay, how about we go visit the ducks?" she suggested.

"Hey, good plan. I have scraps for them." Amanda went over to another counter and brought back a pail.

Margo took the handle and left the kitchen with Julien glued to her side. Once they were out in the central greenhouse, she asked, "What did you want to tell me?"

They stopped at the gate to the duck pen, the gaggle of quacking ducks waddling over to greet them.

"I saw something," he said.

Margo didn't speak. She had no idea how he did it, but the boy could predict future events. He'd done it in the past and he seemed to be doing it again now.

"You can't leave on the *Staffelwalze*," he said with a frown, throwing a crust to the eager ducks.

"Why not?"

"Before, I thought it was only you who was in danger, but now I see everyone is." Julien's manner was far older than his years. "He's waiting for you, and he won't care about hurting the others to get to you."

A chill crawled up Margo's spine. He couldn't mean Nigel. Could he? "Who's waiting for me?"

"I don't know, I just…" He paused for a moment as he distractedly threw more scraps to the ducks. He stopped suddenly and twisted his little body so he could look up at her. "I'm sorry, Margo. I can't control what I see."

"I know. Tell me about what you saw," said Margo, pretending seeing the future didn't creep her out. "Do you see any details?"

"Some, but they don't make sense. I see a storm, rotten vegetables, and a woman without eyes. But I don't understand what all that means," he complained.

Images of storms and rotten vegetables didn't phase Margo. But the woman without eyes? She shuddered. When they'd been speaking, Gary told her about the patients he'd seen at his mother's medical clinic—all of them were suffering ill effects after participating in a consciousness projection experiment, one of which included clawing out their own eyes.

Margo schooled her voice so as not to allow it to tremble. It wouldn't be fair to Julien to let him know that his words terrified her. "What makes you think these things are dangerous?" she asked.

"I just know." He looked down at the ducks. "You know,

there's no one at the other colonies to save. You have to convince Iago not to go. You have to."

Margo sighed. "But, Iago won't cancel anything based on what you say. Besides, we need to go to know what happened to them."

"Then you stay behind," the boy pleaded. "People are going to die. I don't want it to be you." With that, Julien turned and ran back the way they'd come.

She frowned. *The boy isn't always right.* Something in her gut started to quiver and she gripped the bucket's handle tighter. With a sigh she upended the bucket over the fence. Frantic fowl converged on the pile of food, quacking as they jostled for the scraps.

Turning, she looked back at the door to the common room. Julien had already vanished. She had to admit he was right about one thing: nothing felt right about the rescue mission—yet she knew it was necessary and right now presented the best window to get to the other planets.

"I've got to go," she whispered to the ducks. "Hopefully, Julien's visions don't mean what he thinks." Rubbing her butterfly birthmark on the side of her neck, she headed back inside.

Chapter Six

Margo lay on her back on the floor in front of a blazing fire. The radiating heat warmed the skin of her face while the flames danced like the campfires her dad used to make. The air even smelled the same. As she rolled onto her side, the thick Persian carpet covering the floor felt soft against her cheek. She ran a palm along its plush fibres and marvelled at the deep indigo and maroon designs.

Glancing up, she inhaled sharply. A snarling tiger stared down at her. For a fraction of a second, she thought it was real. But it was just the dead animal's head mounted above the mantle. It had been distastefully frozen in time, forced into maintaining a perpetual snarl as it overlooked the chamber. It made her skin crawl.

As she sat up, she pushed hair out of her face and glanced around. A sense of deja vu swept over her. Where am I? *Rising to her feet, she realized the surroundings were familiar, but she didn't know why.*

Two armchairs upholstered in brown leather, their wooden arms and legs carved with an odd collection of lions, tall ships and anchors, were positioned on either side of the hearth. Beside each chair sat an elegant side table. Portraits in elaborate gold frames depicting stern men from a bygone era filled the walls. Behind the pictures, glossy green wallpaper embossed with shiny crowns covered the walls, clashing with the indigos and maroons of the rug. Opposite the fireplace someone had arranged half a dozen ornately carved wooden chairs.

"I've got you now, butterfly girl."

Margo spun around. Nigel Maximilian West, the director of The Conglomerate and the man who'd orchestrated all the trouble her colony had endured, reclined in the chair next to the fire with a pipe in one hand and a cut-crystal tumbler of amber liquid in the other. Dressed for a period movie set in the nineteenth-century, he even wore a cravat cinched around his neck.

Angry tears welled in her eyes. She hated no one more than him. So many people had needlessly died because of his greed!

A sudden coldness welled up from the core of her being as she realized she might have entered Nigel's mind fabrication again. He'd drawn her to this mental lair when she'd projected her consciousness to his space station orbiting Earth. The wormhole had been open then, but it was closed now. He shouldn't have been able to trap her in his mental fabrication. How am I here?

The knot in her gut clenched tighter and her heart raced. If she was back in this megalomaniac's mind… She glared at Nigel, hoping her fear of him didn't show. She wanted out of his fabricated nightmare—the sooner, the better.

"Release me!" she demanded.

Nigel laughed as though she'd told a delightful joke.

In Margo's peripheral vision, she saw the portraits laugh too, but she refused to take her eyes of her nemesis.

Nigel put the pipe to his lips and puffed out a train of smoke rings, each one a perfect circle. The cloying scent made her want to gag.

"You're not in a position to demand anything," he said. With a sweeping gesture, the smoke rings morphed into grey butterflies that fluttered around the room. "I'm in control here. What you see is all my doing." He looked at the butterflies and giggled like a child before once again focusing on Margo. "I have an offer to make. Sit." He nodded to the chair across from him.

Margo frowned. She didn't want to do what he asked even if it was as simple as taking a seat. But she had to figure out how to get out of his fabri-

cated room, a task that required her to remain calm. With her gaze fixed on Nigel, she moved forward and sank into the leather chair.

"What's your offer?"

"Don't listen to him," said Julien, suddenly appearing beside her. His white hair looked almost translucent in the firelight. "He can't be trusted."

Margo leaned an elbow on the arm of the chair so she was closer to the boy, but kept her gaze on Nigel. She was certain Nigel couldn't see Julien, and she didn't want Nigel to be aware that he was in the room with her. Nigel wanted the boy in his grasp almost more than he wanted Margo dead. "I know that," she muttered. "I'm not a fool."

"What he wants is to kill you," said Julien pointing at Nigel.

Nigel laughed.

Margo woke drenched in sweat. A sense of dread washed over her as she pushed her covers back and swung her feet over the edge of her cot—but at least her surroundings were now familiar. She was in her greenhouse, where she'd set up a sleeping area in a private corner. Technically her quarters were in the Hub in a three-bedroom apartment. But Gary lived there, and she had never joined her husband in their assigning living quarters.

The fabric sides and canvas roof of her makeshift shelter made the space seem more like a tent than a home. Right now, it was little more than a barrier from the overhead sprinklers. The area she'd carved out to live in remained spartan, with only a bare concrete pad for a floor. Someday she'd print a rug—but not a Persian one like her dream.

"It was just a dream," she told herself, hoping spoken words would help to convince her. A hint of pipe tobacco remained in the air and she thought she could hear a faint echo of Nigel's laughter.

Running her hands through her tangled hair, she said, "that monster is just a figment of your imagination. He isn't here. Get a grip Murphy."

Butterflies threatened to emerge from the edges of her mind; she pushed them away and focused on her surroundings. She'd positioned her old army barrack box as a bedside table beside her cot. Two photographs, a wind-up lantern salvaged from her childhood and her scroll sat on its surface. Ordinary objects, not fantastical taxidermy mounts, gilded chairs or ornate paintings. Finally, her eyes fell on the packed duffle bag at the foot of her bed.

"Today is the day." Hearing the sound of her own voice seemed to help dispel the last unpleasant visages of her unsettling dream. She hoped.

Julien's warning lingered in her mind. *Is this trip doomed? And can Nigel somehow access them despite the wormhole being closed?* She gulped. *Am I giving too much credence to Julien's warning? Does the child actually know something about future events, or is it some sort of game for him?* She didn't know, but she did know the predictions he'd made in the past held merit.

"That boy's got you so worked up," she scolded herself. "You're letting his warning colour your dreams." She took a deep breath and let it out slowly. The simple act made her feel marginally better.

Twenty minutes later, Margo was ready, even though she was far too early—the *Staffelwalze* wasn't due to depart for another two hours. She tucked her scroll into the side pocket of her duffle bag, hefted it over her shoulder, and stepped into the open space of her greenhouse.

The specially treated glass of the greenhouse's roof, along with an automated timer to create a sense of time, filtered out the perpetual light of Thesan's two suns. At this time of day, it created an early morning glow. The greenhouse was large, three stories high and big enough to fit three football fields. Two thirds of the ground remained native substrate—basically, gravel—and unsuitable for growing Earth-origin plants. Over the other third, Margo had spread a thick layer of soil that now teemed with micro-organisms.

Where there was soil, she had planted. A row of banana saplings already thrived in the greenhouse's tropical environment. Beside them, the first hints of pumpkin vines poked out of the soil. Around the area she'd called her 'porch', she'd planted a circular grove of citrus saplings. One day they would be tall enough to offer privacy to the area where she'd erected her shelter. In front of the trees, her mismatched pair of plastic chairs faced the windows and the over-exposed landscape outside.

The greenhouse was a great space. She loved it, but she felt alone in it too. She wished Gary would let go of the grudge he held against her. Yes, she'd broken her promise to him, but he must see, by now, that her decision to do so had been sound. And the end result had been worth it.

After a last glance around, she ran through a mental checklist of everything that had to be done during her absence. The automatic sprinkling system would keep everything watered, and Devin would check in on her bees. Over at the centre module, Hannah agreed to oversee Margo's plan for the caves. The blueprints for their cave hideout had been made and builder bots programmed, but it would take months before the basic hollowing out was done. She wouldn't be missing much there.

Have I forgotten anything? Her gaze was caught then by the *Staffelwalze* outside the glass walls on the north side of her spoke-shaped greenhouse. She couldn't see it from her present vantage point, but she knew the ship was connected to the *Settler's* engineering airlock, the entrance through which she would soon board.

Margo wondered if she should pop by sickbay and apologize to Gary for doing the consciousness projection. She still didn't think she had anything to apologize for; she'd done what she'd done for the greater good. But just in case Julien's vision meant real danger and the worst happened, she wanted Gary to know that she truly hadn't meant to hurt him.

Boots crunching on gravel drew her back to the present. Someone was approaching.

"Oh good you're still here. Peg couldn't pinpoint your location," said Lucas, referring to the colony's AI as he came into view. "By the time you're back, we should have the upgraded Peggy AI installed."

"I suppose that's good news." Margo let her duffle bag slide to the ground. She plopped into the pink chair and put her feet up on a re-purposed crate, gesturing at the empty green chair. "You might as well grab a seat."

"I'm sorry," said Lucas, taking the chair beside her. "For sending you off on what might be a wild goose chase."

Margo shrugged. "You're not sending me. I'm agreeing to go of my free will. It's necessary." She only had to think about what it would have been like if the *Settler III* survivors had needed rescuing after they'd crash-landed on Thesan—and how badly they would have wanted some other colonizing ship to come looking for them—to know that this mission had value.

"I'd rather lead the mission myself, but if I left Iago behind here, he would take over. We can't have that. His bull-in-a-china-shop tendencies could shatter what we've built here."

"I get it," said Margo. "But you're only delaying the inevitable. He'll make a play for your job when we return. And, if we do bring back survivors, he'll style himself a saviour."

"I know." He rubbed his hand over his chin. "I never wanted the post of commander and I'd love to go back to just being a computer technician here. If it was anyone other than Iago..." He let his voice trail off.

"Well, the good news is I'll be entertained by the sparks Abigail and Yuko set off each other," said Margo, trying to add levity to their discussion.

Lucas barely smiled. "True."

They fell silent again.

"Did you consider swapping Gan out with one of the other engineers?" Margo knew it was a long shot, but if anyone should stay behind it should be Gan. He should be with his pregnant wife.

Lucas shook his head. "No one has experience with ion drives like he does. He's the only one who can get you all home safely." He fell quiet for a moment. "Speaking of ensuring your safety, do you still have Craig's handgun?"

Margo inhaled sharply as she turned to Lucas. Four months had passed, but Craig's betrayal still felt fresh. He'd been her friend since their army days, but he'd sabotaged their colony and tried to kill her, more than once. His orchestrated accidents killed more than twenty of their crew, including Lucas' wife. In the end, Gary had used Craig's gun to kill him, saving Margo from Craig's third attempt on her life.

She bit her lip. When she spoke, her voice quivered. "I've hidden it."

"Take it with you," said Lucas. "Keep it hidden, but take it."

"Why? I don't think we'll be fighting off aliens," she said.

"I want you to have an extra layer of protection." He gave her a playful grin then, and said. "And if Iago takes ridiculous risks with your lives? Shoot him."

Chapter Seven

Cuben fibre walls formed a narrow corridor extending from the engineering airlock out to the *Staffelwalze*. The fabric seemed too light to hold breathable air; yet, it did, saving the passengers from the trouble of having to put on an atmo suit to board the spaceship. Breathable pockets of air existed on Thesan, but they were located in the lowest valleys, not up on the rock-strewn plateau where the colony sat.

As Margo stood staring at the path ahead, the weight of her duffle bag biting into her shoulder, she gritted her teeth. She believed in this mission—she really did. But that didn't mean she wanted to go.

After shifting her bag to the other side, she crossed the threshold into the flimsy corridor, distracted by visions of the walls giving way. Her one time breathing the low oxygen atmosphere outside had been enough—She didn't want to be stuck in that kind of situation again.

The opaque sides of the temporary airlock tube revealed only a small rectangle of the worn grey hull of the ship. At the end, five steps led up to the open door of the ship's airlock. She climbed the stairs, her boots ringing against the metal.

On the other side of the airlock, Margo found herself in a closet-sized room, a vestibule that provided space to don atmo suits. Gan was the only other occupant. He sat on the floor of the small room, in front of the lockers that lined the aft wall. Before him a pile of the ship's orange atmo suits, their stiff shapes looking zombie-like, leaned against a door with the word 'Engineering' on it.

An hour earlier, Margo had seen Lily and Gan eating breakfast together. Lily's thick black hair hadn't hidden her flood of tears as the two of them shared what would be their last meal for at least a month. Even though she knew it would've been futile, she wished she'd argued her case better to have Gan replaced.

There were no benches in the *Staffelwalze* atmo vestibule, This meant putting on a suit would be more awkward than usual. Margo pictured herself hopping around on one leg while struggling to stuff the other leg in. Already, the space felt cramped with just her and Gan, if anyone else entered they'd be tripping over each other. *Good times.*

Gan offered Margo a smile, but it didn't reach his eyes. "I've tweaked our suits." he said. His compact size made him ideal for working in this tight space. "I've upped the sensitivity of the external microphones."

Margo cocked her head. "Why?"

"So we'll be able to hear someone outside our suit talking to us. With this adjustment, two people wearing suits can talk without using their radio," he explained.

"That *is* better," said Margo. The change meant private conversations while in the atmo suits would be possible.

Margo admired Gan's skill. He could fix anything. Plus, she knew he liked tinkering just to make things better, his present task a testament to his relentless penchant for implementing improvements. Best of all, he wasn't annoying—unlike Iago. And Yuko. And sometimes Abigail. Having him be the first person she encountered upon boarding seemed to alleviate some of Margo's anxiety.

She shifted the duffle bag to her other shoulder. "I need to drop off my stuff. Where do we find out cabin assignments?"

"Ask Ash. She's up in the cockpit, although she optimistically calls it the 'bridge'." He turned back to his work.

"Thanks," Margo said with a smile, picturing the ship's schematic she'd studied.

She could've explored the ship at some point over the last two days, but she hadn't wanted to run into Iago. The longer she could avoid him, the better. Behind the airlock vestibule, two ion drives filled the back quarter of the ship. Just forward, a series of storage rooms lined the port side, leaving a narrow corridor along the starboard bulkhead wide enough for one person—which was the route she took.

As she made her way along the narrow hallway, she hefted her duffle onto her back so it didn't hamper her movements. An assortment of pipes and wires snaked along the ceiling just above her head. If she were two centimetres taller, she would've had to duck. On her right, watermelon-sized windows punctuated the outside wall, over-saturating the space with light.

Forward of the storage rooms, the door to the medbay gaped open. She stuck her head inside to see if Abeo had boarded, but no one was inside. Everything a spacefaring medic might need was crammed into the room, which wasn't much larger than the ship's airlock vestibule. An examination table covered in green vinyl—reminding her of the medbay on the Centre Module—dominated the centre of the room. Surrounding it, consoles connected to various medical devices and machines lined three of the walls, including the walls on either side of the doorway in which she stood. The aft wall contained cupboards, which she assumed were stocked with important medical stuff. Tucked in a corner was a tiny, built-in desk with a chair.

She froze mid-breath. A medical bag sat on the chair seat

and she recognized it—it belonged to Gary. The only reason it would be here was if he was coming on the mission in place of Abeo.

Margo bit her lip as mixed feelings about her estranged husband surfaced. She knew their both being on this ship, so much smaller than the *Settler*, would be awkward given their complicated relationship. Hopefully, she wouldn't run into him right away as she needed to take time to prepare what to say and how to act.

Turning her back on the medbay, she continued forward. After passing through a set of airtight doors, she entered the common living area. An open galley ran along the port side, with a large table on the starboard side. Upholstery fabric featuring jaunty pink elephants on bicycles covered most of the banquet style benches, adding an unexpected whimsy.

Overall, the space was clean and well loved, but it showed its age. Flaking paint on the corners revealed layers of different colours. Mismatched cupboard lined the galley as though someone had salvaged them from a space ship graveyard—which might very well be the case.

Just forward of the kitchen, a spiral staircase wound up to the next level. Margo unslung her duffle bag and dumped it on the floor at the foot of the stairs—the cabins were one deck up. Relieved to be free of her load, she continued exploring, moving into the next space.

Open to the galley, it was filled with rows of comfortable seating divided by a centre aisle. In its previous life, the *Staffelwalze* had been a civilian personnel carrier, moving teams of diplomats from Earth to the moon. There were eight rows of over two dozen comfortable chairs arranged facing each other in groups of four. Each pair of seats was separated by a double hand-width plat-form, wide enough to hold a drink and a snack. The configuration looked comfortable and inviting—just right for long conversations.

The original upholstery was a cream-coloured leather.

Diplomats may have once travelled in style here, but that time was long past. Patches now covered many of the chairs—elephant fabric repairs here, floral-patterned ones there. One chair was entirely reupholstered in the same green vinyl she'd seen in the medbay while another was missing its armrests. The ad hoc repairs made the formerly luxurious space homey.

She ran her hand over the headrests as she moved down the centre aisle, then mounted the two steps at the front of the room that led to the bridge.

Dead ahead, a bubble of clear glass gave a panoramic view of the Thesan plateau. A wide dashboard full of multicoloured knobs and levers separated the window from two seats, one for the pilot and co-pilot. Along the aft bulkhead were two more workstations with rotating chairs.

Currently, the cockpit was empty, so Margo headed back the way she'd come, looking for Ash. She found the ship's captain in the kitchen, making a pot of coffee. Ash must've come down from the deck above.

"Amanda has stocked us up well," said Ash, as Margo approached her from between the rows of chairs. "Including enough Brussel sprouts to feed us for months."

Margo grimaced. "I saw them in the store room on the *Settler* and hoped we wouldn't get any."

"Not a fan then," replied Ash with a smile.

"Nope."

Ash chuckled. "How about a cup of coffee instead?" Without waiting for Margo's answer, she opened a cupboard and retrieved a couple of mugs.

"Sure," said Margo. She glanced over at her duffle bag and wondered if she'd earned a black mark from the ship's captain for dumping it on the floor. She hadn't seen a single other item out of place. Ash ran a tight ship. "I was actually wondering what cabin I'm assigned."

"You're in cabin four," Ash replied, handing Margo a

steaming mug, gesturing for Margo to follow her to the table. "You're early."

"Yeah." Margo slid into the seat across from Ash. "I wanted to get settled well before the chaos of departure."

Ash smiled, showing her neat rows of white teeth, a sharp contrast to her dark skin. "Or... You're uncomfortable with the idea of being stuck on a small ship for weeks looking for survivors who may not be out there, but you didn't know what to do with yourself until departure, so you showed up early."

Margo dropped her gaze to her steaming mug. Ash nailed it. Even though she had inhabited Ash's body when she'd done the conscious projection, she barely knew the woman. But what little she knew, she liked. Margo cleared her throat and looked up, meeting Ash's gaze. "Perhaps," she said, before taking a sip of her coffee.

"I've been thinking about what we may find," said Ash. "Since these people haven't responded to our comms, I can't imagine there's anyone to rescue. It's so sad, really. But, I'm curious to know what happened to them."

"Me too."

Before Margo could continue, Iago burst into the space from the hallway leading aft.

"Hey, someone made coffee." He helped himself to a mug. As he poured, coffee sloshed onto the floor. Both women stared at the spill, but Iago ignored the mess. "Ash, let's go over the navigation." Mug in hand, he winked at Margo before he continued on towards the bridge.

Frowning after him, Ash stood. "Some things never change," she said before grabbing a towel and wiping up the spilled coffee. Without another word to Margo, she headed forward.

As Margo took her time to finish her coffee, she considered the tidy state of the galley. Since she needed to stay on Ash's good side—she guessed she would need an ally on this trip—she washed and dried the mug before putting it away. Picking up her bag, she climbed the spiral staircase.

One deck up, the corridor was just as narrow, only this time it went down the centre of the ship. Two strips of soft white lights kept the hallway well lit, showing off the pale green walls and rubberized flooring. A strange combination of lavender and cleaning fluid scents filled the air as though everything had been recently scrubbed and sanitized. This deck wasn't as worn as the deck below—she didn't see chipped paint anywhere.

"I guess the hoards of diplomats spent most their time down below," she said to herself as she looked at the cabin doors lining either side of the corridor. Each had a number at eye level.

She found her door and opened it, the overhead lights automatically came on. Stepping inside, she dropped her duffle onto the single bed. Painted the same pale green as the corridor, the cabin was small, but sufficient. The single bed built into an alcove in the wall and made up with mis-matched floral sheets was narrow but relatively long. She'd fit.

A picture of a kitten with a ball of yarn hung above the bed, while underneath were built-in drawers. A small, built-in desk sat beneath a porthole-like window, covered in a blind. A plain chair was tucked under the desk. When Margo turned, she saw a garishly upholstered easy chair beside the open door. *How could that not be the first thing I noticed?* Covered in red fabric with white polka dots and with a pillow printed with an over-size red rose, the gaudy chair looked both comfortable and inviting.

On her right, on the other side of the desk, was a narrow sliding door. Margo didn't even have to step forward to reach it and slide it open, the room was that small. Inside was a miniature bathroom. It would require an act of contortion to take a shower—but at least she didn't have to share.

"So, this is where you are," said Gary from the doorway.

Margo whirled around, whacking her elbow on the door frame. Ignoring the reminder that funny bones aren't funny, she smiled at Gary. "You must like how clean and tidy the ship is," she said, then bit her lip, feeling like an idiot. Now was not the time to tease Gary about his penchant for neatness.

"Ash seems a stickler for tidy," he responded in a serious tone. "I'm in the cabin across the hall." He pointed to the door with a 2 on it, then ran his palms down the front of his pants.

Margo knew he only did that when he was nervous, and knowing he was nervous somehow made it easier for her. "So, you're coming instead of Abeo?" asked Margo trying to keep her tone light. *Is now the right time to apologize?*

Gary crammed his hands into his trouser pockets. "It was getting a little crowded in sickbay—three doctors and a medic— and I thought, this mission would be better off with a doctor."

"Makes sense."

An uncomfortable silence fell as Margo tried to find the right words to say how sorry she was for breaking her promise. It had been months since she'd woken from her consciousness projection, and the words still remained elusive.

"I should go check supplies in the medbay," said Gary, pointing a thumb over his shoulder..

"I'll see you around," said Margo, as he turned and left.

She shut her door, then turned and flopped down into the easy chair, cursing her inability to apologize.

Chapter Eight

Three hours later, Margo chose a spot in the passenger compartment next to a window. She reclined the seat and gazed outside. Far below, the *Settler III* colony receded, getting smaller and smaller as Ash piloted the ship off planet.

Margo focusing on the view, it was Gary who was on her mind. He'd rejected her attempts at apology in those first days after she'd reawakened in her own body. And now, so much time had passed, she honestly didn't know the right thing to say. What she knew for sure was that she wanted the tension between them to lift, especially now they were both on this mission.

"Hey carrot top," said Abigail, slumping down into the seat across from her. "Planning the revolt already?"

Margo looked over to Abigail and shook her head. "This is way too small of a space to plant a seed of discourse."

"Sadly, this place is perfect. Back when I worked in the domes on Mars, the most discord always came from the groups living in the smallest spaces." As she spoke she fiddled with the magenta scarf she always wore.

"Is the scarf sentimental?" asked Margo, hoping for a neutral topic.

Abigail fell silent for a moment as she ran a finger along the fabric. Her expression remained unreadable. "Yeah, you could say that."

"Um, sorry. I didn't mean to dredge up bad memories," said Margo.

"No worries." Abigail shrugged. "My wife, Vera, gave it to me on our first anniversary. Wearing it reminds me of her."

Margo frowned. Abigail almost never talked about her past —especially not about her time on Mars. She wondered if Abigail's wife had died when things went bad on that colony, but she didn't have the guts to ask. At least her friend had found some happiness with Hannah.

"The colour suits you," said Margo. It was true, the bright shade complimented Abigail's dark skin and it was almost as bold as the woman's personality. "How's your cabin?"

"It's not the worst place I've stayed, so it'll do." Abigail put her feet up on the chair across from her. "Iago has been asking about you."

"Dirty circuits!" Margo let her head tip back into the headrest as her mind shifted to her other awkward social complication. "He just doesn't give up."

"That's the way of the alpha male. You might as well take him for a spin and see how it goes."

"Ugh! Perish the thought," Margo scoffed.

"What you mean is you'd rather take Gary for a spin."

Margo felt the skin on her face heat, a tell-tail sign she was going beat red. She swivelled her head around, checking to make sure the two of them were alone. "We're barely speaking," she said. "I know he doesn't understand my motivation for doing what I did, but I just don't know how to apologize when what I did was the right thing to do"

"That's bat-shit crazy, you dumb ass." Abigail smiled, taking the sting out of her words. "The two of you don't actually need to talk..." Her words trailed off, leaving behind innuendo.

Margo turned to stare out the window, wanting to hide her blush from Abigail. Outside, the brightness of Thesan's landscape had receded to darkness sprinkled with stars. The curvature of the planet was unmistakable. She felt no different than she had on Thesan's surface, a sign the gravity plating was working.

"How did Hannah take the news of you coming on this mission?"

"Changing the topic, are you? Don't think I'm gonna leave your lack of love life alone for long." Abigail slumped deeper into her chair. "Hannah delivered quite the blast over the comms. It's a good thing I didn't have time to go to the Centre Module before we left."

Margo smiled as she pictured dainty Hannah yelling at street hardened Abigail. Her friend put on a tough front, but underneath she was a softy.

"I assume Hannah will be fine out at the Centre Module on her own."

"That shit doesn't phase her," said Abigail. "She fears what might be waiting for us at the other colonies, and that something might happen to me. I don't blame her, considering her other losses."

"Her husband did die right in front of her," said Margo. An airlock malfunction had killed him only a door away from the rest of them.

"It's taken a long time to get her to smile again," said Abigail. "And there are still moments, when she thinks I'm not around, when I catch her crying. I lost someone I loved once, so I know she may never be fully over him."

Margo nodded, thinking of the people she'd lost. Their faces scrolled through her mind and a lump formed in her throat. *What a waste.* She let her forehead rest against the cool surface of the window and gazed into space.

"In other news," said Abigail in a too-chirpy voice. "I overheard Yuko complaining about having us mere colonists on this mission."

"What? Why?" Margo turned towards Abigail.

Abigail frowned. "She said the lot of us are rejects."

"Technically, we all failed the selection process."

"Yeah. But that was due to The Conglomerate meddling,"" said Abigail twisting the facts a bit.

"True." Margo knew it would be easier just to agree.

"Yuko's full of crap. We've proven we can do it."

"She's looking to stir up trouble. That's how she's wired. Just ignore her." Margo shook her head. "Some days, I wonder if inviting them here was a good idea."

"Well, that crowd has changed the flavour of the place," said Abigail. "But, as I understand it, they had nowhere else to go. And, we had room for them."

"True." Margo let herself relax into the headrest again.

Abigail sat up straight, taking her boots off the opposite chair. "I think us colonists need to stick together. We need to watch each other's backs."

"Always," said Margo with a nod.

Abigail stood. "I should go. I promised Gan I'd help him with the atmo suits. Oh, and don't forget—your love life still needs fixing. We'll work on it later."

Margo rolled her eyes at Abigail. When the other woman was gone, she returned her gaze out the window. The gap between the original colonists and the insurgents was wide— putting Yuko and Abigail together for a long trip wouldn't improve that.

As Thesan continued to shrink into the far distance, Margo let her mind drift. For the umpteenth time, she considered how to, once and for all, put an end to Iago's advances. For the umpteenth-umpteenth time, she also considered how she might approach Gary in a manner that would ease the strain between them. But, yet again, no answers were forthcoming.

Some time later, a rumble from her stomach brought her mind back to the moment. Looking around, she saw she was still alone in the seat-lined room.

Standing, Margo decided to try her hand at preparing a meal. After all, no one person was assigned cook's duty. Food preparation would be a shared responsibility, although she'd put money on Iago and Yuko not doing their fair share. She headed aft towards the galley.

A half hour later, she stood at the stove stirring a pot of soup. It was Amanda's mulligatawny, one of Gary's favourites. She hadn't made it, of course; instead, she simply poured it into a pot and heated it. The rich scents of cumin, garlic and ginger filled the air. In that moment, the *Staffelwalze* felt positively homey.

"I couldn't figure out what use Iago had for an entomologist on this mission, but now I see."

Margo turned to see Yuko standing at the bottom of the spiral stairs. *Homey, like when the black sheep cousins come over, uninvited...*

"I'm in no rush to eat hard rations, but if you want to, go ahead." Margo shrugged trying act nonchalant. It was going to be challenging not to give into the temptation to fight with Yuko.

The short, stout woman tucked a lock of black hair behind her ear as she came into the galley. "You colonists are so soft," she observed, helping herself to a cup of coffee. "Like that pathetic display between Gan and..." Yuko paused, and scrunched up her nose. "Whatever her name is."

"Lily." Margo pictured herself picking up the boiling pot of soup and dumping it over Yuko's head. She savoured the image, knowing she wouldn't waste good food. Plus it would put her one meal closer to having to choose between hard rations or Brussel sprouts.

"I almost vomited watching their sappy display of affection at breakfast."

The soup was coming to a simmer, just like Margo's anger. Lily had been crying and Gan had comforted her. They'd hugged, nothing more. And it wasn't sappy. It was genuine.

"I hope you and Gary won't subject us to that sappy shit."

Why won't she shut up already!

Margo glanced up when Iago strode into the common area from the corridor. As soon as he saw her a predatory smirk formed on his face.

"Smells good." Iago stood between the galley and the table, his legs splayed apart as he hungrily eyed Margo. "Yuko, go help Ash with the navigation," he said, keeping his eyes on Margo.

With a sneer but characteristically obedient, Yuko left, leaving Margo alone with Iago.

"I've been waiting to get you alone, doll," he said, stepping into her personal space.

Doll? Margo recoiled, stepping to the side, but keeping her hand on the spoon as she continued to stir the soup. She bit her lip to prevent herself from lashing out at him. For a smart man, it was astonishing he never picked up on the fact that he repulsed her. Margo deflected Iago's previous advances with snapped insults, yet he never stopped. She'd learned it was best not to engage.

"You and I have a connection," Iago stated. "This trip's the perfect opportunity to explore that, if you get my meaning."

Margo stepped away from him, going to the switch in the galley that activated the ship's internal comms.

"Lunch is ready," she announced, hearing her voice reverberate throughout the ship.

"I'm ready," Iago said suggestively from right behind her as he wrapped his arm around her waist. His warmth radiated into her—unwelcome and unwanted.

Margo stiffened. "Get your hand off me," she snapped through clenched teeth. If he touched her again, she would break his fingers—she had the training. But, she didn't want an altercation. If only he'd just stop harassing her.

Iago released her and leaned against the counter assuming a casual pose. "I love it when you play coy. I'll get what I want in the end, doll. I always do."

Before she had a chance to reply, Gan and Max entered the room from back aft, just as Ash and Yuko arrived from the bridge. A moment later, Gary came in, followed by Abigail and Iva.

Max picked up a bowl and went straight to the stove, filling his bowl to the brim and taking several slices of bread that Margo had placed on the counter.

"Thanks, Margo. This smells fantastic." He flashed her an enthusiastic grin before sitting and sliding down the bench on the back side of the table. "We should've brought Amanda with us so we could eat like this every day."

"We need to keep focused on our priorities," said Yuko as she served herself a generous helping. She clearly wasn't interested in breaking out the hard rations just yet.

"We'll be trapped on this ship for some time," said Iago, giving Margo a meaningful look. His loud voice boomed through the space. "Good food goes a long way to keeping morale up," he added in a condescending tone. With his flesh hand, he served up a bowl of soup and handed it to Margo.

Margo took his offering and handed it to Gary. Iago didn't notice as he served himself and took a seat at the table. She stayed by the stove, filling the bowls for the remaining crew.

Gary remained beside her, studying her with a worried expression. "You look tense."

"If I kill Iago, please promise you won't revive him," she muttered, just loud enough for Gary to hear.

Chapter Nine

"How are you holding up, kid?" asked Gary.

He was in the bridge with Ash, sitting in the co-pilot's seat. Beside him, the ship's captain was scrolling through screens on her display. Out of the corner of his eye Gary caught glimpses of fuel usage logs and water supplies. He focused on the video image of Julien projected on the windshield of the bridge.

The boy shrugged. Even the low-res image couldn't hide the black bruise on the side of the boy's cheek that extended from his chin and up, under his googles. It shone dark against his pigment-less skin.

"Neil told me you got into a fight with one of the other boys," said Gary trying to sound neutral about the altercation. According to Neil's interpretation, Julien had been the instigator. Gary knew Julien trusted him; the boy had shown him the artifact, trusted him with the major secret of having it in his possession. Maybe he would trust Gary enough now to tell him the true story of what had instigated that fight. He paused and waited for Julien to respond.

Julien crossed his arms over his chest, and stubbornly looked down at his lap.

When the kid remained silent, Gary tried again, his tone cajoling. "Why don't you tell me what happened? We're friends, you can tell me anything."

The boy stuck out his lower lip and sniffed as he looked up at Gary from behind the whirling kaleidoscope of his prismed goggles. "They didn't believe me. I had a vision that Amanda found Jan's scroll when Jan left it on the floor of the Loop."

"They didn't believe that Amanda found it?" Gary pictured Jan, one of the newly arrived Insurgent children. She had to be about eleven, the same age as Julien.

"Jan said I stole it." Julien balled his hands into fists. "And that I couldn't possibly know what happens when I'm not there."

"You know," started Gary as he ran a hand through his hair. "It is difficult for most people to believe you can see these things. I believe you, but they don't know you like I do."

"Yeah." Julien's lower lip quivered. "I just want them to like me. I want them to be my friends."

"Give them some time to get to know you."

"I have. They've been here over a month."

"Give them some more time," Gary countered.

Julien nodded. "When are you coming back?" he asked.

"Just as soon as we can." Gary tried to inject a reassuring tone into his words. "For sure three weeks yet, possibly more."

"If you come back at all." Julien looked away and bit his lip.

Gary took a deep breath and deliberately didn't glance at Ash. "We're being careful. You can count on us coming back. And when I do, I expect some new jokes out of you."

"I'm working on some," the boy said, perking up. "What did the alien say to the tomato?"

"I don't know. What *did* the alien say to the tomato?"

"Take me to your weeder." Julien laughed.

Gary chuckled. "Good one," he said, even though it wasn't. "Now I need to get going, but we'll talk again soon."

Julien frowned. "You can't go until you tell me a joke."

"Fine. Ever wonder if illiterate people get the full effect of alphabet soup?" Gary asked. He'd been saving the joke for the boy.

Julien grinned and waved goodbye. Gary turned the video feed off.

"Has Julien spent much time around other kids?" asked Ash turning towards him.

"No." Gary said, coming to his feet. "But he'll get the hang of it. I've got to go to the galley. I'm on clean-up duty."

"Iva's already done it," said Ash. "Why don't you go put up your feet."

A crash came from somewhere aft.

"On second thought, why don't you check on that," said Ash.

"Right." Gary turned and left.

————

Gary found Abigail in the galley, scowling and slamming cupboards and drawers.

"Can I help you find anything?" he asked, keeping his distance.

"Sprinkles! I need sprinkles," she practically shouted. The furrow between her brows deepened as though sprinkles were a matter of life-or-death.

"Um, do we even have any on board?" he asked as gently as he could. It seemed unlikely such a thing would be stalked on a spaceship.

Abigail opened up the fridge door, glanced inside, then slammed it closed.

"I need to make cupcakes, and the only ingredient I can't find is sprinkles." She turned and leaned her back against the counter, heaving a sigh.

"What's inspired you to bake cupcakes?" he asked, taking a seat at the table. From where he was sitting, he could see down the windowed corridor heading aft all the way to the airlock vestibule.

Abigail flopped down onto the bench across from him. "When I was kid and I had a bad day, my mom and I used to bake. It always made me feel better," she said. "Right now, I need to distract myself from this shit-storm."

"What happened?"

"Yuko's a bitch," she said through clenched teeth.

"That's not new," he said.

She glanced towards the bridge as though she expected her new nemesis to emerge at any second.

"She's not there," he said. "Last I saw her, she was telling Iago she was heading up to her cabin for a nap."

Abigail seemed to relax a little bit and began fiddling with the salt shaker someone had left on the table. "Yuko's been on me about our terraforming efforts on Thesan," she said. "That bitch keeps citing obsolete papers and questioning my decisions. She's got no right. I know my shit and I don't need to listen to an amateur like her." She slapped her palms down on the table. "I mean she's an astrophysicist, not any kind of biologist."

"She is a dumbass," said Gary, using one of Abigail's favourite phrases in hopes it would defuse her growing anger.

Abigail barked a laugh. "True."

"She did the same to me, you know, when the insurgents first arrived. She marched into the medbay and demanded to know what medical school Neil and I attended and how we ranked against our classmates."

"No shit?"

Over Abigail's shoulder, Gary saw Margo come out of a store room near the end of the narrow corridor, Iago on her heels. Iago reached out and put a hand on Margo's arm, Margo turned to face him. Her back was to Gary so he couldn't see the expression on her face, but her posture was rigid.

Abigail turned and looked at what had captured Gary's interest. "Iago is causing her major grief."

"Should I step in?"

"I doubt Margo would appreciate that. I suspect she prefers to fight her own battles," said Abigail. "You could always try to console her later."

Margo charged down the hallway towards the galley. Her cheeks flushed in a way that made her very pretty—not that he'd ever dare tell her that. She marched through the galley without a word to either of Gary or Abigail, then jogged up the stairs.

Iago had followed her, but he stopped in the hallway, smirking as he watched Margo retreat. When she was gone from view, he nodded at Abigail and Gary, before he turned and went aft the engine room.

"Looks like there's drama everywhere," said Abigail when she and Gary were alone again. She stood. "And we know whose fault that is. Those damn insurgents. I tell you, this place is bat shit crazy," she ranted, then sighed. "Those cupcakes won't bake themselves."

"And I'm sure they'll be delicious, despite the lack of sprinkles," Gary teased, hoping to make Abigail smile. "See you later," he added.

Gary headed up the stairs, stopping at Margo's door with his fist poised to knock. Abigail's suggestion to let Margo fight her own battles came back to him and he paused.

He wasn't trying to come to her rescue. He simply wanted to chat with her. But would she interpret his solicitation as Gary thinking she couldn't take care of herself? He dropped his hand and backed up a pace. Now wasn't the time for a simple chat with Margo, not when they had yet to resolve their issues. Turning, he retreated into his cabin.

Chapter Ten

A week later, everyone squeezed onto the *Staffelwalze's* bridge. Ash and Max were in their seats, with Gary, Iva, and Gan behind Ash, and Margo, Iago, and Yuko jammed in behind Max. Abigail hovered in the doorway. All eyes were fixed, looking out the window at a vista worthy of being on the cover of a vintage science fiction novel.

Thesan's nearest orbital neighbour—the nameless, cold Neptune—filled the bottom half of their view. The blues of its gaseous atmosphere ranged from the pale blue found in the centre of an iceberg to the electric blue of a morpho butterfly's wings. Chaotic swirls danced along rings of latitude, curling and twisting as the rings rotated around the gases below. The colours were dazzling. Margo felt like she could watch it all day.

"Does this planet have a name?" asked Max from the co-pilot's chair.

"Not yet," answered Margo, standing behind him.

"How about we call it Juno?" the young man asked. "You know, Neptune's sister."

"I'd be fine with that," said Margo with a smile.

In the pilot's seat, Ash also smiled.

"Since we should name it after some god of old." Iago's deep voice held amusement. "Juno it is."

His close proximity to Margo meant that when he chuckled she felt the sound resonating through her. As fascinating as the view was, she couldn't wait to get put some distance between her and this overbearing man.

"I'd wager there are icebergs of pure carbon down there," said Yuko, awe in her tone. "Diamonds bigger than houses just bobbing around."

Yuko pushed past blocking Margo's view. Unable to see the planet below, she glanced at Gary standing behind Ash's seat. He seemed to be avoiding looking her way. A week on the ship and they'd barely spoken. Abigail was right, she was bat-shit crazy for letting their silence go on so long. An outsider would think the two of them were teenagers and ill equipped to navigate a relationship.

Ash pointed at an image on her side panel screen. "Everyone, the moon, Geb, *Settler II's* destination, will rise over the planet in a few minutes."

"I love that it's named after an Egyptian god," said Iva.

"Geb is a god's name? Doesn't sound like one." Max twisted to look at Iva.

"Uh, huh," answered Iva. "Geb is the Egyptian god of Earth. I spent a good chunk of my childhood looking into that sort of thing."

Gary spoke for the first time. "Does that mean the moon Geb is Earth-like? Is that why whoever named it chose Geb?"

"We got stuck with the wrong planet, then," Abigail scoffed from behind them. "Thesan's a gravel pit."

"I'll zoom in on the exact point where the moon will rise," said Ash.

She swiped on a side panel and a section of the forward cockpit became a screen. With another adjustment, Juno's horizon expanded. A few moments later the white disc of the moon rose from behind the swirling iridescent blues of the planet. The sight was a once in a lifetime view, and everyone on the bridge knew it.

"Wait. Why is it white?" asked Gary, breaking the silence that had fallen as their ship seemed to inch its way forward, slowly broadening its view of the *Settler II's* home planet.

"That's ice!" Yuko reached over Max's shoulder to access one of his terminals. She scrolled through the long range sensor data as Max leaned out of the way with a scowl on his face.

Iago leaned into Margo to get a better view of the screen. "What do you mean, ice?"

Margo leaned back as far as she could, but there was no room for her to move. Claustrophobia swept over her—an unfamiliar sensation. Out of the corner of her eye, she saw a butterfly flit towards Gary, but she deliberately ignored the imaginary insect. Instead, she focused on Yuko, watching as the astrophysicist commandeered Max's console.

"It can't be ice," Gan said. "No one would send colonists to an ice planet."

"It is ice. Surface temperatures appear to be below minus one hundred degrees Celsius." Yuko stood up straight and turned her head to address Iago. "How could it have been considered a terraforming site?"

"It couldn't have been." Iago shook his head.

Margo shared a look of alarm with the others, and saw bafflement reflected in all their eyes.

"Now that we have a direct line of sight, Ash, try raising them on the comms," instructed Iago.

As Ash began hailing *Settler II*, Margo wiggled her way out from between Iago and Yuko. She stopped just outside the door to the bridge behind Abigail.

"What douche-bag idiot thought it was a good idea to send a colonizing mission to a frozen planet?" demanded Abigail.

"We don't know yet." Margo leaned against the wall.

"The Conglomerate screwed them over." Abigail glanced

forward and pursed her lips. The ice moon was growing in the screen. "They were sent there to die."

"But why?" Margo argued. "That makes no sense."

"I had a friend on the *Settler II*; she was so thrilled to be chosen to go," said Abigail. Margo turned to look at her—it was the first she'd ever mentioned anything about this friend.

"Another survivor from Mars?" asked Margo in a low tone —she didn't want the others to overhear. It was only recently that Abigail had started telling her anything about her time on Earth's neighbour. Margo didn't want to push too hard and compromise their friendship.

"Yeah. Nancy and I worked together." Abigail took a deep breath. "Nancy introduced me to Vera, and she was there the day Vera died."

Margo glanced towards Abigail. The big woman raised a hand and ran it along the fabric of her scarf as sorrow shadowed through her tough veneer. Margo didn't push the conversation further.

Silence descended as they all watched more and more of the moon come into view. A web of red cracks crisscrossed its white surface giving the moon a familiar air.

"It looks similar to Jupiter's Europa," Iva commented in a quiet voice.

"And nothing like a suitable terraforming site." Ash tone was flat.

"Found them," said Max.

Iago and Yuko both leaned in closer over his chair. "You raised them?" Iago asked, his voice booming in the small space.

"No. I found the *Settler II*, though," Max said. "Still in orbit."

"Bring it up on the screen." Iago puffed himself up taking up even more space.

Max tapped a key and the image changed, a speck of white floating above the moon. He manipulated the video feed, zooming in on the ship. When the image reached its max resolution, everyone craned their necks to see the image on the screen. The distinctive ring floated in space.

"Why is it still in orbit?" Margo asked, staying at her spot next to the doorway. No one had an answer. Instead, they all watched in silence as the *Settler II* filled the screen.

"The Centre Module is still attached." Gan's tone was laced with horror. "And it's not rotating."

"Oh, shit." Iago shoved a hand against Max's shoulder. "Move," he ordered.

Without a word of complaint, Max got up and traded places with Iago.

"I don't understand," Gary said. "Why is that a bad thing?"

"No rotation means no gravity." Iago snapped as he scrolled through the sensor data.

"That's terrible." Iva hugged her arms around herself and bit her lip.

"No gravity isn't good, but…" Gary appeared still confused about the significance of their discovery.

"No gravity," Gan said. "Means no power."

"No power means no air," Abigail stated from the doorway.

There was silence—Without power the ship would be unable to circulate breathable air and, even if it was breathable, it would be far too cold to sustain life. The chances of finding anyone alive on board the *Settler II* now dropped from possible to impossible.

"Is there any point in going closer?" Ash asked, turning to Iago.

"We still need to check it out. Maybe they figured out somewhere else to go," said Iago.

"Where?" Abigail demanded in a sarcastic tone. "The big fire breathing dragon on our left? Or the frozen wonderland on our right?"

Margo knew Abigail well enough to know that her tone meant she was trying to hide painful emotions. She really had fanned a hope that her friend Nancy was alive.

"They might have left behind supplies we can use," said Yuko in a matter-of-fact tone.

"What!" Abigail pushed past Margo and jabbed Yuko in the shoulder with a long finger. "Are we space pirates now?"

"Abigail, take a walk," snapped Iago over his shoulder. "It's getting too crowded in here."

"Come on," said Margo, resting a hand on Abigail's arm. Margo breathed a sigh of relief when Abigail willingly left the bridge with her.

Chapter Eleven

In the galley the coffee was still hot. Margo retrieved two mugs from the cupboard and filled them. Turning, she gave a steaming mug to Abigail. The other woman took it and wrapped both her hands around it as though she needed the warmth.

"I've got a bad feeling about this," Abigail said, shaking her head.

"You're thinking of Nancy, aren't you?" Margo couldn't bring herself to acknowledge that Abigail's friend was most likely a frozen corpse.

"I just wanted her to be alive. I loved the idea of us rescuing her. I sure as bat-shit-hell don't want to steal their supplies."

Margo nodded. "As distasteful as it is, Yuko has a point."

"What, you too?" Abigail scowled.

"You'd agree, if you gave yourself a moment to think rationally. What if there's a working shuttle, or builder bots, more domestic printers? Hell, if we could figure out how to get their Centre Module back to Thesan, it could go a long way to improving our lives."

"I still don't like it," Abigail mumbled, taking another sip of her coffee. "It's like, I don't know... grave robbing."

"You're imagining Nancy." At Abigail's nod, Margo continued. "I don't like it either." Margo gestured for them to take seats at the table. "I honestly can't stomach the thought of boarding that ship, not if it's a tomb. And especially knowing one of the colonists was a friend of yours. But Abigail, would Nancy fault us for taking what we need? What would she do if our roles were reversed? Would you want Nancy to benefit from supplies on Thesan?"

"Of course." Abigail grumbled.

"I'm sorry that we can't help Nancy," said Margo. "I'm sorry we're too late.

Abigail sputtered in anger. "We'd have been too late had we come the day after we arrived in this system. Goddamn Conglomerate bastards."

"She was a good friend, wasn't she?" Margo asked.

Abigail nodded. "She and Vera grew up together on Jan Mayen Island. Did I mention Nancy introduced me to Vera?"

"Yeah, you did," said Margo focusing on her friend, glad to see she seemed to be calming down. "Tell me about Vera."

"She was an artist, a maker of whimsical sculptures and other fantastical things." Abigail ran her fingers along her scarf, lost in thought.

Saying nothing, Margo sipped her coffee.

"Vera and Nancy worked as gardeners under the Martian dome. I'd seen Vera around, but it wasn't until Nancy hosted a potluck in her quarters that I finally worked up the nerve to talk to her." Abigail looked out the porthole behind the table and fell silent.

Margo found the idea that this big, brassy woman had to work up the nerve to speak to someone surprising. "You?" She teased. "Too nervous to talk to someone?"

Abigail gave her a ghost of a smile. "She was always out of my league, although she hated it when I said shit like that. But I wasted a long time not talking to her, time we could have been happy together." She frowned at Margo. "Don't you go making the same mistake."

Before Margo could respond, Gary walked into the galley. He stopped when he saw Margo and Abigail, then said, "If you ever need a partner in crime to get rid of Iago, let me know."

"Iago piss you off?" asked Abigail.

Gary seemed momentarily taken aback by Abigail's uncharacteristic subdued manner. He hesitated, then said, "We don't see eye-to-eye." He picked up a mug and emptied the dregs of the coffee pot into it.

"So Iago kicked you out too." Abigail stood and met Margo's eyes, subtly tilting her head towards Gary where he was staring at his half-full mug.

"At least Lucas will listen to reason." Gary complained as he slid into the seat across from Margo.

Abigail finished her coffee and placed the empty cup in the sink. "Call me if anything comes up." She headed up the spiral stairs.

Margo glanced down into her mug and bit her lip, realizing this was the first time she and Gary had been alone since their departure. Swirling the dregs of her coffee in the mug, she felt uncomfortable with the silence that hung between them but at a loss for what to say. For the next few minutes, the only sound came from the ventilation system somewhere in the ceiling.

Gary finally broke the silence. "Do you think Iago will want you to board that ship?"

She looked up at him, saw that he was watching her with an expectant expression. There was tension around his eyes. *He must be worried. Hell, anyone with half a heart would be worried.* She took a deep breath.

"I don't know if you've noticed, but Iago has an annoying habit of making excuses to keep me close, so I would expect so." She noted his half-hearted smile before her eyes skittered away.

Glancing out the window, she stared at the gaseous

atmosphere of Juno below. It had been an awe-inspiring sight before they'd realized the colonists on *Settler II* were all dead.

"I hope Gan can get the ship spinning again," Margo said, hating the awkward silence that kept falling between them. She missed how easy it had been to talk to Gary before. Before she broke her promise. "I hate zero gs," she added

"It was all a blur last time I was in no gravity," Gary said, looking her in the eye.

Margo nodded, remembering waking up in zero gs when things went wrong on *Settler III* the day they crash-landed on their planet. She didn't remember seeing Gary that day. She did remember Linda and her rescuing Tawa and taking shelter in the shuttle. The two of them hadn't survived the crash, but she had. Margo swallowed, banishing those unpleasant memories and forcing a smile.

"Do you think anyone is left alive over there?" Gary turned to look out the window.

Margo shook her head. "Not without power. And even if they had managed to survive for a few days, if they thought they were alone in this solar system, then..." Letting her words trail off, she imagined the fear the colonists must have felt when they realized their new home could never sustain them. She bit her lip again. "It must have been awful for them."

Gary reached across the table and gently cupped her hand in both of his. Neither of them spoke.

Margo didn't withdraw her hands but she couldn't hold his gaze so she looked out the window. The frozen moon had come into view. The closer they got, the more inhabitable Geb's fractured surface looked.

"I've missed being with you," said Gary, breaking the silence.

At his words, her gaze darted back to meet his. His whole body seemed as frozen as that moon as if waiting for her to say something that would either cause a fracture or initiate a melt. *Oh, how she wanted a melting of the tension.*

"When we get back, I want to show you my shelter in the new spoke greenhouse." Margo felt her cheeks warm, but she didn't care.

"Amanda tells me you moved out there," said Gary, visibly relaxing.

"Yeah. I'm living near a banana grove surrounded by citrus trees. Paradise." She smiled, then added, "The shelter's pretty basic right now, but it's nice to get away from the rest of the colony. Our AI can't even reach me out there."

He returned her smile. "Have you hatched out more butterflies?"

Letting go of Gary's hand, Margo swallowed and looked out the window. As she considered how to respond, remembering her first batch of blue morpho butterflies. Margo looked out the porthole at the surface of the moon, but gasped when she saw the multitudes of flapping butterflies, their wings encased in ice. She gulped for air, telling herself the creatures were figments of her imagination. Squeezing her eyes closed, she willed the insects to disappear.

"Hey, Margo." Gary leaned forward and put his hand on her forearm, forcing her to open her eyes and look at him. "Are you okay?"

"Yeah." Margo felt like she'd just run up a dozen flights of stairs. She kept her gaze on Gary's concerned blue eyes, knowing as long as she did that, she wouldn't see the butterflies. "Just thinking about those colonists."

Gary nodded, but concern still lingered in his eyes as he gazed at her.

She liked the warmth of his hand on her arm. *What would he say if I told him about these crazy side effects?*

Margo readied herself, but before she could divulge her terrifying secret, Yuko marched into the galley with lips pursed like she'd just sucked a lemon. "Iago wants the two of you up on the bridge. We've got a good view of *Settler II*."

"Okay," said Gary. He glanced at Margo after he stood,

waiting for her to finish the last sip of her coffee and put the mug in the sink before following Yuko out of the galley.

Back on the bridge, Margo deliberately positioned herself as far away from Iago as she could given the small space. The wheel shape of the other colony ship now dominated the view. Its glossy white exterior appeared pristine and ready to be lived in; yet, it was most likely a tomb.

"Gary," said Iago, still sitting in Max's seat. "I want you to get ready in case we find any survivors."

Gary nodded but said nothing.

Iago glanced over his shoulder, briefly looking from person to person. "All of us except Ash and Max will be boarding as soon as we get close enough," said Iago.

"Since there is no evidence of any atmosphere in there, Gan your first priority is to re-start life support."

"Okay," said Gan, leaning forward to study the other ship.

"Once life support is running, get the ship spinning," said Iago. Gan nodded.

"Margo, you'll need to tell Abigail to suit up."

"Sure," said Margo.

"Then…"

A resounding thunk of impact startled them, the unexpected noise through the windshield made them all jump. For a moment everyone was stunned speechless, staring out of the *Staffelwaltze*'s windshield.

The something that hit the windshield was still there.

Margo swallowed, unable to tear her gaze away from the ghastly sight. It was a man, without an atmo suit, frozen in mid-scream. His exposed skin glistened alabaster white. He'd landed face forward on the glass. Lifeless eyes, frosted over and frozen in wide-eyed terror, stared in at them.

What the hell had happened on Settler II*?*

Chapter Twelve

Silence filled the bridge as everyone stared at the corpse stuck on the outside of their windshield.

"What the…?" Max stepped a pace back into Margo.

"Oh!" exclaimed Abigail as she appeared in the doorway of the bridge.

"What a terrible way to die," said Iva, a hand to her mouth, her eyes wide in horror.

"Yes, that poor man," said Ash in a quiet tone. The man's torso rested against the glass right in front of Ash. She lifted a hand as if to help him, but then let it drop.

"We need to get him in here," said Gary, in an authoritative tone.

Margo glanced his way as she thought that must be how he always sounded in an emergency. She supposed every doctor took on that authoritative persona when needed.

Now over his shock, Max shuffled forward to study the details of the corpse. At Gary's words he turned. "He's a goner, Doc."

"Max!" Ash's sharp tone made Max look sheepish.

"But Mom, I'm just saying the guy's—"

"Max. Think of Tom. What if it was him?"

Margo didn't know who Tom was, but mention of him turned the expression on Max's face from fascination to sorrow. She wondered if Tom had been sent out an airlock. Stories of that kind of vigilante law enforcement surfaced now and then.

Iago rose to his feet. "Dr. Holbrook's right. We need to bring him inside." As soon as he was out of the way, Max slipped back into the co-pilot's chair.

"Hopefully we can identify him." Yuko spoke in a rare compassionate. "That will be the first step in solving what the hell happened."

Margo squished herself against the doorframe as Iago shouldered past her. "Ash, can you tell if there are others out there?" The windshield, not very large to begin with, was rendered useless as long as that corpse was on it.

"Something organic of that size won't show on my instruments."

Gan was shaking his head. "A ship has to be equipped with specialized equipment in order to pick up corpses—this ship has nothing that fancy."

"Like the doctor said, we need to bring him in." Iago turned to Margo. "I want you with me."

"Me?" Margo crossed her arms over her chest and raised an eyebrow. "Why me?" She wasn't opposed to doing a spacewalk, but she was averse to Iago staking a claim on her. Again.

When Iago rested his mechanical hand on her shoulder, it felt heavier than she expected—and cold. "You. Now. Let's go." He turned and headed aft.

Meeting Gary's gaze, Margo shrugged.

"Let's go, Murphy," called Iago from half way down the passenger compartment.

With a sigh, she followed him to the vestibule beside the airlock, cringing at having to share this tiny space while they got dressed. She randomly opened one of the lockers and retrieved an atmo suit. All the suits were identical: one-piece, bright

orange with retro-reflector bands around the biceps and thighs
—and all oversized. These type of generic suits were standard
on all space ships a decade ago. *At least I'll be seen.*

Leaning against the wall and wishing there was a bench to
sit on, she shoved her right foot through the bulky fabric while
trying to come up with an excuse to have someone else work
with Iago. She did her best to ignore the large man, as he
stepped into his suit right next to her.

The suit's attached boots were big enough she didn't even
need to remove her shoes. After pulling the suit up over her
shoulders, she zipped up the front and cinched it at her waist
with the built-in belt. It was still baggy, but at least now she
wouldn't trip over it.

She swung on the air pack, adjusting the straps before buck-
ling the chest strap. After pulling on a soft cap to keep her curls
contained, she retrieved the helmet from the locker's shelf and
put it on. As soon as she sealed it, she performed a full integrity
check, relieved that she'd managed to dress in the suit without
once bumping elbows with Iago.

By the time the light on the wrist control of the suit blinked
green indicating her suit checked out, she still hadn't come up
with a reason why someone other than her should accompany
Iago. When she met his gaze from inside her helmet, he gave
her a curt nod.

"Ash," said Iago over the radio as he activated the airlock.
"We're heading into the airlock chamber."

"Roger that," their captain replied. "I'm holding position 10
kilometres away from the colony ship."

When the light on the outside door flashed to green, Iago
turned to Margo. "Let's move."

Sliding the tinted visor over her helmet's face, Margo
followed him inside the closet-sized airlock. *At least he hasn't called
me doll—yet.* She'd barely sealed the inner door behind them
when Iago flipped the switch to cycle the air. Next, he clipped
on a line connecting his suit and Margo's. As he moved, his

boots clanked against the metal floor—then the sound vanished. They were now in a vacuum. The hum of the air circulation fan in her suit was the only sound other than her breathing.

When the exterior door light flashed green, Iago turned the handle and swung it open. A swath of light from Helios filled the space and would've blinded Margo had she forgotten to put her visor down. In his atmo suit, Margo couldn't tell which of Iago's arms was flesh and which was mechanical. She had to admit he moved with grace, considering he was such a large man and had a prosthesis.

Using a second tether attached to his suit, he leaned out the door and clipped the opposite end onto a metal bar that ran the length of the ship.

"Let's get moving," he said as he stepped past the brink of the gravity plating. With both hands, he pulled himself out the door and disappeared around the hull.

Margo's stomach lurched when she crossed the threshold, making her glad she'd skipped breakfast. Keeping her focus on her hands, she clipped her second tether to the metal bar. At sight of the spots of corrosion on the iron bar, she told herself not to freak out. The rust was superficial, and the strength of the metal wasn't compromised. She hoped.

After her tether was secure, she surveyed her surroundings. *Settler II* loomed above them, seeming much closer than the 10 kilometres Ash claimed. In Helios' light, the hull gleamed white, looking pristine and perfect. It couldn't possibly be a graveyard, thought Margo. It was too beautiful.

"Focus, Margo," said Iago over the radio. He pulled himself forward, his legs floating away from *Staffelwalze*'s hull.

Margo let her feet float behind her as she dragged herself along following him. *Staffelwalze* wasn't big, at least not in comparison to one of the colony ships, so it didn't take long to reach the forward windows. As the front windshield came into view, she saw the corpse was still there. The frozen man wore the standard dark blue uniform of a colonist including rugged boots, cargo pants, and jacket—clothing that would do nothing to protect the wearer from the vacuum of space.

Inside, the concerned faces of Ash, Max, Iva and Yuko looked out at them. Abigail and Gan must be with Gary, Margo thought, transforming medbay into a morgue.

Iago reached the corpse first. Taking hold of the corpse's right elbow, he eased him away from the window, shifting the corpse so his feet drifted towards Margo.

She wedged her boot under the bar to stop herself from floating away and then grabbed the man's foot, controlling his trajectory towards her. He was frozen solid and stayed in the same pose as they manipulated him. When she wrapped an arm around his torso to hold him in place, she noticed he had a name tag on his jacket. Embroidered was a single word: Drake.

"Ash, do we have any records of the names of those on the *Settler II?*" she asked over the comms.

"Standby, Max is checking," said Ash.

"This guy's name is Drake," said Margo.

"Got it, we'll look." The comms line went silent.

Iago pulled himself over top of her and guided the body back towards the airlock door. Margo followed.

"We're not all going to fit in at the same time," said Iago, once they were outside the door. "Especially since this guy is so inflexible."

Did he just make a joke? Margo checked her tether to the ship. Seeing it was secure, she reached down and unclipped herself from Iago.

"You take the body in with you first. I'll wait here," said Margo. Iago was already maneuvering the corpse inside the airlock.

While she waited, she looked back up at the floating colony ship. The more she studied it, the more it reminded her of a toy —inanimate and empty; yet, just like *Settler III*, 25 couples with a dream of a new beginning had inhabited it. Drake had to be one of that 50, meaning there were still 49 people out there somewhere.

Turning her shoulders, she tried to survey the nearby space, hoping there weren't more floating bodies in the vacuum. After a few minutes of seeing nothing, she shifted her attention on the star field behind the colony ship. The tiny pin-points of light were at first beautiful, but then she frowned, puzzled, when they seemed to swirling in her vision. In the next moment, they morphed into a vast swarm of silver butterflies heading for the colony ship.

Margo realized what was happening and squeezed her eyes shut. *Not real, not real, not real.* When she opened her eyes, the colony ship appeared normal again. With a deep breath, she turned and checked the light beside the airlock.

"I regret to inform you that there is no bar service on our outer decks at this time. So, are you coming in or what?"

When she heard Ash's voice over the radio, she realized this wasn't the first question the captain had asked; in fact, Margo had a vague sense that Ash had been calling to her repeatedly. She also realized the light was green. *How long had I zoned out?*

"Coming in now," she stammered, grabbing the door handle. Opening it, she pulled herself inside, then untethered herself from the outside bar. As soon as she closed the exterior door, gravity took hold of her once more and she landed solidly on her feet. She latched the outside door and pushed the button to cycle the air. "I'm in."

She peered out the window into space as she unclipped the tether from her suit. The silver butterflies had returned, swarming around the *Settler II!* For a moment, they looked like they would shift direction and converge on the *Staffelwalze.* Margo swallowed and turned her back on the outside door. *Not real. Not real.*

When the light beside the interior door flashed green, she took off her helmet and returned into their tin-can home.

"Iago wants you in the medbay," said Max, who was waiting for her in the vestibule.

"Why? What do I know about corpses?" Without looking at him, Margo undid her air pack and hung it on a hook.

Max shrugged, ducking out the door. "I'm just passing a message," he said, over his shoulder as he headed forward.

Margo felt unsettled by the hallucination she'd just experienced. *Focus on the task at hand*, she told herself, knowing her hallucinations could risk those around her—a risk they didn't even know existed. She needed to tell someone about them, logically Gary.

Slumping against the wall, she took a deep breath and slowly counted backwards from ten before stripping off her atmo suit. She considered avoiding Iago, but unfortunately, she needed to pass right by the medbay to get anywhere. With a disgruntled sigh, she hung up her suit and headed into the corridor.

As she neared the open door to the medbay, she heard Gary and Iago talking about the corpse. Standing in the doorway, Margo saw the frozen man, now inside a clear plastic bag, lay on the examination table.

"Ah, you decided to stop lounging around outside and join us," said Iago, as she slipped inside.

The medbay wasn't much larger than the airlock vestibule, but Iago still put his flesh hand on her shoulder and steered her towards the examination table. When he needlessly left his hand on her, she shrugged it off. Gary raised an eyebrow, but she didn't respond.

"Alright, Dr. Holbrook, how do you think he died?" Iago pointed his prosthetic hand at the corpse.

"Other than being frozen solid, my preliminary exam shows nothing obviously wrong with him," said Gary, looking down at the corpse. "Since there isn't much in the way of imaging equipment on this ship, he'll need to thaw before I can examine him further." He didn't appear thrilled with the idea. "There is a risk that a pathogen is present."

"What do you think, Margo?"

Margo stared down at Drake, keeping her gaze away from the expression of terror on his face. He wore the standard uniform of their colonizing mission, with a red patch showing he was part of the operations branch.

"Something happened to put him outside without an atmo suit," she answered. "I didn't see any damage to the colony ship's hull, although to know for sure, we'd need Gan to conduct a proper inspection. But I think it's safe to say it wasn't a catastrophic depressurization. An airlock accident, perhaps?"

"Mmm." Iago crossed his hands across his chest. A few moments later, he turned and pressed the internal comms button.

"Ash, did you get access to the colony ship's computers?"

"No, they're powered down. There's not even back-up power. The only way to get into their computers is to get on board," said Ash.

"What's our ETA?" asked Iago.

"We'll be in range to connect in 20 minutes," she answered.

Iago turned back to Gary. "I want you to stay here and figure out how Drake died."

Gary glanced down at the body, nodding. "It will take a whole lot longer than twenty minutes before he's thawed enough for me to examine him. Plus, I'll have to be careful about how much he thaws. We're not equipped with a proper morgue, but I can control the temperature here in medbay."

Iago nodded. "Do what you have to." Then he turned to Margo. "I want you to accompany me onto the colony ship."

"You already said that," said Margo in a flat tone. "Who else are you taking?"

"Yuko, Gan, and Abigail," said Iago, from the doorway. "I'll go talk to them now. Meet me by the airlock in twenty."

The small space felt like it suddenly had sufficient air now that Iago was gone. Margo met Gary's concerned gaze.

"Be careful on that ship," he said. "And be on the lookout for anything, even slight, that is off."

She nodded, tempted again to confide in Gary about the hallucinations. But now wasn't the time. *When was the right time?* "I don't feel good about this at all." Margo looked down at Drake's face.

"Of course you don't. None of us do." Gary's tone was sympathetic.

Margo glanced at Drake's face. "He looks so surprised, doesn't he?" She felt a shiver run up her spine.

"Maybe they had a saboteur too?"

Margo met Gary's gaze. She'd just been thinking the same thing. "With all that happened to us, I wouldn't rule it out."

Chapter Thirteen

Twenty minutes later and back in an atmo suit, Margo stood inside the airlock of the *Staffelwalze* peering out the door window at the umbilical cord-like corridor that was extending toward the colony ship. It was the same tube that she'd passed through from the *Settler III* into the ship—and it still looked too flimsy, but it was their only means to board the colony ship without traversing the vacuum of space. As it moved into place, the stiff tube blocked her view of the other ship.

What will we find on the other side? A knot formed in her gut as she pondered all the gruesome possibilities from frozen bodies huddled together to remnants of cannibalism. Her heart pounded. *Get a grip, Murphy!*

Putting a hand on the thigh pocket of her suit, she traced the outline of the old revolver through the thick fabric. In that moment, she was glad she'd followed Lucas' advice to bring the weapon. Having it reassured her, despite believing it unlikely that any of the horrors they might face could be solved with a bullet. She swallowed back her fear and returned to the vestibule.

Iago, Abigail, Gan and Yuko were also already dressed in

their atmo suits. All five of them held their helmets. Yuko stood beside Iago. She barely came to his shoulder and bristled with confidence. Abigail and Gan stood together against the wall looking like the odd couple, buxom Abigail filling out the one-sized suit beside Gan, whose suit was baggier on him than it was on Margo. In her left hand, Abigail held a portable air sensor, while Gan had a toolbox.

Iago puffed himself up and turned to face the others. "Is everyone clear on our objectives?"

"Find out if there are survivors," Margo said.

"Yes. And we stay together. No one goes off on their own." Iago punctuated his words with an extended index finger.

"So, first to engineering? That'll be the best place to find out what happened to the power and gravity," said Gan.

"It should be easy to get to," said Iago. "This ship is identical to *Settler III*—so we know our way around. First priority is to get the ship spinning and restart life support."

"What about accessing the data on the computers?" asked Yuko.

"That's secondary," stated Iago in a clipped tone.

"Stay focused, no matter what we see," Margo muttered to herself. Despite the fact that she was thinking of her hallucinations when she spoke, the others all nodded.

"Questions?" Iago asked.

A squawk indicated the internal comms being activated, then came Ash's voice. "We're attached to the *Settler II*, and we've pressurized the umbilical with our air. You guys can go as soon as you're ready."

"We are heading out now," said Iago into the intercom box. He turned and looked at the assembled people.

Margo took a deep breath, knowing the others were feeling the same anxiety about what they might encounter on the colony ship.

"Helmets on."

Everyone did as they were told, filling the small space with the sound of their airtight latches catching.

Iago turned and led the way into the airlock, opening the outside door. One-by-one the others filed into the umbilical corridor. Sun light came through walls providing ample illumination. Margo brought up the rear, closing the interior airlock door behind her. When she crossed the threshold of the *Staffel-walze's* exterior airlock door, she pushed back her fear and shut the outside door as well.

Outside the ship, gravity ended and Margo allowed her body to float to the centre of the passageway. Using one hand, she pulled herself forward, the same as her crewmates in front of her were doing. As she pulled herself along, she could make out the outlines of the two ships beyond the translucent walls.

Ahead Iago reached the colony ship airlock, the retro-reflectors on his suit catching the light from everyone's helmets. To avoid a bottleneck by waiting for the others to catch up, he opened it and disappeared inside.

Yuko followed him in. Next was Abigail, who was being uncharacteristically quiet. A moment later, Gan disappeared inside.

"Hey, slow poke," said Abigail over the helmet comms as she reappeared in the doorway to the *Settler II*. "Let's not make this take any longer than it must."

Margo followed Abigail into the colony ship's airlock. Abigail shut the door behind them. It was far darker inside the ship than it had been in the umbilical space. Even though she'd never set foot in this ship before and their helmet lights only illuminated pockets of the surrounding walls, Margo knew the layout. They were in the colony's main airlock.

"I'm opening the inside door now," said Iago.

His voice was unnecessarily loud over their helmet comms, making Margo suspect he was more nervous than he let on. She and her three crewmates watched from behind as Iago turned the wheel. As soon as he swung the interior airlock door open, a riot of loose gear floated in—atmo suit gloves, random straps, woolly caps, and a single boot.

"All clear." Iago pushed aside some of the harmless gear and launching himself into the next compartment.

The others followed.

Once through the large atmo suit change room and in the Loop, it got even darker. Only the beams of light from their helmet lamps illuminated the curving corridor. More floating debris moved through the air like snowflakes.

As Margo propelled herself into the Loop, vertigo hit and nausea threatened to overwhelm her. Instead of the normal up and down of ceiling and roof, she perceived up and down lengthwise along the Loop. One direction was like staring up at a starless night sky, and the other way like gazing down into a yawning black abyss. Darkness beckoned her from both directions. She swallowed and forced herself to focus on the beams of light cast by the others as they inspected the corridor.

"Any idea what these stains on the walls are?" Yuko was shining her light against dark streaks that marred what should have been a pristine white surface.

"Stay focused, Yuko," snapped Iago through the comms. "Remember our priorities. Gravity and power so that we can start the life support. Speaking of, how's the air in here, Abigail?"

Abigail held up her portable sensor unit. "Air pressure is good. Oxygen levels are low, but not fatal. Like the top of Kilimanjaro, or some other high place like that. *Not* what I was expecting."

"Any toxins?" asked Yuko.

"Nothing worth mentioning. Even the carbon dioxide levels are within normal range." Abigail looked up at the others and shrugged. "The cold is the only dangerous thing."

"Okay," said Iago. "We need to get this place running again. Gan, which way to engineering?"

"This way," said the taciturn engineer, with the same soft

voice he always used. Taking the lead, Gan pushed himself forward, and the others followed.

The direction he went felt like up. Margo took a final glance toward her feet. In the dark, far below, she thought she saw the fluttering of a silver butterfly. Before letting it take shape, she spun herself around and propelled herself after the others.

Gan took them to engineering, through the cavernous work space filled with floating tools and on into the engineering control room. He went straight to the main console and hit a button, and the display came to life.

"They have power?" Yuko squawked, holding onto the edge of a workstation to keep herself from bumping into furniture. The others had done the same.

"How is that possible?" Iago demanded.

"First we discover they have oxygen." Abigail gestured with her sensor. "Now we find out they have power. This place is messed up!"

After going through several screens looking at diagnostics, Gan turned towards the others. "It was just off," he said. "At first glance, I don't see any problem."

"Can you turn everything on?" Iago asked.

"Sure," Gan turned and worked through the screens. A moment later, overhead lights flickered on, illuminating the space.

"That's better," said Margo. She hated vertigo, and the dark didn't help. Neither did zero gravity.

Now that the lights were on, Margo and the others—all, but Gan—looked around the room, moving around a bit to see if there was anything obvious that could solve the mystery of the powered-down ship.

Meanwhile, Gan worked through more screens before addressing the others. "I've set the thrusters to spin up the ship again. It'll take a few minutes to reach accelerations of normal gravity."

"Is that it? Power and gravity are on?" asked Iago.

"Yes," said Gan, keeping his gaze on the screens. Margo could see his pinched expression through his helmet's visor.

"But it can't be that simple," Iago argued.

"I'm sure it's not," said Gan. "We just haven't found the problem yet."

"Let's head to the main Control Room," Iago said, leading the way back into the Loop. Here, the space remained dark.

As they floated down the Loop, Margo noticed that her helmet lights illuminated dark stains on all of the Loop's walls. There seemed to be a pattern, but the floating debris made it hard to tell for sure. She wanted to stop and examine it—was it blood?—but Iago was moving too fast and there's no way she wanted to get left behind.

At the open doors of the dark Control Room, the main nerve centre of the ship, Iago paused for a moment before pushing himself in. Yuko followed. Gan was behind Yuko, but he stopped at the doorway, blocking Abigail and Margo.

"The Control Room doors' default is to remain closed," said Gan in a suspicious tone.

"Gan, we need lights in here," ordered Iago from inside, his voice booming over their helmet comms.

"Another detail to add to the mystery," sighed Gan, before pulling himself through the door.

Margo looked at Abigail. "I've got a bad feeling about this."

"Me too," said Abigail.

It surprised Margo the other woman didn't have a snarky comment. Abigail must be as freaked out as her. Then Margo remembered Nancy. She'd been so worried about hallucinating something that she'd forgotten. No wonder Abigail wasn't being snarky. She was likely terrified they'd soon be stumbling across the body of her friend.

"We better get in there." Margo pushed off the wall and drifted into the Control Room, with Abigail right behind.

As she crossed the threshold, the overhead lights switched on. *Thank you, Gan!* The workstations and chairs in the three-tiered space were identical to the Control Room on Thesan. Dominating the far wall was a large screen, but it remained blank. The server room, on the other side of the clear wall remained dark.

An empty coffee cup bounced off Margo's helmet, startling her, and making her heart hammer. She chided herself for not keeping an eye out for floating objects. As she moved she glanced around, having to swivel her upper torso to see properly through the helmet's visor. Everywhere she looked things were floating, pens, scrolls, a half-eaten sandwich, someone's jacket…

"Yuko," said Iago. "It's time to get the computers up and running."

The astrophysicist pulled herself in front of a console and flipped the main power switch. A moment later, it flashed to life, and the screens filled with diagnostic readings.

As Yuko scrolled through the screens, Margo realized the debris of daily life that floated around her was shifting on an angular path towards both the wall on her right and the ground —as was she. The centrifugal force of the rotating ship was starting to pull everything towards the floor, but the counter-clockwise rotation meant the structure was moving before the floating debris—most of the stuff would hit a wall before sliding down to the floor.

Shifting her feet beneath her, Margo touched down on the deck, wobbling slightly.

"What have you found?" asked a now standing Iago.

"Still working on it." Yuko spoke without turning around. "This would go faster if I took my helmet off."

"Temperature is reading minus 146 degrees Celsius, way too cold for exposed skin," said Abigail, before looking at Margo and mouthing 'dipshit.'

"Gary told me the lack of gravity diminishes our immune capacity, making us much more susceptible to allergens," said Margo, knowing the thought of them removing their helmets would horrify Gary.

"Whatever," muttered Yuko, without glancing up.

Margo and Abigail exchanged another look.

"Keep your helmets on for now," said Iago. "Margo, with me." He started towards the Control Room exit. The low gravity bounce in his step was almost comical.

"Didn't you say we'd be staying together?" asked Margo in alarm. She didn't want to leave the group, and certainly not with Iago.

"We're just going across the hall," Iago said as he strode out the door.

"To the stasis room?" Margo asked. "Why?"

"Just come," Iago said, without glancing behind him.

Margo shared an eye roll with Abigail, then followed.

When Iago opened the door, the lights immediately came on. Margo bounced inside the door and stopped beside him.

Inside the large room, rows of 50 stasis chambers were lined up like soldiers on parade. The clear surfaces of the tops reflected the overhead lights, and she couldn't see inside. *Are they empty?* She took a deep breath as tension rose in her body. The room felt suddenly creepy.

To make matters worse, Iago moved uncomfortably close to her and put his flesh hand on her waist and smiled down at her. "It's tough to get you alone." Iago's deep voice was laced with humour as though he'd just told a joke.

"Let's see if anyone is here," Margo said, leaping forward to get away from his touch.

"You don't make things easy." Iago chuckled. "But I love a good chase."

"Not interested," she practically shouted as she approached the nearest stasis pod. She stopped and looked inside. The light from her helmet illuminated the interior. The pod was empty.

Iago chuckled as he headed down the other row. "Everyone always comes around in the end," he stated, glancing into each pod as he sauntered past. "These are all empty."

"So are these." Margo wasn't sure if she should feel relief. *Is it better they're empty?* At the end of her row, she turned and looked to Iago.

"It would've been peaceful if they'd all just died in their pods," said Iago.

"Perhaps."

There was a brief crackle over her helmet comms. "You two need to get back here," said Yuko.

Chapter Fourteen

Gary leaned closer to the window in the main passenger compartment to get a better view of the umbilical corridor. Ash and Max, he knew, were maneuvering it into place using a control panel in the bridge. The tube reminded him of a shimmering tapeworm moving of its own free will as it reached to connect their ship's airlock with the colony ship.

A slight vibration resonated throughout the *Staffelwalze* as the two ships connected. The translucent fabric inflated as the system pumped the mobile corridor full of air. A few moments later, he saw the shadow shapes of his crewmates as they floated between the ships. He studied each one, wondering which form was Margo. His gaze didn't waver from the shapes until the last figure disappeared into the unknown void of *Settler II*.

Iva slid into the chair across from him. "Are they over?"

"Yes." Letting himself relax back into the seat, he studied Iva. The hard edge of her short blunt haircut complemented her heart-shaped face. She smiled at him.

"They'll be fine," she said. He didn't know her very well, but he knew that on their arrival on Thesan, her husband Mihaly had died fighting the fires that had erupted when their ship crash landed. Since then, she'd earned a reputation as someone who could always be relied on—as well as someone rather addicted to playing retro video games on the large screen in the Control Room.

"Do you wish you were with them?" he asked.

"Hell, no." She glanced out the window then back to him. "Exploring haunted ghost ships isn't my idea of fun. Frankly, I would rather have stayed on Thesan—even if it meant working night shifts."

Gary smiled, thinking it best not to mention he'd volunteered to come. "Do the night shifts allow for more video game time?" At her nod, he added, "More than once when I walked by the Control Room, I've heard the electronic soundtracks of your old games."

"You'd always be welcome to come on in and play a round," she said with a smile. When she turned and looked out the window at the other ship, her smile dissipated. "I'll take pixelated ghosts over potential real ones any day."

"Do you think anyone is alive in there?" Gary eyed the pristine hull of the other ship.

"Even though I'd rather not have come on this mission, I really did think the other colonists could be alive. I mean, we had more than our share of disasters, but a lot of us survived. I thought the same might be said for the first two ships. Now, though? After having Drake end up on our windshield? No, I don't," said Iva in a flat tone.

They sat in contemplative silence for a moment before Iva asked, "Do you know how long Drake has been dead?"

Gary shook his head. "Not yet and it'll be hard to get a definitive answer."

"Do you think those colonists all died months ago?"

Gary frowned. "I hate to be that pessimistic. Let's wait and see. Iago, at least, seems hopeful of finding survivors. His determination is why we're here now."

"Iago wants what he wants," she said with a shrug.

Gary eyed Iva. "You mean, to be seen as a saviour?" If Iago was hailed as the saviour who rescued survivors from *Settler I and II*, it would feed right into his ego. Gary didn't voice his other thought—that Iago also wanted Margo, which irked him to no end. At least Margo didn't reciprocate.

Iva nodded. "Uh, huh. It's obvious Iago wants to be seen as the hero. Whether we return with survivors or bring back needed equipment, he's picturing himself as the champion of this solar system. And then, I expect, he'll make a play to replace Lucas as Commander on Thesan."

"Lucas has done a fine job of leading the colony. Given the challenges we've had, I want Lucas to remain at the helm."

"I agree." Iva glanced out the window at the colony ship even though nothing had changed and it was too soon to expect the return of their crewmates. "Lucas had a tough time at first, but now he's found his groove. He's got an inclusive approach. Iago would be a dictator. Plus, Lucas is committed to setting up a democratic system for the long term, as was always the plan. I don't know if Iago would honour that. But, the fact of the matter is, sooner or later we'll be voting for our leader."

"And 'we' colonists are outnumbered by insurgents. Well, only time will tell." mused Gary, then tilted his head as a thought struck him. "Do you think Lucas will even want to run? Maybe calling for a vote will be his way of exiting gracefully?"

The squawking of the comms line interrupted them. They both looked towards the overhead speaker.

"Yuko linked us to *Settler II*'s computers. Why don't the two of you come up front and we can poke around in their records," suggested Ash.

Gary and Iva rose and hurried towards the bridge.

"Have they found any survivors?" Iva asked as they entered the bridge.

Gary had been about to ask almost the same question, but he had 'bodies' on the tip of his tongue rather than 'survivors'.

Maybe he wasn't as optimistic as he at first thought. And maybe Iva was more optimistic than she realized.

"No one yet," Ash answered.

On the bridge, Iva took her usual seat at the console facing the back bulkhead while Gary stood in the door frame behind Max's chair. The young man was focused on his controls and didn't acknowledge their arrival.

"Are they all okay, so far?" Gary asked. It wasn't like him to worry, but Margo was exploring a ghost ship. How could he not worry?

"They're fine," Ash responded.

"They're in the engineering control room," Max said, over his shoulder.

"Okay, Yuko, Iva is here," said Ash, from the pilot's chair. "I'm transferring the remote connection to her console."

Gary saw Iva's display flip to new data, but he didn't know what it meant.

"Yuko," Iva asked. "When you powered the system back up, did the AI come back online?"

"No," said Yuko. Her voice sounded tinny over the radio as though she was far away.

"Good, all AIs go flaky eventually—especially one that had been sitting there with nothing to do like that one," said Ash. "Leave it off and it'll be one less problem we have to solve."

"Mom, look," Max exclaimed pointing to the colony ship beside them. "The colony's begun rotating."

"Right, make sure we match their motion, Max. I don't want to damage our umbilical."

"Does that mean the ship has gravity?" Gary asked.

"It'll slowly return as the ship's rotation reaches the speed to simulate one g," Ash said.

Gary was beginning to realize that Ash never said more than she had to. "That means the ship has power, then? And air?"

"Yes," replied Ash.

"Which makes the death of Drake and that ghost ship over there even more a mystery," Gary stated. No one responded.

Ash turned towards Iva. "You in *Settler II's* system?"

"I'm in but…" Iva's voice trailed off as she leaned in to study her screen.

"But what?" asked Ash.

Gary watched in concern as Iva scrolled through a series of screens, frowning as she went.

"Can you bring up a personnel manifest?" Ash asked.

Iva looked over her shoulder at Ash. "Something is wrong with the colony's computers. Most of the records are corrupt. I can't even get the most basic manifest information."

"What happened to the computers?" asked Ash.

Iva shrugged and turned back to her screen. "Solar flare perhaps?" she suggested as she resumed working. "That ship was never supposed to stay in space this long."

"What about their biotrackers?" asked Gary. Every colonist had a chip inserted into their forearm to help the medical staff keep track of the state of their health. The technology also allowed the colonists to be tracked.

"Good idea," Iva said, her fingers flying on her keyboard. "That would be on their medical server, hang on." Iva kept working. After a few minutes, she stopped and looked up at Gary. "I've got nothing."

"No historical record? Or no current biotracker data?" Gary asked

Iva shook her head. "Neither."

"You mean, the medical server is damaged too?" Ash got up and stood behind Iva, leaning in to view Iva's screen.

"It seems to be fine," Iva said, gesturing at the screen as if the data displayed spoke for itself. "But it's not showing any data on the colonists' biotrackers."

"Another glitch?" asked Gary, moving beside Ash to see Iva's screen, not that he could make heads or tails out of the scrolling data. "Can you expand your search to pick up any biotracker on *Settler II*?"

"Oh, you mean, our guys." Iva worked through several menus. A moment later, a map of the colony ship appeared with four blue dots clustered within the main Control Room.

"Those dots are our people," said Gary.

"We're short a dot," said Ash, a note of alarm creeping into her tone. "We have five people over there."

"Margo removed her biotracker." When the two women looked at Gary, he added, "it's a long story. Don't ask."

Iva glanced back and forth between Gary and Ash. Max remained focused on piloting the ship, maintaining the same speed as the *Settler II* so as not to dislodge or damage their umbilical.

"So, clearly, the system is working. There's power. There's gravity," she said, ticking her fingers. "And there's likely air and heat. Yet…" her words trailed off.

"Yet," stated Ash, picking up Iva's train of thought. "Our five report no sign of colonists, dead or alive. So, where have the colonists all gone?"

"The biotrackers would give a reading even if the host is deceased, provided it hasn't been removed," said Gary. "Can you scan this ship for biotrackers?"

"Hang on." Iva went to work. A few moments later, five dots appeared on the map of the *Staffelwalze*, four on the bridge and one in the medbay.

Gary pointed to the medbay dot. "That's Drake."

"Then that means the biotrackers are working," Ash observed, crossing her arms and frowning down at the blinking dot on Iva's screen. "So, what happened to them?"

"I don't know," Iva replied in a quivering voice. She ran her hands along the fabric of her pants before tapping a few buttons and flipping her screen back to colony computers.

"We may not know what happened to them, but we do know they are gone." Gary nodded his head in the direction of the *Settler II.* "That ship has been abandoned, voluntarily or forcefully we don't know."

"It really *is* a ghost ship," said Max from behind them, a note of awe in his voice.

"Stay focused, Max," Ash chided, giving her son a look of warning.

Max turned back to the flashing lights and screens in front of him. "Under control, Ma," he assured, sounding as cocky as any nineteen-year-old, hot-shot pilot.

Ash gave her attention back to Iva. "Is something blocking the signals?"

"Nothing," said Iva, tapping a few keys to change the readout on another screen. She gestured at the data on the side-by-side screens. The dots were all still there. "The system is picking up everyone's biotrackers."

"Gary, can you assess the data coming from the biotrackers?" Ash asked. Both her tone and expression made it seem like she had everything under control.

"I'll send the data to that terminal," said Iva, pointing to the empty console.

Gary sat down and studied the screen as biotracker data came up relieved to have a task instead of waiting for Margo to return. This data he understood. He went through everyone's vital signs—excepting Margo's—and shared with the others that, although their heart rates were elevated—exactly what he would expect given they were investigating a ghost ship—they were all fine.

"Mom, comms just went dead." Max took his headset off and turned to look at Ash. "I've lost them."

Gary's mouth went dry as he stared out the main window at the colony ship beyond.

"What?" Ash's voice was borderline shrill, exposing a chink in her otherwise calm veneer. She returned to the pilot's seat and fiddled with the comms gear. "Come in, Iago," she kept repeating.

A shard of fear permeated the bridge. Gary ran a trembling hand through his hair. When he glanced at Iva, he saw her face had gone pale as she worked through the comms system's diagnostic screens.

"Everything is working at our end," Iva said, looking over her shoulder to address Ash. "There's no explanation for the comms going out."

"Are we picking up any interference?" asked Ash.

Iva turned back to her console. "Nothing obvious. I'll keep looking."

Gary glanced down at his screen, the four dots were still there, but they didn't include Margo. He knew, as a doctor, he should care about the wellbeing of all five of his crewmates on the ghost ship, but he only cared about Margo. *Please be okay, Margo. Please be okay.*

Chapter Fifteen

Without speaking, Iago and Margo left the stasis chamber room and crossed the still dark corridor back to the Control Room.

"What is it?" demanded Iago, as he strode over to study the screen over Yuko's shoulder. Margo joined Abigail and Gan at the main console.

Yuko glanced up at him. "The computers on this ship have been deliberately scrambled."

"Did you get Iva to take a look?" he asked.

"I was on the line with them, then we got cut off for some reason. It must be some error on their end," she said.

"There's nothing wrong with the *Staffelwalze* system," said Gan. "It's either interference or it's this end. I'll check it out." He moved towards the empty workstation beside Yuko.

"Hang on." Iago put up his hand to stop Gan. "Before we dive into solving the computer issues, which I've already stated are secondary, we need to remind ourselves why we're here. We've got the gravity going, and the power, so now we need to look for survivors. Gan, bring full lighting to the colony. We need to start an old-fashioned door-to-door search. If someone is here, we'll find them."

"That will take some doing," said Abigail as she put her air-quality sensor down on an empty seat. "This is one hell of a big place."

The ship jerked, as if they'd been rear-ended, nearly knocking everyone standing off their feet. Putting a hand out, Margo steadied herself against the nearest wall.

"What was that?" demanded Iago.

Gan scrolled through the nearest console. "I don't know. An engineering glitch perhaps?" He scratched his head. "But, the diagnostics are telling me everything is okay."

"Well the diagnostics must be false," Iago stated.

"Agreed. And to determine what's causing a false report, I need to work in the server room," said Gan.

"Are we in any danger?" asked Iago.

Abigail snorted. "What kind of dumb-ass question is that?"

Margo could tell from Iago's posture that Abigail's comment annoyed him.

"We're on a ghost ship whose crew mysteriously vanished," Abigail scoffed. "Of course we're in danger."

"I mean something more immediate," snapped Iago.

Gan didn't even look Iago's way but kept his eyes trained on the screens and his fingers flying on the console "I have no idea."

"But what makes a ship stutter like that?" Iago demanded.

"It's likely just a…." said Gan.

"Full lighting is up," said Yuko, drawing Iago's attention.

"Let's go see what we can find," he said. "For efficiency, we split up."

Margo inhaled sharply. *What happened to sticking together?* She didn't want to be stuck alone with Iago a second time.

"Yuko, stay here and monitor the ship. Stay in touch. Our comms are working, even if we can't communicate with the *Staffelwalze*." Iago looked towards Margo.

"I'll go with Abigail," Margo stated before Iago could assign himself to her.

Iago's eyes lingered on her. "Fine," he conceded.

Margo let her breath out slowly, feeling relieved, She had to laugh at herself, though. There was a time when she would've thought she was being punished at being partnered with Abigail. A lot had changed since the early days of their mission.

"You two check the living areas," Iago ordered. "Gan, come with me. We'll go through the hangars and engineering. Leave the labs for now. Reconvene here in an hour."

As Iago and Gan strode towards the exit, Iago added, "And stay sealed in your atmo suits."

Margo followed Abigail out into the Loop, but nearly collided with her when Abigail abruptly stopped. The lights were on in the Loop and Abigail was staring at the walls.

"Holy shit!" she said.

Margo stepped forward and stood beside Abigail. Iago and Gan were on Abigail's other side. All four of them stared at the mysterious markings on the walls.

They weren't random stains. A shiver crawled up her spine as Margo studied them. Human hands had made them—more specifically, human fingers. The rust-coloured markings formed indecipherable swirls, Egyptian-looking hieroglyphs, and pictograms. The thick, bold strokes filled the walls from floor to ceiling, stretching the entire length of the loop as far as she could see.

"What do they mean?" asked Iago, breaking the silence.

"More like why in the hell would anyone paint markings like this? On these walls?" Abigail asked, as irreverent of Iago as usual. She gestured at the curving corridor ahead of them. "It's everywhere."

Margo moved closer to better examine the markings. "They're deliberate symbols." The markings were as vague as a conspiracy theorist's notebook and reminded her of Jim. *Could it be the same type of language she'd found in his notebooks?* "Is it a code?"

When Abigail leaned in for a closer view, the bubble of her

helmet almost touched the markings. "Holy bat-out-of-hell shit!" she exclaimed. "That's not paint. That's blood!"

Margo frowned as she stared at the markings. They'd suddenly become gruesome. "Abigail could be right," she said, glancing at Gan and Iago on her right, then back at the wall. "Wait, there's something else strange." She lifted a gloved hand and gestured with her arm as if she was about to start painting the wall. "Look at the height of them."

Iago turned to regard her. "What are you getting at?"

Abigail was nodding. "These markings were made by someone standing on the floor. The colonists were walking around."

So?" Iago demanded, obviously annoyed Abigail had answered instead of Margo.

"It means when they made those markings, they had gravity," said Gan. He turned, so he could look directly at Margo from inside his helmet. "Then why did the ship stop spinning? It doesn't take much energy to sustain rotation—a few solar panels, at most. I know our inspection was hasty, but even so, the mechanical side of this ship seems fine."

"Speculation isn't going to solve this mystery. We'll find the clues we need while we carry on with our search," said Iago, turning and heading towards engineering. "Are you coming, Gan?"

Margo gave Gan a grateful look before he followed in Iago's wake.

As soon as they were out of earshot, Abigail turned to Margo. "Bullshit! He's not interested in 'clues'. That self-serving dipshit is on a treasure hunt." If Abigail let herself get too worked up, she'd start to steam up the inside of her visor.

"Let's not worry about him for the time being. Focus on Nancy. Maybe during our search we can figure out what happened to her."

Abigail sighed. "And her crewmates. Their loved ones deserve to know what happened."

With one last look at the macabre markings on the wall, Margo and Abigail turned and headed towards the residential quarter. Full lights were on, which felt as sinister as the darkness. The Loop was identical to their home, yet the only hint of humanity here was the cryptic writing on the walls.

They remained silent as they walked through the common room. Here the walls were pristine—and perfectly straight and aligned, like *Settler III's* walls had been before they crashed on Thesan. It was messy though; in the dining room furniture lay spread randomly throughout the space, the result of gravity returning.

"This place is creeping me out," said Abigail, as they opened the door to inspect the kitchen.

"Me too." Margo stepped carefully through scattered shards of broken dishes on the floor.

They passed through the food prep space and back onto the Loop without seeing anything enlightening about what might have happened. When they crossed over and went into the Hub —the central courtyard of the 2-storey apartment complex— the frozen garden at the centre of the space caught Margo's eye.

They both paused for a minute at the unexpectedly beautiful sight before them. A veneer of frost covered every leaf and element of the garden. The air flow from the ventilation system made the ice crystals dance, which in turn cast rainbows about the room, creating a child's dream winter wonderland.

"Wow," said Margo.

"Yeah," echoed Abigail. "But why does it look so orderly? Why isn't there a big mess here the same as everywhere else?"

Margo frowned. "Perhaps the plants and soil were already frozen solid when they lost gravity."

"No shit. Let's go apartment to apartment," said Abigail.

"Sure. As long as we stick together."

They headed to the first apartment on the ground level beside a wall of crystallized leafy ferns. Inside, they found the stuff of ordinary life scattered about. They found the same thing in the next dozen apartments. Nothing, so far, gave them any clue as to what had happened.

"Margo," said Abigail, reading the door plaque of the final apartment on the lower level. "This one says Felix and Holly Drake."

"The home of the body we found?" asked Margo.

"It looks that way." Abigail opened the door, but the two of them stood still for a moment. This apartment was no longer that of a random stranger. It felt invasive to saunter in uninvited, even knowing Drake—Felix Drake—was dead and would never return.

Biting her lip, Margo led the way inside, Abigail on her heels, and said over her shoulder. "You check the bedrooms? I'll check the living and kitchen areas,"

Like the other apartments, personal items were scattered everywhere. Margo stooped and picked up a framed picture off the floor. The image showed a moving picture of a happy couple on a beach back on Earth. The face of the man in the image was smiling and happy, nothing like the contorted terror on the face of the frozen corpse, yet this was the same man. Setting it on the coffee table, she ventured further inside. After wandering through the kitchen and bathroom she found nothing of note.

"Anything?" asked Margo, as she and Abigail reconvened at the door.

Abigail shook her head.

"Let's find your friend's quarters."

Through the helmet, Margo could hear Abigail's sigh. "Nancy was always very particular about how she kept her home. She'd hate for us to see it like this." Abigail gestured to the mess in the Drakes' quarters.

"Well, let's check sickbay first before going upstairs."

They found sickbay just as empty of life—and full of mess—as everywhere else. As Abigail checked the examination rooms, Margo inspected the offices. It was strange seeing the duplicate of Gary's office in this abandoned place, but other than the mess returning gravity created, nothing seemed out of place.

"I can't face looking in Nancy's apartment," said Abigail. "Especially since I know there's no one to save."

"I can circle back later with Gan and look. How about we just move on?"

"Might as well check if the terraforming equipment is still okay," suggested Abigail. "If we're going to be space pirates, we might as well get the good stuff."

"Sure." Margo led the way back into the Loop, but stopped abruptly as soon as she opened the sickbay door.

There was writing on the opposite wall. It seemed also to have been written, in blood, by a human hand, but these words made sense.

Butterfly blue, without a clue; Butterfly red, better off dead.

It felt like a giant hand was squeezing Margo's heart. Her breathing became shallow and ragged.

"What the hell?" said Abigail, stepping around her. "Why would everything else be written in indecipherable code, yet this be written in plain English? And strange coincidence it mentions butterflies, don't you think? This shit is getting crazier by the minute." Abigail, looked over at Margo.

"Yeah." Margo couldn't shift her gaze away from the words.

"Hey, you okay?" asked Abigail, resting a hand on Margo's arm.

Margo forced herself to start moving down the Loop towards terraforming. "Let's get this search over with. I want out of here as soon as possible."

Abigail glanced at the strange butterfly quote before jogging a little in the atmo suit to catch up with Margo. "Hey, you're not taking this personally, are you. It's just a coincidence, those words about the butterflies. This place is ghoulish," said Abigail. "Crazy ghoulish."

As the two of them strode down the Loop, Margo glanced back and forth at the strange scrawls and pictographs on the walls, but no other plainly worded messages about butterflies were written on the walls of the Loop. *Am I crazy to think that message was directed at me?* But how utterly strange that the only legible script they'd seen had been about butterflies.

As they passed yet another series of swirls with messy reddish brown dots above, Margo's steps slowed when she noticed one of them moving. She stopped and stared at the dot as it morphed into two dots with a black line between them. The dots shifted, and the transformation into a butterfly was complete. Margo swallowed as the butterfly that couldn't be real lifted off the wall and started fluttering towards Abigail. As the butterfly passed other dots, it seemed to breathe life into them as they, too, morphed into butterflies, creating a swarming cloud in Abigail's wake.

A few paces ahead, Abigail stopped and looked back at Margo, realizing she'd stopped. As soon as Abigail turned towards her, the hallucinated butterflies vanished.

"I know you're freaked, but you gotta let it go. Now's not the time for dilly dallying. Save your art critique for later," said Abigail.

"Yeah," said Margo. She glanced back at the dots on the wall. They had returned to being stationary and cryptic. Then she turned Abigail's direction "I'm coming."

Once inside the terraforming room, they set to work checking the terraforming gear starting with the oxygen producing algal generators.

"Good news. It looks like nothing has been touched," said Abigail at last. "Everything is here, and it's all usable."

"Let's check out the seed library," said Margo.

The two of them headed further down the Loop. A squawk over their helmet comms brought them to a stop.

"Margo? Abigail?" Iago said over their atmo suits' comms. "I need the two of you to come to the shuttle hangar right away. Gan's had an accident."

Margo stopped in her tracks. "What's happened?" she demanded, immediately picturing Gan bleeding or dead.

"Gan?" Abigail called on the helmet radio at the same time. "Are you okay?"

"He's fine. Just get to the shuttle hangar." Iago snapped.

Abigail clicked off her helmet comms, then said to Margo, "I guess things aren't going smoothly for Mr. High and Not Mighty."

The two of them broke into a jog. Their large boots and the atmo suit gear—helmet, gloves, air pack—made jogging difficult, but they were both concerned about Gan. A few minutes later, breathing heavily, they entered the hangar and rushed over to where Gan sat with his back against the wall beside the tool bench.

A web of cracks covered the clear bubble of Gan's visor.

"Has your suit lost integrity?" Margo rushed to kneel beside him, Abigail taking the same position on the other side. Margo glared briefly over her shoulder at Iago. "His suit has lost integrity! How can you say *he's fine?*"

Sharing a disgusted look with Abigail, Margo inspected the damage to Gan's helmet. The cracks reached all the way through as she could see blood on the inside of his helmet, likely caused from shards of the shattered visor.

"I *am* fine," Gan insisted, although his tone was strained. "There's breathable air."

"No toxins," Abigail reported, consulting the internal sensor read out on the wall.

"Are you hurt anywhere else?" Margo asked.

"No, just my face."

Abigail glared over her shoulder at Iago, a clumsy move given she had to turn her entire upper torso to do so. "Why didn't you attempt to patch up the cracks?" Her accusing tone squawked unpleasantly over the helmet speaker.

"What's the point?" Iago gestured defensively. "Like he says, there's oxygen. Besides, if there is some toxin in the air, he's already inhaled it. So I called you instead. You can take him back to our ship."

"Gary will insist on quarantining me," Gan said with a grimace.

Margo wanted to punch Iago for being such a casually selfish idiot, but instead addressed Gan. "And so he should."

Relieved that Gan wasn't on death's door, Margo rose and took a moment to take in her surroundings. The hangar bay was just like the one in *Settler III*, except undamaged, with all the doors perfectly aligned within their door frames. Two shuttles were tethered to the hangar floor just like the two shuttles in *Settler III* when they'd left Earth's orbit.

The fact that the shuttles sat in pristine condition was telling. "Both shuttles are here," Margo stated.

"And still tethered. They didn't even attempt to use them to escape whatever it was that went wrong," said Abigail.

Margo returned her attention to Gan. "What the hell happened? How did you get injured?"

"We'd split up, Iago was in here," said Gan, looking around the hangar space. "I was across the Loop checking for clues in the ventilation room.

Margo and Abigail both turned on Iago. "You split up?" they demanded in unison.

"It made sense," Gan insisted in a raspy tone.

It didn't make sense, Margo wanted to argue, but instead she looked down at Gan. "What happened?" she asked.

"I was looking around the CO_2 scrubbers. I caught sight of something shiny blue moving in my peripheral vision. When I turned to look, it slammed into the front of my helmet."

"Did you see what it was?" asked Margo.

"No. It moved too fast," said Gan.

"But gravity is in place now. Nothing would've fallen. There's only one thing that could cause a projectile," Abigail said, looking at Iago.

Maybe Lucas was right about how dangerous Iago was, Margo thought. She ran her hand down the pocket on the outside of the suit, reassured by the shape of the pistol. "First you split up and then you throw something at him?" she accused, heat rising within her.

Iago had been standing a few paces away, but now stepped forward and grabbed Margo by the arm. "Of course not," then snapped over his shoulder at Abigail, "Stay with Gan."

He pulled Margo with him into the first shuttle. When they were alone, he let her go and turned to face her.

"Don't you dare question my orders or accuse me of harming my crew ever again."

Margo crossed her arms across her chest and glared at Iago. "Well, how the hell did Gan get hurt?"

"I don't know. But I also don't know where these colonists went. So, instead of accusing the leader of this mission of a heinous act, let's instead add that to the list of mysteries that need solving. Can you do that, Margo?"

Margo thought of the butterfly phrase written in English. That was a mystery. A rather chilling one, in her mind. Maybe Iago was right; some odd force of some kind was behind Gan getting hurt. She would concede that point. But that didn't change the fact that Gan had only been hurt because he'd not been with Iago inspecting the hangar. "But you risked Gan's life by splitting up. You shouldn't have done that!"

"I'm in charge of this mission and don't have to explain anything to you," said Iago, staring Margo down.

"You've risked Gan's life; we need to get him back to the *Staffelwalze*."

"Just you," he said.

Margo frowned. "What do you mean?"

"Haven't you noticed?" said Iago. "This abandoned ship is a

treasure trove. These supplies will make our lives back on Thesan better, and safer."

"We still don't know what happened to the colonists," said Margo. "They might have taken refuge somewhere."

"It's clear they aren't here," said Iago.

"But we haven't looked everywhere yet," said Margo, gesturing angrily towards the Hub. She explain that she and Abigail hadn't taken the time to explore the second story of living quarters, instead allowing themselves to be diverted to the terraforming lab. "We haven't had time to do a thorough inspection. They might come back."

"Unlikely. I'm staking a claim on this gear on behalf of Thesan." Iago gestured to the shuttle they were in. "We'll load as much as we can in the two shuttles and send them back to our colony."

In that moment, Margo realized she truly hated Iago. He was way too willing to sacrifice others to get what he wanted.

"Abigail and Yuko can help me start loading the shuttles. You take Gan back to the *Staffelwalze*. Then return with Max and Iva to help load these supplies."

"Fine," said Margo. Turning her back on Iago, she stomped out of the shuttle and headed back to Gan. "But you're on your own convincing Abigail to help you *rob these people*."

Chapter Sixteen

"Iago! Come in," called Ash over the radio. She pinched her lips together when only silence greeted her call.

Even though this felt like the millionth time Ash had tried to communicate with their team on *Settler II*, Gary still expected a response. Without a task to focus on, he paced in the small space between the two forward chairs where Ash and Max sat.

Everyone had something to do—except him. Ash focused on re-establishing comms. After the colony ship's rotation became steady, Max set the autopilot and was now splitting his attention between monitoring their motion and keeping a close watch on the camera looking down the passageway between ships. Iva sat hunched over her console, her fingers flying as she adjusted displays and her brow furrowed.

Gary turned his gaze to the scene beyond the small windows of the bridge. Below, the stark white of the colony ship, the panoramic vista of the malignantly beautiful planet below filled the bottom half of their view. He forced himself to exhale slowly as he eyed the swirling colours, his mind swirling with questions mimicking the clouds below.

"What's happened to them?" asked Iva. The technician was

paler than normal with pinched worry lines running across her forehead. "Surely, they would've come straight back if there was a problem."

"Only *if* they are able," commented Ash, without turning around.

Gary glanced at Ash, who sat rigidly in the pilot's seat, then over at Max. Max's shoulders were hunched, betraying his tension.

"Maybe there is something blocking the signals," said Gary.

"Iago! Come in," repeated Ash, toggling switches on her dashboard.

Gary felt himself get tenser as the minutes ticked by. Still no reply.

"Yuko? Anyone? Can you hear me?" Ash worked through several diagnostics screens on her console. From where Gary stood, he could see that the comms system in the *Staffelwalze's* bridge seemed to be working. Which meant the problem had to be on the colony ship side.

"Bloody hell!" Ash suddenly slapped the top of her console. "Why hasn't Iago noticed we've lost comms?"

Gary was startled by Ash's uncharacteristic display of impatience and fear. Up until now, she'd shown only calm confidence.

"Wait!" Iva adjusted her display. "I'm picking up a broad spectrum electromagnetic source." She pointed at her screen. "I didn't notice it at first as it seemed part of the background radiation here. It wouldn't affect our signal, but it might mask the weaker comms units our team has."

Ash twisted to face Iva. "Is the source on the other ship? Can you pinpoint it?"

"Working on it." Iva scrolled through screens so fast, Gary had no idea how she was absorbing the information.

Feeling useless, he sat at the empty console, spinning the chair to face the others. He wanted to badger Iva with questions, but he kept quiet to let her work.

"Got it!" She rotated to look at Ash. "The interference isn't coming from the colony ship. It's noise emitted from the storms on Juno."

Max grinned over his shoulder before resuming his focus on keeping the *Staffelwalze* aligned.

The others peered out the window on the port side at the bands of spinning cyclones on the gas giant below. The inner rings of the storms were laced with flashes of occasional lightening—a sure sign of significant electrical activity.

"Can you work out a transmission scheme to get around the interference?" asked Ash.

"Yuko would know more about that than I do," said Iva, turning back to her display.

"We'll get Yuko to do an evaluation when she gets back," Ash said.

Gary appreciated that their captain didn't say "if" they get back.

"Just come up with a kluge that'll do for now."

"Wait! There's movement in the umbilical," cried Max, leaning closer to the small video display on his side of the dashboard.

"Who is it?" asked Gary, standing and moving so he could see over Max's shoulder.

"Put the view up on the main screen," directed Ash.

With a tap on a key, Max displayed the video feed on a portion of the forward windshield. Iva turned in her chair and the four of them watched, hungry for confirmation that their crewmates were safe. Light glinted from reflective bands on multiple atmo suits, creating lens flares that obscured the camera's view.

Gary leaned forward as if doing so would make the video feed image clearer. Iva was standing beside him doing the same thing.

"They're pulling themselves along the rungs," said Iva, pointing. "But, I can't tell how many people are in there."

Gary could finally make out individual arms and legs. "There are only two people," he said, his tone betraying his concern.

"Look," said Max, pointing. "I think this person is injured. Whoever it is, they can't see properly."

They all watched in silence as the figure reached for a rung, groping with a hand a few time before finding it.

"And where are the rest of them?" asked Ash.

"Something must have happened." Gary stood up straight. "I'll go meet them at the airlock."

Turning, Gary strode off the bridge, finally filled with purpose. On his way aft, questions raged through his mind. *Is Margo in the tube? Of not, where is she?* He stopped briefly in the medbay and grabbed his medical bag. Drake still lay on the examining table, and he paused momentarily, realizing he hadn't once thought about the original occupants of the *Settler II*. His concern had been so focused on Margo, he'd forgotten about them.

Once in the airlock vestibule, he set his medical bag on the floor and then went to peer through the small window into the airlock, Gary was alarmed to see only one person. He couldn't identify who it was aside from it not being large enough to be Iago or Abigail. Regardless, there had been two people in the tube. *Where is the second person?*

It was excruciating to have to wait for the air to cycle. The amber flashing light told him the person inside had set the airlock to decontaminate. That alarmed Gary further. After a moment, there was a flash of UV light before the interior door light blinked green and it opened.

It was Margo.

Relief swept over him as he realized she was okay. Forcing himself not to leap forward and pull her into his embrace, he stuffed his hands in his trouser pockets waiting for her to remove her helmet.

"Why aren't you guys answering our comms?" she

demanded, pulling off the cap covering her hair and releasing her titian curls.

"Iva thinks the gas giant is creating interference," said Gary. "Why are you alone? Weren't there two of you in the tube? Where are the others?" Although he had more questions, he waited to give her time to respond.

Instead of answering she gathered up an unused atmo suit.

"What are you doing?" he demanded, stepping forward. He wanted to grab her and pull her back into the vestibule. "You're not going back there?"

"No. Gan got hurt and his suit is compromised," Margo stated in a clipped tone. "He needs to change into an airtight suit before coming onboard."

Gary watched as Margo deposited the suit in the airlock. She sounded angry, but he was certain it wasn't directed towards him. Not this time, anyway. When she stepped out of the chamber and was about to close the door and hit the button to cycle the air, he stopped her.

He strode into the airlock, and looked out the exterior window, seeing Gan on the other side, one arm holding onto a rung. Gary sucked in his breath on seeing how badly damaged Gan's visor was. If that had happened where there was no oxygen, he'd be dead. He lifted a hand to acknowledge Gan, but Gan didn't see him.

"Can he hear me?" he asked Margo over his shoulder.

"No."

"You think he breathed in toxins? Is that what happened to the colonists?"

"No toxins registered on our sensors."

"Regardless, he needs to be in an undamaged suit while I process the samples and take tests. I'm not set-up for a proper quarantine. And I need to be in here when he changes," he said, striding back into the vestibule. "I'll take blood samples. And from the damage I saw, he's likely got cuts all over his face."

"He does," Margo confirmed as she began peeling off her suit.

Gary stepped to the intercom and gave an update to the others in the bridge before reaching for an atmo suit.

"Are you sure there weren't toxins? Is Gan reporting any breathing difficulties?"

"None. Aside from the cuts, he claims he's fine, although we're all unsettled about how this could have happened."

"Did you find any colonists?"

Margo shook her head. "Neither dead nor alive."

"Any sign of where they are? What happened to them?"

When Margo paused, Gary thought she looked frightened and wondered what she was thinking.

"How did Gan get hurt?"

Instead of answering, Margo turned to Gary. "Iago ordered Abigail and Yuko to stay," she stated, her voice rising with unveiled disgust. "Abigail was about to mutiny, but Iago railroaded her. *That man!* So, now they're packing supplies in the shuttles. Can you believe it? Our mission leader is a goddamned space pirate. You know what? I think he intended this all along. He hoped we wouldn't find survivors so he could scoop us their leavings. What a bastard!"

Gary hadn't seen Margo this angry since she'd discovered pockets of breathable air on Thesan and realized they'd been lied to by The Conglomerate. He was about to agree that Iago was, indeed, a bastard, but Margo hadn't finished her tirade.

"He ordered me to bring Gan here and then come back to the shuttle with Iva and Max. To steal from those colonists. Can you believe it? Bloody hell!" she cursed as she struggled to remove her clunky atmo boot. "This damn room needs benches!" she added in an angry undertone.

"Here, let me help." Gary was wearing the bottom half of his suit already, and gestured for her to lean on him as he stooped to remove her stubborn boots. "So what happened? How did Gan get hurt? You said his suit is compromised?"

"Thanks," Margo said, balancing her weight on one foot and resting her hand on Gary's back as he bent to help her out of her boots. "A projectile of some kind hit his face shield."

As Margo stepped out of her atmo suit, Gary straightened and looked at her in shock. "What do you mean, *a projectile?* Is there a saboteur onboard that ship too?"

Margo stared at him for a moment. "Crap. I didn't even think of that."

"What were you thinking?"

"I accused Iago of throwing something at Gan."

Gary winced. "That couldn't have gone over well." *But maybe Margo's accusation was off-putting and the man would finally cease and desist his unwelcome advances.* Gary finished dressing. The only thing he still needed to don was the helmet.

"Why does everything end up with me having to put on an atmo suit?" he asked with a sigh. Margo knew full well how much he hated the things.

"You seem to have that kind of luck," she responded with a smile.

Gary was glad to see, now that she'd vented her anger, that she could smile again. *And at me.*

"Now would be a perfectly appropriate time for you to curse."

"Fine. This is rubbish."

Margo giggled and Gary felt himself relax as he fit his helmet on over his face. It was fun to banter with Margo. He'd missed it. Far more than he realized.

"Let me make sure it's all on right," Margo said.

"Hey," Gary said in surprise. "I can hear you. A little muffled, yes, but I can hear you perfectly."

"Yeah. Gan tweaked the suits. As long as we're within a few metres, we can hear each other."

"Even if you're wearing a suit too?"

"Yep."

Gary looked towards the airlock chamber. "Then I'll be able

to communicate with Gan whether his suit is on or off. We don't need helmet comms?"

"That's right." Margo answered as she walked slowly around him, checking the connections and seals. "You're good," she said with a slap on the shoulder.

When she handed him his medical bag, he realized his gloved hands made his movements awkward. He test squeezed his hands into fists, hopefully he had enough mobility to take blood.

Just then, Ash, with Iva following on her heels, walked into the space. Ash took one look at him dressed up in his atmo suit and raised an eyebrow.

"I'll let you explain," he said to Margo as he stepped into the airlock chamber.

Chapter Seventeen

"Can you hear me, Gan?" Gary asked over the suit's comms as he approached the exterior door.

"Yeah," said Gan.

"How do you feel?"

"Like an idiot for letting my suit get compromised." Gan sounded weary.

"Nonsense," said Gary. The light on the exterior door flashed green. "I'm opening the door."

When Gary opened the airlock door, Gan half-floated, half-walked into the chamber using his hands to feel his way. Gary guided the injured man to sit on the floor against a side wall, before he closed the outside door.

After hitting the button to cycle the air, he addressed Gan without using the atmo suit comms. "I like how you tweaked the suits. Makes communication easier." He tried to keep his tone light.

"It seemed an obvious thing to do."

"I'm not set-up for a proper quarantine, so you'll have to change into an undamaged suit." Gary pointed at the suit Margo had deposited in the chamber before realizing Gan wouldn't be able to see it. "Margo put an extra suit in here before I entered. You'll have to hang out in that while I process the samples."

"Yeah, makes sense," Gan agreed, although it was clear he wasn't happy about it.

The light flashed green. "You can remove your helmet, now," Gary said

When Gan removed his helmet, Gary inspected the man's injuries. There was a lot of blood, but that was to be expected on facial lacerations.

Gary turned to Margo, who he saw was looking through the window of the interior door, and gave her two thumbs up, then opened his medical bag and removed supplies to clean Gan's face. Although there were multiple superficial grazes, there were only two significant cuts—one a few millimetres above Gan's left eyebrow and the other on his cheek.

"Any idea what hit you?" Gary retrieved a skin fuser and a pre-moistened cloth from his bag. The thick gloves reduced his dexterity, making him clumsy.

"Don't know," said Gan. "I thought I saw something and turned." He dropped his head to look down at the damaged helmet. "Then this happened."

"Head up, and hold still." Gary cleaned the blood off the two cuts before fusing them closed. "These wounds are minor. Are you experiencing any breathing difficulties? I'm concerned about the air on that ship," he added, jerking his head towards the *Settler II*.

"Nothing. I'm sure the air is fine. By now, I'd know if it wasn't."

"True," Gary said, helping Gan up. "Let's get you into that new suit."

Gary packed his things back into his medical bag as Gan stripped off the rest of his atmo suit, exposing the T-shirt he wore underneath. Gary used an auto syringe to take a blood sample, an easier task in his gloved hands than fusing the small cuts. As soon as he finished, Gan dressed in the other suit and put on the helmet.

Once Gan was dressed, Gary stuffed the other suit as best he could into the helmet then opened the outside door. In the corridor, he clipped the helmet onto the first rung on the ceiling, hoping it didn't impede the others when they returned. Closing the exterior airlock door, he cycled the airlock on decontamination mode, closing his eyes when the warning beep sounded that the UV light was about to flash. A second beep told them it was safe to open their eyes.

When the interior door light blinked green, he opened it, pleased to see Margo still waiting for them in the tiny vestibule. There was no sign of Ash and Iva.

"It will take an hour or so to process the blood samples," he said to Gan. "You might as well wait in the passenger seating area. With that helmet on, there won't be anywhere else comfortable enough to sit."

Gan nodded, looking dejected as he exited the room. Gary removed his helmet and turned to Margo.

"He said he couldn't see what hit him," Gary said, as he began removing his suit. "Did you ask Iago if he saw anything?" Gary smiled at Margo. "That is, before you accused our fearless mission leader of throwing the projectile himself."

Margo pulled a face, looking pleased with Gary's teasing, but then she grew serious again. "Even though our rule upon entering the colony ship was to stick together, Iago ordered Yuko to stay in the main Control Room, and the rest of us to start inspecting the ship. When it happened, Gan said he was alone in shuttle hangar. Iago was…" She scratched her head. "Somewhere else. And Abigail and I were in terraforming."

Gary shook his head, stepping out of his atmo boots with more ease than Margo had. "He should never have split you up."

"Preaching to the choir," Margo stated.

"Well, someone launched a projectile at Gan."

Margo frowned and bit her lip. "I know."

"Come with me while I process Gan's samples," Gary said, picking up his med bag and leading the way out of the vestibule. Once inside the medbay, he shut the door behind them.

"I have to mention the body in the room," said Margo, nodding to the sheet-covered corpse on the examination table.

Gary smiled. "Hopefully you can ignore him. It'll be a while until he's thawed enough to examine."

He retrieved Gan's blood sample from his bag and put it into the DNA/RNA sequencer, programming it to seek anomalous sequences and analyze.

"I look for anything that doesn't match human," said Gary as he swivelled his chair and faced Margo.

Leaning against the closed door, she stifled a yawn. She looked tired and probably didn't need any lessons on what his equipment did.

Do you think there's a saboteur alive over there?" Gary nodded towards the colony ship. "Waiting for a Conglomerate ship to come and rescue him. Or her?"

"But that wouldn't make sense, would it?"

"Why not?" Gary asked. "We had a saboteur, and a Conglomerate ship orbiting Thesan ready to claim the spoils."

Margo gave Gary a telling look. "But that's just it. There are no spoils."

Gary was about to argue, but then began nodding slowly, realizing what Margo was getting at. "An ice moon. No indium. Or other valuable resource."

"Exactly."

"But someone had to have launched that projectile, whatever it was, at Gan."

Margo nodded. "I know. But who?"

"Or *what*?" Gary suggested in a teasing tone. "What about Max's theories about aliens?"

Margo scoffed. "Boys his age read far too many alien invasion novels, and it makes them lose sight of reality."

Gary was revelling in how natural it was to converse with Margo again. She was distracted, and he didn't think she even noticed that they'd resumed their once easy friendship. At least for now. "But maybe there is a saboteur onboard," he said. "Only it's for a different reason than why we had a saboteur on Thesan. We can't dismiss that possibility just because we can't establish why The Conglomerate's might do this for *Settler II*."

Margo shook her head. "The colony ship is too cold for anyone to survive. Even the plants froze solid." She tilted her head and gazed into the distance. "It was a strange sight—and quite beautiful."

"I can imagine."

Margo met Gary's gaze, her look earnest. "No, you can't," she said, leaning forward slightly. "Gary, the ship is eerie. And not just because it was deserted and the power and gravity had been shut off."

Gary frowned. "What do you mean?"

"For one, picture our Loop before we crashed with all the walls and doors perfectly aligned." She continued after Gary nodded. "Well, someone—or maybe a lot of someones—wrote on the walls. I walked at least half the length of the Loop, and the writing was everywhere. I can't imagine how much time it would've taken to do that."

"What did it say?"

Margo hesitated, looking down. "It was gibberish," she said.

Gary wondered if she wasn't telling him everything. *Did she see something that scared her? More than having to explore a ghost ship?* He thought of asking her these questions but was afraid she'd shut down or leave. Instead he watched as she took a deep breath.

"Are you okay?" The room was so small, all he had to do was reach out with his to rest a hand on her arm. She didn't shift away. "I'm worried about you."

She smiled. "I'm just spooked. There's so many unanswered questions over there. And the feeling of déjà vu..." She shivered.

Taking a chance, Gary stood and wrapped his arms around her. To his surprise, she hugged him back. Her cheek against the side of his neck felt right, as if that's exactly where she belonged.

After a moment, she pulled away. "The place creeped me out," she confessed. "Especially the writing on the wall—it could have been blood."

Before Gary could respond, a knock sounded on the door. Gary slid the door open to reveal Iago still in his atmo suit minus his helmet. He looked from Gary to Margo, then back to Gary again.

"So this is why you didn't return like I ordered?" he asked, smirking at Margo. "Getting cozy with your husband? With a corpse in the room?" He shook his head. "No accounting for taste."

"Try not to be such an ass," Gary said. He didn't care that a spark of anger flared in Iago's eyes. The man was an idiot. "Is someone injured?"

"No." Iago said. He glanced from Gary to Margo, and seemed to want to make a retort, but instead said, "change in plans. I'm calling an all-hands meeting in the common room. Be there in fifteen minutes. There are things we need to discuss."

Chapter Eighteen

When Margo and Gary arrived in the kitchen-cum-common area, the others had already gathered. Arms crossed over her chest, Ash leaned against the side of the last cupboard in the galley with Max right beside her. She was glaring at Iago, and Margo guessed their mission leader and ship's captain had just had a confrontation. Margo wondered what had happened.

Iago dominated the room with his size, and stood like the lord of the manor, filling the pulpit-like alcove forward of the spiral staircase. Yuko, Iago's loyal sidekick, sat on the chair closest to him, analyzing data from *Settler II's* computers on her hand-held scroll.

Someone had made a pot of coffee and most had a mug in their hand. Margo went to the counter and filled two mugs, handing one to Gary. Without a glance toward their mission leader, Margo headed to where Abigail sat, sliding into the seat beside her friend. Gary took the last empty seat across from them, next to Iva. Gan, still wearing his bright orange atmo suit, stood in the aisle near the passenger seating area as though in self-imposed exile.

"What's this about?" Margo asked Abigail in an undertone.

But Abigail just shook her head in disgust and muttered, "Damn space pirate."

By now everyone on board was up to speed with what they had seen on the other ship—no survivors, gibberish written on the walls in what looked like blood, and a huge supply of undamaged equipment. Margo could tell from the chatter that Abigail hadn't told anyone about the butterfly—and she was grateful for that. She wasn't sure she could have it discussed and not see hallucinated butterflies.

For the next few minutes they debated what might have happened to the other 49 members of *Settler II*'s crew. The dialogue soon shifted to whether the marking on the walls had, if fact, been written in blood.

Iago cleared his throat, directing the conversation to the real reason he'd called this meeting. "The shuttles over there are in pristine condition. Since our colony only has one working shuttle, we would benefit significantly from using what *Settler II's* poor lost souls no longer need." He cleverly modulated his voice to be both melodious and sympathetic.

He continued in this vein, surprising Margo with how clearly he could articulate his argument and how convincingly he spoke about how they wouldn't be harming anyone by taking *Settler II's* equipment. Margo felt torn by his argument, almost willing to agree with him that they weren't behaving like grave robbers, but then she thought, *this is Iago!*

As Iago spoke, his eyes kept drifting to Ash as though she was the one he needed to convince. Margo wondered again what might have caused their altercation.

"The question that needs to be answered," Iago said, interrupting another argument about whether they had the right to take from *Settler II*. "Isn't, do we allow ourselves to benefit from this windfall, it's will we be foolish and abandon this opportunity when we all know the resources it would take to make a second trip to this destination?"

Ash addressed Iago then, tight-lipped and angry. "It's pointless loading the shuttles if we don't have pilots to fly them."

As Margo assessed the glares between Ash and Iago, for the first time she wondered about their history. Along with the other insurgents, they'd been in hiding on the abandoned moon-base for years, living like outlaws. She guessed this wasn't the first time there'd been disagreements between the two. Both had strong personalities, although Ash's, at least, was tempered with basic human kindness.

"Max can pilot one and Abigail the other," Iago stated as calmly as if he'd just assigned kitchen clean-up duty.

Ash stood up straight and squared herself off, clearly ready to do battle. "Even if we agree that it's right to steal from *Settler II*. At top speed, they'll be in those shuttles for at least six days."

"Seven," said Yuko with a smug expression as she tapped her scroll.

"Fine, seven days. That's way too long for someone to fly solo." Ash glanced over to her son.

Max looked both torn and eager, like anyone his age would when presented with an opportunity for adventure. "But Mom, I can do it," he said. "I'm betting both those shuttles have solid autopilots."

Ash sighed, then nodded. "I know *you* can. I was thinking of Abigail." She turned to Iago. "It's safer and smarter to send one shuttle, with Max as pilot and Abigail as co-pilot. Allowing Abigail to pilot on her own is foolhardy." Ash looked towards Abigail. "No offence, but you're too green."

"Can't argue that, cuz I agree," said Abigail. "It'd be a dumbass plan for *anyone* to ask me to fly alone for an hour let alone seven days."

"I have an idea," stated Margo in a loud voice before more arguments could resume. "Let's all keep going to Nak together —the *Staffelwalze* and the two shuttles. The shuttles can connect to the *Staffelwalze* and we can swap people back and forth. We can even pack a lot of extra gear in here," she added, gesturing at the passenger seating area. The idea of confiscating more gear would appeal to Iago, at least.

A loud murmur of agreement spread through the group in the room, excepting Yuko, but Iago's loud voice overpowered and silenced them.

"That would bring too many elements into play and dilute our focus," said Iago. "We need to stick with Ash's schedule, which means we leave for Nak and keep things simple for our journey by sending the two shuttles back to Thesan." Iago's reference to Ash's schedule was a not-so-subtle ploy to make it sound like Ash was onboard with what Iago was proposing.

Iago paused and looked around the room. When he spoke, his tone sounded sincere. "Don't you want to find *Settler I* as soon as possible? Find survivors instead of..." Iago gestured with his prosthetic hand towards the colony ship outside the window. "This?"

Yuko sat in front of Iago, nodding like a brainwashed convert staring up at an evangelical preacher.

"I, for one, want to find survivors." Gan stated into the silence. "I've had my fill of ghost ships." His voice sounded weary.

"There might be people to save on *Settler I*. We can't let them down," said Iago. "We depart for Nak in six hours. There's a lot of work ahead of us."

Iago glanced at Gan before resting his gaze on Gary. "So? Did Gan get exposed to anything dangerous?"

With a glance at Margo, Gary rose from the table. "I'll go check if the sequencer is done." He headed towards medbay. As he passed Gan, he added, "Come by as soon as you can."

"Max, you're the lead shuttle pilot," said Iago. "Head there now and make sure everything about those two shuttles are flight worthy. After that, orient Abigail with anything she'll need to know. And Max?"

"Yes, Iago?"

"When you're in flight, you stay within sight of each other.

I'm holding you responsible for the success of your mission. Are you up for it?"

"Yes, sir," he said, nodding enthusiastically before hurrying out of the room.

"Abigail, what would you most need on Thesan from *Settler II's* terraforming lab?" Iago looked at her.

"The small algal generators," Abigail replied.

Iago turned and looked at Gan. "Any engineering gear that would be useful to take?"

"The builder bots would top my list," said Gan.

Iago nodded. "Yuko, you're in charge of getting the shuttles loaded." He jerked his head towards the exit, making Yuko jump up and follow Max and Abigail towards the airlock chamber. "Iva and Ash, suit up and go help. I'll follow shortly. And I'll send Gary and Gan, as soon as Gary gives us his report."

He watched as Iva and Ash left the room, then turned to Margo, looking at her like a predator eyeing its prey. "Margo, *I want you* to pack enough food for both shuttles. The one thing we won't take from *Settler II* are the food provisions."

Margo felt certain he deliberately embedded his orders with the phrase *I want you.* It made her stomach turn. One of these days, that man was going to make her puke for real. "Fine," she said.

"Gan, let's go see Gary." Iago gestured for Gan to follow.

"I don't know about this plan," Abigail stated in a a low voice when she and Margo were alone in the galley.

"You're a natural pilot, Abigail. Max said that every time he took you up. And Max will be both visually present for you and within easy comms distance. He can coach you through anything." Margo stood, pausing a moment to pat Abigail on her shoulder. "I better go get your food packed."

When Margo headed to the pantry, Abigail followed.

"I still don't like this," said Abigail.

"Yeah, I hate splitting us up too, but at least you'll be away from Mr. Insufferable."

Margo opened the pantry door, ignoring the large bin of Brussel sprouts right next to the enterance. She wouldn't subject her worst enemy to those—certainly not a friend. "I guess 'I'll pack hard rations for you guys."

"I don't give a shit about the food," said Abigail. "I don't want to be stuck in a stupid shuttle by myself."

At the uncharacteristic wobble in Abigail's voice, Margo turned to regard her friend. Her usual bristly manner had evaporated and was replaced with apprehension. "I'd go with you if I could," said Margo.

Abigail snorted. "I'm not sure having someone who keeps losing her mind as a co-pilot would be much better."

Margo frowned. "What do you mean?"

"I know you saw something over there. After we saw that butterfly quote?"

This time Abigail was soothing Margo, something Margo hadn't previously thought possible. She was about to argue, but then realized she didn't have the energy. "It's just in my mind," Margo said, dropping her head and rubbing her temples.

"How long has this…" Abigail waved a hand to encompass Margo. "Whatever it is, been going on?"

Margo leaned against the wall and crossed her arms, reluctantly meeting Abigail's gaze. "Since I did the consciousness projection," she admitted. "Hallucinations are, apparently, on the list of possible side-effects."

Abigail stared at her open-mouthed, for once, it seemed, struck speechless. "That was four months ago!" she finally said, putting her hands on her hips. "Why the hell haven't you done something about that crazy shit?"

"Like what?" Margo challenged.

Abigail put her hands on her hips. "Like consulting the expertise of the bloody doctor who invented the process. You're the one who brought him to Thesan. He could make it stop. Couldn't he?"

Margo shrugged. She'd been avoiding Paul since he arrived,

scared he wouldn't be able to offer a solution. After all, the side-effects were well documented. That meant there weren't solutions for them, didn't it?

"Ah, shit," said Abigail putting a hand on Margo's shoulder. "You haven't told Gary either, have you?"

"I couldn't. He was so mad at me for breaking my promise not to do the consciousness projection. We've only just gotten back on speaking terms," said Margo. "I'd forgotten how much I like his company. I don't want him to get mad at me all over again."

"But what if he can stop these mind tricks?"

"I doubt it's that simple," said Margo shaking her head.

"Don't be such an dunderhead, girl! You haven't even asked him."

Iago strode into the galley, interrupting them.

"I thought I heard voices. No time for dilly dallying," he reprimanded. "Abigail, get out there. Margo, we need that food packed."

"What were the results about Gan?" Margo asked as Iago turned to leave.

"He's fine," he called over his shoulder, without pausing in his stride.

Abigail glanced at Margo and shrugged, then followed Iago.

Margo turned back to the cupboards and pantry. Before she could pack food, she needed to get bins from the storage room. The *Staffelwalze* felt deserted as she headed aft, as though everyone had also vanished from this ship. It felt unsettling and eerie.

The medbay and the airlock space were empty. She opened the door to the storage compartment and stepped inside.

Grabbing two bins, she began tossing in assorted hard rations. Filling them to the brim gave each pilot enough food for three weeks—four if they had to stretch. If nothing went wrong, they'd each only consume a third of what was in the bin. She put the lid on each, then hefted one.

"There you are," said a deep voice behind her.

She turned to see Iago. With a wolfish smile, he entered the cramped space and closed the door.

"I was hoping to have a few moments alone with you," said Iago.

Margo glared at him. She'd had enough of this asshole. "You can carry this to the airlock," she said, forcing him to take the bin she thrust at him.

Iago didn't even appear disappointed. "I was thinking we could spend a few moments getting to know each other," he said, turning and setting the bin on a shelf beside him.

"I'm not interested," spat Margo.

"That's because we haven't become properly aquainted."

He stepped closer to her, and raised his flesh hand, running a finger along her jawline.

Margo had nowhere to go. She was already backed up against the shelves, but at his touch she swatted his hand away.

He chuckled, his voice reverberating through the space. "My, aren't you a feisty one."

Instead of backing down, she craned her neck to look up at the tall man and pushed her face close to his, then said in a scathing undertone."Touch me again, Iago, and you'll regret it." Margo slammed her hands into his chest, forcing him to step back, then pushed around him. "You take the food bins. I've got better things to do," she said as she opened the door and left.

Chapter Nineteen

An hour later, Margo ran out of excuses for delaying going back to the colony ship to help load the shuttles. At the very least, she wanted to see Max and Abigail off. But first, there was something she needed to do.

Alone in the *Staffelwalze's* airlock while waiting for the air cycle to complete, Margo checked the integrity of her atmo suit, then confirmed the two vials and butter knife were accessible in her suit's front pocket. When the green light flashed, she opened the exterior door and stepped through. Gravity melted away. With a push, she propelled herself along the fabric corridor towards the colony ship.

After opening the *Settler's* door, she felt gravity pull her in. Her feet naturally shifted beneath her until she was standing once again, supported by gravity. Closing the door behind herself, she pressed the button to cycle the air, waiting in the large airlock chamber for the green light to flash.

Her plan wasn't to help the others prepare for sending the shuttles back to Thesan just yet. Instead, she had another mission in mind. Maybe she should have told someone she was investigating on her own. *Gary perhaps?* She bit her lip as self-doubt gnawed at her guts. *No, I've got this.* The green light flashed and she opened the door and stepped inside.

Even fully lit, the colony ship felt haunted. Butterflies formed in her stomach instead of her mind as she entered the Loop. As creepy as before, the pictograms still coated the walls. Smothering her apprehension, she strode towards sickbay, staying close to the outside wall where there were no drawings.

As the coloured line on the wall changed from red to purple, she stopped and looked back the way she'd come. For a fraction of a second, she thought she saw movement, but the Loop was empty. Her mouth went dry when she remembered something had attacked Gan. *Do I need to worry?*

Feeling fearful now, she slowed her pace, giving herself time to peer through the windows into the common room, checking for movement. Nothing stirred within. The double doors to the Hub were closed, and she stopped and peered through the windows at the frozen garden. Again, nothing seemed threatening in the space. Continuing on past the closed door, she paused to investigate both the dining room and kitchen. Both rooms appeared threat-free.

At the sickbay doors, she stopped and took a deep breath. Turning, she faced away from the door to study the wall. The phrase scrawled across the surface seemed to taunt her. Despite her trepidation she approached the wall, removing the sample vial and butter knife from the front pocket of her suit.

Her pulse hammered in her ears as she reached forward and scraped pigment into her bottle from the 'B' of the first butterfly. As soon as she had a few flakes, she put the knife in her pocket and screwed the lid on, tucking it next to the knife.

With a second vial, she repeated the process on one of the dots on the wall above her head, the ones that had morphed into butterflies. Nothing happened as she worked. After stashing the second sample in a different pocket, she backed away from the wall until her airpack touched the closed sickbay doors.

A hum from behind the closed doors startled her. She spun

around as the doors slid open. The warm lighting from the soft green space within was exactly the same as their sickbay on Thesan—yet this room felt haunted. Telling herself she was being silly, she strode inside and examined every nook. Everything was the same as when she'd been there with Abigail.

She left sickbay through the Hub door, stopping to study the ice-encased leafy courtyard. The frost on the tree limbs now resembled the hoar frost she'd only read about. Thick bands clung to every branch, weighing them down and causing them to bend towards the ground.

As she walked on the pathway that wove through the courtyard garden, she noticed a thin film of what looked like snow coating the ground. She paused and glanced behind her, seeing the large footprints of her atmo boots in the thin white coating.

The winding route would take her to a bench in the middle of the garden. She followed it, and found the bench exactly where it was on *Settler III*. She sat.

She gazed at each apartment window in turn, both at the ground floor where her and Abigail had investigated and at the upper floor, where they hadn't ventured. Drawn blinds on the windows prevented any view inside, an aspect she hadn't noticed before. Even though her suit was temperature controlled, a shiver ran up her spine as if she could feel the oppressive cold.

Where did the colonists go? How long did they live circling a moon they could never land on? What did it feel like to realize they were all alone out here?

Out of the corner of her eye movement along the ground caught her attention. With a racing heart she jumped to her feet and twisted to see what it was. Nothing was there. *What the hell?*

Forcing herself to steady her breathing, she walked towards where she'd thought she'd seen movement. At the junction between the path she'd been on and a path leading to the main Hub doors, she turned around and looked back the way she'd come.

She inhaled sharply as she spotted a second set of footprints going down the same path, then turning off towards one of the apartments—footprints that hadn't been there when she'd approached the bench.

Heart thumping in her chest, she retraced her steps until she came to this other set of footprints. The boots had the same oversized treads as hers. Glancing around her, not sure what she expected to see, she followed the new set of footprints to an open doorway to one of the apartments.

Was this open before? When she peered inside, all she could see was a darkened corridor.

"Hey, Margo," said Gan, approaching her from within the dark corridor.

She let out a ragged breath.

He paused at the threshold and smiled at her before pressing a gloved finger on the light control switch. "Did I startle you? You look like you've seen a ghost."

"I'm kinda on edge in this place." She smiled back and followed him into the apartment. She realized it was Drake's residence. "Why are you here?"

Gan gestured for her to follow as he turned and went back into the apartment. "I thought we should know a bit about our corpse," he said over his shoulder. "Gary confirmed that he died from exposure. Which means he was alive when he went into space without an atmo suit. How does that happen?"

"I don't know," said Margo, looking around. She'd already been in this apartment. Nothing had jumped out at her then and nothing jumped out at her now. "Abigail and I searched this place. We didn't find anything suspicious. What are we looking for?"

"Nothing unusual. I simply want his scroll," said Gan, opening drawers in the kitchen and rifling through the contents.

"What about downloading the ship's servers?" asked Margo as she distractedly began re-examining the contents of the room. She saw the framed photo she'd earlier retrieved from the floor.

"They've been wiped, we aren't going to find anything there."

"Wiped?" She paused and turned to face Gan. "Why would they be wiped?"

Gan opened a cupboard and was moving things aside in his search. "I haven't determined if it was deliberate or an accident."

Margo turned her attention back to the mess on the living room floor, kneeling to pick up a blue case not much bigger than an extended scroll—it could fit a computer or a few books. She set it on the coffee table and opened it. A flock of silver butterflies fluttered out. "What the…"

"What did you find?" asked Gan, joining her at the coffee table.

"I don't know," said Margo, closing her eyes in an effort to make the hallucination go away. When she re-opened them, the butterflies were gone. She saw the case contained only a single data drive.

Gan picked up the memory device. "Good find," he said, putting it into his pocket. "Find more of these Margo, and we might just solve the mystery of this ship."

A crash came from the Hub. Them sprung to their feet and looked down the corridor to the open door.

"What the…" Gan's words trailed off.

"Let's check it out," said Margo trying and nearly succeeding to sound calm.

She strode to the exit, with Gan close behind. One pace past the threshold, she stopped and looked around. The source of the noise was immediately apparent. A branch had broken off the largest tree and landed on the bench where she'd been sitting a few minutes before.

After retracing her steps down the path to the base of the tree, she spotted the cause of the broken branch. "Gan, come here. You have to see this." She knelt to get a closer view.

He squatted beside her. "A working petbot?"

The size of an ordinary house cat, its head, tail and boots were dark grey while its body was covered in a short iridescent blue fur. Gan reached out and flipped the cat-like robot over.

"It must have activated itself when I switched the lights on. I wonder if this is what hit me?" He extended a narrow cord from his scroll and connected it to the petbot, displaying the diagnostics on his screen.

"Find anything?" asked Margo.

"Yeah. The drivers on this thing are scrambled. I can fix that," he said, picking up the petbot.

"So, you're adopting it?"

"Why not? We don't have any petbots on Thesan. I don't know why I didn't think of making one for Lily. She misses having a cat." He smiled at the mention of his wife.

"Then this is the perfect find," said Margo.

"Yeah. This one looks like a blue point Siamese, just like Mackerel, the cat Lily had when we first met. It's a high end model, with the most realistic behaviour programming. It won't take much for me to reboot the drivers. She's going to love it."

Margo was shaking her head at how animated Gan had become. He wasn't usually so talkative, but the petbot had peaked his interest. "So you're going to give your wife a robot that attacked you?" she mocked.

Gan held the petbot out in front of him. The cat's iridescent fur glinted in the lights. "We don't know it attacked me. And don't be a such a pessimist." He grinned at her. "I think I'll call him Mackerel II."

Chapter Twenty

Once back on the *Staffelwalze*, Margo paused outside the closed medbay door. The two vials of scrapings weighed down her trouser pockets—one in each to keep track of where she got them. Staring at the door, she bit her bottom lip.

"Tell Gary everything," she ordered herself in a whisper. A fluttering sensation filled her belly. *I've avoided telling him for way too long.*

After taking a deep breath, she knocked on the antiquated metal door. A moment later, Gary slid it open. His eyes lit up when he saw her.

"Come in," he said with a smile, gesturing inside.

Margo stepped in and Gary closed the door behind her. She immediately noticed that the examination table where Drake had been was empty. "What did you do with…" She pointed.

"Iago and I moved him to *Settler II*," said Gary. "We put him in a stasis pod. Fitting, in a weird way. We aren't set up to transport a body, especially since we're carrying on to *Settler I*. Eventually, we can come back for him and bury him on Thesan." He leaned against the counter next to the door.

Trying to act casual, Margo rested her hands on the table.

"You went over to the ghost ship?" She raised eyebrow knowing how much he hated being confined in an atmo suit.

"Iago didn't give me much choice." Gary shrugged as though it was no big deal. "I saw some of the writing on the walls. It must have taken a lot of time and effort to make those pictograms."

He made no mention of the butterfly phrase that haunted her—he mustn't have seen it.

Gary met Margo's gaze. "Did they remind you of anything?"

"Like what?" She held her breath waiting for his answer.

"Jim's notebooks."

She let out a long exhale. "It has to be a coincidence. I went back and took samples of the pigment," she said, retrieving the two vials from her pocket and holding them out to him. The rust brown powder inside shifted. "Abigail thinks its blood."

"That's typical Abigail. Being quick to see the worst?" He rubbed a hand on the back of his neck. "I'll test them and find out for sure. I really hope it's not blood, though. On top of everything else, that would be too gruesome."

Margo nodded, handing Gary the vials. "I agree."

Gary put the vials inside his microwave-sized isolation chamber and closed the door. "It's an old piece of equipment," he said while he worked. "The analysis will take a while."

Using a robotic arm, he dumped the contents of each vial into different sample trays, then put both into the DNA/RNA sequencing machine and started it running.

Just as Gary turned to her, Margo's stomach audibly grumbled. She winced in embarrassment.

"Have you eaten recently?" he asked.

"Not since we arrived at *Settler II*. Iago has kept us busy."

"True. How about I heat us up some soup?" he asked, gently touching her elbow as he stood. "Amanda has taught me a thing or two."

"She had to *teach* you how to heat up soup? As in, step one, open microwave door? Step two——"

"Enough already," Gary interrupted with a laugh. He held out a hand in invitation. "Come on, Margo. You need to eat. Let me impress you with my microwave prowess," he teased.

"Soup sounds good," she said with a smile. Standing she took his hand and let him lead her the two steps to the door.

As the corridor was too narrow to walk side-by-side, Gary gestured for Margo to precede him to the galley. She took a seat at the table facing towards the passenger compartment, grateful no one else was around. Leaning back into the elephant patterned cushion, she told herself to relax. She still needed to tell Gary about the hallucinations—any hope of relaxation evaporated. *Do I have to tell him? Yes, Murphy, you have to!*

If only they all were heading back to Thesan instead of heading further into the solar system. *Will we also find tragedy on* Settler I*?* As she closed her eyes, Drake's frozen eyes looked back at her. A shiver ran up her spine. She re-opened her eyes and ran a hand through her curls. *Get a grip Murphy! Freaking out will solve nothing.*

The sound of the door closing on the microwave brought her attention to Gary as he moved about the galley. The pungent spice of Amanda's Mulligatawny soup wafted her way and she realized she really was starving. With his back to her, Gary retrieved bowls and spoons, moving with a grace Margo hadn't noticed before.

"It'll just take another minute," Gary said as he came and joined her at the table.

With a smile, she gazed into his eyes. The two of them were so close they were almost touching. Just being next to him was comforting. Leaning towards him, she rested her head on his shoulder.

He briefly stiffened, and then relaxed. His scent was a mixture of cedar and soap. She remembered that from before she'd done the consciousness projection, when they'd just started forming a friendship.

"This place is getting to me," she said.

"Iago plans for us to be on our way soon. Perhaps *Settler 1* will be a thriving colony, happy to see us." Gary wrapped an arm around her shoulders and drawing her closer.

"That would be nice. Overly optimistic maybe, but nice."

When the microwave pinged and Gary stood, Margo sighed as a wave of cool air replaced his warmth. A moment later he set the fragrant soup in front of her and she was more than happy to dive in. A comfortable silence enveloped them as they ate.

As Margo finished her soup, she set her spoon in the empty bowl. *I should tell him about the hallucinations now.* She opened her mouth to speak, but paused when she heard footsteps coming from behind them. They both turned to see who was coming.

"Did you tell Gary about Mackerel?" Gan asked when he entered the galley area. "I think I've got it working," he added before she could answer, setting the petbot on the table.

When Gan sat opposite to them, Gary asked, "Did you just come from next door? Are the shuttles loaded?"

Gan waved a hand. "Yeah, they're pretty much done."

Gary picked up the empty bowls and took them to the sink.

"Are you sure it's safe to have that?" Margo eyed the feline-shaped robot with suspicion.

"Why would you ask that?" Gary asked, returning to his seat.

Gan grinned at Gary. "She thinks Mackerel is what attacked me."

Gary raised his eyebrows. He looked from the petbot to Margo to Gan. "That doesn't seem likely, does it?"

"I agree." Gan unrolled his scroll and set it on the table. "This here is a top end model, indistinguishable from a real cat."

"Except it's blue," said Gary.

"I don't know a lot about biology, but I'm sure someone out there is breeding blue cats. After all, Margo's butterflies were blue."

Margo opened her mouth to explain the fallacy of comparing a mammal's colouration to an insect's. But she decided not to say anything. Gan was genuinely excited about this gift he'd found for his pregnant wife. He was the happiest she'd seen him since they left Thesan.

"On the plus side, there'll be no litter box to clean," said Gary.

"Exactly. Lily is going to love this." Gan flashed another grin before looking at the data on his scroll, swiping through screens.

Margo stared at the benign-looking robot cat. It looked soft, and part of her wanted to reach out and pet the blue fur. An ear twitched and a moment later the robot opened its perfect yellow eyes and looked at her. She laughed. No longer able to resist, she reached out to pet the cat. Her reward was a loud, deep purr.

"You're right, Lily will love this."

As Margo scratched the robot cat behind its ear, Ash came down from the bridge and stopped beside them, her forehead creased in a worried frown. She barely gave the petbot more than a glance as she turned to Gary

"Gary, can you help me check the contents of the medkits for the shuttles?" she asked.

"Sure," said Gary. He met Margo's gaze and smiled. "I'll catch up with you later." He followed Ash towards the medbay.

"She sure seems worried about Max leaving," said Gan without looking up from his scroll.

"He's capable, but still very young," said Margo, staring towards where the two of them had disappeared into the medbay. "And Abigail is a green pilot. That's heaping a lot of responsibility on someone Max's age."

Gan looked up at her. "I'd go in Abigail's place if Iago would let me," he said. "Except, I've never piloted a shuttle in my life." He sighed.

"You're worried about Lily?"

"I'm sure she's fine." He shook his head. "It's just that, after all that's happened to us, I don't like being separated from her." He leaned forward and scratched the cat's chin, causing the volume of the petbot's purr to increase.

"I guess I should check over those shuttles one last time." He picked up the cat and headed aft.

Standing, Margo headed up the spiral stairs to see if Abigail was in her cabin, packing. On the top deck only one door was open—Abigail's. With her hands in her pockets, she sauntered over.

"Can I give you a hand?" she asked, leaning against the door frame.

This cabin was nearly identical to hers—down to the polka-dot easy chair. The major difference were the pale pink walls, as if a little girl had been a former occupant of the room. Abigail had two bags open on the floor and all her stuff spread out over her bunk. She turned and looked at Margo, then flopped down on her arm chair with a dramatic sigh.

"This sucks," she said.

"At least you'll be back with Hannah soon than we expected," Margo said.

"True. I wonder if Gan will let me have his petbot? He can spend his time on the ship making another one for Lily. A gift like that would go a long way to getting Hannah to forgive me for leaving."

"You hardly volunteered for this trip," said Margo.

"I think Yuko is the only volunteer." Abigail stood and took the one step required to reach her bed. "Maybe you could talk her into planting her ass on *Settler II* and you guys could pick her up on your way back."

"I'd way rather plant Iago's ass there instead. Or, better yet, both of them," said Margo. "Need a hand packing?"

"Yeah, sure," said Abigail. "I hate this shit."

Margo moved over to the bed and started shoving clothing

into Abigail's bags. "I found a chocolate cake Amanda hid at the bottom of the freezer. I put the whole thing in the bin on your shuttle."

Abigail burst out laughing again.

Margo looked at her and raised an eyebrow. "And here I thought chocolate cake was a serious matter," she said, chuckling at Abigail's response. "What's so funny?"

"I'm just picturing Max's expression when he flies close enough to see me eating chocolate cake in the pilot's seat."

Abigail zipped closed the bag she'd packed and sat on the bed, watching Margo struggle to zip closed her second bag. "On a different note, I've noticed a general warming between you and Gary."

Margo finished her task and sat on the end of the bed next to Abigail. "Maybe."

"What do you mean maybe?" said Abigail. "You need to be on top of that kind of thing, brainiac."

Margo grinned, lifting and raising her eyebrows suggestively. "On top?"

"Get your mind out of the gutter." Abigail paused thoughtfully for a moment. "For now, anyway. But do something. Make a move on him. I know you want to. And so does he. I gotta tell you, watching the two of you tippy-toe around each other is painful."

A gurgle of static announced that the internal comms to Abigail's room had been activated.

"Abigail?" Ash's voice asked.

"What is it?" Abigail's tone sounded annoyed.

"Iago wants you over in the shuttle bay *on Settler II* in 10 minutes. I think he's planning a pep talk," said Ash.

"Good times," said Abigail. "I'd better be going."

"Need a hand with your gear?" asked Margo, standing.

"Nah." Abigail grabbed a bag in each hand and headed towards the door. "But I do want you to do something for me."

"Sure," said Margo.

"Stay safe."

Margo nodded, smiling at her friend. "You too."

Abigail disappeared into the corridor, then turned and stuck her head back in the open doorway. "And get *on top* of the situation with Gary," she added, her laughter echoing from the corridor as she walked away.

Chapter Twenty-One

A few hours later, everyone except Max and Abigail crammed onto the bridge once again. Tension hung heavy in the air. In the pilot's seat, Ash focused on the dashboard before her as Iva slid into the co-pilot's seat. With both personality and physique, Iago filled the space between them. Gan and Yuko sat at the two back consoles. Just in front of the door, Gary stood next to Margo, close enough that their shoulders brushed.

Ash had already retracted and stowed the umbilical corridor. The *Staffelwalze* now sat five-hundred metres from the colony ship, leaving a clear path for the shuttles to pass. From his angle, Gary could see the open hangar door on the *Settler II*.

"Pulling Shuttle 1 out of the hangar now," said Max over the radio, his voice calm and confident. In a fluid motion, he guided his shuttle out.

"Look out, here I come," said Abigail, with typical irreverence. Her shuttle barrelled out with as many course corrections as an orb in a pin-ball machine. It was amazing she didn't hit anything.

Muting the comms, Ash looked up at Iago. "This is a bad idea."

"They'll be fine." Iago crossed his arms over his chest and didn't even bother to look in Ash's direction. "She'll be fine."

Ash opened her mouth to retort, then clenched her jaw closed. She turned and faced forward again.

"Be safe," she said, after re-opening the comms link.

"See you soon, Mom," Max replied, his tone eager.

The crew on the bridge of the *Staffelwalze* watched as Max fired the thrusters on the first shuttle.

"You guys be safe, too," radioed Abigail from the second shuttle. "Don't do anything stupid. And Margo, do what I told you to do. And Gan, build me another petbot while you're sitting on your ass doing nothing. And Gary—"

"That's enough." Iago cut her off. "Set your course to stay on Max's tail." He reached in front of Ash and closed the comms link.

The second shuttle fired its thrusters and performed an awkward turn before following Max's path. As Gary watched the two shuttles recede into the distance, he felt Margo's fingers touch his palm. He looked over at her and they shared a smile as he took her hand in his, giving it a gentle squeeze.

"Right," said Iago, turning so his back was to the windshield.

"Set a course to Nak at full speed."

"Already done. ETA is just under a week," said Ash in a flat tone.

Iago glared at Gary. "I'm sure we can all figure out something to fill our time." He pushed past and left the bridge.

With a scowl, Yuko followed.

"I guess I have plenty of time to work on that petbot," said Gan.

Ash swivelled her chair so she faced the engineer. "Before you get too engrossed in that, can you look at the port side water reclaimer? It's acting up again."

"Sure," Gan said before leaving.

"I'll get started on dinner," said Iva, sliding out of the co-pilot's seat. "How does Pad Thai sound?"

"Good," said Margo. "Anything but Brussel Sprouts."

"Let's reconvene for a meal in an hour," Ash said before turning back to her displays.

"Your analysis should be done by now," said Gary to Margo. Reluctantly, he let go of her hand. "Let's go look."

She nodded and the two of them went back to the medbay. As soon as he slid the door closed, she wrapped her arms around him.

"I wish we were heading back with the other two," she said.

"Me too." Gary brushed a ringlet away from her face. This was the first time he'd touched her hair—he'd wanted to touch it for ages—its softness surprised him. "But, on the positive side, we have a whole week to spend together."

Margo flashed him a lopsided smile as she slid her hand down his back. "And what were you thinking we could do, Doctor Holbrook?"

Gary pretended to think hard as he ran a hand up the back of her neck into the tangle of her hair. "You could always teach me how to play bridge?" Without turning away from her, he reached behind him with his free hand and flipped the latch to lock the door.

"Sadly, I don't know that game. I'll have to improvise." Margo pulled him close and their lips met.

———

Later after having just gotten dressed after their 'bridge' game, Gary sported a lopsided grin of his own as he took a seat at the console and began scrolling through the results from the scrapings Margo had provided. Cheeks flushed, she leaned against the wall beside him, a contented smile on her face as she watched him work.

But as he read the results, his grin faded and his brow furrowed. "Abigail was right. It's human blood."

"Crap." Margo moved behind him. She rested her hands on his shoulders and leaned forward to view the results. "I think I convinced myself it couldn't be true. But it is. Shit."

Gary gestured at the screen. "But the two samples are blood from two different people. Neither matches Drake." He swivelled in his chair so that he could loop a comforting arm around Margo's waist.

"The writing went all the way around the Loop, on both sides," she said, leaning into him.

"Assuming it was all written in human blood, they would have needed a lot of it." Just the thought of it left a bitter tang in Gary's mouth. Imagining the logistics of how it must have been done started a churning in his gut. He rubbed his free hand over the back of his neck.

"But why would anyone do such a thing?" asked Margo.

Gary shook his head. "That's just one question of so many. Why would they write gibberish on the wall in the first place? Why in blood? Who did it? Where are they now? The list goes on and on.."

At Margo's hesitant look, Gary tilted his head to the side and gave her an inquiring gaze. "What?" he prompted.

She seemed ready to speak, but then the intercom box on the wall squawked. "Dinner's ready," announced Iva.

Margo stepped out of his embrace, and Gary turned, switching off the display. He stood and faced her, pulling her into his arms as he gazed down at her. "So?" he asked. "Do we tell the others what we've discovered?"

Margo nodded soberly. "We have to, I think."

Gary nodded. "I agree."

They stood looking at each other for a moment for the sheer pleasure of doing so, or so it seemed to Gary.

"I guess we should go," Margo finally said, lifting her hands and adjusting her shirt. "Am I presentable?"

Gary responded with a warm smile. "You look gorgeous." He saw that his enthusiastic compliment made her blush. With flushed cheeks, she was even more beautiful.

"That's not what I meant," Margo protested "I just wanted to know if I'm properly dressed." She ran her hands down her pants.

"You're perfect." He pulled her in for a quick kiss. "Maybe after dinner, we could play bridge in my cabin?" he suggested.

Chapter Twenty-Two

Heart thumping, and feeling an urgent need to hide, Margo turned to view the corridor behind her. Lit by grimy overhead panels, the grungy hall seemed to go on forever in a featureless form. Without visible exits or hiding places.

She turned to face forward; the view was virtually the same.

The glowing panels in the ceiling suddenly caught her attention. Are the lights getting dimmer? *She glanced over her shoulder as the hairs on her arms rose.*

In the dimming lights behind her, she spotted movement in a shadow. Her leg muscles tightened as her flight response kicked in.

She sprinted down the corridor as fast as her legs would carry her. As she ran, algae began creeping over the overhead lights, casting a green tint to the dimming lights. She'd been here before, she was sure of it, but where was here? *And how could she get out?*

As soon as she rounded the first corner, she stopped dead at the sight that greeted her. Chest heaving from exertion, she considered the stairwell before her. She could go up or down. Neither option seemed worse or better than the other. Above the sound of her pounding heart, she heard distant footfalls approaching. Whoever was chasing her was catching up. Who is after me? And why?

Uncertain of the best option, she went down—simply because it took less effort to run down than to run up. With a hand on the metal rail, she descended one level and then pushed through a set of doors. The hallway here seemed to be a doppelgänger to the one she'd just left.

"Crap!" She looked back at the stairs. Should I go back up? "No, keep going," she told herself.

She sprinted down the corridor. When she reached the first corner, she skidded to a stop at a door and tried the handle. It opened and she slipped through.

Inside, lights automatically came on, exposing a deserted medical lab. She locked the door, then turned to take in her surroundings.

An examination table dominated the centre of the small room. All the equipment was powered on, their LED lights flashing. Like the two corridors, this space felt familiar. Circling the room, she stared at the examination table. The green vinyl was well worn and even flaking away in places. Dark stains marred the surface. She didn't want to think what had made those.

Motion at the door drew her attention, and she froze. The door handle slowly rotated. Will the lock hold? Her limbs quivered as she backed away from the door. Whoever was on the other side kept twisting the handle back and forth as though the repeated motion would unlock it. When it didn't, whoever was out there rattled the doorknob as though they were frustrated.

She turned around. Breathing in ragged gasps, she searched for an alternate exit. The far wall contained a sliding door! Margo leapt towards the door, opened it without hesitation, and ran through.

On the other side, a third hallway extended both ways and lit with the same algae-infested light panels. Turning right, she broke into another sprint, but when a cramp formed in her side, she slowed to a jog. The sight of a T-junction up ahead left her with a sense of hope. Is this the way out?

When she reached the junction, markings on the wall caught her attention. Written in a dark brown substance that looked suspiciously like dried blood, the bold letters spelled words she'd seen before:

Butterfly blue, without a clue; Butterfly red, better off dead

Taking a deep breath, she glanced back the way she'd come. No one was visible, but she could sense someone was back there somewhere. Turning, she studied the words, stepping forward until she was an arm's length from the wall. Forcing herself to tear her gaze away, she turned right and began walking.

The hallway soon opened into a large common area. A play structure for kids and raised garden beds full of vegetables filled the space. She continued to a picnic table that looked familiar, but she couldn't place it either. Running a finger along the plastic woodgrain surface, she circled around. This place feels so familiar.

"Where am I?" she asked aloud.

"Hey, bug girl," came a voice from where she'd entered the space. "You can't outrun me."

Her heart skipped a beat as fear nearly paralyzed her. With a deep breath she turned and looked. Thousands of butterflies lifted off from the ground in unison, temporarily obscuring her view. Then the swirling mass of insects separated, and she saw who had been chasing her—Nigel Maximillian West.

"You can try, but you can't out run me. I'll be coming for you," he said.

At the chilling sound of his laugh, she began to scream.

Heart pounding and drenched in sweat, Margo opened her eyes. She was on the *Staffelwalze*, safe in her cabin.

"What the hell?"

She rolled over and sat up on the edge of her bed. Taking deep breaths, she waited until her heart rate slowed to a reasonable level. *It's just another nightmare.* As she started to calm, she noticed the dim outlines of the furniture in her cabin. The slit under her door allowed a soft glow to enter, creating interesting, yet ordinary shadow shapes.

"Dirty circuits," she muttered under her breath as it dawned on her she'd get no more sleep that night. Lowering it to the dimmest setting, she flipped on the panel light above the bed.

Standing in front of her sink, she turned on the tap, allowing water to pool in her hands before splashing it over her face. Images of her dream flashed through her mind. Her legs felt rubbery as though she really had been running.

"Nigel, why are you haunting my dreams?" she asked, looking her reflection in the eye.

The low light blurred her image in the mirror. The contours of her face were barely discernible, the details masked by shadows.

Will Gary be up? Is this the right time to tell him about my nightmares? How about the hallucinations?

More than once, she'd been ready to tell him, but every time they'd been interrupted and the moment passed. She knew that waiting for the perfect time was procrastination—there was never going to be a perfect time. Now that they'd become lovers —more than lovers; friends again—she didn't want to do or say anything that might jeopardize that.

Nevertheless, she had to tell someone, and the obvious 'someone' was Gary—but they were due to enter Nak's orbit in a few hours.

After getting dressed, she left her cabin. Out in the hall she paused at Gary's door. If their beds hadn't been so narrow, they'd be sleeping together. He would likely have realized she'd been having a nightmare. In his arms in the dark would have been the perfect time to tell him.

Margo leaned against the wall beside his door, smiling a little as she pictured how she would alter her greenhouse shelter to accommodate two. *I'll have to set up a bit more storage space... Maybe an entire bedroom...* As she let her mind mull over her ideas, calmness descended over her. With a soft sigh, she turned her back on Gary's door and headed downstairs. He deserved a proper night's sleep.

In the galley, she set a pot of coffee to brew and sat down to wait. It would be another two hours until their normal breakfast hour. She yawned and listened to the water percolate through the coffee grounds.

"Merrrp." The petbot leapt onto the table and directed its electric blue gaze at her.

"I guess Gan has lost track of you," she said, reaching out and stroking the synthetic fur. "What's your name again?"

"Merrrp," said the cat as it purred and arched its back towards her hand.

"Tuna? No. Herring?"

The coffee pot beeped. When she got up to pour herself a mug, the petbot stopped purring, then started again as soon as she resumed her seat. "Mackerel!" she exclaimed, finally remembering the name. "I knew it was something fishy."

The cat crawled onto her lap and settled in. Margo relaxed, stroking its fur and sipping her coffee as she continued planning how to expand her shelter in the greenhouse to accommodate Gary.

A half-hour later, footfalls on the stairs drew her attention. She glanced up, hoping it was Gary. Instead Gan entered the galley, carrying his tool box.

"You're up early," he said.

Margo shrugged. "Couldn't sleep."

"Me neither. I keep worrying about *Settler I*. I wish they'd answered our comms. I don't want a repeat of what we saw on *Settler II*. It all just keeps replaying in my mind"

"Me too," Margo said.

Gan spotted the petbot on Margo's lap. "Ah, that's where Mackerel got to." He gestured with his toolbox. "Thought I'd spend some time working on it."

Margo set the petbot on the table—it looked as grumpy at this mistreatment as a real cat. Without the warmth of the fake cat in her arms, she felt cold, so she stood and went to refill her coffee, seeking its warmth.

Gan sat at the table, setting his toolbox on the bench beside him. He opened it up and rummaged through as Margo returned to her seat, setting a mug of coffee at Gan's elbow.

Bent forward over the petbot, his scroll open on the table in front of him, Gan's black hair looked glossy under the overhead lights. He was already intently focused on the robot, and had removed an access panel on the bot's side, exposing the complex circuitry inside. He turned something off, and the cat became lifeless, like a discarded marionette.

"Did you find any useful information on that thumb drive we found in Drake's quarters?" Margo asked.

"Dead end. The data was all corrupt."

"That's too bad," Margo said. "Have you heard from Lily lately?"

Gan nodded, without looking up. "I got a message from her yesterday. She says she's sick of being pregnant."

"Fair enough." Margo sipped of her coffee.

"And Lucas finally relaxed his ruling banning use of the domestic printers. Lily and Amanda have been printing all sorts of baby things." He took out a device and did something to the robot's interior—Margo didn't know what—but the front leg twitched.

"Smart Lucas. It would take a braver man than him to deal with two pissed off pregnant ladies," said Margo.

Gan grinned in response then pulled out a circuit and held it up to the light. It looked just like the other circuits. Margo wondered how he knew which circuit led to what feature. "The cat Lily had when we first started dating hated me." He put the circuit down and rummaged through his tool box again, retrieving a circuit board that, at least to Margo, looked the same.

"Cats can be finicky that way." She yawned, and leaned back in her seat, watching Gan install the new circuit board. Grateful he'd risen early too, otherwise she'd have little to distract her from her sleep deprivation and the fact they would arrive at Nak today.

"That beast nearly ended our relationship before it even got the chance to start." He looked up at Margo and smiled. "He was a Siamese, and more temperamental than his peers."

"So, you won't be programming Mackerel to be like its namesake?" She took the final sip of her coffee before setting the mug on the table.

He put down his tools, and closed the access panel. "Hell no, there's not enough blood in my body for another cat like that. This here cat isn't just going to like me, it's going to *love* me."

Chapter Twenty-Three

"What are we looking at here?" Iago pointed his prosthetic hand at the view beyond the windshield, commanding everyone's attention. He stood in his usual spot between the pilot's and co-pilot's chairs taking up more that his fare share of the limited space.

"The home of *Settler I*," stated Margo from her seat in the co-pilot's chair.

She hadn't needed to answer, nor had Iago needed to ask. Everyone gathered on the bridge staring at the yellowish orb filling their view knew it was the planet Nak. Clouds cloaked the entire planet, hiding its surface from view. Everyone also knew they still hadn't made contact with *Settler I's* crew.

Ash, as usual, was in the pilot's seat. Yuko stood behind Ash, as close to Iago as she could reasonably get. Iva was the only one not looking out the windshield; instead her face was scrunched in concentration as she scrolled through the sensor readings.

Margo turned to glance over her shoulder at Gary where he stood by the door beside Gan. His casual posture, she knew, belied his concern about what they would find. She smiled at him and he relaxed enough to smile back. Untwisting to face forward once again, she studied the planet as the *Staffelwalze* approached.

"The main constituents in the atmosphere are carbon dioxide, water vapour, and oxygen." Iva announced.

"That's not so bad," said Iago, leaning forward to examine Nak. "Sounds like Earth."

"Wait…" Iva hovered a finger near the screen as she read the data. "There are also nasty amounts of sulphur dioxide and hydrogen sulphide."

"Is that all?" asked Iago.

"Nope." Iva turned. "Ash, watch out for the clouds. They're made of enough sulphuric acid to strip the paint off the ship. And they're concealing raging electrical storms."

"You're right," said Ash, nodding at her dashboard displays. "This planet is going to be a problem for this ship."

"Which means it also would have presented a problem to *Settler I*," Yuko said, consulting the scroll in her hand.

"There's more," warned Iva, turning to look towards Ash again. "The atmosphere is laced with hydrogen fluoride."

"None of these are insurmountable problems," said Iago, a little louder than necessary. "Is that all?"

"The average wind speed in the upper atmosphere hovers around 360 kilometres an hour." Iva's tone was flat. "I should point out—"

"This planet exhibits the phenomenon of super-rotation," interrupted Yuko. "The upper atmosphere is circling faster than the planet is rotating."

Margo turned, noticing Iva casting a glare at Yuko's back.

"I should point out," Iva started again, enunciating each word with care. "That hydrogen fluoride mixed with water creates hydrofluoric acid. That wouldn't just strip off the paint from the *Staffelwalze*—it would strip off *the hull*."

Ash shifted in her chair, looking back at Gan. "How long can we stay in the atmosphere?"

Iago put a hand on her shoulder. "We'll get to the technical details later," he said before Gan could answer.

Ash scowled as soon as she turned back towards the planet.

"The ship would only have hours until hull integrity would be compromised," Gan stated, ignoring Iago's attempt to control the conversation.

Iago directed a glare at Gan before focusing on Iva. "What's under those clouds?"

"We can't know for sure. The clouds block our optical imaging. I'll start a radar scan." Iva continued working through her screens.

Iago glanced at Yuko, who shrugged. "There's likely acid rain," she said.

"And *Settler I* landed here?" Iago put his hands on his hips.

Everyone fell quiet as they stared at the mustard-toned orb below.

"I'm picking up the colony's beacon." Ash placed her hands on the ship's controls. "I'll maneuver us into a geostationary orbit right above it."

The heads-up display showed the *Staffelwalze*'s movement relative to the planet, yet the view didn't appear to change as Ash shifted the ship's position.

Iago turned to Margo. "Is this world even a candidate for terraforming?"

Margo studied the muddy-yellow cloud formation above the planet. "From what Iva says, the atmosphere sounds like Venus." She looked up at Iago. "Abigail could have given a better answer, but I'd say this world isn't a good location for a colony. The acid content in the air alone would rule it out, at least for humans."

"Not to mention the toxic gases that would leach into every structure built," added Iva.

"Your analogy to Venus doesn't quite hold," Yuko argued. "For one, the atmospheric pressures aren't as high. From what I can see, at ground level, pressure is only twice that of Earth.

And this planet has virtually no magnetic field, which means the solar winds from Helios continuously spew parts of Nak's atmosphere into space."

"I have radar data compiled," interrupted Iva.

Iago turned to her.

"The surface is mostly solid, but there might be liquid bodies —can't tell if that means water. And volcanism is rampant down there."

"From plate tectonics?" asked Yuko, her tone puzzled.

"Never mind that." Iago put up a hand to prevent Yuko from asking more questions. "Can you image the colony?" he asked Iva.

Margo was surprised to see Yuko glaring at their mission leader. It was the first hint of friction she'd seen between them. Perhaps Yuko was finally chafing in her subservient role of side-kick.

"Hang on..." They waited in silence for Iva to continue. "Here it is."

A false-colour image appeared on a subsection of the wind-shield. It showed a flat region near the base of what looked like a chain of mountains. As the details resolved, the ring-shape of the *Settler* colony became visible.

"They got their dome up!" Gan stated in triumph, stepping closer to the view screen.

A cheer went up from everyone on the bridge, except Iago. This was more progress than the *Settler II* had made.

"There will be people to find this time," stated Iva with a grin. She zoomed the image to its maximum resolution. The large triangular panels that made up the greenhouse within the donut-hole shape of the ship were visible. "That's as good as we'll get. Our radar is limited to one metre resolution."

"They've put up two of their spoke greenhouses—just like we have," Gan observed in a pleased tone. "They must've applied a coating to protect it from the acidic conditions."

The false colour of the image told Margo nothing about

possible crops in the spoke greenhouses. "They wouldn't be able to grow the crops directly in the ground like us. They'd have to use a membrane under the soil." She turned to Gan as a new thought hit her. "Is there enough solar radiation passing through the clouds for their solar panels?"

"I don't know," said Gan. "We'll have to wait and see."

Margo turned to make eye contact with Gary. He gave her a smile. *Perhaps there's enough time for a brief side trip to one of our cabins before we head down to the surface...* She shook her head—now wasn't the time for such throughs.

"Any luck with comms?" asked Iago.

"I've established a comms link," announced Iva. "Ash, you can call them."

"*Settler I* come in," called Ash.

Margo studied the planet, barely hearing Ash's attempts to raise the *Settler I* on comms. *Was it luck of the draw that put* Settler III *on a terraformable planet?*

On their next comms window to Earth, they'd have a lot to report to the Colonizing Council. *No, the Colonizing Council either was part of the conspiracy or incompetent.* She'd run her idea past Lucas next time she communicated with him, but it was possible that the Colonizing Council was in the pocket of The Conglomerate. During their next comms window with Earth, the Thesan colony needed to share this information as wide as possible. But Nigel would likely not allow the wormhole to open on schedule. *Are we cut off from Earth for good?*

"No one is answering," said Ash, drawing Margo's attention back to the group.

"All right." Iago paused until all eyes were on him. "Take us down and we'll knock on the front door."

"Wait," said Gary, stepping into the bridge from where he'd been leaning against the door frame. "If the atmosphere contains hydrogen fluoride gas, breathing in a microscopic drop could destroy our lungs." He held up his bare forearm and pointed to it. "A small splash here would interfere with how our bodies use calcium, resulting in almost immediate cardiac arrest."

"No one is suggesting we walk bare-faced around on the surface," said Iago, his tone condescending. "We'll have our suits on."

"There's one more point we need to consider," said Iva. "What if the colony didn't stay sealed from the ambient atmosphere?"

Everyone fell silent for a moment. If what Iva stated was true, there would be no survivors on *Settler I*. It was a sobering thought.

"We'll keep our suits on until Gary gives us the all clear," Iago finally said.

Gary nodded. Margo could tell that he didn't believe anyone should venture into *Settler I*, even in an atmo suit. But she also knew he knew, as they all did, that it had to be done.

"I'll drop you on the surface, then return to orbit," said Ash. "I can't risk too much damage to the hull."

"Okay," said Iago. "Ash stays with the ship. The rest of us, suit up Hopefully, we'll find the settlers alive and well."

Margo didn't think he sounded remotely sincere.

Chapter Twenty-Four

Margo pocked her head into the median. "You ready?"

Gary looked up from where he was checking the equipment in his bag on the examination table. Even though he smiled at her, his eyebrows were drawn together. He took a deep breath and rubbed the back of his neck. "Let me guess, Iago is getting impatient."

"He seems to think speed is the path to glory," she said, with a smile of her own as she stepped inside.

"How are you holding up?" Gary's tone was soft as he snapped his bag closed. The air-tight seal would keep the toxic atmosphere from contaminating his medical supplies. Leaving it on the table, he circled the green vinyl monstrosity and approached Margo.

When Gary reached out and claimed her left hand in both of his, the warmth of his touch radiated through her. She glanced down at their intertwined hands, then up at his face, at his kind eyes.

"I'm lucky to have you," he said. "And I think Iago is the only one who isn't horrified by the thought of going in there."

"Don't forget Yuko. She seems in her element," she said.

"True." He lifted their clasped hands and kissed the back of hers. "Promise me you won't take any unnecessary risks."

They stared at each other for a moment, acknowledging the elephant that came into the room along with Gary's words.

Margo bit her bottom lip, then said, "Last time I made you that promise, I had to break it. I don't want to break another promise to you." She lifted her free hand and ran her fingers along the line of his jaw. "We didn't speak to each other for months."

"We're both to blame for that. I could have been less stubborn, and you could maybe have tried harder." He smiled, taking the sting out of his words. "I didn't know what to say to fix things between us."

"I didn't either," she said.

A silence fell between them for a few moments.

"I miss the days we spent together going through Jim's notebooks," he said.

Margo smiled. "There are still plenty of those to look at when we get back."

"It's a date, then."

She leaned in and wrapped her arms around him. Gary did the same, holding her tight. Up close, his distinct scent of cedar and soap comforted her. She reached up and ran a hand through his hair.

The comms unit in the wall squawked, shattering their moment.

"Gary get to the airlock. We'll be leaving ASAP," transmitted Iago.

Margo sighed. "That's our cue." She savoured Gary's warmth a moment longer, before stepping away.

"We should get going before he shows up in person," said Gary, holding her gaze.

Margo wished they could stay behind. She wanted to spend a whole afternoon studying the gold flecks in Gary's blue eyes. Instead, the two of them had to face who-knows-what on the silent colony. A sour taste formed in her mouth. *What are we going to find?*

"One more thing," she said, keeping her tone lighter than she felt.

She leaned in and kissed him. Gary took his free hand and cupped the back of her neck, turning what she intended as a quick kiss into something more intense.

The intercom squawked again and Iago's baritone boomed over the speaker. "Gary, is Margo with you? I can't reach her. Tell her to get to the airlock. Now!"

The couple stopped kissing, but stayed in each other's arms, their gazes locked in an acknowledgement of shared passion.

"I could do with more of this," said Gary. He jerked his head toward the intercom speaker. "And a little less of that."

"Can we disengage the intercom? And lock the door?" Margo suggested. "Or perhaps move up to a cabin?"

Gary smiled and wrapped his arms around her waist. "Now, *that* suggestion sounds far more appealing than—"

"Hey, love birds!"

Gary and Margo broke apart and looked towards the open door.

Standing in the doorway, Iva laughed.

"Iago is itching to go, so we might as well get this over with. There'll be lots of time for that," she waved a hand between the two of them, "on the way home." With a chuckle, Iva left, heading aft.

Heat rose in Margo's cheeks.

"Like Iva said, let's get this over with. I've just had a brilliant idea, by the way," Gary said, picking up his heavy medical bag.

"What's that."

"We crowbar my bunk out of my cabin and set my mattress on the floor, with yours beside it."

"And here I thought marrying a doctor would put me in the lap of luxury," Margo teased as she followed him out of the medbay.

"Margo, Yuko and I will go through the airlock first," announced Iago in a too loud voice. He stood in the small vestibule with his back to the airlock door facing the remaining six members of the crew.

They were crowded into the tiny space and out along the hall, dressed in their orange atmo suits and holding their helmets. Already, Margo's neck ring chafed. One-size-fits-all suits meant they fit no one comfortably. Shifting her helmet to her other hand, she tried to ignore how sweaty her palms felt within her gloves, or how the knot in her gut was threatening to expel her last meal. *What will we find on* Settler I*?*

"We'll wait on the other side of the airlock for the three of you. Okay, helmets on," Iago ordered.

Margo glanced over at Gary before putting her helmet over her head. It clicked into place and she confirmed the suit's integrity. She was good to go—except for her churning stomach. She'd even packed the pistol again in the unlikely event she'd need it.

Through her visor, she watched Gary secure his helmet, and then frown in concentration as he did his integrity check. A slap on the shoulder from Iago brought her focus to him.

"Come on Murphy, let's go." He didn't wait to see if she followed as he strode into the airlock.

Yuko was already inside, her expression behind her visor smug. Margo wanted to tell her that being chosen to cycle through the airlock with Iago was no prize, but she kept her thoughts to herself as she stepped in. There was just enough room inside for Yuko to manoeuvre the door shut behind her. No one said a word as the air cycled. When the exterior door light flashed green, Iago opened it and stepped outside.

As soon as Iago's bulky form cleared the door, Margo paused and gaped at the view. After a prod from Yuko, she descended the five steps down to the planet's surface. Even though Helios was high in the sky, it didn't disperse the yellowish mist that clung to the surface like fog, obscuring the distant landscape. The subdued ambient light created a strange twilight-like effect. The three of them turned on their helmet lights.

Huge flakes of volcanic ash floated in the air, drifting slowly towards the ground. She held out her hand until one fell onto her gloved palm. It dissolved into powder as soon as it touched her.

The ground looked nothing like rock-strewn Thesan, instead covered in a moist substrate. Overall, her surroundings reminded her of a yellowed and vintage Christmas card depicting a winter wonderland. It surprised her she found it so pretty.

"You okay, Margo?" asked Iago.

His soft, concerned tone surprised her. "Yeah," she replied. "Just...wow."

A slight breeze shifted the mist, exposing the hulking form of *Settler I* directly ahead of them. Ash had landed the *Staffelwalze* about fifty meters from *Settler I's* main airlock. Margo knew its exterior had once been as pristinely white as its sister ships, but now the same yellow as the world it inhabited tinted its exterior. Darker splotches appeared randomly scattered on its surfaces like structural chicken pox.

"Hey, look at this," said Yuko. Iago and Margo joined her where she'd crouched down, running a gloved finger across the ground.

Margo knelt beside the astrophysicist, for once curious about what Yuko had to say. She dug a couple of fingers into the soil as if making a hole for a seed. The texture of the ground reminded her of moist soil. The first centimetre was mushy, but it was more solid below that. A film of it stuck to her glove. She raised her finger up to examine it in her helmet's lights. "It looks like a thick jelly. Do you think it might be alive?"

"How would I know," Yuko responded in a testy tone.

Margo rolled her eyes. *Abigail should be here!.*

When Margo stood up, she noticed their three sets of footprints leading from the ship were already partially erased by the floating flakes. It wouldn't take long before no hint they'd ever been here remained.

"Yuko, take a soil sample," Iago ordered.

Yuko pulled out a vial and filled it with the goo.

Light from the ship's airlock spilled onto them as the door opened again. Gan stepped out first, his small form easily recognizable. Next came Iva, then Gary. Margo eyed Gary in concern as he tentatively stepped onto the ground.

"Everyone set?" asked Iago, glancing from person to person. When everyone responded affirmatively, Iago lifted his wrist and turned on the comms that would allow him—any of them—to communicate to Ash in the *Staffelwalze*, "Ash, you're free to take the *Staffelwalze* back to orbit. We'll contact you once every two hours, on the hour. If we go silent for four hours, come back down."

"Roger," Ash said. Her voice came through on all six of their helmets. "I'll wait until you are inside *Settler I* before lifting off."

Margo pictured the *Staffelwaltz's* captain sitting in the pilot's seat concentrating on the video feed showing the six of them. Margo lifted her head and waved in the direction of the nearest camera. "Be safe up there."

Gan, Iva, and Gary had been looking around, just as Margo had done, but now Gan said, "I see a light on the airlock door. They have power. I'd expected to have to go through the airlock manually."

"They have power; yet, no one answered our hails," said Iva, stopping beside him.

Margo noted that every one of the *Settler I's* windows was dark. For a moment, it felt like the inky blackness held a malevolent presence staring back, daring her to enter. A shiver snaked up her spine. She averted her gaze.

"Let's go," said Iago, heading towards the colony's main airlock.

Gary fell into step beside Margo as the five of them followed Iago.

In her peripheral vision, the floating flakes of ash morphed into a group of grey butterflies. Margo tried to ignore them, telling herself they were just another of her hallucinations. Then a butterfly fluttered right in front of her helmet. She raised a hand to it but it disintegrated into powder, like the last flake she'd tried to touch. *Ignore them.* Another butterfly appeared. This one landed on Gary's shoulder. She forced herself to turn away from it and focus on Iago's broad back as he led them toward the colony.

Chapter Twenty-Five

When the exterior light of *Settler I*'s main airlock flashed green, Iago turned the large handle and opened the door. A light blinked on inside, illuminating a pristine white interior identical to the main airlock on Thesan.

"We'll all fit, so let's stick together." Iago showed no hesitation as he led the way across the threshold.

Turning, Margo glanced back at the *Staffelwalze*. Through the yellow haze and floating flakes, she could still see the ship—a little ancient, but solid and friendly. For a moment, she debated running back to it. *If I left now, what would Iago do?*

"Get moving," said Yuko as she charged past Margo into the airlock and stopped beside Iago.

After sharing an encouraging gaze with Gary, Margo entered the airlock right behind him. Inside, they stood so close their shoulders touched. Iva stood on her other side, her eyes wide and darting around the space as though she expected a ghost to pop out at any moment. When Iva made eye contact with her, Margo gave what she hoped was a reassuring smile. Iago and Yuko were both peering through the interior door's window into the change room, but they didn't say anything so Margo assumed there was nothing to see.

As the last one in, Gan sealed the outside door, shutting out the murky yellow sky and floating ash. With the door closed, there was no choice but to face what was inside.

"Okay Ash, we're in," said Iago over the radio comms.

"Roger that." Through the helmet speaker, Ash already sounded far away. "Stay safe, and I'll see you all soon."

Through the inset window in the airlock's exterior door, Margo watched the *Staffelwalze* lift into the sky. The thruster's downwash scattered the floating ash. As she watched, they reformed into non-existent butterflies and she forced herself to focus on the ship. The bulky old hull lifted higher and higher until the haze above swallowed it. Ash would be alone up there. Margo didn't know what was worse, being alone up there, or having to explore another ship that might be just as as gruesome as the *Settler II.* At least Ash got to wait in a familiar environment.

"I'm putting us through a full decontamination cycle," said Gan from the controls. "When the alarm sounds, close your eyes."

A moment later, a klaxon went off and Margo squeezed her eyes shut. The brightness of the UV light was still visible through her closed eyelids. She cringed as she wondered if the radiation was enough to keep the outside environment at bay. The alarm ended as soon as the light levels returned to normal. Margo opened her eyes.

"I hope there's nothing awful in there. Please don't let there be anything awful." Iva's voice started sounding more and more hysterical.

"Iva! Enough," snapped Iago. The door light flashed green, he reached forward and opened it.

Margo put a hand on Iva's sleeve and the other woman turned to look at her. "We'll figure this out together," she said. Iva nodded in response.

The six of them spilled out into the large roomy change room. The overhead lights automatically came on flooding the space with cold, bright light. After her eyes adjusted, Margo felt the same overwhelming sense of deja vu she'd felt stepping on *Settler II*. The main airlock's atmo suit change room in *Settler 1* was identical to the *Settler II* and the one back home.

Iva turned to Margo. The other woman's skin tone looked ashen beneath her helmet. "No one came to greet us."

"No." Margo bit her lip, not wanting to voice her suspicion that the reason there was no welcoming party was because no one was alive for them to rescue.

"Yuko, how's the air in here?" asked Iago in a business-like tone.

Yuko detached an instrument from her belt and waved it around. After a moment, she stopped and looked at its display. "The air checks out," she reported sounding surprised. "Oxygen levels are more than sufficient and carbon dioxide levels are low. Temperature is a perfect 21 degrees. We could take our suits off right now."

"Hold on a minute," said Gary, stepping between Yuko and Iago. "Nobody takes off their suits! Not your helmet, nothing! The atmosphere may be survivable, but we don't know if there are pathogens or toxins in the air. Since the power is on, there will be instruments to test the air more thoroughly in the sickbay."

"That's unnecessary," said Yuko. "My portable unit is more than sufficient to test the air."

"We don't know the state of the ventilation system," said Gan, looking up at the vents in the ceiling. "I'm with Gary. We should wait until we do further tests."

Gary stared Iago down. "Iago, it would be utter foolishness to allow anyone to remove any part of their atmo suit."

Iago was silent for a moment and Margo held her breath. *Is Iago foolish enough to listen to Yuko and risk breathing the air?*

"Let's err on the side of caution, for now," said Iago.

Margo exhaled and glanced at Gary. He looked tense. She might be out of her element, but he was light years out of his.

"We'll break into two groups," said Iago.

Everyone except Yuko protested.

"What?" Margo demanded. "Didn't you learn from what happened to Gan on *Setter II*?"

"I'm running the show here," Iago commanded. "And it's ridiculous to waste resources. This is too big of a ship for us not to split up. Gary, Gan and Yuko, head to sickbay and run further tests on the air quality. Iva, Margo and I will go to the main Control Room and see if we can get the computers up and running. Everyone, keep an eye out for survivors."

"I'd be more use in the control centre." Yuko's voice carried a whiny edge.

"You have your orders," said Iago, not bothering to meet Yuko's gaze.

Yuko flinched, stomped to the door of the Loop and opened it, exposing the well-lit corridor beyond and the red line denoting they were in the operations quadrant. She stepped through and Gan followed.

Margo turned to Gary. "Be safe." If they hadn't been wearing helmets, she would've kissed him. She didn't care who witnessed it.

"You too," He said, then turned and followed Yuko and Gan. The three suits looked extra orange against the white walls of the Loop before they vanished out of sight.

Once he was gone, Margo slowly exhaled. *Please come back to me.*

———

Margo watched as Iago opened the door to the side room for suit maintenance and stepped inside.

"Might as well check everywhere in case of survivors," said Iago. A moment later, he returned. "No one there, let's get going." He strode to the open door to the Loop.

Iva followed, looking nervous and timid behind their over confidant mission leader.

As Margo made to follow, an image of the Loop on *Settler II* flashed into her mind. *Butterfly blue without a clue; Butterfly red better off dead. What did that mean? And was it directed at me? How could that even be possible?* She froze as butterflies threatened to emerge in her peripheral vision and squeezed her eyes shut. After a brief moment, with no report from Iago or Iva of pictograms covering the walls, she opened her eyes.

"Margo!" called Iago over the helmet comms.

Stomach quivering, she stepped across the threshold to the Loop and glancing one way and then the other. The walls were pristine, like theirs had been before the crash landing onto Thesan.

"Keep moving," ordered Iago.

Iva and Iago were already well ahead forcing Margo to hurry to catch up.

Unlike *Settler III*'s Control Room doors that had been warped during the crash landing on Thesan, these Control Room doors automatically slid open when they arrived. As the three of them stepped inside, the overhead lights came on, but the screens stayed dark.

"Iva, get the computer system up and running," ordered Iago, striding down the first set of stairs to the middle platform that housed a half-dozen workstations.

Iva followed and went to the main console, perching on the chair as best she could, given the air pack on her back. After a few moments of tapping clumsily with her atmo gloves, all the screens came to life.

A mosaic of internal camera feeds showed both the interior and exterior of the colony, including the shuttle and rover hangars, the common room, the Hub and various locations along the Loop. Margo immediately began looking to see where Gary, Gan, and Yuko were, but there was no movement on any of the views.

"I don't see the others anywhere," said Margo, feeling her heart-rate elevating as she glanced from image to image.

"That's weird." Iva stared down at her console. "Those aren't live feeds, just static past images."

"Oh." Margo stepped down onto the same platform as Iva and Iago. "Can you bring up live video feeds?"

"I can try." Iva flicked through more screens on her display.

"Focus on finding the AI first," said Iago leaning over Iva's shoulder. "It might be able to report what happened here and I'm sure the others are fine."

Margo sat at the workstation beside Iva and started looking for the live video feeds on the console's small monitor.

"I can't find an AI," Iva said after a few minutes. "Maybe they removed it."

"Are the other systems operating within acceptable limits?" asked Iago.

Iva scrolled through more screens. "Yeah, the colony seems to be functioning fine."

"Okay, keep looking for a record of what happened here. Margo." Margo raised an eyebrow as Iago turned to face her. "Come with me, we'll check the commander's office. Hopefully, the commander kept a log."

"Right," she said using the console's structure to push up to her feet. She followed Iago as he strode to the side door that led to the commander's office. The door was unlocked. Like everywhere else they'd been, when the door slid open the lights inside came on.

"What was the Commander's name again?" asked Iago. "Reeves, River, R…"

"I don't know. I didn't follow the media blitz on the first colony ship," Margo said, roaming around.

"Riemer, that was it." Iago stood in front of the Commander's desk and picked up a framed photo. "Ah, yes…" He studied the image. "I remember, Stella Riemer. Such a pretty thing."

"Hmmm," said Margo, keeping the desk between her and Iago. She opened the top drawer and found what had to be the commander's scroll. Sitting down, she unrolled it and turned it on, then set it on the desk's surface. *What are the chances the commander didn't have her scroll password protected?*

Iago saw what she'd found and put the framed photo back on the desk. "Are there logs?" he asked, coming around the desk to stand behind her.

Too close.

Margo gritted her teeth when she realized she'd allowed herself to be trapped. "I'll take this to the Control Room and display it on the large monitor. It will be easier to read the data."

"No you won't." Iago moved closer, preventing her escape. He gripped her shoulder with his prosthetic hand, then leaned over her, resting his big gloved hand on the desk beside hers. "I've been waiting to get you alone," he said in a sickeningly playful tone.

Margo tried to push her chair back and escape his grip, but she was jammed between the desk and his powerful body.

"Stop resisting me, Margo. I, for one, am done chasing."

She forced herself not to struggle, knowing she wouldn't be able to overpower the iron grip of his prosthetic hand. She did, however, scowl up at him. "On a ghost ship? In atmo suits?" Her tone dripped disdain.

"Why not? The air is fine, Yuko's always right. Your doctor is overreacting."

"My *husband*," Margo corrected through gritted teeth. His grip on her shoulder was beginning to hurt.

"Whatever. I sent him off to do his 'tests' to keep him out of our hair. There's just not enough space on the *Staffelwalze* to get you alone. Once you've been with me, you'll dump your doctor."

When he removed his hand from her shoulder Margo almost sighed in relief. Then he unlatched her helmet and removed it in one motion.

"What the hell!" Margo shoved as hard as she could on her chair, sending herself backwards and knocking Iago off balance. He took a step back to steady himself, and she used the extra space to scoot away from him. She put the massive surface of the desk between them and glared at him.

"You pompous asshole! How many times do I need to say no to you?"

He still had her helmet.

The air smelled wrong, there was an organic scent underpinned with the smell of rotten eggs, but she could breathe. Gary would flip if he found out she was exposed this way.

"Give me back my helmet!" she said.

"I know you feel it too," he said, putting her helmet down on a shelf behind him. He then took his helmet off. "Women like you always fall for the alpha male."

"That's ridiculous."

"One kiss will convince you," he said. "Just give in."

"Fuck you," Margo said and stomped out of the room.

Back in the main Control Room, Iva looked up as Margo walked in. "Margo! Why did you take your helmet off?"

"I don't want to talk about it," snapped Margo.

A moment later, helmet in place, Iago came out of the office and walked towards them. "Any luck with the AI yet?" he asked.

"Still checking," Iva responded, giving Margo a baffled look before she resumed her work.

Still fuming, Margo returned to the commander's office to retrieve her helmet from where Iago had left it on the desk. After she jammed it back on, she had to pause and steady her breathing. On the desk, next to where her helmet had been, she noticed that the commander's scroll wasn't password protected.

Sitting down, her heart rate finally normal again—*Iago is a fucking bastard*—she initiated a search for the commander's logs.

In no time, she found them. The last one was dated two weeks earlier.

Just as she lifted her hand to open the file, she heard Iva scream. Grabbing the scroll, Margo ran to investigate.

Chapter Twenty-Six

Out on the Loop, Gary fell into step beside Gan as Yuko strode ahead. Their footfalls seemed extra loud in the hushed environment.

"Keep up. You don't want to lose me," she said, without looking back.

"Yeah, we do," muttered Gan. His tone was low enough that only Gary's helmet could pick up his words. Since dissenting comments of any kind were uncharacteristic for Gan, Gary concluded the tension of the situation must be getting to the engineer. *It's getting to me too*, he thought.

The line on the wall changed from red to purple. They were in the domestic quadrant now. *Settler I's* Loop was the same as theirs—except the place was deserted. *Where is everyone?* Gary saw that Gan was doing as he was, looking left to right, searching for clues. But, all the doors were shut leaving nothing but the white corridor.

As they passed the common room windows, he glimpsed the dark outlines of plants in the ship's inner-ring greenhouse. He wondered if the *Settler I* colonists had built a fish pond like they had on Thesan in their inner-ring greenhouse. Or if someone had smuggled in butterflies like Margo had. He smiled at the thought of Margo, but was interrupted in his musings when Gan spoke.

"What could have gone wrong here?" Gan asked.

"I was just thinking the same thing. In fact, it looks like life on *Settler I* started out much more smoothly than *Settler III*, all going according to plan. They landed in the spot they intended. They built their greenhouses. What went wrong?"

"Let's go through the Hub," said Yuko, stopping and letting the other two catch up. Before her both sets of doors to the Hub stood wide open. "You never know, we might find someone to save."

Neither Gary nor Gan responded, but they followed Yuko into the Hub. The garden at the centre contained as many plants as theirs on Thesan. But even to Gary's non-gardening eye the foliage didn't look right. *Margo would know what the problem is.* He toyed with the idea of calling her. Iago might hate it, but he was certain she would defy Iago and come if Gary called. As he debated what to do, Gan walked right into the middle of the nearest garden bed.

"Something is coating these plants." Gan leaned in for a close look before rubbing his gloved fingers across a branch. From where Gary stood, he saw a film of shiny goo come off onto Gan's glove.

"What is it?" asked Yuko, walking over to investigate.

"A sticky film is covering everything," said Gan. Stepping out of the garden bed, he stopped beside Yuko.

She examined the goo on his glove, then glanced up at the tree behind him. "Whatever it is, it hasn't outright killed the plants."

Motion from the two-story high greenwall caught Gary's attention. He cautiously took a few paces closer—the greenwall was far from thriving. Irregularly shaped grey blots like mould spotted most of the leaves and whole swaths of plants were yellow as though starved of nutrients. As he watched, the leaves moved again, caught in the breeze from the overhead ventilation.

Although he didn't attempt to touch anything, it looked like the same goo that Gan found also covered these plants. *Is what's killing the plants dangerous to people?* He saw that Yuko had already begun taking samples. He would need to examine them to find the answer.

He glanced back the way they'd come. From where he stood, the open doors of the Hub aligned with the doors of the dining room and the doors leading to the central greenhouse. Staring through the line of open doorways, he tried to make out what was growing in the greenhouse. The panels on the dome were at their darkest level, shading out the light of the two suns. The only light spilling into the space came from the Loop. Beyond the first few metres, there was only only a void of darkness.

"If something is killing the plants in here, what is it doing to the plants in the greenhouse?" he asked.

"That's not our primary focus right now," said Yuko, her tone inpatient. "Remember, we're supposed to go to sickbay, not take an inventory of plant health."

Gary made eye contact with Yuko. "No. Our primary goal is to find survivors and, barring that, find clues to help us determine what happened to the colonists."

"Yeah." Yuko gestured impatiently. "At sickbay, like Iago ordered. Are you coming?"

"Yes, I'm coming," he answered. But first he turned to take a last glance down the line of open doors towards the central greenhouse. He was about to turn away when motion in its shadowed depths again caught his attention. He snapped himself fully around as adrenalin surged through his system. For a moment, he thought he saw a black tentacle-like shape writhe in the shadows. The hairs on the back of his neck stood on end.

"What are you waiting for?" demanded Yuko.

"Something moved in the greenhouse." Gary pointed.

"You sure?" Gan stood beside Gary and looked in the direc-

tion Gary pointed. The two men stood in silence staring—
nothing moved. No Lovecraftian beings lurked in the darkness.

"Sickbay is this way," urged Yuko.

"My eyes must be playing tricks on me." With a sigh, Gary
turned away and followed the others to *Settler I*'s sickbay. It was
strangely comforting to be in a space where he knew he
belonged, where he was the expert. He went straight to the
small lab next to the washroom. Yuko and Gan followed.

"I'll take the samples." Gary held out his hand.

She gave him the two vials, one marked as NS—Nak soil—
the other as PG—*plant goo?* Gary set the vials on the counter as
he booted up the sampling machine. Various LED lights flashed
on and a diagnostic protocol started on the main screen. In the
bright lights of the lab, he noticed that the contents of the vials
looked identical. They were the same colour and even had the
same level of transparency.

"They look exactly the same," said Gan, as he bent closer to
the vials.

Yuko came to stand beside Gan. "That seems odd."

"Contamination from outside?" said Gary, as he slid the
sample from outside into the machine. "I'll start with a general
mass spectrometry analysis to assess the chemical makeup."

"How long is this going to take?" Yuko put her hands on
her hips.

"Assuming the equipment functions properly and there's
nothing too exotic in the samples, not long. Five minutes?" Gary
crossed his arms and watched the main screen. "Gan, can you
check the air quality readings?"

Without a word, Gan went to the other display and scrolled
through screens. Yuko followed him and watched over his shoulder.

Gary picked up the second vial and raised it up to his visor.
It reminded him of a slime he'd made with a chemistry kit as a
kid. As he studied it, the goo seemed to churn, like water just on
the verge of boiling. Then its surface bubbled, and an antenna-

shaped arm of goo started reaching towards the lid. He nearly dropped the sample.

"Wow! You need to see this. This sample is behaving like it could be alive," said Gary, steadying himself.

"Impossible," said Yuko. "This planet was vetted—the initial probe found no signs of life." Despite her claim, she joined Gan beside Gary. All three of them stared at the contents of the vial. The thin arm reaching for the stopper was thickening and continued to move on its own.

"Yet, the sample moves," said Gary. He could hear the awe in his voice. Or maybe it was fear. Whatever it was, he was getting a bad feeling in his gut.

"There has to be another explanation," Yuko said, turning back to the air quality readings. "Perhaps it's just a non-organic crystal forming."

Gary held the vial up close to his visor. The substance's movements were not orderly like a crystal, but there was no point arguing with Yuko when the equipment to prove the point was right in front of him.

The mass spectrometer dinged, signalling it was done analyzing the first sample. Setting the vial down, Gary, with Gan peering over his shoulder, read through the results, but he was struggling to make sense of what he saw. According to this analysis, the goo consisted primarily of sulphur-based structures. When he zoomed in close, he could've sworn he was looking at living cells.

Are they alive, or is the structure a coincidence?

"I'm no scientist, but that's a living organism, isn't it?" Gan asked.

"Looks that way to me," Gary said.

Hearing their conversation, Yuko came over from where she'd been working on the air quality machine and suggested, "Test the other vial."

Gary swapped the vials and analyzed the other. They had to

wait another five minutes, but the result of the second sample was the same as the first.

"The substance we encountered outside is the same as that inside," said Gary. "Both look structurally similar to earth-based cells. On a first look, I'd say the samples are alive—life based on sulphur instead of carbon."

"Is it dangerous?" asked Yuko.

"The scanner detected no toxic compounds," said Gary. "But it's premature to tell if the substance is harmful. There could be an airborne component we haven't identified yet, or the sulphur-based cells might interact with ours in an unexpected way."

"I'm sure you're overthinking things," said Yuko dismissively as she studied the air quality readouts. "Well, the air all over the colony is just fine." She gave Gary a told-you-so look. "But as Dr. Cautious, I suspect you'll never concede the air is safe to breathe."

When Yuko lifted her hands and started to work the clasps to remove her helmet, Gary and Gan both stepped forward and shouted, "Don't!" But they were too late to stop her.

Yuko, smiling triumphantly, held her helmet in front of her and took her first breath of Nak air.

When she started to cough, Gary and Gan both sprang to her side. She waved them off.

"I'm fine," she said waving a hand in front of her nose. "It's just the stench."

"What do you smell?" asked Gary.

"Rotten eggs," she said.

"Elevated sulphur levels are being detected throughout the colony," said Gan, reading off the display. "Not at dangerous levels though." Gan put his hand on the latch to his helmet.

"Hold on," said Gary, but he was too late Gan had removed his helmet.

After taking a deep breath, Gan said, "rotten eggs is an understatement."

Gan and Yuko removed their atmo suits as Gary watched in horror. The suits were uncomfortable, but they were the only barrier they had to mitigate exposure risk. He had no idea what the consequence of exposing themselves to the alien life would be.

"Okay, let me look at your goo," said Yuko. She picked up the vial on the counter and held it up to the light. "You're right, it's movement makes me think it's alive."

Gary turned his attention back to the machine's display. The computer had ideas what the substance might be.

"Assuming it's alive, it most resembles a slime mould," said Gary.

"Congratulations, you've found alien life," said Yuko, in a tone that had to be sarcastic. She put the vial down. "Now lets figure out what happened to the colonists. Gan bring up the biotrackers."

A burst of static crackled over their helmet speakers. "… come to the Control Room right away," said Margo over the radio. "We've found someone."

Chapter Twenty-Seven

As Margo rushed back into the Control Room, she found it empty, but the door to the server room off the lowest of the three platforms gaped open. Her atmo boots resounded loudly on the floor as she ran to the room. Once inside, she saw Iva standing next to a bank of servers staring at something near where Iago crouched on the floor. They didn't even look up when she entered, but Margo could see the horror etched on Iva's face.

Shoving the scroll into a pocket, she hurried around the server stacks. "Oh, crap!" she said, stopping beside Iva. In front them was a body.

The slight blonde woman lay on her back slumped against one of the server towers. Her dark blue colonist uniform had the red patch of the operations group on her shoulder. Coagulated blood coated her clothes and hands, with more dried blood coating the flaxen hair hiding her face. Bloody fingerprints covered the floor and equipment around the body. Whatever happened hadn't been slow and the blood was still red enough to suggest it was recent.

Iago was kneeling beside the woman, and reached out his flesh hand to brush the hair out of her face.

He jerked back in alarm. "Christ!" he said.

"Oh-my-god-oh-my-god," muttered Iva, turning away and putting her hands over her mouth.

Bile rose in Margo's throat at the sight. Someone had gouged out the woman's eyes leaving bloody sockets.

Iago recovered first. "According to her name badge, this is— was—the colony commander." The overconfident edge in Iago's voice was gone. He shifted back to his heals and looked down at his hands.

Taking a step closer, Margo stepped around the blood and dropped into a crouch beside the woman on the opposite side of Iago.

"Oh, that poor woman," Iva said remaining standing. "Who would do such a thing?"

An image of the photo in the commander's office surfaced in Margo's mind. The vibrant, confident woman in the picture had little in common with this blood-smeared, eyeless corpse.

After a moment, Iva pointed at the woman's hands. "I think she...she did this to herself," she whispered, a tremor to her voice.

At Iva's words, Margo sucked in a breath, thinking of what Gary had told her about the patients in his mother's ward back on Earth—they had also gouged out their own eyes. "We can't know that," she argued.

"Look at her fingernails." Iva crouched down and picked up a discarded plastic cable tie from under the server housing next to her and used it to lift one of the woman's fingers. "Look at her fingernails."

The woman's fingers were bloody—especially around her fingertips. Margo studied the edges of bloody fingerprints on the floor. A yellowish slime formed thick haloes around every spatter of blood.

"Why would she do that?" Iago gestured with his prosthetic hand. "This has to have been some sort of accident."

"What could possibly do this by accident?" Iva's words mirrored Margo's thoughts. Iva stood and turned in a circle, examining the room, then leaned back to study the ceiling. With a frown, she looked down at her companions. "There's nothing here but computers."

"There's nothing we can do for her now." Iago stood and backed away from the corpse. As he headed towards the main room, he said over his shoulder, "We have even more reason now to figure out what happened here."

"Iva." Margo said when the two of them were alone in the server room. She swiped a bit of slime onto her gloved fingertip and held it up. "What do you think this is?"

"I don't know," she said eyes fixed on Margo's glove. A tremor went through her body.

"Why don't you wait outside with Iago?" suggested Margo.

Iva nodded before turning and following Iago.

After taking a deep breath to steady herself, Margo activated her suit's radio. "Gary you need to come to the Control Room right away. We've found someone."

"One of the colonists? Alive?" asked Gary.

"One of the colonists, yes. But she's dead. We're in the server room. Can you come right away?"

"Of course. Are you guys all okay?"

"We're fine," Margo said. She wouldn't let herself think about the consequence of having breathed the air for the few minutes she'd been without her helmet. *It was only for a minute...* She wished they were finished their inspection of the colony and back on the *Staffelwalze*, heading home.

Margo shifted to sit on the floor outside the pool of dried blood. As she waited she scanned the server room. Blinking green lights suggested the computers were running as they should. Everything about the room looked normal—except for the dead woman on the floor who might very well have gouged her own eyes out.

As she glanced through the glass walls, Gary, Yuko and Gan entered the Control Room. What she saw made her scramble to her feet. "Dirty circuits," she swore. Yuko and Gan had not only removed their helmets, they'd taken their suits off. Margo couldn't hear from inside the server room, but she saw Iago speak briefly with Yuko and then, for the second time, remove his helmet

"Is the air okay?" she asked when Gary entered the server room, medical bag in hand. Through the clear plexiglass walls, she saw Iago stepping out of his atmo suit and tossing it onto one of the chairs.

"Too soon to say." Gary jerked a thumb over his shoulder towards Yuko. "But she's too stubborn to listen to reason."

Margo watched as Gan and Yuko join Iva and Iago at a console, consulting data that Iva had pulled up on a screen.

"Oh!" he said, stopping when he saw what had been done to the woman.

"Sorry, I didn't think to warn you," said Margo. "This is, I mean *was*, Stella Riemer, the colony commander."

Gary knelt down beside Stella, being careful to step clear of the blood on the floor. From his bag, he pulled out a portable scanner and waved it over her. Lights flashed on his instrument, and he turned it to read the display.

"She's been dead at least a few days." Gary leaned in to examine where her eyes had been, then glanced up at Margo. "It's highly probably she did this to herself." He picked up one of her hands and looked at the blood on her fingers.

"Could mutilating herself like that have killed her?" She gestured to Stella's face without looking at her.

Gary shook his head. "I don't think so," he said. "I'll need to take her to sickbay to determine her cause of death." He put his sensor back in his bag, then stood beside Margo. "You look pale, are you okay?"

She forced a smile. "I'm just looking forward to getting out of here. There's nothing right about this place." She gestured to the others. "And I can't believe Yuko's being so reckless."

"Me neither. She's putting too much faith in the air quality sensors. There's simply too many unknown variables to take such a foolish risk," he said. "You'll never believe what we discovered." He explained about the evidence of life in the slime, including that the exterior and interior samples matched, and there were no apparent toxins.

News of alien life left her feeling both confused and horrified at the same time. "Take a look at this here," said Margo, pointing to the slime surrounding the blood stains on the floor.

Gary knelt on the floor to take a closer look. "It could be the same substance," he said, then retrieved a vial from his bag and took a sample. "I'll have to test it." He paused then, and looked thoughtful. "I wonder... could the slime be feeding on the blood?"

"Or, could it drive someone to do that?" Margo pointed at Stella.

"I don't know enough about it to even hazard a guess," he said, coming to his feet. "There was slime on the plants in the Hub, yet sickbay was clear." He looked around. "And there's no more than a small amount in here, and it's contained within range of the organic matter near the body."

"So what do we do now?" Margo asked.

Gary nodded at the body. "Find a stretcher and take her to sickbay."

Chapter Twenty-Eight

Gary gripped the front handles of the stretcher they'd taken from the first-aid station just inside the Control Room. Margo held the other end at the corpse's feet. As they maneuvered down the Loop and into sickbay, the others followed. It was a good thing their corpse was a slight woman as none of the others offered to help with the load.

Once through sickbay's doors, Gary headed through to examination room one. Inside, he and Margo stopped parallel to the green vinyl covered table.

"On the count of three, we lift her up," he said.

Margo nodded.

"Three... two... one." The two of them hoisted the stretcher up and slid it onto the table.

"She can stay on the stretcher," said Gary backing away from the table. Beneath the thick gloves covering his hands, his palms were sweaty. Moving a corpse in his atmo suit had been awkward—he could see the appeal of removing it like the others had, but he wasn't willing to take the risk. He turned and smiled at Margo and was pleased to see her smile back. Then he glanced down at Stella.

"I need to know what killed her." Iago stood in the doorway holding his atmo suit and helmet in his arms. He was the most muscular of the group, and it irked Gary that Iago hadn't volunteered to help move the body. In fact, their leader hadn't said a word since Gary and Margo loaded the body onto the stretcher.

"So do I," Gary said in a deliberately neutral tone.

Iago gave a curt nod before disappearing from view. Gary assumed he joined the others in the waiting room. Margo was the only one who'd volunteered to stay with him in case he needed help.

"They're being foolish," he said in a low tone. The two of them were close enough to talk without the need for their helmet comms. They wouldn't be overheard. He glanced over at Margo, glad she, at least, still had her helmet on. "It's way too early to know if the atmosphere in here is safe to breathe."

Through the faceplate of her helmet, he saw Margo bite her lip.

"Don't worry. As long as your suit has maintained its airtight seal, you haven't been exposed," he added trying to sound reassuring.

Margo opened her mouth as though she was about to launch into a debate, but then she simply said, "Yeah." As she leaned against the counter, she kept her eyes averted from the body, instead studying the equipment in the room as though it was fascinating.

He shifted his attention to the examination table. Stella Riemer's flaccidity told him that rigour mortis had passed, and she'd thus been dead for at least two days, if not longer. The bright overhead lights exposed every detail of her mutilated face. Self-inflicted or not, the wounds were superficial and the blood loss insufficient to have resulted in death.

"Why did you die?" he asked aloud as he moved closer to examine her face.

"How are you going to find that out?" Margo asked.

"I'll start with a full body scan."

After pulling the scanner down from the ceiling, his movements only slightly hampered by his atmo gloves, he initialized the most detailed sequence. The light on the side of the contraption blinked as a wand slowly passed over Stella. A processing bar popped up on a display behind him. A quick glance told him the scan was only 2% complete—this could take a while.

Margo leaned in to look at the screen. As the shoulder of her atmo suit grazed his, he turned to her. It was too bad the safety of their atmo suits prevented actual physical contact.

"Assuming she scratched her own eyes out—hard to assume otherwise, given the evidence before us—we want to know why. But more importantly, we need to know the cause of death."

"Something must have made her mentally unstable here, since arrival," said Margo. "I'd expect, back on Earth, they vetted her for pre-existing physiological disorders."

"True. So, let's conclude she didn't have a pre-existing condition.

The display read 78% complete—the processing was going faster than he'd expected. Moments later, a three-dimensional rendering of Stella appeared on the display. Gary pressed a few buttons so that the view showed all Stella's major systems. One thing jumped out at him.

"Huh, that's odd."

"What's odd?" Margo leaned in closer to the screen.

"She has two biotrackers," said Gary, pointing to their locations on the screen, one in her forearm and one near the base of her brain.

"Is that weird?" Margo asked.

"Not necessarily. They might've decided redundancy made sense for this first mission." Gary continued to scan the results, then gave a satisfied nod. "These preliminary results at least confirm that losing her eyes didn't kill her."

"What did?"

"I need to do a more detailed analysis, but with these clumsy gloves…" He held up his hands. "It'll take a while."

"What can I do to help?" asked Margo.

"First, we should take blood and tissue samples. How about you go through the cupboards and find the sampling kit," he asked.

Margo turned and searched as Gary once again bent down to examine Stella's face. Deep scratches ran down her face from her hair line to her jaw. Where there wasn't blood, her skin was patchy as though she'd been suffering from a skin condition of some sort. The coin-sized patches were raised slightly from the surrounding skin, and the flaked skin formed an unusual pattern. In addition, the patches appeared to have different ages, some spots appeared older than others.

He lifted Stella's right hand noticing the raised spots extended all down her arm. Rotating his grip, studied her nails. With his other gloved hand, he shifted the overhead light's angle, shining it right on her finger tips. There was definitely flesh under her nails—most likely she'd done the damage herself. *But why?* An exotic pathogen could cause extreme reactions and seemed a reasonable hypothesis; it was something he could test.

"Will these do?" Margo handed him a tray with standard sampling gear.

"Yes, thanks. You know," he said as he carefully sliced off a tissue sample from Stella's face. "I remember reading once about a fungus that would infect jungle ants back on Earth. It would completely alter the ants' behaviour." Gary dropped the tissue sample into a vial.

"*Ophiocordyceps unilateralis*," said Margo, as though it was on the tip of her tongue.

Gary paused and smiled at her, realizing that of course she'd know the latin name.

Margo continued, "An infected ant is basically a dead ant that's still moving. The fungus drives it to climb to a high location where conditions are optimal for spore dispersal. These zombie ants inspired some of the first zombie flicks."

Gary shivered at the thought of zombie-inducing slime. He'd never been a fan of zombie vids. Turning back to the sampling equipment, he put the tissue sample in. "This will take a few minutes," he said, and Margo nodded.

A commotion in the waiting room drew both Gary and Margo's attention. Before they could head out to investigate, Gan appeared in the doorway.

"Yuko's gone nuts," he said in a rapid, high-pitched tone. "It was like a switch was flipped. And she started clawing at her face."

Gary shot past Gan and rushed over to where Yuko was on her back on the floor of the waiting room. Iago and Iva were on either side of her, doing their best to control Yuko's flailing limbs. Blood oozed from a gash on her forehead.

"LET ME GO!" Yuko screamed, twisting from side-to-side.

She managed to rip her arm out of Iva's grasp before twisting to slash at Iago. He dodged her attack and shifted so that his body weight pinned her to the floor, giving Iva a chance to grab onto Yuko's free arm.

Gary's mind raced to analyze the situation. It was almost as though Yuko had become stronger. *Could an air borne pathogen do that? Flood her system with adrenalin?*

"What happened?" asked Gary, as he knelt down beside Iva next to Yuko's head.

The astrophysicist had stopped struggling, at least momentarily. He examined Yuko's eyes. Even inside the bubble of helmet and without a penlight, he could see that her pupils were severely dilated. Tiny patches of inflamed skin were forming on her cheeks—smaller, but the same shape as the spots on Stella.

"Let me look at the skin on her arm," he said.

Iago shifted his weight to free Yuko's left arm, but in the instant he moved, Yuko vaulted out of his grasp and threw her weight against Iva, knocking away Iva's grasp on her other arm. Yuko rolled away, then jumped to her feet.

"Don't let her get away," shouted Iago.

Everyone but Iva, who was still regaining her balance, lunged for her. Margo was the closest, but Yuko dodged away from her grasp and fled into the second examination room.

Gary quickly slid the door shut, trapping Yuko inside. "There's no other exit," he said, turning back towards the others. "What happened?"

Gan went to Iva and offered her a hand, pulling her to her feet. Iva took a seat on one of the built-in benches that lined the two walls of the waiting room. Iago stood, his feet wide apart and his arms crossed as he stared at the closed door. Margo walked over next to Gary, by the closed door of the examination room, while Gan went to collect his atmo suit from where he had discarded it earlier.

"We were looking at the results from her air quality metre on her scroll." Iva gestured at the rolled-up device that had skittered across the floor when Yuka had dropped it. "She suddenly started muttering gibberish—something about blue and red butterflies," recounted Iva with a shake of her head. "And then she raked her fingernails down her face."

"Do you think it's an air-borne pathogen?" asked Gan. Eyes wide, he held his atmo suit as though he intended to put it back on. "Should we suit up again?"

Gary wanted to say, *a little late now, don't you think?* but they all jumped when Yuko kicked the door from inside, making it vibrate.

"You're going to need to sedate her. I'll get your medical bag," Margo volunteered before disappearing into the examination room where Stella lay.

"Gary," Iva said in a tone laced with panic. "What if Yuko is on the same path as the commander? She might hurt herself unless you do something."

"Margo and I will go in," said Gary, as he accepted the bag

from Margo with a nod of thanks. He set it on the floor, before crouching beside it to remove a syringe. Then he glanced up at Margo where she stood next to the door of examination room two. They all heard the resounding crash from inside. "You ready?" he asked Margo.

She nodded, and he opened the door.

When Gary entered with Margo close behind him, he saw that Yuko must've shoved a metal tray onto the floor from off the counter top—the source of the noise. Now she crouched between the far wall and the examination table, her arms wrapped around her knees. He heard rather Margo close and lock the door behind her.

"No, no, no, no," whimpered Yuko upon seeing them. "You can't make me do it!"

"Who are you talking to?" Gary spoke in his steady doctor's voice and approached her slowly, keeping the syringe out of sight. More scratches covered her face, but her eyes remained undamaged—so far.

Yuko stared at Gary, seeming, for a brief moment, to recognize him. "He's in my head," she whimpered. Then madness seemed to descend like a veil as she rocked back and forth and shook her head. "No, no, no, no!"

"Who's in your head?" asked Margo, leaning over the narrow examination table to look down at the whimpering woman. At Margo's words, Yuko shifted her focus to her.

"You!" she breathed. "He wants me to tell you, *butterfly blue without a clue; butterfly red better off dead*." She spoke the phrase like a chant, then laughed.

Gary cringed at the sound of Yuko's laughter. He'd heard something very much like it in his mother's ward when she'd been treating patients who'd gone mad after projecting their conciousness. The sooner he got the sedative into Yuko, the better, or she really would do damage to her eyes.

He felt Margo's hand on his shoulder. He turned and saw her gesture at him to let her squeeze past towards Yuko. Her face was abnormally pale and her eyes flared with fear, yet she gave him a fierce look that clearly meant, *let me talk to Yuko.* Hoping she could talk Yuko off whatever edge she was on, he moved aside and let Margo pass.

Margo knelt down in front of the fretful woman, "Who's in your head, Yuko?"

"You know! *Him!*"

Yuko launched herself at Margo, shoving hard with both hands against Margo's chest. Margo stumbled backwards against Gary's legs, and the two of them crashed into the cupboard, causing the doors to rattle. Margo kept her wits about her and managed to grab a hold of Yuko's ankle just as the possessed woman tried to leap over the table to escape.

Bouncing off the cupboard, Gary lunged forward and stabbed the needle of the sedative into Yuko's hip. She screeched and flipped her body, loosening Margo's grip on her ankle, then reached for Gary in fury, grabbing the front of his suit.

Gary wrapped his arms around the much smaller woman, pinning her and preventing her from pounding on him. In her mad state, she was fiercely strong, and he was thankful when Margo regained her balance and grabbed the other woman from behind, sandwiching the struggling woman between the two of them, Yuko's struggles soon lessened as the tranquilizer took effect. A moment later, she went limp. Margo stepped back as Gary lifted Yuko and lay her down on the table.

"You okay?" he asked, looking at Margo.

"Yeah, I'm fine."

Gary frowned at her. "You don't look fine."

At his comment, she straightened and, avoiding his eyes, opened the door, poking her head out and telling the others that Yuko was successfully sedated. When she turned to look at Yuko, Gary felt certain she was deliberately avoiding his gaze. *Why would she do that?*

"Yuko's behaviour is far from her normal," said Gary. "I think we need restraints so she doesn't hurt herself."

"I agree," said Margo. "And I'm not saying that because she's a bitch."

Just like in his examination rooms back home, the padded restraints were in a side door of the bed. It didn't take long to slip them onto Yuko's limp limbs.

He pushed up Yuko's sleeve to examine the skin of her forearm. Like he suspected, more patches of red skin ran up the inside of her arm. *Are these patches new since removing her suit? Or had she had skin issues before stepping on Nak?* Whatever the cause, he'd only find answers by conducting a more thorough examination of her and of Stella. He took a blood sample and put it in the analyzer. Then he set the scanner running.

"She should be out for a while. Let's go talk to the others," said Gary.

The two of them went back out to the waiting room. Both Gan and Iva had put their atmo suits and helmets back on. The only one still breathing the air was Iago.

"Is she going to be all right?" Iago asked immediately upon seeing Gary.

Gary thought he could detect a sincere note of concern in Iago's voice. *Did he actually care about the wellbeing of the sycophant who trailed after him like a loyal lapdog?*

"I don't know. But if it's an air-borne pathogen, all of you have been exposed. I want to take blood samples from everyone," said Gary.

Chapter Twenty-Nine

A half hour later, Margo was still trying to temper her reaction to Yuko quoting the same word's she'd seen on *Settler II*. Allowing herself to freak out would not help the situation. *But, how had the other woman known those words?* Possibilities churned through her mind, almost eclipsing her fear of what she might have been exposed to.

She watched as Gary put the last vial of crimson blood into the wire rack with the other samples, all clearly labelled. He'd taken a sample from everyone except her. He still thought she hadn't been exposed, but she had and the thought of it caused the knot in her gut to tighten. So far, no one else had gone off the rails like Yuko—so perhaps her reaction was an idiosyncratic response to whatever toxin was present, or something else entirely.

"I'll go start the analysis," said Gary, looking briefly at the other four occupants of the waiting room before picking up the rack. His expression was calm and focused, yet the samples trembled in his hands as he headed towards examination room one where Stella lay.

"I'll be out here if you need any help," she said, trying her best to give him a reassuring smile. She sat beside Iva on one of the benches, with Gan across from them on the opposite bench. On Margo's lap was the scroll she'd taken from Stella's office.

"Thanks." Gary offered a tight smile before disappearing into the examination room. Without explanation, Iago followed Gary.

Reminding herself that important clues might be in the commander's logs, Margo turned on the scroll and started reading them in chronological order. At first things for *Settler 1* had gone well. But, within a few month's of arrival, the colonists were getting sick.

"There must be something we can do," said Iva, eyes fixed on the door that contained Yuko.

"When are we due to check in with Ash?" asked Margo.

After checking her scroll, Iva sighed. "We still have about 20 minutes."

Iva's face looked pinched. Beside her, Gan sat slumped and miserable-looking as he stared down at his scroll. This whole experience had been a huge strain on all of them. Margo felt like they'd been on *Settler I* for hours, but it had been less than two. She wished they could leave. Now.

Iva pursed her lips. "We'll have to go back to the Control Room to get the message to Ash."

"I'd rather we stay together," said Gan, standing next to the other two. His expressive face seemed frozen except for his eyes, he was blinking rapidly and looking around as though he expected an attack at any moment. "I can pipe our suit comms through their system from here."

"You can?" Iva's voice held relief. "That's a great idea. I don't want to explore this place any further. I just want Ash to get here so we can get back on the *Staffelwalze* and off this planet."

Gan went to the comms unit in the wall beside the chief medical officer's office and removed the access panel. After pulling out a few tools from pockets in his atmo suit he crouched down and went to work.

Margo glanced back down at the scroll and frowned. The logs weren't helpful. Rolling it up, she put it back in her pocket before wandering over to the open door to examination room one.

Inside Iago and Gary stood side-by-side while they stared at the workstation's display. Stella still lay on the examination table, and one of the men had pulled a sheet over her. Not wanting to disturb them, she continued over to one of the padded benches and slumped down, letting her airpack rest against the wall.

Her nose itched, but her visor kept her from scratching it. She closed her eyes, and the image of Stella's mutilated face popped into her mind. With a sigh, she opened her eyes and watched Gan work. Iva, she saw, had joined him and hovered at his elbow.

"You put everyone at risk," said Gary, as the two men re-entered the waiting area.

Margo turned to watch them, listening to their conversation.

"But there never was a pathogen," said Iago with his normal certainty. "You just showed me the evidence of your test. Both Stella and Yuko are clean."

"That's not the point," Gary argued. "We didn't know that when you and Yuko encouraged people to remove their atmo suits. Besides, maybe those tests came back clean, but there's no arguing, this place isn't benign. I just haven't done the test yet that pinpoints what's malignant."

Margo stood, noting that Gan and Iva were paying attention as well. "What do you mean?" she asked.

Gary turned to Margo. "There's a sulphur deficit in every-one's samples," he said. "The deficit is much more pronounced in Stella due to long term exposure."

"Exposure to what?" asked Margo.

"The same thing that's killing the plants in the Hub, the slime-mould-like local life," Gary explained. "I'd need to do more tests to know for sure, but it appears the substance produces a denaturing agent and enzymes that break cysteine bridges, then pull out the sulphur from methionine and cysteine attached to tRNA. The damaged tRNA then makes malformed proteins and cell functions are impaired."

"Hold on, what does that all mean?" asked Iago, his tone impatient.

Gary looked glum. "The slime is ripping apart the proteins in our bodies to rob the cells of sulphur. Once the slime got into the colony, it would have affected all life, from crops to people."

"Is it permanent?" asked Iva.

"Let's hope not as we won't be here long." Gary paused and glanced at Iago before continuing. "An exposure of a day or two poses little risk to us. Once we leave and clean off the slime, we can replace the missing sulphur through diet. Daily servings of Brussel sprouts should do the trick."

"So, we're actually going to have to eat them?" asked Margo, raising an eyebrow.

"Looks like it," said Gary.

"Is the slime the smoking gun?" Iago drew himself up as tall as he could. "Did it kill off the colonists?"

"Not necessarily. They could've figured this out as easily as I did," said Gary. "If they monitored it, they could've kept the slime out of the colony. They seemed to have successfully done this, at least for a while."

"So, something changed the colonists behaviour, making them less diligent. Then the slime got into the *Settler*," said Margo. "And you've ruled out exotic pathogens?"

Gary nodded as he sat on the nearest bench. "Based on the minimal short-term risk, I'm comfortable taking off our atmo suits."

As if to demonstrate and prove his theory, Gary removed his helmet and put it on the bench beside him. With a half-hearted cheer, everyone did the same.

"So, how did Stella die?" asked Margo.

"I just went back through the scans." Gary ran a hand through his hair. "She's effectively dead, but there's still some activity in her body."

"What?" Iva asked in a credulous tone.

"There is zero consciousness—in fact, the cerebrum has started to decay. However, other parts of her body are functioning at an absolute minimum," Gary explained.

"You mean her heart's beating?" Margo stood. "How did we miss that?"

"It's beating at less than one beat per minute," said Gary. "I can't classify her as alive. She is past the point where anything can be done to save her. Basically, she's dead."

"What did this to her?"

"I don't know." Gary looked tired, frustrated that he didn't have the answers he needed to solve these riddles.

Margo wished they were alone, so she could smooth out the worry lines in his forehead, first with a caress and then a kiss. She didn't like feeling so helpless in the face of his frustration. She sat next to him and gave him a brief smile. Gary's eyes warmed when he looked at her.

"Would long-term exposure to this slime cause people to gouge out their eyes?" asked Iago crossing his arms over his chest.

Gary turned to look up at Iago. "People would behave just the opposite. They'd become apathetic and/or lethargic, but that wouldn't make them rip out their own eyes or commit murder," he said, rubbing the back of his neck. "I'm out of ideas."

Although Iva had taken a seat, Gan still stood by the access panel. "Didn't you say before that she…" He pointed to Stella's examination room. "Had two biotrackers?"

"Yes."

"Are you sure they're both biotrackers?" Gan walked over and looked into the room.

"No. I got distracted from that." Gary looked hopeful as he glanced at Gan. "I know little about that kind of technology."

"Let me look." Gan went into the examination room. From where Margo sat beside Gary on the bench, she could see how Gan avoided looking at the covered corpse as he approached the workstation and monitor. Less than a minute later, he returned.

"The second is a Conglomerate chip," Gan announced, an edge of tension in his voice.

Margo sucked in her breath as an image of Lucy Snow on the roof of the Central Module flashed through her head. That day, Nigel Maximillian West had taken control of her thanks to The Conglomerate chip in her head, forcing her to try and kill Margo. When Lucy failed, Nigel made Lucy to kill herself.

"Vince—he's a top-notch whiz when it comes to electronics," said Gan. "He told me those chips have serial numbers that start with MS—for Maximilian Station where they're made."

"They can use those chips to control the host," said Margo, slowly rising. "But how could Nigel, or anyone in The Conglomerate, do any of this? The wormhole is closed. It can't be someone off world and we have the only ship in the system."

Everyone fell quiet. Gan, a frown on his face and clearly needing to be doing a task, went back to fiddling with the sickbay comms unit.

"Iago, assuming the chip is to blame for Stella's death, do any of your people have them?"

"You mean Yuko? She left her post with The Conglomerate about…I don't know, eight months ago?" Iago looked worried as he glanced at the closed door to the room Yuko occupied. "You're suggesting she might have a Conglomerate chip implanted?" At Gary's nod, he continued. "And you're wondering who, besides Yuko, might also have them? *Me?* Others from the insurgents?"

"It's a fair question," Iva stated.

Margo glanced at Iva. She usually wasn't so bold in challenging Iago, but Iva was, Margo knew, all about being fair.

Instead of answering, Iago turned to Gary and asked, "Can the chips be removed?"

"I assume they put the chips in with specialized equipment. Getting them out without that equipment would be tricky," Gary said. "They're deep in the thalamus right next to important structures that support motor and sensory signals. It's a region of the brain that's difficult to access."

"Is there the tools here to do that?" asked Iago.

"Yes, but I can't work alone," argued Gary, realizing where Iago was going. "This is sophisticated surgery. It needs a team of medical professionals to ensure success."

"Margo's a biologist, I'm sure she could help," said Iago.

Margo inhaled. Iago couldn't be serious. They were far more likely to kill Yuko on the operating table than successfully remove the chip.

"I've got the comms working," announced Gan. Everyone crowded around behind him.

Iva looked at her wrist. "We're only five minutes late in contacting Ash."

Gan activated the comms link. "Ground team to *Staffelwalze*."

"*Staffelwalze* here," replied Ash immediately. "Glad to hear from you. How are things going down there?"

"We need you to come get us," said Iago, stepping in front of Gan.

At his words, Margo felt the knot in her gut release. *Yes!*

"Bad news on this end," reported Ash. "The hull took more damage than expected going through Nak's atmosphere. I need three hours for the bots to finish resurfacing the exterior. Can you guys hang tight that long?"

A reverberating crash echoed through the waiting room. Everyone whirled to look behind them. Yuko emerged from the room where she'd been strapped to the examination table holding a large set of scissors in her hands. Through the gaping door, Margo saw the examination table lying on its side. *It had been bolted to the floor!*

Blood dripped from from her damaged hands as she stopped to stare at her crewmates. What Margo saw in Yuko's face terrified her—just like Lucy Snow, Yuko's face was blank. Before Margo could draw a breath and cry a warning, Yuko spun around and ran for the exit doors to the Loop, faster than expected. The doors automatically whooshed open, and the astrophysicist darted out.

"Stop!" Margo sprinted to the door, the others on her heals, then paused in the Loop. There was no sign of Yuko.

"Look!" Iva shouted.

Margo turned and saw a smear of blood on the wall. Beyond that, another, and another. Yuko had left a trail to follow.

"Margo and Iva, with me," ordered Iago, charging past Margo. "We'll bring her back."

Chapter Thirty

With everyone except Gan out hunting for Yuko, Gary returned to examination room one where the body of Stella Riemer lay covered with a sheet. Relieved to be free of both the helmet and bulky airpack, he skirted the table and sat at the workstation set into a small desk on the far wall.

He brought up Stella's scan results again, scratching his head as he re-read them. No brain activity—she was clearly dead. Yet, her system was still pumping blood, albeit slowly, preventing cell decay. Nothing in the slime mould could do this to her.

"What happened to you, Commander Reimer?"

With a sigh, he looked back at the workstation display and brought up his victim's blood sample analysis. The screen displayed a list of organic compounds—none of which explained why she gouged her eyes out or why she'd shut down.

It had to be The Conglomerate chip, Gary concluded. It was the common denominator for both her and Yuko's behaviour—except when he'd seen it used before someone had been the puppet master. He examined the scans of the chip and how its location related to the functions of that part of the brain. Someone purposely put the chip in a location difficult to work in. He zoomed in closer.

A faint groan sounded behind him. He spun his chair around, asking, "Who's there?" But he was alone in the examination room. The only sounds were Gan out in the waiting room working with something mechanical and the ventilation system humming above.

This place is getting to me he thought, shaking his head. He swivelled his seat around. "Where was I?" he asked himself, zooming the image of the chip in even closer. A model of the chip's programs was a place to start and it was an easy duplication to perform. After initiating the program, he started a diagnostic to check for malfunctions. As he waited for it to run, he retrieved Stella's medical file and started scrolling through it.

Another groan sounded behind him—louder this time. When he turned and stood, he noticed the sheet covering Stella had shifted. It had been straight when he'd covered her—he cared about things like that—but now it lay across her at a slight angle. *Is there a breeze in here?* Gary toyed with the idea of calling in Gan. Instead he went over to the head of the examination table and reached a hand up to the ventilation duct above. Air blew past his hand—explaining why the sheet moved. He readjusted the corpse's covering and sat back down.

"Wow," he said to himself, turning back to the screen. "You're turning into Dr. Paranoid."

He pulled up the mission records from *Settler I*'s chief medical officer. "Dale Nader," he read the man's name aloud.

The name sounded familiar. Then he remembered why. Dale and his wife... her name was unusual. The name was on the tip of his tongue... *Aqila!* Several years ago he'd met them at a dinner hosted by Neil and Amanda.

Gary started a search through the records for anything concerning the second chip in Stella's brain. When the results came, he leaned forward and his jaw dropped. Dale had implanted a chip into everyone on the colony. *But why?*

There was a rustle behind him. Assuming Gan had entered the room, he said, "Gan, look at this."

Still scrolling through the results, he heard an odd gait approaching. Worried that Gan had hurt himself again, he turned, but then froze, staring wide-eyed at the person in front of him. Racing, his heart threatened to explode from his chest.

The eyeless form of Stella stood before of him. She was studying him—*looking at him*—as if she not only had eyes, but as if she were alive.

But you're dead! he wanted to scream. *You're dead!* He'd been sure—no brain activity. Her brain was decaying. He couldn't be wrong about that—and neither could the scan. A shaking sensation sweep through his limbs as the dead Stella took a step towards him.

"Stella." He was surprised he could even find his voice given what he was looking at. "You need…you need to lie down," he said, tripping over his tongue. He wasn't sure why he said that, but he was a doctor. Isn't that what doctors say? *To animated-yet-dead patients without eyes?*

She made a low growl somewhere in the back of her throat, which made Gary's heart hammer even more erratically.

"Gan!" he called, but his voice was shaky and the sound didn't carry.

Alarms were going off in his head—none of this was possible—but when Stella took another step forward, he finally managed to stand. He moved towards her. "I'm just going to guide you back to the bed."

"Gan!" he called a little louder this time, at the same time hearing a muffled hammering from his look-alike office. *What is Gan doing?*

Gary reached out a hand to guide Stella back to bed, but paused. Swallowing, he found the courage to lay his hand on her upper arm. The flesh was cold. As soon as he touched her, Stella lashed out, raking her fingernails across his cheek.

He twisted away in the same way he'd dodge a right hook

from Neil in the boxing ring. Crouching, he put his arms up in a defensive stance. Next, he shimmied to the side, his foot falls silent on the rubberized flooring. He didn't understand how her body had become animated, but she was blind, and therefore wouldn't—*no shouldn't*—be able to follow him.

But when she turned and angled her face directly at him, Gary realized she was tracking him some other way. *How is she even moving, let alone tracking me? None of this is possible!*

"Gan!" he shouted. This time his voice didn't betray him.

Gary backed away, circling slowly around the examination table. She stood, turning a little so that she continued to face him as he moved. Something about her stance shouted malevolence. He could see no expression in her absent eyes, yet he knew she was intent on attacking him. He needed to escape the room, get to Gan. He reached the end of the table. Now all he had to do was cross the open space between himself and Stella to reach the door.

With a burst of speed, Gary sprinted for the door. He drew a breath to shout for Gan, but Stella leapt forward, tackling him around the waist and tumbling them to the floor, knocking the air out of his lungs. He tried to roll away and catch his breath at the same time. Before he could, she scrambled on top of him and grasped one of his wrists in a cold, vice-like grip. He shuddered in revulsion as his eyes locked on her mutilated face above his.

"Gan!" he shrieked. "Get in here!"

Gary put the heel of his free hand on her forehead above the empty eye sockets and shoved with all his strength. She pushed back, refusing to give way. Twisting his other wrist, he managed to pull free from her grip.

Stringy mats of her hair fell out where his fingers contacted her scalp. With a snarl, she repeatedly opened her jaw then snapped it closed with a sharp clack each time. He pushed harder against her, determined not to let her bite him.

As he shrieked for Gan again, a swatch of her hair fell across his open mouth, changing his scream to that of a frightened five-year old. Pulling himself together, he blew the fallen swatch of hair off his lips and sucked in a deep breath, then shouted, "Gan!"

Gary worked a knee free and drove it with all his force into her belly pushing her away. He scrambled to his feet and bolted into the waiting room, slamming the examination room door shut before Stella could follow. He slapped his hand on the panel beside the door and heard the satisfying sound of the lock fall into place.

Only then did he let himself relax, leaning against the door and sucking in air as if he'd run a marathon in record time. He lifted a hand to his face, thinking to wipe away sweat, but saw a smear of blood instead. He'd forgotten she'd raked his face with her fingernails.

Gan sauntered into the waiting room from the store room, carrying what looked like a battery pack. He stopped when he saw Gary. "What's going on?"

Gary jumped away from the door behind him when Stella began thumping her fists on the other side.

Gan's eyes widened. "Yuko came back?"

"Can you ensure this door doesn't open?" Gary asked. "I don't trust the lock."

"Yep," said Gan. He opened the control panel and pulled out a couple of wires. The lights on the panel flicked off, and the word 'lockdown' appeared on the panel screen. "That should do it. How did Yuko get back without the others? Is she having another meltdown in there?"

"Not Yuko. Stella…" Gary paused and took a deep breath. "I don't even know how to say this, but she…"

At Gary's hesitation, Gan shifted his eyes toward the door to examination room one. Every now and then the door vibrated as Stella kicked it from within. "You're not saying…?"

Gary knew there was a wild crazed look in his eye when he stared at Gan. He suspected that look would be in his eyes for some time to come. *How is any of this possible?* "Yes. I'm saying she got up."

When he finally uttered the words that shouldn't be possible, he felt weak at the knees. *Shock setting in,* he evaluated, assessing his own symptoms. Keeping a hand on a wall for support, he walked over to the nearest bench and collapsed onto it. Gan stared at him as if he were the walking corpse, absently reaching up and wiping the blood from his cheek with his shirt sleeve.

"It shouldn't be possible."

"Stella's dead, Gary," Gan stated in a decisive tone, glancing towards the exam room door. It sounded like Stella had begun methodically slamming her fists against it. "You're honestly telling me the person making that racket is Stella? She woke up? And she did that to you?" Gan nodded at Gary's wounded cheek, then retrieved a first-aid kit from off the wall and handed it to Gary.

Gary met Gan's disbelieving gaze and took a deep breath before speaking. "It's true. She got up. She attacked me." He bent his head to unlatch the kit and retrieved some alcohol and wipes, saying as he did so, "I don't know how. I don't know why. Shit, Gan, I don't feel like I know anything anymore."

With trembling hands, Gary dabbed some alcohol on a cloth and held it against his cheek. It stung, but the pain helped to clear his head.

"It shouldn't have been possible for her to animate," said Gary. "Her heart's not beating. Her brain isn't working." He let out a ragged exhale.

The thumping on the other side of the door died away.

"Lotsa things are happening here that shouldn't be possible. Yuko turning into a banshee for example."

"The automatic door opener is deactivated, but the door isn't locked," said Gan crossing his arms across his chest and frowning. "She could get out if she uses the manual leaver."

"We need to go back in," said Gary, setting aside the blood-stained wipe and putting his elbows on his knees.

"We?" Gan moved further away from the door. "Can't we keep zombie woman locked in there? I could weld the door shut."

"I need to understand what's going on with her." Gary rubbed his hands over his face. His heart rate was back to normal now and his brain churned with questions. "Perhaps if I can figure out medically what's going on with Stella, we can solve the mystery of what happened to the other crew members."

Gan scoffed. "You're a scientist, Gary. You cannot draw any conclusion from what happened to one subject—the only subject in this study—and conclude what happened to the other forty-nine—who we've yet to find."

Gary nodded. "I know."

"And besides," Gan argued. "We didn't come here to solve a mystery. We came here to rescue survivors. We haven't found any. It's times to leave, don't you think?"

"I suppose," Gary conceded. Now that he'd recovered from the shock of what had happened, he was finding it difficult to suppress his curiosity how such a thing was possible. When would he ever get to study such a fascinating specimen ever again? "But Gan, Stella caught me off guard. With the two of us, we should have no problem getting her back on the bed and putting on restraints."

"How about you sedate her?"

"She's dead. I doubt that would do anything," said Gary.

"Restraints didn't hold Yuko," said Gan in a soft tone.

"I'll put more on." Gary looked down at his hands, noticing a long strand of blonde hair hung between his fingers. He flicked it off. "If I figure out what's going on with Stella, I might be able to help Yuko."

Gan sighed. "That makes sense. They'll likely be back soon with her."

They both stood and went to the door's control panel.

"Are you ready?" Gan asked.

Gary's heart rate was spiking again as he stood in front of the door. He nodded at Gan, signalling his readiness. Then the door slid open and the two men peered inside.

"Stella?" said Gary from where he stood within the doorway.

At first glance, the room appeared empty. Gary took a step into the room and looked around. When he didn't see any sign of her, he knelt down to see under the examination table. Stella slouched with her back against the wall in the farthest corner of the room. Her head was angled to the side, and with her legs splayed out in front of her and her arms hanging limply at her side. She looked like a discarded marionette.

Gary gestured to Gan to go one direction around the examination table while he went in the other. Slowly, the two of them closed in on her. She gave no indication of being alive, let alone aware the two of them were there.

"Stella?" Gary knelt down in front of her. She didn't move.

Gary glanced up at Gan. "You grab one arm and I'll grab the other. We'll drag her up onto the examination table."

"Then you're tying her down?" asked Gan.

"Yes. Wait," he added, stopping Gan from touching Stella. "I think it was when I touched her, trying to get her back to the table, that she went berserk. Be prepared."

As expected, as soon as they touched her, Stella began thrashing and grunting her indignation.

"Holy crap!" Gan held Stella's right arm immobile. "I almost didn't believe you."

"I know," grunted Gary, trying to keep Stella's flailing left arm in his grip.

Gary and Gan managed to pull her up onto the table, with Stella, grunting and growling, struggling against them the whole time.

She suddenly jerked the lower half of her body up, slamming her knee into Gary's nose so hard, he lost his grip on her arm.

Seeing Gary momentarily incapacitated, Gan used his weight to pin Stella down. She began hammering at his face with her free arm.

"Gary! Restraints!" said Gan through clenched teeth.

Ignoring the blood gushing from his nose, Gary caught Stella's arm and managed to wrap the soft restraint around her wrist. Once it was secure, he pulled the restraint tight, pinning her arm against the table. Keeping his body angled away from her flailing legs, he grabbed one of her ankles and secured first it and then the other. With Gan's help, he did the same for her other arm, and then slipped a fifth restrain across her forehead, effectively pinning her onto the table.

Once Stella was secure, Gan and Gary stood looking down at her. Despite the restraints, she continued thrashing, reminding Gary of patient he'd once seen having a seizure. He realized that wasn't quite right though, because Stella's movements were jerky, almost mechanical. She snapped her jaw at the air, the sound of the clack-clack-clack of her teeth filling the air.

Rubbing the back of his neck, Gary eyed the corpse. Beside him, Gan crossed his arms across his chest.

"No heartbeat, you say?"

Gary nodded. "No obvious heartbeat or breathing. No brain function."

Reaching for the scanning equipment, he started another round. In mute silence, the two of them watched the equipment lower from the ceiling and begin shining its beam up and down Stella's still convulsing body.

Chapter Thirty-One

The bloody handprints contrasted against the white walls of the Loop, but the print's creator was already out of sight. Taking measured steps, Margo followed the row of smeared hands. Most were smudged as though Yuko was having trouble keeping her balance.

Iago and Iva kept pace with her as they advanced down the corridor.

"This is my fault," he said.

Margo looked up at Iago, surprised to see him frowning. *Is he worried for Yuko?* It surprised her that Iago cared about the astrophysicist. He mostly treated her with disdain.

"You couldn't have known," she said, glancing over her shoulder at Iva. The other woman's eyes were wide at Iago's admittance of culpability.

As they came to the entrance to the kitchen, Iago said, "we should've left when no one came to greet us."

Astonished, Margo paused, as did Iago and Iva. Both women stared at Iago. His tone actually sounded remorseful. *Is he sincere?*

Iva pointed to the closed door leading to the kitchen. "Look at the blood smears. She must've gone inside."

"We need to stay focused on finding Yuko." Margo aimed her remark at Iago. When she saw him nod, she turned to the door. The hand prints were so dense, the fingers merged into an abstract form that reminded her of a group of butterflies. She shook her head. *Stay focused, Murphy!*

"Wait," Iago said as Margo lifted her hand to the door. "Before we go any further, I must apologize to the two of you." He looked earnest, his machismo had evaporated.

"As soon as we have Yuko, we'll take one of the colony's shuttles and get out of here. Ash doesn't need to risk damaging the hull a second time."

Margo's heart leapt at the thought of leaving this dreadful place. Iva's eyes lit with anticipation at the thought as well. Instead of agreeing, she said, "First things first," then, taking a deep breath to steady herself, she opened the door. And nearly vomited.

A wave of rotten food stench washed over them. In layout the space was identical to Amanda's kitchen on Thesan, yet this one was barely recognizable as a place to prepare food. Open food containers littered the entire room. Many were ripped open, their contents spilled over the counters and floor.

"Disgusting!" exclaimed Iago.

Iva turned away, both hands over her mouth as she gagged.

Holding a hand over her nose, Margo took a step into the room, then another, as she scanned the space for Yuko. There was no sign of the woman, but she did notice that all the exposed food was covered in a layer of slime. When her gaze went to the corner by the stove, she sucked in a deep breath.

Amidst the strewn food was a severed hand already well decayed. Margo's gut heaved, and she remained rooted to the spot as she allowed the wave of nausea to pass. Behind her, Iva wasn't so lucky. The sound of her retching filled the space.

"Yuko!" Iago called.

"Right," said Margo, forcing herself not to look in the direction of the severed appendage.

The view from the windows on the far wall showed only darkness in the central greenhouse beyond. Beside the industrial-sized stove, an opening caught her attention.

"Look." Margo pointed to the entrance to the storeroom. "The storeroom door is open. And there's blood on it. See?" She clenched her jaw as the knot in her gut told her things were about to go very, very wrong.

"Wait. I want to make sure the Loop door is wedged open," said Iva. "Just in case we need to leave in a hurry."

"Good idea," said Margo.

Iago nodded. "Do it. We'll wait."

"Done," said Iva, rejoining them a few seconds later.

Staying close together, the three of them walked farther into the kitchen, carefully stepping over the debris on the floor. At the open storeroom door, they stopped, peering into the darkness beyond.

"The lights should be on since the door is open," said Iva in a quivering voice.

"There's an emergency light mounted on the wall by the door to the dining room," said Margo, walking over and retrieving the flashlight. Fortunately, it worked. Standing at the mouth of the gaping door, she shone the narrow beam of light inside, illuminating a mess just like the kitchen's.

"Why aren't the overheads lights on in the storeroom?" demanded Iago from behind Margo and Iva.

Margo glanced his way, saw that he was standing in his superman pose with his arms across his chest. *Their so-called fearless leader held his chest out like a strutting rooster; yet, he was letting her take the lead.*

"Something else to add to the long list of things that are off about this place," stated Margo. Then, with a glance at Iva, she took a step across the threshold, stopping just within the door. "Yuko," she called. "Are you in here? We want to help you."

All three of them froze when they heard a weak voice coming from the direction of a darkened corner. "I can't fight it," said Yuko.

Following the sound of her voice, Margo shifted the torch until the light fell on the other woman. Yuko sat on the floor in the back corner hugging her knees to her chest. Her eyes were wide and her lower lip quivered.

"What can't you fight?" asked Margo, staying in the doorway. Wanting to free up her hands before advancing on the unpredictable woman, she handed the light to Iva.

"There's someone in my head," Yuko whined in a little voice, "forcing me to do things." Yuko covered her face with her hands and sobbed before she began rocking back and forth. "Please, make it stop."

Iago advanced past Iva and Margo towards his sidekick. His bulk blocked the light, casting Yuko in shadow. He moved slowly —the same way one would approach a wounded animal.

Iva shifted to the side, keeping the beam of light trained on Yuko. Margo stayed where she was knowing that, if anyone could influence Yuko, it was Iago.

"Yuko, " he said in an uncharacteristically gentle tone. "You need to come with us. We'll take you back to Gary. He'll help you. Then we'll all get off this forsaken planet."

"I...I...can't...control it," stammered Yuko between sobs.

"I'll get you out of here." Iago reached a hand towards the woman. "I've gotten you out of bad situations before. Remember what happened on New Egypt Station? I saved you then and I can save you now. Trust me."

Yuko lifted her head to look at him. Even in the glare of the light, Margo saw hope flare in her eyes. "I've always trusted you," she said, then her face fell as she shook her head. "But I can't control this."

Witnessing Yuko's abject sorrow, Margo and Iva shared a brief glance from where they stood just inside the door.

"Yuko." Iago now stood less than an arm's length from her,

bent forward a little as he spoke. "We're here to help you."

"I'm sorry," Yuko sobbed, giving him a beseeching look. Then her body suddenly went rigid.

Iago's soft tone didn't change. "You don't have to be sorry. We've figured it out. It's the chip in your head. Here, take my hand." Iago held out his flesh hand.

"I can't," Yuko wailed. She let her hands fall to the floor, beyond the narrow beam of light.

In the darkness, Margo thought she saw something gleam briefly at Yuko's hip, but was distracted when Iva put a hand on her forearm.

"Margo," urged Iva, in a quivering whisper. "Look at the door to the Loop."

Margo turned her head towards the door they'd left open. Her breath caught in her throat as she saw the crowd of colonists gathered at the door.

They stood, still and silent, staring at Margo and Iva. Most had blood on their faces, and all of their clothing was in tatters. But it wasn't the blood or their attire that made her pause; it was their gazes. Their faces were blank, reminding her of zombies in the old action vids she used to love.

Her mouth went dry and her knees felt like they'd give out at any moment. By the way Iva gripped her forearm, she knew Iva felt the same. Adrenaline zinged through her veins as if shouting at her to flee.

"Hello?" called Margo, without moving. The colonists remained in the hallway—none acknowledged her greeting.

Margo glanced at Iago, who was helping Yuko to her feet. "We need to go. Now!"

Behind her, the crowd of zombie colonists laughed in perfect unison. Margo spun to look at them again, the chilling sound eerily familiar. She knew that laugh, and her veins turned to ice.

"Iago! Back away!" she said, whirling to face Iago. Her throat closed when she saw what Yuko held in her hand. She heard Iva gasp beside her.

Yuko's right fist held a butcher knife. She must have taken it from the kitchen before entering the storeroom. From Iago's angle, Margo knew he couldn't see it in Yuko's hand. But before she could even leap a half-step forward to intervene, Yuko's arm arced forward, the blade reflecting the light a second time before it plunged into Iago's chest.

Iago barely had time to lift his hand when the blade found its target. His face registered his shock.

Margo leapt forward, shouting for Iva to steady the light.

Iago, with the last of his strength, turned his head towards the sound of Margo's voice and said in a weak voice, "Get out. Run!"

As Iago's knees started to buckle under him, Yuko jerked the blade out of his chest with seemingly super-human strength. Then, with no hesitation, she swiped the blade across his neck, severing the carotid artery.

Iago's blood spewed onto his diminutive attacker, disappearing into the darkness outside the beam of light that now wobbled thanks to Iva's shaking hand. He made a final, sickening gurgling sound. Paralyzed with horror, Margo watched him collapse to the ground.

Yuko calmly turned to Margo as though she hadn't just murdered someone. "Butterfly blue, without a clue," she chanted.

Iva tugged Margo's arm. Blinking, Margo turned and looked at her.

"Shit, Margo! We need to go." The panic in Iva's tone made her voice shrill. "Or we'll be next."

"But...Iago? We can't just leave him," Margo argued, even knowing it was too late to do anything for him. But she was already turning and running beside Iva, heading for the exit to the dining room on the opposite end of the kitchen from where the animated dead watched them.

Just before the door closed behind the escaping pair, the zombies chanted in unison, "Butterfly red, better off dead."

Chapter Thirty-Two

Gary returned to the waiting room and found Gan sitting on one of the benches. The other man's skin was abnormally pale and his black hair stuck straight up as though he'd been pulling at it. He stared back at Gary with wide eyes.

"What did you find?" asked Gan.

With a yawn, Gary sat on a bench beside Gan. He rubbed his hands over his face before looking at the other man.

"Well, I'm not losing my mind. Stella is dead," Gary reported. He glanced back through the open door of the examination room where the corpse still struggled against her restraints.

Gan tilted his head, following his gaze, then shivered and looked away. "Creepiest thing I've ever seen."

"I'm not sure how it's possible, but that chip is reanimating her," said Gary. "Stella's corpse is being manipulated by whoever is controlling the chip."

"So, who's controlling the chip?"

"I don't know," said Gary.

"Is there anything in that room you need to access?"

Gary frowned. "What do you mean?"

Standing, Gan turned to Gary. "If you don't mind, I'll secure that door closed. I can hear her moving, and it's giving me the jitters." He glanced over his shoulder towards Stella, then focused on Gary. "Are you forgetting Yuko? She broke out of her restraints. I think it would be prudent to give us an extra layer of protection for her, just in case she goes berserk."

Gary inhaled, then nodded. "Go ahead. There's nothing more I can do for her." He gestured towards Stella, hating that he was way too late to help her.

He watched as Gan closed the door and removed a wrench from his side pocket. Next Gan opened up the door's control panel and undid several bolts. As soon as the internal workings of the pocket door were exposed, Gan shoved the wrench in wedging the door shut. Gary sighed and dropped his gaze, looking down at his hands. He was surprised to see they were trembling.

"This place is a living nightmare," he said. "I don't know what I expected, but it was not this."

"Me neither," Gan said over his shoulder as he worked to stream the video feed from inside the examination room to the screen outside the door. A few minutes later, he returned to his seat beside Gary. He let out a long, ragged sigh and leaned his back against the wall.

"I feel slightly safer." Gan looked over to the main doors to sickbay. "Maybe, I should lock us in on the off chance there are more animated corpses like Stella. If they found us here, we could be trapped."

"While I agree I don't want to be trapped in here, we can't lock out the others. They should be returning soon, hopefully with Yuko," said Gary. *Is Margo safe?* He knew better than to suggest going hunting for them, but doing nothing to try and help Margo and the others felt wrong. "They should've taken their suits. As things stand, we have no way to communicate with them."

"I'm sure they'll be along soon," Gan said, but his words

were rote. He was obviously thinking of something else. He turned to Gary. "What do you know about how the chips operate?"

"Me?" Gary rubbed his neck. "Sadly, almost nothing." Gary turned to Gan. "How much do you know about the day Lucy Snow died?"

Gan gave a humourless grin. "The only thing that seemed important about that event was that she was dead."

"Nigel Maximillian West used The Conglomerate chip implanted in Lucy Snow's head to take control of her body. He was able to transfer his consciousness into her," said Gary. "Then she—controlled by him—attacked us. When Margo got the upper hand, he made Lucy jump off the roof of the Centre Module to her death."

"I didn't know that." Gan stared at nothing for a moment, then turned to Gary. His voice sounded almost enthusiastic. "Did you retrieve the chip from her brain?"

Gary snorted. "Had I the foresight to know that information about the chip would help us four months later, I would have. But, no. At the time, I didn't even think of it."

As the two of them fell silent, the only sound came from the ventilation system above. Gary let his head fall back until it leaned against the wall. He looked up at the air vent on the ceiling, imagining the tentacle-like system of ducts running through the maintenance between this level and the upper level of the ring-shaped ship.

"How does consciousness transfer work?" asked Gan, interrupting Gary's thoughts.

"Not like that," said Gary, pointing at the video image of Stella. Her body continued to convulse, thrashing sporadically. The restraints, thankfully, held. "Plus, in order for Nigel West to take over the body of someone who has a chip in their brain, the wormhole needs to be open."

"And it's closed," said Gan.

Gary nodded.

"Maybe there's a puppet master here who's pulling her strings," suggested Gan with a nod at the image of Stella.

"Maybe. But why? More importantly, by whom?"

Gan thumped the heel of his hand against his forehead. "Biotrackers," he announced, jumping to his feet. He hefted the tool bag and turned to Gary. "I forgot all about checking for *Settler I*'s biotrackers."

Gary stood. "And if there is only one biotracker that registers a sign of life, then we've identified the puppet master. Let's use my office." Gary paused, realizing they weren't on Thesan. "Sorry, Dale Nader's office."

Gary approached the office that was his on Thesan and slid the door open. The furniture layout of the desk, chairs and workstation were the same, but that was where the similarity ended. Half-drunk mugs of coffee, dirty plates, medical supplies, and stacks of paper cluttered every horizontal surface of the space. Removing a stack of random medical supplies from the desk chair, Gary sat at the main console, Gan standing behind him. But nothing happened when Gary switched the console on —the screen remained dark and blank.

"This computer isn't working."

"Let me try," Gan said

As soon as Gary was out of the way, Gan knelt down and looked under the workstation. The engineer retrieved something from his pocket, then stretched out on his side on the floor. "I'll do a manual override and restart the system in recovery mode."

"Will that work?" Gary asked. "If it doesn't, we can try the computer in Neil's office. Or in the examination room where Stella is. That computer is working."

"This'll work," Gan stated in a determined voice.

Gary wondered if the steel in Gan's voice was because he didn't want to use the computer in Stella's room.

A moment later, the console screen flashed to life. Gan moved out of the way and Gary sat back down with Gan leaning over his shoulder. Gary swiped through various screens, looking for the biotracker dashboard.

"It's not here," said Gary. "You don't think someone has deleted them, do you?"

"Let me look." The two men changed places.

While Gan tapped the keyboard, Gary went to the window and opened the blinds. Like *Settler III*, sickbay was situated on the outside of the ring and its windows looked out at the planet.

Outside, the muddy yellow sky appeared darker than before reducing the visibility. Floating ash flakes swirled in the the wind, which seemed to have picked up as predicted. As sheet lightning lit up the clouds above, he could just make out the walls of one of the spoke greenhouses, the one identical to Margo's. A bright flash of chain lightening punctuated the view.

Gary turned to Gan as a thought crossed his mind. "Can this colony handle lightning strikes?"

"Yeah," replied Gan, engrossed in his task.

Gary turned back to the window and saw three more bolts of lightening slam into the ground, creating a momentary shimmer of white-yellow in the slimy substance that covered the ground. The weather conditions were worsening, and fast.

"I think we're in the midst of a bad storm," said Gary. He hated the idea of the storm delaying Ash from coming to get them.

"Got it!" crowed Gan.

Gary came to stand behind his shoulder.

"The biotracker info wasn't deleted, but someone took a lot of pains to hide it." He leaned back and gestured at the screen. "There it is."

"The biotrackers show 55 people on the colony," said Gary.

Gan frowned. "That's one short."

"Margo removed her biotracker," said Gary, as he studied the results.

"Removed her biotracker?" Gan asked, looking up at Gary. Then he frowned. "How?"

Gary gave a humourless smile as he studied the data. "She cut it out," he said without elaborating further.

"That takes guts," commented Gan in a tone filled with newly inspired awe for his crewmate.

"Yes," said Gary distractedly. "She's got that in spades. Look." He pointed at Stella's name. "Here's Stella. She's flat-lined, with no brain activity at all."

As Gary scanned through the rest of the names, he sucked in a breath and felt his mouth go dry.

"What is it?" asked Gan.

"Everyone's readings are the same as Stella's." His eyes skimming over the data. "Wait! Except…" His voice trailed off for a moment and he stood straight. "Dale Nader. The Chief Medical Officer on this mission. His readings are abnormal," Gary said, gesturing at the screen. "But he's alive."

"The only one still alive?"

"Yes," said Gary. "I met him once."

"What's he like? Could he be the puppet master?" asked Gan.

"I hardly know him. Neil knows him better. But I can't imagine why he would do such a thing." Gary tried to bring up the medical records like he had for Stella, but this time a password was required. "That's weird."

"What?" asked Gan leaning in closer.

"Only a few minutes ago I could access the medical records and now I'm locked out," Gary said. The he turned and looked at Gan. "Can you get in?"

"Iva would be way better at hacking confidential medical records than me," said Gan. "But I'll try."

While Gan attempted hacking magic, Gary checked the video view of Stella. She was finally laying still. On the monitor, the holes where her eyes had once been showed up as pools of darkness. He thought of the other 49 colonists, 48 of whom were just like Stella, even if he didn't know where.

"What a waste," he muttered. None of these colonists

deserved this. *And for what?* He understood the motivation—sort of—of The Conglomerate planting a saboteur on Thesan. Their planet was rich in indium deposits and The Conglomerate wanted to claim those riches. But this planet? What was here that The Conglomerate wanted?

"I'm in!" shouted Gan a few minutes later.

Gan stood and gestured for Gary to sit in front of the screen. All the colonists medical records were listed. Gary clicked on them, one by one, searching for the date their chips were implanted; 17 had the chip implanted while on Maximillian Station—The Conglomerate's home base in orbit around Earth. *Settler I's* chief medical officer and the rest of the colony's medical staff were included in this number. Since arriving on Nak, Dale Nader had systematically implanted chips in the remaining 33 colonists.

"Did they know that's what their chief medical officer was implanting when they had the procedure done?" Gan asked.

"I'm guessing not. Why would non-Conglomerate crew agree to that? No." Gary shook his head. "Dale did this deliberately, and obviously on the instructions of The Conglomerate. And since the wormhole is closed, that can only mean Dale is the puppet master. Most likely he locked us out as well." Gary looked over his shoulder at Gan. "Can you use the biotracker data to find out where he is?"

"Sure. We can find out where everyone is." Gan shuddered. "I don't know if I want to know. But first I'll find this Dale Nader."

Gan and Gary changed seats. Gary leaned against the desk and watched Gan work. "Ive just realized," Gary stated, his tone grim. "Dale must've done this to his own wife." He shook his head in disbelief. "None of this makes any sense." He ran his hands through his hair. "Why would anyone agree to do this?"

"It looks like he's in his quarters," stated Gan, leaning over to point out the location of Dale's biotracker. "We could use the internal comms to call him."

Gary shook his head. "Bad idea. We need to surprise him. We need to show up at his door," he said. "Otherwise the puppet master could send an army of zombie minions after us." He shuddered at the thought.

"We can't go until Iago and the others return," Gan stated in an impatient tone.

Gary nodded. He was worried about what was taking Margo and the others so long to return. "Hopefully they get here soon—I hate not being able to communicate with them."

"Well, if we ever find ourselves on a planet infested with zombies again, I'll first make sure to fit us with comms devices before we start exploring."

Gary grinned up at Gan, thankful for his attempt at humour. "Believe me, once we're back safely on Thesan I'm never leaving again."

Chapter Thirty-Three

As the kitchen door slid closed behind them, Margo and Iva paused, panting in fear, and scanned the shadows surrounding them.

Margo's heart was hammering. *Butterfly blue, without a clue; butterfly red, better off dead.* The words echoed in her head over and over even as her eyes darted around the room, following the path of Iva's light. *How is it possible....* Butterflies started to emerge from the shadows, all heading her direction. She forced herself to take a deep breath, then another.

"Get a grip Murphy," she said under her breath, letting Iva get ahead of her.

Iva swung her light around the space, checking the corners, as the overhead lights hadn't automatically come on like they should have.

Margo squeezed her eyes shut and willed the butterflies away. "Focus," she said to herself.

"What?" said Iva turning back to her.

Feeling herself again Margo put a hand on Iva's forearm. "Turn off your light," she urged in a whisper.

Iva switched the light off and the two of them stood still, letting their eyes adjust. Through the windows to the Loop, Margo saw the hallway was filled with colonists—likely the same group they'd just encountered. Faces blank, they all just stood there unmoving. None looked their direction, but they completely clogged the Loop.

"We're trapped," whispered Iva.

"Let's cut through the greenhouse," suggested Margo in a low voice, turning to look through the windows on the opposite side of the dining room. Only inky darkness looked back.

"What if more colonists are there?" Iva's whispered voice was quivering.

"I don't think we have another choice," said Margo.

Keeping their eyes on the colonists in the Loop, they walked backwards to the double set of doors leading to the greenhouse. The first door slid open when Margo hit the release button, and the two went inside the small alcove, waiting for the door behind them to close before releasing the door to the greenhouse.

When the doors opened, Margo almost gagged as the wave of hot, humid air that reeked of decay hit her. It had to be Nak's indigenous slime turning the entire greenhouse into a neglected compost pile, multiplied by a hundred.

"Whoa, that stinks," Iva complained in a low tone, her hand over her mouth and nose. She looked up at the black dome above. "Helios is still up. Why is it pitch black in here?"

"For some reason, they've blocked out the light." Margo peered into the darkness, but could only distinguish vague forms against the black shadows.

"Is it safe to use my light?"

"I think so," said Margo, then added, "I hope so."

Iva turned on her light and swung it in a slow arc in front of them. The greenhouse was overgrown and the plants were unrecognizable. Like a field strewn with dismembered tentacles, a chaotic mat of yellow-tinged vines extended out as far as the light could illuminate. There was no obvious path.

"Let's aim for the engineering airlock. It'll be at two o'clock from where we're standing," Margo said, holding her arm as if it were a clock-hand. "Then we can climb up to the mainte-nance ring. Going through the maintenance corridor will be safer than traversing the Loop. I'm certain no colonists will be in there. From there we should be able to drop out into the Hub, right by sickbay."

With her memory of the centre greenhouse back home to guide her, Margo stepped into the mat of vines and headed towards the engineering airlock. Iva stayed beside her, shining the light ahead of them. The vines seemed to willfully attach themselves to her boots, forcing her to regularly pull herself free. The ground under their feet made a sticky, squelching sound with each step.

"Is this the result of the same slime we found in the Hub?" asked Iva, picking her way along beside Margo.

"More than likely."

Margo stepped onto what looked like a hard crust, but it gave way. As her boot passed through, a pungent aroma was released that punched through the ubiquitous reek. When she pulled to step forward, a heavy mass of slime clung to her foot.

"Shine your light on my foot," she said.

When Iva paused and swung the arc of light towards Margo's feet. Margo had stepped into a rotten pumpkin; under the light, it appeared covered in a semi-transparent goo, just like Gary's samples.

"Shit! It's getting all over our clothes." Iva shone the light on her legs and then Margo's, illuminating glossy splotches of goo

"Gary said it isn't immediately dangerous."

"That's not reassuring," Iva scoffed. She looked behind them towards the door. It was just visible in the beam of light, about twenty metres away. "Let's get out of here."

Margo rested one hand on Iva's shoulder as she scraped the rotten pumpkin off her boot with her other foot. When she glanced back at the dining room windows, she couldn't see the colonists—so at least they hadn't been followed. But would they stay still where they were in the Loop? She swallowed as the knot in her gut tightened.

"We need to pick-up the pace," she said picturing the colonist spreading out, seaching for them.

The two of them ran through the field of rotten pumpkins. Vines, rotting fruit and vegetables, and slime made it feel like a they were running through a sticky bog. The effort left them gasping for breath. All around was a sea of darkness, without even pinpricks of stars for guidance.

As she ran, Margo caught a glint of something metallic, like the gleam of metal from Yuko's knife blade, or the exoskeleton of an insect—and it was moving. She tripped and fell, her face cracking open the crusty top of a rotting pumpkin.

"Oh shit! You okay?" said Iva, coming to a stop. She shone her light back on Margo.

Spitting out rotten pumpkin and slime, Margo pushed herself up to sitting. She began frantically wiping the gunk off her face. The fruit tasted worse than it smelled and the palms of her hands burned from stopping her fall. She stared forward into the darkness and saw nothing. *All I saw is yet another hallucination. It had to be a hallucination.* She glanced up at Iva.

"Gary's going to hate that I'm covered in this…" She shook her hand and a wad of goo flew off. "Stuff."

"Look!" Iva said, pointing. They could see the small green light on the door panel of the engineering airlock. "There it is. Finally!"

Margo's heart leapt at the sight. She walked carefully towards the door, wanting to avoid another face plant in a pumpkin moment at all costs.

Once they reached the door, Margo leaned against the wall as Iva hit the button to open it. As Margo stared back into the dark void of the greenhouse, she thought she saw swarms of glossy midnight-blue butterflies swirling against the shadows. They seemed to all land on something at the same time, a bulky form rising from the ground that she couldn't distinguish.

Iva pulled her through the door and slammed it shut behind them.

"I hate this place," Iva said as Margo opened the inside door and stepped into the cavernous engineering workroom. This time the lights came on.

"We made it," said Margo as she looked around the room. The workshop was orderly as though colonists would be there to work at any minute.

"Where is the nearest access door to the maintenance corridor?" asked Iva.

"I'm just going to collect a few things," she said, then pointed at a cabinet. "Look in that tool cart there and grab the biggest wrench you see."

Margo found an empty duffel bag and began filling it with a cutting torch and a random assortment of other tools.

"What are you doing? Why do we need that stuff?" Iva asked over her shoulder as she opened the doors of the cart and began searching through the tools.

"I believe in being prepared," Margo said. "My gut tells me getting off this planet isn't going to be as simple as arriving."

"But how do you know what to take?" Iva handed Margo a wrench as long as her forearm.

"I don't. It's totally random. But having these makes me feel safer than not having them," she stated. Adding the wrench Iva gave her into the bag, she zipped it up and slung it over her back, then swiped a nearby flashlight.

"There's an access ladder in the Loop just outside the main engineering door. Hopefully we don't see any colonists," said Margo.

Faking confidence, Margo strode forward to the door to the Loop, Iva at her side.

"I really don't want to go out there," said Iva. Her wide eyes reflected Margo's fear.

"Me neither, but we can't stay here," said Margo.

At the door, Margo paused, gave a look of mostly fake encouragement to Iva, then hit the button to open the door. Both women poked their heads out of the opening and glanced both ways.

"The coast is clear," Margo said, making no attempt to hide the relief in her voice. "We need to move fast."

With the awkward duffel bag bouncing off her back, Margo darted into the Loop and opened the access panel revealing the ladder disappearing into a yawning black hole above her. After tucking her flashlight into the band of her pants, she started up. The bulk of the duffel bag on her back barely fit in the tight space, forcing her to keep her body as close to the ladder as she could. She heard Iva softly close the access door behind herself and start up the ladder.

Once in the second story maintenance corridor, Margo put the duffel bag down and stood, swinging her light around. The overhead lighting remained off, and they didn't have time to troubleshoot the problem. Their handheld lights were going to have to be the only defence against the darkness.

Her beam of light revealed various ducts and pipes snaking down the gently curving tunnel as though human occupation was an afterthought. The bright spot of her light was hardly a comfort given it created deep shadows that felt alive. On the edge of the light, she thought she saw something move and the hair on the back of her neck rose. Heart racing, she flicked the light to a gap between two ducts, then higher to a where multi-coloured cables formed a thick cord, but nothing was there. Her imagination was playing tricks on her.

When Iva reached the top of the ladder, Margo was grateful for the second beam of light, which forced the shadows to retreat a little farther away.

"Come on" Margo whispered. "Step as quietly as you can and keep any talking to a whisper."

She picked up the duffel bag again, shifting the weight of it onto her stooped back. It was heavy, and she considered ditching it, but the idea of not having it was worse than struggling with the weight of it. "This way," she said, turning and leading them in what she hoped was the shortest route to the Hub.

Iva was short enough to stand upright everywhere, but every few paces, Margo had to duck under tubing of some sort. The two of them took care to keep their footfalls silent—a tricky thing considering the floor was made of a metal grid.

As they continued forward, the hairs on Margo's arms rose. She turned and flashed her light into the darkness they'd come from expecting to see a herd of zombie colonists, but her flashlight glinted only on metal. She shook her head and continued on.

After they'd been walking for a few minutes, Margo whispered over her shoulder, "The exit to the Hub is just ahead."

A moment later they stood near a hole in the floor with a ladder heading down.

"You sure?" Iva asked, looking around for some kind of marking to show where they were. "I don't want to come out in the middle of a zombie support group."

Margo smiled at Iva's weak attempt at injecting some levity in their frightening situation. She shifted the bag to her other shoulder. "I hate to admit it, but I'm not sure about anything." They shone their flashlights down the dark tube of the ladder, but it revealed nothing but more shadows. "There's only one way to find out," Margo added.

She tucked her flashlight under her belt, slung her duffle bag and started down the ladder. As there was no room for the two of them to stand at the bottom, she couldn't wait for Iva to join her so she took a deep breath to steady herself and then opened the access door.

The Hub was empty with the overhead lighting cycling to dark.

Margo stepped out into the space as quietly as she could,

wincing when the tools in her duffle bag shifted and clanged together. Then she stood and waited for Iva, all the while looking up and down the corridor. Iva exited the passageway and closed the panel.

Without a word, they jogged towards the sickbay doors. When they tumbled into the waiting room, Gary rushed forward to take her into his arms. She had to hold out a hand to stop him as she set down the duffel bag with the other.

"I'm covered in gunk," she said, gesturing towards the spatter marks from the rotten pumpkin. Then she noticed the scratch marks across his face. "What happened here?"

"I'll tell you, but first…" Gary stepped forward and wrapped his arms around her. "I was worried about you and I don't care about the gunk."

"Wait," said Gan. "Where's Iago?"

Reluctantly pulling away from Gary, Margo shared a morose look with Iva before responding to Gan. "Yuko slashed his neck. He's dead."

Gan and Gary's expressions mirrored their shock at this unexpected news.

"She tried to fight what the chip was telling her to do," reported Iva. "I never liked her, but I'll give her full points for determination and courage. Iago was trying to help her, but the chip won. There was nothing we could do to stop her."

"A group of colonists gathered in the Loop between the kitchen and here. They were just lurking, but it was damn creepy," said Margo as a shiver went through her. "It was obvious the chips were controlling them too."

Gary nodded towards his counterpart's office. "We did some research and learned that 17 of the colonists already had Conglomerate chips implanted before embarking on this mission, including the chief medical officer. After arriving here, he implanted chips in all the others. Gan accessed their biotrackers. Their lifesigns are the same as Stella's," Gary added in a monotone voice.

"So everyone here is dead?" Iva asked.

Gary frowned. "Mostly, we'll talk about that in a minute, but there's something you need to see first." He took Margo's hand. "Come look at this. Iva? You'll want to see this too."

Chapter Thirty-Four

Unsure of what to expect, Margo let Gary lead her into examination room one. The corpse of Stella Riemer lay on the table in the centre of the small room—now with straps pinning the corpse to the table. Gary stopped at the foot of the examination table and turned to face the corpse, still holding her hand.

Iva remained in the doorway, unwilling to step further into the room where the disturbing corpse lay. "What the..." Her words trailed off as she stared at the corpse.

"Gary." Margo spoke in a suspicious tone. She was avoiding looking at Stella's face—she didn't need to see her gouged out eyes again. "Why did you put restraints on a corpse?"

"Yeah," Iva said from the doorway. "Why?"

"Just wait."

A moment later, Stella's pinky finger twitched.

Margo inhaled. Iva brought a hand to her mouth and stared wide-eyed.

"Oh crap," Margo finally said.

"Did she just..." Once again, Iva's words trailed off.

Starting with small jerking motions, Stella's body began to spasm. Within seconds, her movements escalated into what resembled a full-on seizure. As she twisted back and forth, her jaw clacked open and closed. The snapping sound of her teeth reverberated through the small space.

"Oh my god! I can't watch." Iva turned and fled.

Shivers swept through Margo, as she found it hard to watch too. She turned her head towards Gary, tucking her face against the steadying presence of his solid shoulder.

"How awful," she said, her words muffled. Then she realized something and raised her face to regard Gary. "Those scratches. She attacked you?"

At Gary's nod, Margo leaned forward and kissed him on the lips, then tilted her face and kissed the scratch marks. Drawing back, she looked up at him. "Not sure if that will make it better."

Gary smiled, bringing her hand up to his lips and kissing it. "Already better."

Still holding her hand, Gary led her out of the room to where Gan and Iva were working in the corner. Once back in the waiting room with the examination room door closed, Margo stood watching Stella through the streaming video. The seizure-type thrashing seemed to be waning but, even viewed remotely, the sight was disturbing.

"Are you sure she's dead?" asked Margo.

"Yes," said Gary. "The Conglomerate chip is animating her corpse by sending an electrical impulses through her nervous system, which is intact." He gestured to the screen. "That's the result."

"The Conglomerate has been researching all sorts of things, but why would making zombies be on their list? And why here, on Nak?"

"All their lifesigns are the same as Stella's," Gary said in a monotone voice.

"So everyone here is dead?" She raised an eyebrow.

"No, there is one colonist with vital readings that suggest he's still alive," said Gary. "It's the colony's chief medical officer, Dale Nader, and he put in most of the chips.

"The chief medical officer put Conglomerate chips in his fellow colonists?" Margo couldn't believe it.

"Yes, including his wife."

"We should look at his biotracker info, see where he is."

"Gan and I already have. He's in his quarters now—the equivalent apartment as mine."

Margo waved towards the video feed. "Maybe this is reversible. Maybe if we talk to him, he can tell us how to—"

Gary interrupted her. "The colonists are dead, Margo, except Dale Nader. There's no bringing them back," said he, his tone flat. "But maybe there is something we can do for Yuko."

Margo turned and looked at him. Bluish bags had formed under his eyes, and he'd hugged her even knowing unsavoury goop covered her. Although he acted like he was holding it all together, she could see that he was beginning to fray around the edges. She leaned in close, enfolding him into her embrace, offering him what comfort she could.

———

"I've got the external comms routed through here," said Gan. "And I've amplified the signal, it should be able to get through the storm now."

Margo and Gary went over to where he and Iva had been working.

"Ash, this is Iva, come in. Over," said Iva. The line was quiet, and Iva repeated her request. Margo bit her lip. Out of the corner of her eye she saw Gary flicking at the cuticle of his left thumb.

A squawk of static made them all jump. "Ash here."

At the sound of Ash's voice, Margo felt tears welling up— Ash was their lifeline. She looked around at the others, and saw that they'd all relaxed a tiny, but perceptible bit, upon hearing Ash's voice over the comms.

"When can you come and get us?" asked Iva.

"There's a giant electrical storm above your hemisphere. It's too risky to bring the *Staffelwalze* through it. The models estimate another six to eight hours," reported Ash.

Margo bit her lip. *Another six to eight hours?*

"Roger," said Iva, her calm voice didn't match the look on her face. "We'll continue to check in every two hours. Iva out."

When silence fell and Iva turned to look at her, Margo realized everyone was looking at her. Somehow she'd ended up in charge. She hadn't been in charge of anyone since the fiasco at Clearwater River that resulted in her court-martial. And she didn't want to be in charge now. But she also didn't want to be on a colony infested with zombies. *Life didn't always give you what you wanted.*

She took a deep breath, then addressed her crewmates. "Okay, first rule? We stick together. Agreed?" She waited for the three nods. "Let's go find this colony's head doctor. If the biotracker information is correct, he'll be right next door."

———

In single file, Margo lead the four of them out of sickbay into the Hub stopping in front of Dale's door. They were all nervously glancing over their shoulders expecting to see the other colonists. Dale's position as chief medical officer meant his quarters were on the first story right beside the sickbay's doors—on their home and doppelgänger colony on Thesan, it was the same location where Gary lived.

"Iva, keep watch out here," said Margo. "We don't want anyone sneaking up on us."

Standing between Gary and Gan in front of the door, Margo patted the pistol in her side pocket—she'd taken the time to transfer it from her atmo suit. In that moment, she was glad

Lucas insisted she bring it. After taking a deep breath, she nodded at Gary. He knocked.

They waited a moment, but there was no answer.

"I suppose a criminal mastermind wouldn't just answer the door," said Margo.

Gary tried to open the door, but it was locked from the inside.

"Gan?" asked Gary.

As Gan moved to the door panel, Margo glanced over her shoulder, confirming no colonists were in sight. She avoided looking at the Hub's dying greenery, afraid it would trigger hallucinations of butterflies. *Hallucinating now will only put everyone at risk.*

She turned back just in time to see the door slide open, exposing a black interior. A faint noise came from somewhere deeper inside.

"Did you hear something?" whispered Margo, well aware they weren't being truly stealthy.

"I did," said Gary. He shone the flashlight into the living room, highlighting two ordinary couches and a coffee table.

Shoulder to shoulder, Gary and Margo stepped inside. Behind them, Gan followed, turning on the overhead lights.

A pile of used hard-ration packages scattered across the coffee table indicated that someone has been camped out in this unit. In the living room, the colony computer console mounted in the living room of every apartment had been smashed. On the floor beside it was a destroyed scroll. Gan picked it up and turned it over in his hands, but he said nothing.

With Gan on their heels, Margo and Gary approached the smallest of the three bedrooms. The door was closed. Gary waited for her nod before he hitting the button. When the door slid open, Gary reached around the door's threshold and turned on the light. Margo stepped into the room with Gary right behind her. Gan stayed at the threshold, keeping watch.

The room was being used for storage. Along one wall,

medical supply crates had been stacked on top of a single bed. Beside it was a pile of pristinely white atmo suits that looked like they'd never been used. Other boxes and crates were stacked in relatively neat rows.

Gary pointed to the hard rations crates stacked in a corner and went over to inspect them while Margo walked silently to the closet door.

She felt the hair on the back of her neck rise. *Something isn't right.*

"Gary," she whispered.

He looked up from the crate he'd been examining. She gestured towards the door and he nodded. Holding her breath, she took the gun out of her pocket and released the safety. She raised the barrel, pointing it at the closet door.

Standing out of the way, Gary slid it open. Inside was clothing—uniforms and street clothes—hanging on hangars. With a ragged exhale, she lowered the gun, meeting Gan's gaze where he stood at the threshold looking in.

Just as Gary and Margo turned to leave, a running form smashed into Gan from behind. Gan fell forward and knocked into Gary. Gary staggered back, but both men stayed on their feet.

Margo shoved past them, shouting, "stop!"

Dale didn't heed her shouts, continuing toward the exit to the Hub. But, at the threshold, Iva, whom he hadn't seen, stuck out her foot and tripped him. He tumbled forward into a garden bed, landing face first onto the slime-covered soil. Keeping her gun trained on him, Margo followed.

"Stay where you are or I'll shoot," she said, in her best don't-mess-with-me voice. She addressed Iva over her shoulder, saw Gary and Gan tumble out into the courtyard. "Keep an eye out for colonists. This might've attracted their attention."

Margo turned back to Dale. He was still on the ground but he'd turned to look at them.

"If we stay out here, they'll come," he said.

"You mean the other colonists?" said Margo. In her mind she was thinking, *why isn't he surprised to see us? Did he know we were here?*

"They're all dead." Dale lifted a hand to wipe the gunk off his face, the slime making his dark skin gleam.

In the back of her mind, Margo also registered that the chief medical officer wasn't freaking about about being covered in slime.

"He's controlling them," Dale whined, his voice on the verge of hysteria. "He'll send them in here any minute—we've got to get somewhere safe."

"Get up. We're all going back to sickbay," ordered Margo, gesturing with the barrel of the pistol.

Dale kept his eyes fixed on the short hallway that connected the Hub to the Loop. Then he stared at Margo for a moment before looking at each of the others.

"Who are you?" Dale asked, wiping his face.

"No time for that now. Let's go," said Margo.

Standing, Dale took one last fearful look at the path to the Loop before turning to sickbay. Once the five of them trooped into the waiting room, Dale slumped down on a bench. The others stood in a half-circle around him, Margo still holding the gun, kept it pointed at the ground in front of Dale's feet.

Dale looked at each of them in turn. "Did he send you?"

"Who's 'he'?" asked Margo. Then she looked at Gan. "Can you lock us in? We don't want any uninvited visitors."

Gan nodded and went to work at the panel beside the door.

Dale sat up straight for a moment and looked at each of them one at a time. "How do I know he didn't send you?"

"Dale," said Gary as he put a hand on the gun Margo still held. He gently pushed down until she had the gun pointed at the floor. "We met once back on Earth. Do you remember?"

"Yes," said Dale after studying Gary's face for a moment. "You are one of those Holbrook twins from Cape Town." Dale ran a hand through his short, wiry hair. "I'm sorry, I don't know which one you are."

"I'm Gary," he said. "My brother and I both took posts on the *Settler III* mission." Next, Gary introduced his three crewmates.

Dale looked shocked as he eyed each of them, then finally asked, "You don't work for Nigel West?" At their vehement denial, Dale slumped back against the wall in relief.

Margo engaged the safety mechanism to the gun.

"We know Nigel is controlling the other colonists through the chips in your heads, but we don't know why," Gary stated, pointing to the video screen at the door to examination room one. Stella was still at the moment.

Dale poked his head forward to better view the video screen. "That's Commander Reimer?" he asked. When they nodded, he said, "She was going to shut down our off-world comms. We thought it would stop the madness."

"You mean, you linked the altered behaviour of the colonists to the chips in your head?" Gary asked.

Dale nodded.

"How?" Gan asked from where he was fiddling with the wires in the door panel.

"That's not what's important, I mean, not right now, " Margo stated before Dale could respond. "What I want to know is, why aren't you affected?"

"I don't know," he said, burying his face in his hands. He lifted his head suddenly, his eyes shining with hope as he looked up at Gary. "You could take it out! You could remove it!"

Margo put the gun back in her trouser pocket, turning towards Gary and Iva. "Well he's clearly not the mastermind," she said in a low tone. "Where does that leave us?"

Chapter Thirty-Five

"You've got to get the chip out of my head," repeated Dale, pinning Gary with eyes filled with desperation.

Margo bit her lip at the realization Dale was talking about brain surgery. She glanced at Gary, but he had his eyes fixed on Dale.

"Look, it's the only way I can be sure he won't take over my body like he did all the others." Dale paused and gulped, clearly terrified of what he was suggesting, yet suggesting it anyway. "If you don't do it, I'll never be free. And I'll be a danger to you."

"It would be tricky," said Gary. Deep wrinkles had formed across his forehead. "I don't have any trained assistants and that chip is in a difficult place to access."

"All the equipment you need is right here." Dale gestured around the space.

Gary let out an audible exhale and ran his hand over his face. "I need to get a better look at the chip's position."

Dale nodded and headed into the empty surgical suite.

"Margo, will you help me?" asked Gary.

"I'm not sure how much help I'd be," said Margo, noticing

both Iva and Gan were avoiding making eye contact with Gary. *They don't want to help with brain surgery any more than I do.*

"You have a biology background," said Gary.

"Most of my studies centred on chasing butterflies through the rainforest," she said, before realizing his request was more about needing moral support than technical help. "But, yes, I'll help you."

"Thanks," he said. "We might as well get started."

Margo followed Gary into the surgical suite. The space was spotless, like a real hospital back on Earth. The gleaming white walls gave her a glimmer of hope that brain surgery could be successfully performed.

Dale followed them into the room and sat himself on the table by the scanning equipment.

Margo asked, "How can I help?"

"Before we can even think about surgery, we'll need to do some detailed scans," Gary said, sitting down in front of the computer console controlling the scanners. Margo pulled over a chair and sat beside him.

I've already set the scanners to the highest resolution," said Dale, turning his head to watch Gary.

"Don't move then, just stay still," said Gary without looking over his shoulder. Margo watched him push a button, and the scanner unfolded out of its compartment in the ceiling. The long bar containing the sensors was supported on either end by a series of mobile joints that reminded her of a stork's legs.

Dale let out a series of coughs. His head lifting from the table with each.

"Lay still," Gary chided. "You know as well as I the results are compromised if you're not completely still."

Margo glanced over her shoulder at Dale. Redness was spreading out from his cheeks and getting worse with every cough. She rose in alarm, asking, "Are you okay?"

Dale nodded as best he could, but kept coughing.

"Gary, something is wrong!" Margo said.

Gary stood and they both approached the patient. Dale's face had turned a molten purple colour. His hands were on his neck, clawing as though he was trying to remove a noose.

"He's choking," said Gary, as he rushed to the head of the table, Margo rushing to the other side.

Pop!

The pristine the examination room changed in an instant. Margo jerked her head back and squeezed her eyes closed as warm bits of brain matter and blood sprayed her face. She choked down a need to vomit, and instead opened her eyes, staring in shock at the sight before her.

Small chunks of grey matter, bone fragments and hair coated Gary's chest, hands and face. His eyes were wide as he stared down at the patient in front of him.

Margo shifted her eyes down and looked down, then regretted it. Dale's jaw was all that remained of his head. Where the rest of it had been was nothing but a pulpy, blood-soaked mess. She turned, fell to her hands and knees, and vomited

She sat, hunched over and panting, uncertain of whether another spasm would overwhelm her. Then Gary was at her side.

"You okay?" he asked.

Margo felt her stomach settle. "Yeah. But get me away from…" She gestured weakly at the soiled floor. It was difficult to say where her vomit started and Dale's brain matter began.

Gary helped her to her feet and eased her over to the large sink, turning on the faucets. "Wash," he insisted. "No. Scrub. Use this." He gestured at the disinfectants, then shrugged out of his jacket, tossed it aside, and began to wash.

Slipping out of her jacket, Margo tossed it on the floor near Gary's. They remained silent as they scrubbed themselves clean. Finally, Margo pressed a towel to her face. As she dried her hands, she watched Gary—more focused than she needed to be on watching a man wash and dry his face and hands. But shifting her gaze to the alternative was not an option. She kept her back to the table where what was left of Dale lay.

Margo was thankful when Gary finally straightened, grabbed a towel, and turned to meet her gaze. His eyes softened when he looked at her, and it grounded her.

He lifted a hand and gently stroked a finger on her cheek. "Are you okay?"

"I will be. That was…"

Gary glanced over his shoulder to look towards Dale. Margo kept her eyes on Gary.

"That was…" Gary didn't seem to know how to end that sentence. "I didn't even touch him."

Nodding, she took a deep breath, and stood straighter, keeping her back to the table. She put a hand on his arm.

"Gary. Someone else did this," she said.

Gary nodded. "Nigel?"

It was Margo's turn to nod. "Let's get out of here." She took his hand and led him out of the examination room and into the waiting room where Iva and Gan were both assessing data on scrolls. They stood when they glimpsed inside the examination room before the door closed.

"You're done already?" Gan asked.

"That was fast," commented Iva.

"We're not done. The chip…" Margo let her words trail off as she looked at Gary.

"The chip exploded before we even touched him," said Gary, his tone dull.

"It exploded?" Iva looked like she was about to puke.

"While still in his head?" Gan looked towards the operating room with horror.

"Yes. His whole head," said Margo, lifting her hands and gesturing outwards to signify and explosion.

"I need a minute," Gary said, heading for the office that was his on Thesan.

Margo glanced at Iva and Gan, saw that Gan wanted to

peak inside the operating room. She wasn't going to watch him do that, and instead said, "I need to brush my teeth," then walked over to the washroom and shut the door behind herself.

She rooted around in the medicine cabinet for a toothbrush and toothpaste, noticing for the first time that her hands were shaking.

"Calm down Murphy," she said to her reflection in the mirror. "These people need you to keep it together." As she spoke, she saw a blue morpho butterfly fluttering behind her reflection.

"How can I possibly be expected to keep it together when you keep showing up?" she asked the hallucinated insect. Fortunately, it didn't answer. She took a deep breath and began scrubbing her teeth.

Drying her hands a moment later, she studied her reflection. She looked like shit. Her skin had taken on an ashen tone, blueish bags had formed under her eyes and her curly hair was a tangled mess. *How much longer until we can get off of this world for good?*

After taking a deep breath, she rejoined Gan and Iva in the waiting room. She couldn't tell if either of them had looked in on Dale, and she didn't ask.

In silent agreement, the three of them headed to Gary's office, and found him sitting in front of the workstation. Margo and Iva both took seats in the two chairs, while Gan stood leaning a shoulder against the doorframe.

"If they're somehow controlling these people from Maximilian Station, how do we stop them?" asked Gary to no one in particular.

"We shut down the off-world comms," said Margo.

"We'd have to do that from the Control Room," said Gan.

"Wait," Iva said. "Isn't that what Stella was doing when…" Iva's voice trailed off to nothing. She frowned and looked down at her feet.

"The difference is, we don't have chips in our heads," said Margo. "We'll succeed."

"Nigel can still send the colonists to spy on us. If the colonists see you near or in the Control Room, he'll direct them to attack." said Gary. "Your gun won't stop them."

Gan moved to Gary's console, tapped a few keys over Gary's console. "The colonists are still in the common room," he announced.

"All 48 of them?" Margo asked.

Gan tapped another key, bringing up a colony schematic. "Yup," he said.

"How do we get there without them seeing us?" The common room had walls of glass. There was no way to access the Control Room without walking past the common room—or going the long way around the loop of a colony.

"We can get into the maintenance ring from the Hub. There's an exit at the back of the Control Room," said Margo.

"We shouldn't split up," said Iva.

"I agree," said Gary.

"As much as I hate to say it, Gary and Gan, you need to stay here. Gary needs to figure out how to safely remove the chips," said Margo. "We can't save the colonists, but maybe we can save Yuko,"

"I'll see what I can find, but I still hate this idea," said Gary. "And I want the two of you to wear your atmo suits."

"That'll just slow us down, and you've already shown that a pathogen isn't causing this," said Margo.

"If someone remotely controls the colonists," he argued. "Then there is no reason they couldn't just cycle in some outside air to kill us off."

"Good point," Margo said, nodding.

"I hate this plan," said Iva.

"Do you have a better idea?" asked Margo.

"No. Shutting down external comms is the best option. But I still hate it." Iva stood. She looked over to Gary. "And I hate you've put the idea that some remote person would kill us by making the air toxic. Thanks for that." She sighed. "I'll go get my atmo suit on," she added in a resigned tone as she headed out of the office.

Margo rose. "Gan, can check in with Ash? See how much time until the storm passes?"

When Margo made to follow Gan from the room, Gary snagged her wrist, tugging on it and forcing her to plop onto his lap.

Gary and Margo remained silent as they watched Iva and Gan leave Gary's—Gary's counterpart's—office.

"Come here for a moment," said Gary in a low tone. He settled his arms around her waist. "Promise me you'll be careful."

"I promise," she said, then leaned in for his kiss.

———

Sealed into her atmo suit, Margo picked up the duffle bag. She didn't know if she would need the tools, but she wasn't taking any chances.

She turned and looked at the others. With her atmo suit sealed, Iva stood beside with Gan by the door ready to let them out, while Gary stood nearby. Everyone's faces looked weary, Margo saw. *Shutting down the colony's off-world comms has to be the solution*, thought Margo. Because if it wasn't, they were out of options and they would have to abandon Yuko when Ash finally came for them. Ash had reported that the storm would move past their location in four hours.

"We'll all keep in touch using the suits' comms," she said. *So much for an inspiring pep talk.*

"I've turned on the lights up there," said Gan, pointing up to where the maintenance corridor was.

"Thanks," said Margo. "We'll be back as soon as we can."

Margo nodded to Gan and he opened the door. Five paces

took her to the access panel door in the Hub. With Iva at her side, she unlatched the door and opened it exposing the ladder inside.

Out of the corner of her eye, Margo saw the sickbay doors slide shut. She took a deep breath, clipped the duffel bag to her belt and started up the ladder. The bag weighed her down and made climbing difficult, but she didn't reconsider her choice to bring it along.

At the top, Margo cleared the ladder, unclipped the duffle bag and set it on the floor. She looked around. The dim lights left dark shadows between the tubing and equipment. In her peripheral vision the shadows seemed to move—undulating arms of darkness unwinding into the light, but when she looked directly at them they were just shadows. It was all just her imagination playing tricks on her. The corridor was benign.

Taking a deep breath to calm herself, she glanced down to see Iva almost at the top, then she looked the direction they had to go. After Iva was in the corridor, Margo slung the duffel bag over her shoulder and started walking.

A clicking sound that reminded her of insect feet against a metal roof sounded behind them. Both women spun to see what had made the noise.

"It sounded like there was something right behind us," said Iva in a whisper.

The two of them stood still, staring down the maintenance corridor. Margo saw the shadows beginning to morph. In places they stretched, in other places they became darker. She recognized the signs—she was about to see butterflies that weren't there.

"It's nothing," she said looking away. "Let's keep moving."

The two of them turned and resumed walking.

The hair on the back of Margo's neck rose as she glanced over her shoulder. Something skittered out of view. *It's just a hallucination.* Turning her attention forward, she picked up the pace.

"Did you see something?" asked Iva.

"No," said Margo. *Just figments of my own imagination.* Steadying her breathing, she stopped at the top of the ladder down to the Control Room. "You first." Iva didn't argue and started down.

Yet again, Margo looked back the way they'd come. Something was unfurling from a shadow. Spindly limbs with red joints slowly extended. *It has to be a hallucination—but this time it's not a butterfly. An arachnid perhaps?* In the shadow's darkness, she thought she could make out an eye, glowing red. *Not real.*

"I'm clear," said Iva from below. Margo turned her back on the nothingness that was in the shadows and went down the ladder.

Chapter Thirty-Six

"We'll be back as soon as we can," Margo said before following Iva out the door.

Gary hated being separated from her once again, but he also recognized that it was necessary. *I want off this blasted planet!*

As soon as the door shut behind the two women, Gan re-locked it, checking his work several times. Then he turned towards Gary.

"Now what?" he asked.

Without a word, Gary sat on the nearest bench and pulled on his suit. Gan shrugged and did the same.

"First, I'll take another look at Stella's chip," said Gary as he stood to zip up the front of his suit. Once the suit was on, he turned and reached for his helmet. Stopping, he studied his hands—they now had a slight tremor to them. He squeezed his hands into fists, then relaxed them before he grabbed onto the helmet's neck ring.

"I'm not going anywhere near her," said Gan as he glanced towards the closed examination room door with Stella on the other side.

"Neither am I, I took a full scan of her earlier." Gary got up and returned to Dale's office.

Through the window, he could see the storm raging outside. The flashes of lightening were nearly constant and the visibility had reduced since the last time he'd looked.

"It's looking crapier and crapier out there," said Gan as he leaned against the door frame.

"Ash said it will pass," said Gary as he sat at the console and brought up Stella's scans. He scrolled through the three-dimensional image of her brain, magnifying the region where the chip had been inserted. *It should be possible to remove Yuko's—but it will be tricky. One false move and she'll be left brain dead. Perhaps there's another option.* He zoomed in closer to get a better look at the actual chip.

"Gan, can you take a look at this?"

Gan came to stand behind Gary and studied the screen over Gary's shoulder.

"Can you see if there is some way to deactivate the chip? That's a better option than surgery."

Gan scratched his head and leaned in closer. He was quiet for a few moments. "It's impossible to tell from the image. I'd need an actual chip to test."

"Maybe Dale has extra stored somewhere," said Gary, looking at the messy desk.

"Is anyone there?" came a faint voice over the internal comms.

Both men shifted their attention and stared in astonishment at the wall box beside the door.

"Hello?" said the voice again. Gary finally recognized the voice as Yuko's. Her voice sounded strained.

Gan stood up straight. "Do you want me to get that?" he asked.

"Okay," said Gary.

Two paces took Gan back to the comms unit, and he pushed the transmit button. "Yuko? Is that you?"

"Help me," she said, her voice quivering.

Gan looked at Gary before responding. "What's wrong?" he asked, his tone suspicious.

"I'm in engineering. Some equipment fell on me," she said. "I hurt my leg and I need help."

Gan took his finger off the transmit button and looked at Gary. "What should we do?"

"Do you think it's a trap?" Gary stood.

Gan went over to the console and scrolled through several screens. "Yes," he crowed. "It looks like Iva shut down the main servers. That should take down the off-world comms."

"But does that means it's safe to go to engineering?" asked Gary.

"I have no idea," said Gan.

"I can bring up her biotracker info." Gary turned back to his screen and tried to bring up the right screen. The computer froze, leaving him staring at a blank screen. "I guess whatever Iva did shut down our access to the data."

"Now what?" asked Gan.

The two of them stared at each other for a moment.

"Hello?" said Yuko over the comms again. "Please help me. I'm myself again. I feel like something terrible happened, but I can't remember. And I don't know how I got here."

Gary ran a hand through his hair. "We can't do nothing. If the chips have been deactivated, she'll be confused on top of any injuries she might have sustained."

"This is all based on the assumption that the chips were controlled by someone off-world." Gan looked at him and frowned.

"Margo was hopeful that was the case," said Gary. "It sounds like Yuko really needs our help."

Gan nodded and pressed the transmit button. "Hold on, Yuko. We're coming."

———

Gary packed up his medical bag and then put on his helmet. He looked around sickbay for something he could use as a weapon, but there was nothing big enough to bother with. For a moment, he wished Dale had been an avid baseball fan and left a bat in his office. *What good would a scalpel do as a weapon against a zombie? The zombies are gone,* he told himself, but he still felt queasy with unease. *We should stick to the plan and just stay put. Margo must be on her way back by now.*

"Margo, come in," he said through the suit's comms. He'd been calling her ever since hearing from Yuko, but she still wasn't answering.

"If they are still in the server room, our signal is probably blocked," said Gan. He'd found a huge wrench and was test swinging it. The tool doubled effectively as a formidable weapon.

"Then we might as well get going," said Gary, hefting his medical bag. "You should put on your helmet."

"I'll keep it close but, I'd rather not put it on," said Gan, clipping the helmet to his back. "I'm sweating too much. If I wear the helmet, I won't be able to wipe it off." As if to demonstrate, he dabbed the sweat off his brow.

Gary stared at Gan.

"Now that the zombies are neutralized, the risk is low." Gan squirmed a bit under Gary's gaze. "I have a portable air sensor clipped here." He pointed to a small device attached to the strap of his air pack. "It'll give plenty of warning if the air is bad."

"Fine. Let's go."

Gan unlocked the door to the Loop and stuck his head out. "It's clear. I'd rather not go through the maintenance corridor, so let's pass through the gardening quadrant."

"That'll take us the opposite direction to where Margo and Iva are," said Gary. Gan just looked at him, then Gary remembered the gathering of colonists in the common room—they shouldn't be animate now, but... he really didn't want to see them. "Fine, lets move."

They turned right down the empty hallway. The white walls of the Loop were broken only by occasional doors and the coloured band changing from purple to green to blue. The only sound was their own footfalls. It was so quiet, it made Gary's skin crawl.

He thought back to the brain scans he'd been studying. It was well within his skill set to remove the chip and there were surgical facilities on *Settler I*. *Should I remove the chip from Yuko here?* The medbay on the *Staffelwalze* was too basic and taking her all the way back to Thesan would be a huge risk—one he could mitigate if he put Yuko into a stasis pod. He thought back to the state he'd left the operating room here on *Settler I*. What was left of Dale was still there. A lot of cleaning would be required to use that space. And there was the issue of the tremor that still hadn't left his hands.

At least he'd already checked the original colonists on Thesan for implanted chips; he'd have to check the Insurgent group who had arrived on the *Staffelwalze*. He added that to his mental to do list.

Gan stopped and looked up.

"What is it?" asked Gary, his heart rate spiking.

"I heard something above us."

"Could it be Margo and Iva still in the maintenance loop?" Gary looked up at the ceiling—all he could see was the lighted panel enclosing the space.

"No, it wasn't the right sound. Besides, even if they returned to sickbay through the maintenance corridor, they wouldn't pass above us here." Gan continued to look at the ceiling. "Maybe it was my imagination, we should keep going."

The two of them started walking again, but in less than twenty paces Gan stopped.

"As soon as we moved, the sound started again," said Gan in a barely audible tone. "It's still there. Sounds like something mechanical."

Gary listened, but he couldn't hear anything other than his

own breathing. Then he heard it; a faint clicking of metal on metal somewhere above.

"What would make that sound?" he asked. His voice low, in a whisper. "The ventilation system perhaps?"

"No." Gan pointed to the ceiling. "That's the sound of something moving above." Gan cocked his head to the side.

"In the maintenance corridor?" asked Gary noticing the sound had stopped. He walked forward another dozen paces and the sound resumed, then stopped directly above.

"It's like it's tracking us," said Gan.

"But what is it?"

"There's no way to know without going up there," said Gan.

"First we need to see to Yuko. Then we investigate the corridor up there," Gary insisted. "Better yet, let's gather everyone up and get off this planet."

Gan nodded, and the two of them walked faster towards engineering, the sound of their footfalls obscuring whatever was making noise above them.

Once they reached the doors to engineering, Gan paused at the access panel to the corridor above.

"I'll feel a whole lot safer if this panel is locked from the outside." He pointed to the panel.

Gary glanced up at the ceiling, then down to the panel. "Do it."

As Gan worked, Gary stepped to the outside wall of the Loop and looked both ways, hoping to see Margo and Iva approaching them, but the Loop remained empty. A few moments later, Gan opened the doors to engineering, and they went inside.

Gan turned on all the lights.

Fully illuminated, the space looked just like their own engineering space back home. The workbenches were clear, and the tools were put away. Everything was orderly, and there wasn't even any evidence of the slime mould. Still, the space felt wrong somehow, but he couldn't put his finger on the cause.

Gan walked around the workbenches searching for Yuko, while Gary, after setting his medical bag on a work bench, stuck his head in the chief engineer's office, but nothing was out of the ordinary.

Back in the main workshop, Gary found himself alone. He didn't know the intricate ins and outs of the space like Gan did. A door at the far end of the space stood open—Gan must have gone through.

"Why didn't you wait for me?" asked Gary stopping in the open doorway.

Chapter Thirty-Seven

The door led to a short hallway lined with more doors—an place Gary had never been to before even on Thesan. He went to the first door on the right; it opened into a small workroom with specialized tools. Gan wasn't there so he stepped back and closed the door.

Gary switched on his helmet comms. "Gan, where are you?" he asked, but there was no answer.

He went through the next door. Inside was an empty meeting room with wall-to-ceiling windows along one side. The lights were off, and the only illumination from the mustard-hued storm outside. Yellowed tones highlighted the table and chairs, leaving streaks of dark shadows.

Motion in the clouds drew his attention to the scene outside. He walked right up to a window and put his hand on it. The storm was getting worse. From within the pea soup coloured clouds, near continuous flashes of lightening continued. With each flash, the clouds lit up, exposing the writhing air masses above. The sky looked alive, boiling in a frenzy.

"Gary," said a quiet, feminine voice behind him.

With a surprised yelp, he spun around. Yuko stood at the door. She was in shadow, so he couldn't make out her features.

"Are you okay?" he asked, taking a step towards her.

Lightening flashed just outside the windows, illuminating the space. And Yuko's face.

"Oh!" For a moment Gary froze, trying to process what he'd seen as the lightening faded.

Dark pools filled the space where her eyes should have been—she'd gouged them out just like Stella had. Blood still dripped down her face and hadn't yet begun to congeal. Blood smeared her clothes as well. Somehow able to sense his presence, Yuko took a few steps towards him, the yellow light from outside cast her in its sickly glow.

"I need your help," she said lifting her right hand.

Gary's heart raced as he retreated until his back hit the window. Something about her motion wasn't right.

Halting mid-step, Yuko cocked her head as though she could see and was studying him. Her right arm hung at her side like it was weighted down. She'd crossed her left arm across her mid-section and gripped her right forearm. She took another step forward. As she moved, she kept her left shoulder angled towards him. He couldn't tell if she was holding something in her right hand or was just injured.

"Please help me." She took another step towards him.

He edged along the window, hoping to put the table between them. Multiple flashes of lightning pulsed outside, creating a series of strobing lights. The whole scene felt straight out of a stop-motion animation film of old. In each frame, Yuko lifted her right hand a little higher. Only once it reached shoulder height did Gary realize she held a heavy crowbar.

As she arced the crowbar at him, he bolted to the side, around the table. The crowbar slammed into the table's faux wood surface.

"You can't escape!" she howled, chasing after him.

Gary picked up a chair and turned, raising it like a shield. A fraction of a second later, he felt the impact of the crowbar slamming into the chair. It nearly knocked him off balance, but he remained on his feet and the angled end of the crowbar had stuck in the chair. *A weapon!* He held the chair with one hand and made a grab for the crowbar, but she was faster. She gripped his arm, and pulled him towards her.

Whatever was controlling her had made her strong. Gary struggled to break free of her grasp.

Twisting, Gary pulled away. The chair with the crowbar embedded in the seat fell to the ground, distracting Yuko. For a moment she looked confused then she reached down to retrieve the weapon. Gary grabbed another chair and slammed it down on her back. The impact sent Yuko sprawling on the floor, away from the weapon.

Picking up the crowbar in both hands, Gary brought it down as hard as he could onto the back of her skull. With a wet crunch, the bone caved in. Ignoring the squishing sound, he pulled the weapon free.

Gasping to catch his breath, he took a pace backwards. His hands were shaking, forcing him to tighten his grip on the weapon. The crowbar was all that stood between himself and whatever Yuko had become.

Without blinking, he stared at Yuko's motionless, prone form. *The chip was controlling her—there was nothing I could've done to save her.* A bead of sweat dripped down his forehead and along the side of his nose. The fan in his helmet switched onto maximum to help clear the moisture.

He didn't know how long he waited, but his breath had slowed and she still hadn't moved. The only motion in the room was the quivering of the tip of the crowbar.

Dropping the gore coated weapon at his feet, he backed out of the room, closing the door. He let out a ragged exhale and felt himself slump against the wall. His hands trembled so hard, he didn't think he could pick up anything.

We need to get off this world. The sooner the better.

"Gan!" he called over his helmet comms.

Silence stretched out as he waited for a reply—none came.

"Gan, where are you?"

Gary walked further down the corridor, poking his head into a series of storerooms. Gan wasn't in any of them. He went back into the main engineering workshop. Everything looked the same.

What if Yuko got to Gan before she found me?

"Gan," he called again, using his suit's comms. He walked out to the Loop and looked both ways.

"I'm in terraforming," said Gan over the suit's comms.

"Why are you there? And why the hell didn't you tell me?" Gary was furious with Gan as he retrieved his medical bag and hurried out of the room. He turned towards terraforming and started jogging.

"I thought I saw Yuko," said Gan.

"Well you didn't," he snapped. "Yuko's dead."

Gary switched the comm's link to broadcast to Margo. "Margo, where are you? Yuko's dead," he said, but there was no response.

As he jogged in the heavy atmo boots down the Loop, the line on the wall changed from purple to green. By the time he got to the door of terraforming, he was gasping for air. He opened the door and went inside.

All the lights were on and Gan stood calmly at a console—a perfectly ordinary scene. Gary clamped a hand to his side, the long jog had left him with a cramp. As he waited to catch his breath, he looked around. The cavernous space was filled with the same gear they had back home. Algal generators lined the wall, ready to be set up and used. He shifted his attention back to Gan.

"What are you doing?" asked Gary. He licked his lips, craving a drink of water but not willing to remove his helmet. He wanted to scream at Gan, but he'd give him a dressing down later, once they were safely back on the *Staffelwalze*.

"I'm trying to raise Margo and Iva," Gan said, dabbing sweat off his forehead. Gary's eyes shifted to Gan's helmet clipped on to the airpack.

"Is there still something blocking their signal?"

"Looks like it," said Gan. His expression became more and more perplexed as he worked.

"Let's just head to the Control Room and find them." Gary turned towards the main door.

"Hang on," said Gan. "What the heck? It looks like the two of them are outside. What are they doing there?"

"Outside?" Gary wished there were windows to see outside.

"Yeah. But they're about to come in the terraforming airlock. Let's go meet them."

"Why would they be outside?" demanded Gary. A fluttering feeling formed in his gut. "That wasn't the plan. Margo wouldn't deviate from the plan without telling us."

"We can ask her in a minute." Gan turned and led the way to the airlock. It was a small one, with a tiny change room. The airlock capacity was three people.

"They're in the airlock, cycling the air," said Gan, resting his hands on his hips as he waited for the interior door to open.

From where he was standing, Gary couldn't see anyone inside the airlock. "Something's not right about this," he said.

"Agreed. And they'll need to explain," said Gan.

As soon as the light beside the interior door flashed green, Gan stepped forward and opened it.

A gust of wind pushed into the space, nearly knocking Gary off his feet. Ahead of him, Gan screamed and began fumbling with his helmet. Air quality alarms started going off as Gary realized the outside door was open—Gan was breathing the toxic atmosphere.

As Gan fell to the ground, Gary pushed against the gusts of wind, fighting to get to Gan. Gan hadn't been able to unclasp his helmet and now he was convulsing.

"Shit!" cursed Gary, as he moved past Gan and put his weight against the airlock door, pushing it closed

With the door closed, the small room was suddenly quiet, the hum of the ventilation system trying to clear the air was the only sound.

As Gary knelt at Gan's side, he realized he was too late. Gan had inhaled toxic amounts of hydrogen fluoride gas. There was nothing he could do for him. Gan was dead. The helmet that could have saved him still clipped to his back.

Chapter Thirty-Eight

Margo exited the maintenance shaft behind Iva and stepped onto the highest platform in the Control Room. Beside them, the door to the Loop was closed and the room was quiet—unnervingly so.

"And here we are." She ran her hands down the legs of her atmo suit in a foolish attempt to dry her sweaty palms inside her gloves.

"Right," said Iva. Her face had taken on a pallid hue. "I'll get to work." She went to the centre console and started it up.

Margo followed and stood behind Iva's chair to watch the diagnostic screens scroll by. Indicators blinked red across the screen—*Settler I* was in bad shape. The slime, or whatever that alien goo was, was taking its toll.

With the next swipe of her hand, Iva brought up the off-world comms. "That's weird," she said, as she scrolled through a few more screens.

Margo raised an eyebrow. "Weird good?"

"No." Iva twisted to look up at Margo. "The off-world comms are not functioning. In fact, they're locked out and seem to have been that way since the colony's arrival. I'd need the correct biometrics to gain access to them."

"So when things went bad, the colonists couldn't call for help? Not even when the wormhole opened?" asked Margo. A sick feeling knotted in her gut as she realized the colony commander's last mission to shut down the comms had been futile.

Iva wrapped her arms around herself. "That explains why we could never reach them."

"How are we talking with Ash?"

"Gan augmented the signal from our suits, because he couldn't access off-world comms from sickbay." Iva still studied the screen before her.

"If the comms are locked off, then who's the puppet master?" Margo took a pace back and glanced around the room. "It has to be someone on this colony."

As if in response to her words, the lights in the Control Room started flashing like a strobe light.

"Let's get out of here." Margo grabbed hold of Iva's arm and pulled her to her feet.

"Oh shit!" said Iva.

They'd been so focused on their task, they hadn't realized the door to the Loop had opened. With each flash, more and more colonists spilled into the room. But with the strobe light, it was like they weren't moving; instead, each time the light died, it seemed an unseen hand shifted them from position to position.

"Server room." Margo grabbed her duffel bag and twisted it over her shoulder.

The flashing strobe light gave Margo a sense of vertigo as they fled to the computer room on the lowest level. As soon as Iva pulled closed the clear door, Margo retrieved a screwdriver from her duffel bag and studied the door, a tricky task given the flashing lights. Unfortunately, the door opened out, wedging the screwdriver through the latch was the best she could do.

"We're trapped," shrieked Iva, eyeing the approaching

colonists through the clear walls. The top two tiers of the space were now filled with re-animated corpses.

As soon as Margo locked themselves in, she began searching through the room, her brain scrambling for an alternate exit. She noticed that the servers were completely powered down—a strange thing given these machines were needed to serve the needs of fifty colonists. Margo stopped suddenly, thinking the flashing strobe light was playing tricks with her vision. The server in the back corner was the only one still powered on. Pursing her lips, she tried to reason what that meant.

When they'd first arrived, they'd found Stella's body in this room. She'd been laid out like a discarded doll. *But why had she been in this room in the first place?* Then Margo remembered the colony commander's logs.

Margo hurried back to Iva, saw that the colonists were continuing to file in. They came forward and pressed themselves against the clear walls, but they didn't try to get in through the door.

"Iva, she stopped logging," announced Margo. *The puzzle pieces were finally beginning to fall into place.*

"What?" asked Iva, tearing her fear-filled gaze away from the silent colonists to frown at Margo.

"Stella stopped logging." Margo put her hands on her hips, looking frustrated that Iva wasn't keeping up with her logic. "Maybe she thought someone was reading those logs."

"Huh?"

"For everyday since landing, she made a log entry—then two weeks ago she stopped. Things here were going downhill fast. The only reason I can think of why she wouldn't record what was going on was because someone was reading her logs to gain an advantage."

"Someone, as in the puppet master?" asked Iva.

"Exactly. But, I think we've been assuming the puppet master is flesh and blood."

Margo scanned the ceiling, looking for a camera. The

puppet master was watching them, watching the whole colony from who knew how many cameras. She spotted it then, mounted in a corner. "Come on," she said, grabbing Iva's arm and heading directly to the camera.

She stopped under it, as close as she could get to the camera and stared up at it. "You got us," Margo said in a loud voice. She hoped the sound carried through her suit and to whatever microphone was rigged to the camera.

As soon as Margo spoke, the flashing lights stopped. The sick sound of Nigel's demented laughter floated out from the speaker. But how was it possible? The wormhole was closed. Nigel shouldn't be able to see or hear anything in any of the three *Settler* colonies.

They both whirled around when the colonists in the Control Room joined in Nigel's laughter. Their expressions were mechanical and the sound of their laughter stuttering and void of life.

Margo turned back to look up at the camera. "Why are you doing this?"

At her challenge, the colonists went quiet. She turned again, and saw them standing as still and expressionless as store mannequins.

A voice floated from the speaker. "*Butterfly blue without a clue; Butterfly red better off dead.* Margo Murphy, I knew you would come once you got my message."

And then everything clicked for Margo. It was Nigel West's voice, but it wasn't him. She turned to Iva. Pulling a scrap of paper and a pen off the top of a nearby server. She began to write, turning her back to the camera:

It's a Nigel II AI—can you remove it?

After reading the note, Iva's eyes widened momentarily. Then she nodded and stood in front of a nearby computer, her fingers flying and swiping across the touch screen and the accompanying keyboard.

Margo crumpled up the piece of paper and let it drop to the ground.

"Why did you think I would come?" asked Margo, turning and looking back up at the camera.

"It was foretold. And now I get to have the pleasure of watching you die too," said the AI.

"Iva? Any luck?" asked Margo.

"Almost there," she said.

"Stop that!" demanded Nigel II, as the colonists started pounding on the wall.

"Are we doing something that's bothering you?" asked Margo. The pounding was getting loud. *Will the wall hold?*

"Thirty more seconds," said Iva.

"I see what you're doing, but even if you're successful, it doesn't matter," said the AI. "You'll never get out of that room. You'll starve, trapped."

The pounding suddenly stopped. Margo turned to regard the colonists. The silence felt more ominous than their pounding on the wall.

"Got it," crowed Iva with a final flourish of her wrist.

The chips in the colonists' brains simultaneously detonated. In unison, all their heads exploded, and the headless corpses collapsed atop one another on the floor. Margo's knees almost buckled at the sight. In her peripheral vision, she saw Iva grab the edges of the computer desk with both hands.

Iva and Margo stood in silence just staring at the gore, then turned away as if together deciding it was too unsightly to look upon for any longer than they had to

"I deleted him from the system," said Iva. "He doesn't have control anymore."

"Good work, Iva," Margo said. "But I still want to know

why an AI would do this? I thought there were safeguards against an AI assuming control and turning vigilante."

"There are." Iva said. "The AI didn't do this alone. Someone programmed Nigel II to do this."

Iva sighed and looked at Margo. "Can we go home now?"

Margo saw the dark bags under Iva's eyes. Likely she didn't look any better. The strain of the last few hours was taking its toll.

"Let's go home," Margo said.

They both walked over to the server room door and saw that a dozen or more headless corpses were blocking the door. Margo pulled out the screwdriver she'd used to jam the door closed.

"Oh shit," said Iva, seeing the problem. "The door opens out."

They both put their shoulders to the door and pushed with all their strength, but nothing happened.

"There's no other exit," Iva said in a shrill voice filled with panic. "The AI was right. We will die in here."

"Not if I can help it." Margo pulled out the cutting torch from her duffle bag now glad she hadn't ditched the heavy bag. "What's behind these walls?" she asked, gesturing at the three walls that weren't made of plexi-glass.

Iva grinned at Margo. "There," she said, pointing to the far wall. "Behind that wall is the change room for the main airlock."

Margo picked up the duffel bag and walked over to the far wall, Iva beside her. Tapping a screen on the wrist control pad of her atmo suit, Margo dropped the darkest visor on her helmet, the one used if they went out on Thesan's surface when both suns were overhead.

"Can you get a message to the Gary and Gan?" asked Margo, as she dumped the duffel bag on the ground in front of the wall. "Tell them we'll meet them at sickbay shortly. Hopefully we can find Yuko. Oh shit!" She turned to Iva. "Do you think the chip in Yuko's head exploded too?"

Iva looked pained at the thought. "Probably? I'll ask Gan to locate her biotracker."

Margo nodded. "And fingers crossed Ash can land soon. Get us the hell off this planet."

She started creating a hole in the wall that would be big enough for them to get through in their atmo suits. The torch cut easily into the metal. As she worked, she could hear Iva trying to call the others.

"Any luck?" asked Margo, pausing for a moment.

"No. They aren't answering," said Iva. "What if something has happened to them?"

"If they've stayed put, then they're fine." Margo was not going to let herself lose focus by worrying about Gary. *But please, Gary, please be okay!*

Repositioning the torch, she continued cutting, finishing soon after. She turned the torch off, set the tools aside, and then stood with Iva for a moment admiring the lopsided, woman-size outline she'd cut. "Ready?" she asked Iva. At Iva's nod, Margo, resting a hand on Iva's shoulder for balance, put her foot on the centre of the cut and pushed inwards. The loosened piece of wall clanged against the deck beyond. "Let's get out of here."

"That's the best idea I've heard all day," said Iva with a relieved smile.

After putting the cutting torch back in the duffle bag, Margo threw it through the hole, then ducked through. She looked around. The atmo suit change room was quiet and, more importantly, absent of zombie colonists.

She turned back to the hole in the wall. Iva hadn't followed her through. "Are you coming?"

There was no response. After a minute, Margo stuck her head through the hole. The other woman stood looking at the pile of decapitated corpses.

"Iva!"

Iva turned to Margo. "Sorry. I just wanted to say a silent poem for them." she said as she approached the hole in the wall. "It sounds silly, but I wanted to leave them with a sense of peace, you know?"

"They were dead before we arrived," said Margo knowing that wasn't true for everyone—at least one person had been alive.

"I know. It's silly of me."

"No, it's not. It's kind. And thoughtful. Good on you, Iva. Now, let's get back to the others and make a plan for getting off this hell hole."

Iva ducked through the hole as Margo backed up to make space.

Chapter Thirty-Nine

Leaving the main airlock change room, Margo, with the duffel bag over her shoulder, followed Iva out to the Loop. The way was clear in both directions. Iva turned right, the most direct route to sickbay, and strode off ahead. Eyes focused on the hall ahead, Margo stopped and blinked. *Something is wrong.*

A split second later, a kaleidoscope of black and red butterflies appeared around the corner ahead and barrelled down the Loop directly towards them. Her skin prickled and her heart rate sped up as she fought an urge to run. Twenty paces away, the flock of insects dipped low. Then their shape became an arachnid, all spindly black limbs with red, bulbous joints. It stopped in the corridor, blocking their way. Although its eight legs were stationary, its eyes focused on her while its fangs opened.

"Oh, shit!" Iva turned and ran back towards Margo. As she passed, she grabbed Margo's arm and pulled her along. "Margo! Let's go!"

She let Iva drag her in the opposite direction, looking over her shoulder—awkwardly in her atmo helmet—at the arachnid. If Iva was seeing it, *it is real!* As disturbing as it was to have an arachnid twice the size of a wolf blocking their path, it was a relief to know it wasn't a hallucination. As soon as she realized it was one of the colony's builder bots, its spider features morphed to the spider-shaped robotic reality—*that's what Iva saw.* Margo's mind snapped into place allowing her to focus on escape.

The builder bot walked toward them. Turning full around, she and Iva started to sprint. A few paces on they skidded to a stop as a second builder bot approached from the opposite direction.

"Hangar bay," said Margo. It was the only door between the two bots.

Margo punched the door release button and the door slid open. Iva darted inside. As Margo followed, she slapped the button to close the door. The two women turned and faced the door while backing away from it. Before it could close again, one bot launched itself towards them, the door whooshing closed just after it passed through. It landed on all eight legs, it's forward cameras trying to focus on both women at once.

Unslinging the duffle bag, Margo squatted down to set it on the floor. At her motion, the bot turned towards her and jumped. She pushed off from the bag, in attempt to launch herself out of the way, and nearly succeeded. Most of the bot passed by, but she got clipped by a hind leg and fell to the ground.

"Margo!" shouted Iva from the other side of the bot.

The bot held its ground between them. Swivelling the main sensor array on it's head between Margo and Iva as though it was trying to decide who to target first.

Keeping her distance, Margo moved deeper into the hangar nearer to where the two shuttles were parked. She considered calling Gan and Gary for help—but they would never arrive in time. How many builder bots does the colony have? She swallowed when couldn't come up with an exact number. *Five maybe? Six?* Gary and Gan were better off staying put where they were. She licked her lips. *Focus Murphy, you can defeat it.*

From it's post blocking the door, the builder bot continued scanning them. It took a step forward, before, pausing as though undertaking multiple calculations.

"Iva, back away," said Margo, noticing the other woman was closer to the bot than she was.

As though the bot had come to the same conclusion, it shifted to face Iva.

"What do we do?" asked Iva.

Margo glanced around—she had a clear path to the duffle bag. She sprinted towards it as soundlessly as possible, trying not to draw the bot's attention.

Seeing what Margo was doing, Iva waved her arms keeping the bot's attention. "Stay on me," she shouted.

At the bag, Margo knelt and unzipped it quickly, then pulled out the cutting torch. She pushed the ignition button and held the glowing white flame out in front of her. Taking a deep breath, she stood.

As Iva continued to wave her arms and back away, the bot kept it's focus on her. As she took her next step backwards, she tripped and fell. In a single motion, the bot leapt on top of her and impaled her through the left thigh with it's front leg, pinning her to the metal floor. Iva's screams filled the hangar, chilling the blood in Margo's veins.

Margo charged, aiming for the bot's body, the abdomen had it been an actual spider. Iva continued screaming from where she was pinned, but Margo kept her focus on the bot, pushing the flame in where she hoped the control board was. The metal robot twisted and lashed out with a back leg as though it was in pain, it caught her mid-chest and sent her sliding backwards across the room. The cutting torch dropped from her hand and spun away. She tumbled to a stop next to the tool bench.

Ignoring the pain from her fall, Margo grabbed the nearest thing on hand, a small sledge hammer, and leapt back to her feet. Iva had stopped screaming now, leaving only eery silence beyond Margo's overloading helmet fans. She charged the bot a second time.

With it's back legs, the bot made another swipe at her. This time she dodged to the right. As she moved, she raised the hammer and smashed the upper 'shoulder' joint of the leg pinning down Iva. The bottom part of the leg broke off—still stuck in Iva's leg—and the bot skittered away on seven legs, spewing blue hydraulic fluid as it went.

"Iva!" Margo knelt down at the injured woman's side, keeping one eye on the damaged bot as it stopped next just in front of the shuttle. Iva didn't answer.

She wanted to drag Iva away, move her behind the tool cart to protect her from more attacks, but the severed robotic leg held her in place. Just then, the door whooshed opened and the second bot charged through. The second bot stopped five metres from her.

Margo glanced back and forth between the two bots. "Crap!"

The glowing flame of the cutting torch caught her attention. It lay on the floor a few paces away. She scrambled towards it. Grabbing the torch, she turned back to Iva, but the bot at the door had already rushed forward and was standing over the woman as if claiming its prey.

"Did you really think I had myself all in one place," it said with the voice of the Nigel II AI. "You are a foolish one, butterfly girl." Both bots laughed.

Margo swallowed back her fear, knowing she needed to smother it to save her friend. But then Iva reached up and ripped open the access panel on the under side of it's abdomen on the bot above her. She grabbed a handful of wires and pulled.

The bot's mechanical laughter was cut off mid-laugh. As the bot begin to collapse towards her, Iva twisted out of the way, giving a grunt of pain as her movements yanked the robotic limb impaling her leg free from the floor. She dragged herself towards Margo, sobbing in pain, the limb sticking out of both sides of her thigh.

Margo looked around for the first bot, but it had hidden itself.

"Crap, did you see where it went?" asked Margo as she rushed to Iva's side and helped her to her feet. In her other hand, she kept the lit torch at the ready.

Margo clicked her helmet comms on. "Gary! Are you there? Iva's hurt." But Gary didn't respond.

"The bots don't have enough memory to run an AI," said Iva, gasping in pain. Through the faceplate of her helmet, her skin had taken on an ashen hue. "The AI must run off the colony's computers. Somehow it decentralized itself."

"If that's the case, what can we do?" Margo asked as she put Iva's arm over her shoulder and started moving them towards the door. She kept the torch lit, careful not to let the flame touch either of them, but feeling safer with it lit than turning it off.

"Not that way," gasped Iva. She pointed to the console beside the workbench. "I need to cut the power. I can do that from the terminal in here."

Margo shifted direction and helped Iva to the console. The computer tech slumped into the seat, her injured leg out in front of her. She activated the workstation and the four screens flashed to life. For a moment Margo felt optimistic, and moved to the side, searching the room for the other bot.

"Shit! It's just like a…" Iva's words were cut off as the seven-legged bot dropped onto her from the ceiling, ripping her away from the console and stabbing one of its legs through her chest.

"No!" Margo screamed, swiping at its back legs with the lit torch. The flame bit into the metal, releasing more hydraulic fluid. When the bot twisted towards her, she struck again with the flame. One of the bot's front legs clanged to the floor. She backed away as more fluid squirted out.

Balancing awkwardly on its remaining five legs, the bot lurched towards her, but it skidded on the spilled fluid, bowling into Margo's legs. She fell forward, shifting the torch so as not to cut into her atmo suit, and landing on the bot. She stabbed the flame at the robot's back.

It screeched and tried to buck her off, but its movements were weak and Margo managed to maintain her perch. She melted the metal and then the circuitry inside and, a moment later, the bot collapsed and lay still. She turned off the torch and scrambled off the bot. Standing, she panted as she eyed the bot making sure it was truly fried. After letting out a long exhale, she turned to Iva.

"Iva!" She ran over and knelt beside the slumped form of Iva.

The robot leg stuck up from Iva's thigh, and blood seeped through her suit from where she'd been impaled in the chest, leaving a dark patch amongst the blue spatters of hydraulic fluid. Margo looked down at Iva's face through the helmet's visor. Iva's pale eyes were open, staring at nothing. *I'm too late.*

Margo turned away, squeezing her eyes shut against the tears. There was nothing she could do for Iva now.

It took a few minutes until thoughts of Gary percolated through her mind. She could still do something for him and Gan. She opened a channel on her suit's comms.

"Gary, are you there?"

For a long moment there was no reply. She swallowed and tried to keep herself together.

"Gary, come in."

"I'm here," he said in a hushed tone. His voice sounded off. Wobbly.

"Are you okay?"

"I'm not hurt."

"Where are you?"

"In the terraforming airlock vestibule. But the airlock exterior door has malfunctioned."

"Is Gan with you?"

When Gary didn't immediately respond, Margo knew there

would be bad news. She closed her eyes, steeling herself to withstand what she knew Gary was about to say. "Yuko called us for help. We tried to save her, but couldn't. Gan's dead, Margo. I was too late. I couldn't save him."

Margo understood now why Gary's voice had sounded off. She closed her eyes and ducked her head for a moment, choking down a scream. Instead, she sucked in a breath and, with a last glance at Iva—and wishing she knew an appropriate poem to say as a farewell to her kind-hearted team-mate—she stood.

"Gary," she said, walking over to the console where Iva had been working. "It's not your fault, okay? You would have saved him if you could, but none of this is your fault."

"I know," said Gary. "It's just…"

Margo was about to reassure Gary again, but she was distracted by the warning that had come up on the screen, demanding confirmation: *Are you sure you want the entire power grid to be turned off?* Margo sucked in a breath. *All I need to do is tap the screen and the Nigel II AI would be no more!*

"Gary, I think I have a way to end this," she said in a tone that held a mixture of eager disbelief. She paused for a moment to think about the consequences and ripple effect of turning off the power grid. She was no computer expert, but she guessed it was a last-ditch fail safe if glitches to the system needed to be rebooted. She took a deep breath. "Iva and I figured out that the colony AI, a Nigel II, is the puppet master."

"The AI?" Gary's tinny voice registered his disbelief. "But shouldn't that be impossible? Look, Margo, where are you two? I'll make my way to wherever you are. We shouldn't have split up. Or are you and Iva close to where I—"

"Gary," Margo interrupted. "Iva is…" Her words trailed off as she glanced behind her at the still form of her crewmate. She didn't make it," Margo stated simply

"Oh, Margo! I'm sorry."

"Me too." It was only the two of them now, Margo thought,

and Gary sounded so far away—. Margo blinked back her tears. There would be time for that later.

"Where are you?" Gary asked.

"The hangar."

"Where are the colonists?"

"They're dead. Well, *more* dead. We saw their chips explode, all at the same time."

"Shit!"

"Yeah."

There was a brief pause before Gary's voice crackled once again over the helmet comms. "Margo, what did you mean, *you know a way to end this?*"

She turned and eyed the shuttle parked a dozen paces away. "I'll be turning the power off. Can you get to the spoke greenhouse that's the same as mine? It's next to terraforming, just a short walk…" She bit her lip, picturing him wandering around the colony alone.

"Yes. I can get there."

"Go through the greenhouse to the far end. There's an emergency airlock there, it's completely manual—cutting the power won't affect it." She squeezed her eyes shut, picturing the airlock. The AI would never have access to it—it wouldn't have been able to mess with it in any way. It was the safest way for him to go.

"I'm going to pull out one of the shuttles and pick you up there, then we're leaving this place."

"Okay," he said, sounding far away.

"Promise me you'll make it," she insisted. But all she could hear was static and her helmet fan.

"Gary? Gary!"

"I'm here," he said. "I'll see you soon."

Chapter Forty

"Ash come in," transmitted Margo for the seventh time. Like every other time there was no reply—it was clear she didn't know how Gan and Iva had reached the ship.

After confirming her atmo suit's integrity, she turned to another screen and brought up the hangar airlock controls and opened the exterior door. As the outside door lifted into the ceiling, it exposed the putrid yellow landscape beyond. Lightning forked down from the sky, electrifying the pools of slime on the surface. Turbulent winds were unleashed into the hangar, bringing in ash that would soon coat everything.

Turning back to the first screen, Margo hit the button to confirm that, yes, she wanted to shut down all power. The hangar lights clicked off. Illumination now came from her helmet light, which automatically clicked on, and the yellowish light from outside the hangar door.

Margo moved to kneel beside Iva's lifeless corpse. She still hadn't thought of a poem—she didn't know any poems—but she silently thanked Iva for her kindness, her willingness to always lend a helping hand—on Thesan and during this mission —and mostly, her unfailing courage. Tears welled up as she rose, but she swallowing them back, then headed for the shuttle's side door, stopping only to pick up her duffle bag.

Crouching down just outside the hull, she looked under the shuttle. There were no tie-downs—the shuttle was clear to take off. She stood and stepped into the shuttle, depositing her duffle bag on the floor next to the cargo netting beside the ramp. After closing and sealing the door, she headed forward.

Once sitting in the pilot's chair, Margo pressurized the ship, then ran through all the procedures from starting the shuttle, pretending Max was in the chair beside her. She'd completed her check-through by the time the air was ready to breathe, and she took off her helmet, and put it on the co-pilot's seat. Scratching her nose, she took a deep breath.

The hangar door gaped wide, letting the sickly yellow glow of Nak fill her vision. The sulphur rich atmosphere obscured the horizon, the reduced visibility would force her to rely on the shuttle's sensors—something she'd never done. Wind was another factor she'd never dealt with. She bit her lip.

"Keep it together, Murphy," she said aloud as she focused on the scene before her. "You can do this."

Swallowing back her fear, she took hold of the controls, then released them and took a moment to adjust her seat; she'd never pulled a shuttle out of the confined space of a hangar before. *How did Max do this so effortlessly?* Lifting the shuttle's skids only a few centimetres off the ground, she guided the craft forward at a snail's pace.

Margo heard a single banging sound of something colliding with the shuttle, on the starboard side belly of the shuttle. Had the storm caused something to shift in the hangar bay that slammed into the shuttle? "Crap!"

Her heart accelerated as she tried to maneuver the shuttle forward. Something was dragging at the starboard side. She looked down at the controls. *Should I gun the throttle? Or will that make things worse?* She needed the shuttle to be space worthy or it was pointless even making the attempt to exit the hangar.

She didn't want to go outside again, but she had no choice. At least the danger from the puppet master was gone. With the power off, Nigel II was no longer a threat. Margo put on her helmet and headed to the aft section, then hit the button to start the air cycling.

For a moment she pondered pulling out her pistol out of her side pocket. But what would be out there for her to shoot? Instead, she retrieved the large wrench from her duffel bag. She didn't think she needed a weapon, but she wasn't taking any chances. When the green light flashed, she opened the door, exiting the shuttle on the port side.

Stepping back onto the hangar floor, she looked around. The brightness from outside cast long shadows in the dark interior, and she was thankful for the beam of light shining from her helmet. Getting down on her hands and knees and gripping the wrench in her right hand, she lowered herself onto her belly, then rolled onto her side to look under the shuttle. Her helmet light revealed nothing amiss no matter where she looked

As she rolled away, she thought she saw motion in her peripheral vision. Her heart rate accelerated as she turned this way and that, searching for what she might have seen. She rolled out from underneath and got to her feet.

It's just your mind playing tricks on you again, she told herself as she began inspecting the rest of the craft's exterior.

Once she was all the way around, she swung the beam of her helmet light back and forth to see if anything was in the shadows. Everything looked normal. Except... she shone the light on the ground. A steel-wire tie-down extended from a hard point on the hangar floor and disappeared beneath the shuttle.

She walked over and shone her light along the wire. *Did I miss this? I thought I checked.* She knelt down and unclipped the tie-down, then stood and shone her helmet light in a slow arc into the depths of the hangar one more time before retracing her steps and boarding the shuttle.

Leaving her helmet on this time, she moved the controls to

ease the shuttle out of the hanger. It wasn't graceful, but she managed it. Once hovering in the air outside, the blocky craft shimmied in the wind.

Struggling to maintain control of the shuttle in the blasting storm, Margo gained a metre of altitude, then flew to the long end of the spoke greenhouse where the airlock was located. With a couple of bounces, she set the shuttle down as close to the door as she could. After landing, she powered down.

A gust of wind briefly cleared the sky. Helios was about to slip out of view, but it was too misty to see Nak's actual horizon. Unlike the perpetual light of Thesan, this planet would experience full darkness—the cloud cover would prevent even starlight from getting through.

"Gary I'm here," she transmitted. There was no response. "Gary where are you?"

Margo tried to make out details within the greenhouse, but the blowing ash made it difficult. He was supposed to meet her at the door. Where was he? The knot in her gut twisted as she ran through scenarios. *What if there were more builder bots? What if…*

"Get a grip, Murphy," she said as she stood and headed aft. "Just go get him."

———

As soon as she stepped out the side door of the shuttle, the wind nearly knocked her to her knees. It took all her weight to force the door closed long enough to latch it.

As she staggered forward, it felt like wading through deep water. She was breathing heavily by the time she made it to the greenhouse's airlock. It it was like hers—a system independent from the colony. Even if Nigel II managed to re-power himself, he couldn't touch this airlock as it wasn't linked to any colony computers.

Once inside, she cycled the atmosphere. When the light by

the inner door flashed green, she stepped inside, looking this way and that for Gary.

"Gary, I'm at the airlock. Where are you?" she transmitted. Again there was no reply.

As she hurried past the slime-covered plants, she noticed the vines moving, twisting and probing. Like alien tentacles, they reached towards her. Ignoring what she knew was the start of a hallucination, she turned her gaze away and walked towards the colony, stepping carefully around the overgrown vines on the floor so as not to trip and once again trying and failing to raise Gary on the comms.

She stopped, her heart in her throat, when a life-like Nigel West appeared in front of her.

"I killed him," Nigel said in a tone as benign as if he were giving a weather report. "My builder bot skewered him just like Iva."

I'm too late! Gary is dead!

Margo ignored the hammering of her heart and sucked in a deep breath, telling herself that this Nigel was just a hallucination. *This is no AI controlling the colony.*

"Get out of my way, you're just my mind playing tricks on me," she said, charging ahead. Nigel fell into step beside her.

"You can't get rid of me."

"Shut up and go away." Margo tried to focus on the ground ahead of her. *Where is Gary?*

"Butterfly girl, it's my pleasure to tell you that, when we fought back on my station, you drew me into your mind. Remember your construct—an uninspired version of your Earth-based greenhouse."

Margo remembered. It had seemed like a good idea at the time, bring him into her environment so she could control it. *Did I really bring him into my mind?*

"That day, part of me got left behind," he said. "Since then, I've been making myself at home. Creating butterflies for you has been deliciously fun—putting the bugs into the bug girl."

The sound of Nigel's laughter sickened her, but then Margo stopped as she absorbed the impact of his words. She looked at him in horror. *Am I really carrying around a piece of this vile man?* She shook her head. *It's not impossible—but he could be lying to me.*

"Surprise," he said, with a boyish grin, shaking his spread hands at his side. *Damn those jazz hands.* "You got stuck with a piece of me."

Margo's surroundings morphed into a luxuriously minimal office. Three walls were bare and pristinely white, while floor-to-ceiling windows extended along the fourth wall. Through the window she could see Earth. The scene had to be Maximillian Station, yet it was a place and a perspective Margo had never seen.

"I'm ready to take control of you now."

"This isn't real," stated Margo in a loud voice. She expected, by speaking, she could make the hallucination evaporate, but it didn't. Instead, she found herself walking over to the floor-to-ceiling windows. Below, the rotation of Earth revealed the browns of Africa.

Margo looked over her shoulder, and saw Nigel shrug as he sauntered over to a built-in bar behind his over-size desk. He took out two glasses and poured amber liquid in each. He walked up beside Margo and handed a glass to her. She took it, lifting an eyebrow, before raising the glass to sniff its contents—hints of smoke tickled her nose.

"It's real enough," he said.

Swirling the viscous liquid, she watched its legs form on the side of the glass. The drink wasn't real. She took a sip. It tasted real. It was a well-aged scotch and felt smooth going down. For a figment of her imagination, the drink was superb.

"This is a trap," said Julien.

Margo turned and saw that the boy had appeared at her other side. He looked up at her wearing his usual prismed goggles. His sudden appearance was weird, but so was everything else. She took another sip of the scotch.

"You need to destroy this fragment of Nigel," said Julien.

"How?" she asked the boy.

"I don't know." Julien shrugged. "But if you don't, we'll never be safe."

Margo turned back to look at Nigel. He was regarding her, leaning against the edge of his desk as though this was a friendly, every day visit. As soon as she looked at him, he chugged what remained of his scotch. Nigel seemed unaware of Julien's presence.

Gulping down what remained of her drink, she pondered permutations of what she was experiencing. *Is Julien also a figment of my imagination? Or a figment of a figment?* She shook her head.

"No," said Julien. "They created me to be a conduit for other consciousnesses—being able to project myself is a side effect."

Margo looked back at Julien. The boy shrugged.

"Margo, my dear," said Nigel. Margo jumped, Nigel was beside her again. Both their empty glasses were gone.

"Why did you kill all those colonists?" she demanded.

"That wasn't me. The AI did that," he said. "Didn't you know the Nigel II AIs are flakey? Put an idea into its code and voila. Mayhem." Nigel accented his words with those damn jazz hands again.

"So you admit you're responsible for what happened here."

Nigel nodded towards the view. "Not here," he said, shrugging.

Margo slammed her right fist into his face.

Staggering back, he put both hands over his bloody nose. His expression stunned.

What was he expecting me to do? She flexed her fist in anticipation of hitting him again.

"We'll be reporting to the Colonizing Council what went on in these colonies," she said, advancing on him.

Nigel took a few steps back as he laughed, the harsh sound echoing off the bare office walls.

"Who do you think funds the Colonizing Council?" he challenged. "Complaining to them won't make a difference. Only if you..." His face suddenly went blank.

"Only if I what?" Margo advanced on him, lifting her fist as if ready to swing again.

Strangely, her action evoked fear in his eyes. *If his existence truly is a part of my mind, perhaps I have a good measure of power over him, and over how this unfolds.*

"Nothing," he said, taking another step back from her and bumping into the front of his desk.

"What are you not telling me?" said Margo, backing him into his desk and going eye-to eye with him. "I'm guessing it takes just a thought on my part to destroy you."

"No! Wait," he exclaimed, his voice quivering. Beads of sweat were forming across his unlined forehead. "I can tell you things."

"Like what?" She took a pace back and crossed her arms over her chest. She noticed Julien standing at her side again, looking towards Nigel

"The wormhole. I can tell you how to control the wormhole," he offered.

"Okay, so tell me."

"There's a series of harmonics, like an alien version of morse code. We found them engraved into the side of an alien artifact."

"That sounds like a load of horse shit," said Margo. "The wormhole is natural."

"No, that's just what we led the public to believe."

Chapter Forty-One

Feeling a sense of deja vu, Gary rushed through the colony's entomology lab. He looked out the windows towards the spoke greenhouse beyond. The plants, which in Margo's space would've been green, were yellow-hued—even he could tell it was a garden gone wrong. He went through the open airlock—there was no need to ever close this now that the spoke greenhouse had been built—and into the greenhouse. The roiling, stormy sky above combined with the slime-covered plants made him glad his helmet protected him from the scents and the elements.

A pair of lights beyond the dome caught his attention. Letting out a sigh of relief, he realized it was the shuttle. He'd be with Margo soon, then they'd get off this world. He stopped and watched as the small spacecraft flew out of the hangar.

A knot formed in his gut as he remembered Margo's forte wasn't flying. *I'd rather take my chances and fly with her than stay a minute longer than necessary on this hellhole.*

His thoughts went back to Gan then, and how the AI had tricked him into thinking Margo had gone outside. *Is this another trick?* He felt the muscles in his neck and shoulders tense. *Did I really speak with her, or was it the AI?*

He watched as the shuttle swung towards the greenhouse, it's motions jerky. One side dipped as it landed, and the landing was so hard, one skid got buried into the ash-covered surface. As the shuttle levelled out and settled onto the ground, ash plumed out.

Would an AI fly so poorly?

The flight pattern could only be indicative of a rookie pilot —Margo had to be at the controls. He let out a ragged exhale of relief and he felt his shoulders relax. *Soon this horrid place will be behind us.*

He moved forward in a zig-zag pattern, stepping over and around the jumble of rotten foliage sprawled across the ground. Picking his path carefully, he kept moving towards the end of the greenhouse. The plants became too thick to walk around, giving him no choice but to step on them.

As soon as the airlock at the end activated, he smiled. Margo was here. Speeding up his pace, he kept his eyes glued on the airlock door.

His foot slipped, and he landed on his back with memories of old comedy routines where someone slipped on a banana peel for laughs. *Nothing about my circumstance is funny!* But too much had gone wrong, he needed a release. He laughed at his ridiculous predicament.

When he rolled to his side, he saw Margo at the far end of the greenhouse.

———

"So you're saying there's an alien artifact," said Margo, sharing a disbelieving look with Julien. The boy was nodding solemnly up at her. Margo assumed her hallucination of Julien was agreeing with Nigel. *That kid was always strange.*

"The Vikings found it in the tenth century." Nigel's eyes

darted around as though he were looking for an escape—or attempting to delay her.

"In the Middle Ages, it was brought to Paris and hidden in a basement, guarded by a secret society. In the late 1800s, Professor Plum and my namesake Nigel West found it and brought it to London."

Margo realized she'd heard a version of this same story before from a different source—Peggy Plum, the wife of the late Professor Plum.

"My ancestor dedicated his life to studying this priceless and powerful artifact."

That part of Nigel's account matched what Peggy Plum had told her. "What makes you think it's an alien artifact?" asked Margo. While she kept Nigel talking, she tried to figure out what to do, how to exit herself—permanently—from these shared hallucinations with Nigel.

"Oh, it's alien alright. It has properties that..." Nigel's voice trailed off for a moment. "Properties that can't be explained. They need to be demonstrated. And anyone in the artifact's actual presence is left with no doubt it's an alien thing."

"So, you want me to just take your word for all this?" Margo asked, still stalling, her mind whirling in the background. *How to stop this? How to get out?*

Nigel gave her a telling look. "Butterfly girl, you know when I speak the truth. We're practically one, aren't we?"

Margo grimaced at the thought, sharing a horrified look with the boy beside her. "Why wasn't it made public?"

"Too dangerous," he said. "It would've destabilized the world."

Margo scoffed. "It's your actions that are destabilizing the world."

"Hardly. Everything I do is to create a new and improved version of the future. We can do that together, butterfly girl."

Margo shook her head. "Your story is all bullshit."

"It's true, Margo," Julien said in a whisper even though it didn't appear that Nigel could see or hear him.

Margo looked down at the boy.

"I have the cube."

"You have it? On Thesan?" asked Margo raising an eyebrow.

The boy gave her a solemn nod. Margo wished she could see his full expression, but his prismed goggles hid his eyes.

Margo ran her hands down the pants of her atmo suit, stopping when she felt the outline of the gun in her pocket. This was all a complex hallucination. *It's not real. Focus Murphy.* She needed to find Gary and get off this hellhole.

Nigel smiled and began to approach her. She held her ground. *I'll punch him again*, she thought.

Before Margo could move, Nigel landed a foot in her gut. She doubled over, felt the air rush out of her lungs, and fell to her knees.

———

An overwhelming wave of relief swept over Gary as he saw Margo step into the greenhouse. He lifted an arm and spoke her name over his helmet's comms.

She didn't answer.

"Margo!" he called again, flicking the comms switch on and off, but she still didn't appear to hear or see him.

A knot formed in his gut. She might not be able to see him but she most certainly should be able to hear him. *What's wrong?* He got to his feet and walked towards her stepping carefully on the slippery plants.

She was walking towards him, but it was clear she didn't see him. There didn't appear to be anything misting her visor, as she was stepping over any plants that were in her path.

When she suddenly stopped, Gary looked around. Wondering what she'd seen, but there was nothing and no one in the greenhouse but the two of them. Fear clawed at his gut. *Something weird is going on.* He moved towards her as fast as he could.

As he got closer, he saw her suit was stained with bluish translucent patches—what had caused that?—and a dark red that he knew could only be blood. *Is she okay?* But, he reasoned to himself, if it was on the outside of her atmo suit, it wasn't her blood. *Iva's.* He hadn't had time to ask how Iva had died, but it hadn't been like Gan, who hadn't shed a drop of blood, that much was evident.

Gary continued to walk towards her, but Margo remained oblivious to his presence. When he came within a few feet of her and could finally see her face behind the glass of her visor, he saw that she was looking over his right shoulder and appeared to be talking to someone. He looked around them again, but there was only the two of them present.

For a split second in his peripheral vision, he thought he saw something move behind the shuttle, but dismissed it as the storm outside gusted ash from the ground.

He turned his attention back to Margo, and then leapt towards her when he saw her fall to her knees.

———

Nigel stood over Margo, laughing. "Gotcha good," he said with jazz hands.

Margo rolled to her side and pushed herself back to her feet. Scanning Nigel's office, she realized Julien had vanished. Turning, she faced Nigel. "You're not actually hurting me you know. My body is fine. Your prank has accomplished nothing."

When Nigel smirked, she took a step forward to punch him again, but that hadn't accomplished anything either. She paused. Something important was teasing her at the edge of her memory.

"Have you chickened out?" Nigel mocked.

"Yes." From the side pocket of her suit she pulled out the pistol and pointed it at him. Her gloved finger could just fit onto the trigger. She released the safety and aimed at the centre of his forehead. Her arm was steady. "Your time is done."

Nigel took a step forward, still grinning. "Go ahead. Shoot me," he said. Then, like a child of three, he stuck out his tongue at her.

Anger welled up within Margo. She wanted this bastard dead.

She started to squeeze the trigger.

———

A few paces away from her now, Gary stopped in his tracks. Margo had pulled out the gun. She raised it up, aiming at his head.

"Margo?" he said, his mouth dry.

Chapter Forty-Two

Nigel laughed, a cackling sound that Margo felt right down to her bones.

This isn't real! Nothing I'm seeing is real. Margo forced herself to picture the spoke greenhouse she'd entered with its tentacle like plants rotting on the floor. The office on Maximillian Station melted away. She could see her real surroundings once more.

Gary stood in front of her—right where Nigel had been. She gasped and dropped the gun. *Nigel almost tricked me into shooting Gary!*

"Margo?" Gary asked again.

"Crap!" She sank onto her knees into the muck of rotting plants, then looked into Gary's face as he knelt beside her. "I almost shot you."

"But you didn't," Gary responded in his doctor's voice, resting a concerned hand on her shoulder. "What happened, Margo? What did you think you saw?"

How can he sound so calm when a minute ago I had a pistol aimed at his head? She swallowed and looked at him. "Nothing. I...I was confused," she stammered, wishing she'd told him the truth earlier. This certainly wasn't the time. "Crap," she said again, sitting back on her heels. She needed a moment before she could look Gary in the eye.

"Come on. Let's get off this world," said Gary helping her to her feet.

The two of them headed to the end of the greenhouse and into the emergency airlock, the abandoned pistol left behind on a bed of rotting plants.

———

In the pilot seat of the shuttle, Margo flicked the switch on the control panel to cycle the air. While the ventilation system filtered the air so it was fit to breathe, she began a quick run-through of the take-off procedures. A moment later when the air was breathable, she took off her helmet. The lingering scent of sulphur remained, but the air was fine. She looked back as Gary entered the cockpit.

Seeing her helmet off, he removed his helmet and tossed it aside, then came over and kissed her. "I'm so glad you're okay," he said, dropping to his knees beside her seat and wrapping his arms around her.

She leaned into him, resting her forehead on his shoulder, avoiding the hard edges of the neck ring. She felt her body trembling with the shock of almost having killed him. "I almost shot you," she said, her voice on the verge of a wail.

"It's okay, we're both okay now," said Gary, pulling her in tighter.

"No, it's not okay." She pulled back and looked him in the eye. Her words came out in a rush. "I thought you were someone else. I should've told you long ago. Ever since I projected my consciousness, there's been side effects. I…"

Her words trailed off as she struggled with how she could explain without sounding crazy. *But then, maybe I am crazy.*

"Margo," said Gary. Cupping her chin in his hand, he turned her face back towards him. "Tell me," he said in a gentle tone. "What's been happening?"

Taking a deep breath, Margo looked down for a moment. *Where to start?* She exhaled, then met Gary's gaze. "I see things. At first, it was just butterflies in my peripheral vision." Her hand lifted and she made a brief, fluttering motion. "Then it escalated into nightmares. They felt so real though, as if I was consciousness projecting in the dream. Then I started getting waking hallucinations." She swallowed. "Just now? Back in the greenhouse? I was talking to Nigel West. Actually, I was in his office on Maximillian Station looking at Earth. Africa," she added. *As if that mattered!*

Margo saw Gary close his eyes briefly. When he opened them and met her gaze, she saw anger, but she also saw warmth and understanding and love.

"I wish you'd told me sooner," he said.

Margo nodded. "Me too. But Gary, this time I learned something new."

"What do you mean?"

"When I fought Nigel before, I pulled him into my illusion. At the time I didn't realize I was basically inviting him into my mind." She stopped and took a deep breath. "Just now? He told me a piece of him had been left behind. Is that even possible? Medically, I mean?"

Gary's expression had been serious but now it became grave. "I don't know, Margo. It's not my field of expertise. Paul Dogan would know. Have you told him about these hallucinations?"

Margo shook her head. At Gary's look, she said. "I know I should have. I'm regretting that now."

"When we get to the *Staffelwalze*, we'll get Paul on the comms, I'm sure he'll have suggestions."

"You think he'll be able to stop the hallucinations? I've seen so many butterflies that aren't actually real, that I've been hesitant to hatch out the next generation of morpho butterflies on Thesan."

"Is that why? I'd wondered." Gary pulled back. "Margo, I'm sure Paul can help."

"Nigel also claimed that the wormhole wasn't entirely natural. That there is an alien artifact with a code written on it that can control it," said Margo. She looked unseeingly out the windshield at the storm. "Weirdly, Julien was there." She turned to Gary and pulled a face. "And then that bastard Nigel tricked me into pointing the gun at you, and I almost pulled the trigger!"

"But you didn't," said Gary in an insistent reassuring tone, hugging her again before shifting into a more comfortable seat in the co-pilot's chair. "Margo, there's something I haven't told you too, but it was because it wasn't my secret to share."

"What?"

"You're experiencing more than just the hallucinatory side effects of consciousness projection."

"What do you mean?"

"Julien has an alien artifact. He showed me once. There are symbols all over it," he said.

Margo frowned. "Are you thinking what Julien has is the alien artifact Nigel is talking about? And that's why Julien was in my hallucination?"

"Yes."

Margo shook her head. "But that doesn't make sense. Nigel made it sound like this artifact was in London, and it was hidden, maybe even guarded."

Gary nodded. "It was hidden on Maximillian Station. Julien's dad stole it from there."

Margo still looked disbelieving. "Just because Julien showed you a strange looking object doesn't mean it's the alien artifact—"

"It is," Gary interrupted. "I've seen it. And if you saw it, you would know. It's alien. And it's powerful. And scary," he added.

"I didn't know," said Margo, feeling cold. She remembered the cube Peggy Plum had shown her. *Are they all the same artifact? And it's on Thesan?* "We'll never be safe from The Conglomerate if the real Nigel knows we have it."

"We have to assume he knows and be on guard for that," said Gary, reaching out and squeezing her hand.

A nearby flash of lightening illuminated the shuttle's interior. Gary let her go to look outside.

"Can we get out of here?" he asked.

"Max kicked me out of his shuttle flight training," said Margo. "He didn't know it, but it was because of my hallucinations. Seeing things that aren't there do not make for a skilled shuttle pilot."

"I wish I could help but I've never touched a shuttle's controls in my life," said Gary, as he looked at the unfamiliar dashboard. "But I have full faith in you, Margo," he added with a warm smile in her direction. "You can get us to the *Staffelwalze.*"

Margo nodded. It might not be a smooth ride, but she knew what to do. She activated the comms to call Ash just as a fork of lightening hit the ground outside the shuttle.

"Ash come in," said Margo.

A moment later there was a reassuring crackle over the radio. "Ash here."

"We're leaving the planet surface in one of their shuttles," said Margo. "I'll call you when we're in orbit."

"Roger that. See you soon," said Ash and the line squelched off.

"I think we should put our helmets back on just in case," Margo said, before putting hers over her head and latching it on. Gary did the same.

She lifted the shuttle off the ground and circled around the colony. It looked pristine from the air, like it was ready to be lived in. But Margo knew better. No colony would thrive here. The winds had died down below the clouds, and the shuttle was easy to control. Above she could see the bottom surface of the pea soup cloud.

The undulating surface of the cloud appeared like it was a solid mass—much like the boundary between a liquid and a gas. Every few moments, sheet lightning lit up sections within.

Both hands on the controls, Margo looked over at Gary. Beneath the helmet, his face looked resigned as he stared out the windshield. Swallowing back her fear, Margo pulled the controls towards herself. The shuttle lurched higher and into the clouds.

As soon as they entered the swirling cloud layer, the shuttle began to jerk and twist, at the mercy of the turbulence. Margo tried to keep their path upwards steady, but it took all her strength. Visibility was limited, and only briefly increased with the regular flashes of lightning. The wind tossed the shuttle around as they continued to ascend. Thankfully, and despite her anxiety, no hallucinations materialized.

In the next moment, they emerged above the clouds. They'd escaped the clutches of gravity and everything was suddenly still and tranquil. A multitude of stars hovered in the vast canopy above them. It was beautiful.

A voice suddenly crackled over the comms. "Unidentified shuttle, come in," said Ash.

"We made it," said Gary, turning to Margo with a grin.

"Yeah." Margo didn't share that she wouldn't feel like they made it until she safely landed the shuttle.

She hit the transmission button. "Ash, it's Margo. We made it." Margo's thoughts drifted to Iago, Yuko, Iva and Gan as a lump formed in her throat. She would tell Ash face-to-face about their terrible losses. Margo knew she was letting Ash assume by "we" she meant six crew members. She was sorry for that, but Ash would understand, once everything was explained to her.

"I'm 200 kilometres away. Setting a course to intercept," said Ash. "Just maintain your course."

"Roger that."

"You'll have to abandon the shuttle," Ash added. "The *Staffelwalze* isn't big enough to bring it with us."

"Fine by me," Margo responded. *I don't want to bring anything back from that cursed planet.*

Margo activated the autopilot and released the controls. She reached out a gloved hand to Gary and clasped her hand in his.

Chapter Forty-Three

With their atmo suits still sealed, Margo and Gary stood at the window of the shuttle's side door watching as the *Staffelwalze's* umbilical extended towards them. The tentacle-like corridor no longer seemed fragile and flimsy, but was instead a friendly, reliable hand coming their way. She smiled when the translucent fabric tube clamped onto the exterior of the shuttle with a faint thud.

Margo found herself holding her breath as she waited for the go head to open the shuttle's door. She exhaled, slowly, then inhaled again. As usual, it calmed her.

"The shuttle is secure. You can cross over now," announced Ash, sounding as calm as she always did.

Gary turned and put a hand on Margo's shoulder. "We're safe. We're finally safe."

Margo let her smile grow into a happy grin. Exhausted wouldn't come close to describing the fatigue she felt, yet her heart raced. She half expected one more damn thing to go wrong. *That's what you get for going uninvited to an inhospitable planet.*

"We're heading over now," transmitted Margo.

"Coffee's on. See you all soon," said Ash.

Gary opened the shuttle door, exposing the long hall to the ship. The door of the *Staffelwalze* seemed to beckon to them. All that was between it and them was a short length of zero gravity. *Shower*, Margo thought, listing to herself the order in which she would fill the next twelve hours. *Coffee. Amanda's mulligatawny soup. Sleep.*

Margo gestured for Gary to go first. He pulled himself into the tube, moving awkwardly in the zero gravity. As he moved, his feet kept drifting into the walls of the tube, making his progress slow. An overwhelming urge to giggle swept over her— her ridiculous response was due to her utter and sheer exhaustion.

She gave a last glance behind her. In the zero gravity of the shuttle, the trusty duffel bag she'd taken from engineering was floating towards the cockpit. Had they planned to return to the shuttle, she would have gone back and tied it down, but it no longer mattered. This abandoned shuttle was doomed to a decaying orbit around Nak.

As soon as Gary was a few body-lengths ahead of her, Margo grabbed onto the rungs on the ceiling and launched herself into the tube. Hand-over-hand, she propelled herself along, keeping well back of Gary's flailing feet.

About halfway through the tube, Margo felt her pent up tension start to drain away. *We're safe. We're heading home.* She looked at Gary's back in front of her and smiled. *Soon the two of us can start a life together...*

Just as she was about to release her left hand from gripping one of the rungs, the tube floor suddenly ripped, exposing a slice of the cloud-covered planet below. For a second, Margo didn't understand what had happened, but the wave of vertigo almost caused her to lose her grip

"Hold on, Gary!" she instinctively shouted.

"What's going on?" Ash demanded.

Grabbing the rung she'd been holding with both hands, Margo watched in horror as the rip got longer, pulled wider apart. A wave of panic twisted in her gut as the air within the tube and shuttle rushed out the hole. She wrapped an arm around the rung, wedging her shoulder in place as the escaping atmosphere tried to pull her through the hole and into space. "Gary! Hold on! Just a moment longer!"

"Holding," Gary said. His voice sounded like he spoke through clenched teeth.

She kept her eyes trained on his flailing body. She couldn't see his hands. *Please, Gary, please hold on!*

"Don't let go," she urged. Just when she thought her strength would give out, the pulling sensation stopped. The air in the tube voided.

She relaxed and loosened her grip. On the other side of the hole, she saw Gary do the same.

"We're okay," she transmitted.

"What the hell happened?" asked Ash. "The tube shouldn't have failed."

Turning to look behind her, Margo assumed the failure had been how the tube connected to the shuttle. But as soon as she saw what was pulling itself through the rent in the bottom of the tube, she froze, unable to breathe. It was one of the builder bots —the one she'd severed two legs from.

"What the…" Gary's words trailed away.

Margo backed up as fast as she could, towards the shuttle, then saw that Gary was about to come to her aid.

"Gary! Get into the *Staffelwalze*," she ordered, still retreating towards the shuttle. "Ash, make him go inside."

With one of its knife-like forward limbs, the builder bot sliced the umbilical in half and then crawled on its five legs into Margo's side of the tube. Gary, Margo saw, was close to the *Staffelwalze's* door in his half of the tube. She was in the other half with the shuttle behind her and the Nigel II-possessed arachnid in front of her.

Margo's pulse spiked and she lunged to get away from the advancing bot, but then lost her grip on the rungs. Her panicked momentum smashed her into the side of the tube. She flailed her hands, finally grabbing a rung, preventing her from bouncing off the surface into the void of space.

Smothering her fear, she pulled herself towards the shuttle as fast as she could. She flung herself through the open door of the shuttle, grabbing the handle on the inside of the door and, bracing herself by wedging her foot under some gear, slammed the door shut in the arachnid's mechanical face. When the door sealed, the shuttle automatically began pumping in new air.

"Margo, are you okay?" transmitted Gary. He and Ash had been calling to her the whole time, but she'd tuned them out..

"I've got Gary inside the *Staffelwalze*. We'll pull off to 50 metres," said Ash. "Gary just told me about the others." There was a pause, and then Ash added. "Keep the comms lines open Margo. We're not losing you."

The shuttle wasn't large, and from where she was at the side door Margo could see through the cockpit window. She saw the *Staffelwalze* moving away and it filled her with dread. *Now what?*

Scratching at the door drew her attention—the builder bot was trying to get in. Pushing herself away from the door, she backed into the cockpit, only stopping when the pilot's seat dug into her back. She glanced down at the controls.

"Shit!" There were no locks on either the door or the ramp of this model of shuttle. Then she saw the duffel bag floating behind the co-pilot's seat. She scrambled to it, and retrieved the torch. It wouldn't last long on its internal storage of oxygen; when it came time to use it, she'd have to act fast.

Facing forward, she eyed the side door, her muscles coiled like springs while her heart felt like it would pound out of her chest.

A moment later, the door opened. The atmosphere rushed out once more and Margo was suddenly floating again. The whoosh of air would have blasted the bot, but the shrewd arachnid had stayed to the side of the open door. As soon as the air was gone, the bot pulled itself inside. It was much better adapted to fighting in a zero gravity environment than she would ever be.

"You didn't think you'd get away that easy," the bot said as it morphed into Nigel.

Margo saw Nigel standing on the shuttle's deck as though there was gravity holding him down. She knew it was the bot, but all she saw was Nigel. And a hallucination didn't have to obey the laws of physics.

"I'm so disappointed you didn't fall for my rouse," Nigel said as he advanced on her. He, or rather the bot, was only a few paces away now. "I loved the look on your face when you realized you were pointing your gun at your unlikely husband." He stuck out his bottom lip in a mock sad face. "I almost cried."

"Did I tell you, with the alien artifact one can see possible futures." He paused as though waiting for Margo to answer. She said nothing as she waited for him to get close enough so she could use the torch. "I saw how you will mess up with my future plans. I can end that potential future now." Nigel started to laugh. "How could you ever be powerful enough to stop me?"

"If you don't think I could ever stop you, why are you trying so hard to mess *with me*?" Margo taunted.

Nigel frowned in anger. "Time for you to die, butterfly girl," he spat, waving his extended hands at his waist.

"I hate jazz hands," countered Margo as she swung the cutting torch from behind her back, clicking the starter. A hot flame whooshed out as she launched herself at Nigel. He retreated, and they both paused, facing each other in the cargo area.

Nigel was now superimposed on the back of the builder bot arachnid. Margo couldn't delay her attack, or the torch would no longer serve as a weapon. She pushed off the ceiling, arcing the flame at the arachnid. The image of Nigel vanished, leaving her alone with the bot.

It dodged, then lifted a front leg and swatted her aside.

Margo hit the side of the shuttle, barely keeping a grip on the lit torch.

Then the bot was practically on top of her, and she waved the flame, swiping at the left front leg. The leg severed and drifted away, the hydraulic fluid floating out in pretty bubbles of blue.

On the down sweep of her arcing attack, she aimed the torch down into the bot's front sensors. It writhed as though it felt pain and retreated, drifting without control, its legs clawing crablike at the air.

Margo turned and hit the button by the side door to pressurize the shuttle.

The bot swiped at her again, this time throwing her aft onto the closed ramp. When she landed, she lost her grip on the torch, and it flickered out, empty of fuel. Pulling herself over to the ramp controls, she wrapped an arm and leg into the cargo netting there. Panting heavily, she tried to focus on her next steps.

In her view, the bot morphed into Nigel again. She realized the AI Nigel and her hallucinated Nigel were two separate things—unable to work together. Two separate problems, and in that moment she only needed to deal with one. The robot needed to go.

Ignoring Nigel's laughs, she glanced around for a solution. She spotted the answer—the emergency release for the ramp. It was a big red button, just to the side of the cargo netting. It would be a stretch, but she could reach it.

With his jazz hands out, Nigel advanced, superimposed over the AI controlled builder-bot. "Bye, bye butterfly girl," he said, then added, "I'm going to miss you, you know."

Just before he reached her, Margo slammed her fist into the red button. The ramp's explosive bolts fired. The ramp fell way from the shuttle and the bot, caught off guard, was blown out into space. She clung to the cargo netting, hoping it would hold until the shuttle's atmosphere was gone.

Less than a minute later, Margo could move again. She unwrapped herself from the netting and looked out at where the ramp had been.

"Good riddance," she said, before taking a deep breath. The she turned on her comms. "Ash? Gary? It's over."

"Margo! Are you okay?" Gary demanded.

"I'm okay."

"And the builder bot?" asked Ash.

"Yeah, it's gone" said Margo, still looking out where it had gone. She thought she saw a black spec out there against the yellow atmosphere of the pond scum planet. The builder bot's orbit would decay, eventually it would fall through the atmosphere and burn up. It was no longer a threat to anyone.

"We're coming back in to get you," said Ash. "I'll bring the *Staffelwalze* in as close as I can. Margo, you're going to have to jump."

"After everything else we've been through? A simple jump is no problem," said Margo.

Chapter Forty-Four

After taking a ridiculously long shower, Margo wiped the condensation off the mirror in her cabin and studied her reflection. The dark bags under her eyes confirmed her exhaustion.

Am I really safe? Will the piece of Nigel in my head try to trick me again?

Taking a deep breath, she spoke aloud as if scolding herself. "You're as safe as you decide you'll be," she said, knowing it was up to her to deal with whatever came. At least they were on their way home again. And now that Gary knew of her struggles, she had someone to turn to. Together, they would enlist Paul's help. She didn't dare contemplate whether he could offer a permanent solution. As of now, she could only take one day at a time.

Pulling on her coziest pants and an old knit sweater, she actually felt herself again. They'd only been on the *Settler I* for a few hours, yet if felt like she'd been gone for months.

She turned to leave, but was overwhelmed suddenly by a wave of emotion when she realized again that there were only two other crew members on this suddenly too large ship. Her knees buckled and she dropped into her comfy chair. Their original crew of eight—Max and Abigail were safely on their way back to Thesan—were now only three. She hadn't liked Yuko, and had despised Iago, but they hadn't deserved to die. And Iva. She would miss Iva, miss her kindness, her passion for video games, her sense of humour. And Gan. How would his pregnant Lily manage without him? Their child, never to know his father. All four of them deserved to have come home, to step foot once again on Thesan.

Margo lifted a hand and wiped tears from her wet cheeks. She hadn't realized she'd begun to cry but the thought of Lily and Iva, and the others, it was too much. Dropping her face into her hands, she wept, her shoulders shaking with grief.

She didn't know how much time had passed when she stopped. After blowing her nose, she took a few deep breaths. Then she stood, running her hand through her curls as she glanced around her safe, cozy cabin. Turning, she opened the door and stepped into the corridor. Ash had promised coffee.

Margo heard Gary before she saw him.

"Hey," he said, as she came down the spiral stairs.

Looking freshly showered, he rose from his seat at the table and came to greet her, hugging her when she got to the bottom of the stairs.

Margo sighed and smiled, relaxing into his welcome embrace. *Yes, I'm safe.*

She pulled away after a moment and looked up at him, cupping his face in her hands. How had she ever thought this warm-hearted, generous man was snobbish and stand-offish?

Their kiss was warm but all too brief.

She asked, "Are you okay?"

"Yeah," he said. He smoothed his hands over her damp curls. "Are you?" He resting his lips against her temple for a moment before once again meeting her gaze.

"I am now. Never let me go?"

Gary smiled. "Never."

"Promise?"

"I promise."

They were interrupted when Gan's petbot entered the galley from the passenger compartment, its shiny fur showing the same iridescence as the fish it was named for. It sauntered up to Gary and rubbed against his leg. As he reached down to pet it, it scooted over to rub against Margo's leg.

"It's as fickle as a real cat," observed Margo, with a laugh, stooping to pick it up. The synthetic fur was softer than a real cat's.

"I'll pour you a coffee," said Gary, going over to the galley and filling a mug. He brought it to the table, setting it in front of Margo, then took a seat beside her. "We should dig into those Brussel sprouts on the way back."

She pictured the box full of them sitting in the store room. "How about we send them out the airlock instead?"

"After being exposed to the slime mould, we'll need to replenish our sulphur—Brussel sprouts are teaming with that element." Gary smiled.

"Really?"

Gary nodded before turning to look at the petbot. "How much processing power is in that robot?"

Margo gave Gary a wide-eyed gaze as she realized the reason for his question. "Are you thinking it's infected with a Nigel II AI?" she asked, shifting her gaze to the robotic cat. It looked up at her and started to purr. *Is it just biding its time until it finds a time to attack?* She swallowed and she set the cat down on the cushion beside her.

"I'll be right back," she said to Gary as the cat jumped up onto the table.

In the storage room, she searched for a large bin with lock-down handles. She found one, but it was full of spare electronic parts. She dumped the contents onto the floor, unconcerned about the mess. The box was perfect.

She returned to the galley and set the open case on the floor beside her seat. She saw Gary's approving nod, but he didn't speak.

"Come here, Mackerel," she said, but the cat ignored her, staying where it was on the other end of the table.

She smiled at Gary, showing her patience, then resumed her seat. The cat strode down the middle of the table and dropped back into her lap. In a single motion, Margo lifted the petbot, put it into the case and closed the lid, snapping it shut, clipping the plastic handles down into the lock position. From inside the cat hissed.

"Schrödinger would be proud," said Gary, smiling at her.

"I'll get Vince to check his software when we get home," Margo said. "Do you want another cup of coffee?" she asked, standing.

Gary grabbed her hand before she could move towards the galley and swung her onto his lap.

She giggled, and wrapped her arms around his neck. "Why don't we go up to my cabin? I need to sleep, but first…"

Gary ran a hand up her back and into her hair. "First?" he teased, "Now that we are safe from possibly possessed robotic cats."

Just as Margo was about to kiss Gary, an image flashed into her head—Abigail and Max piloting separate shuttles full of builder bots. *Builder bots that could be infected with a Nigel II AI.*

She abruptly pulled away from Gary and he gave her a quizzical look.

"We have to warn them!"

Chapter Forty-Five

Standing before the bank of floor-to-ceiling windows that ran the length of his office wall, Nigel Maximilian West scowled down at the view below. The browns and blues of Earth rotated past, but he wasn't really watching. Instead his mind was stuck on that annoying, inconsequential, little colony in another system. It posed a problem he couldn't easily solve. At first he'd thought destroying it was the answer, now it was clear the Thesan colony had something he needed.

"We need to take control of the situation." Nigel turned and glared at the only other person in the room. "What if we keep the wormhole closed? Once we have a plan in place, then we open it."

"I advise against that plan," Fran said as she got up and walked over to him. Her high heels clicked against the real slate floor with every step she took.

"But as soon as we open the wormhole, they'll continue to transmit their lies against us," he said, balling his hands into fists at his sides. "Every time they do, our stocks drop a thousand points. Hell, even the Colonizing Council have been talking of opening a formal investigation into our dealings."

"Is that the endgame you fear?" asked Fran, her expression serine as she stared out the window at the Pacific Ocean.

Nigel followed her gaze. Only the brown dots of the Hawaiian Islands broke the ocean scene—everything below was ugly.

"No," he said feeling manipulated.

She nodded as she studied her profile. His advisor's salt-and-pepper hair was pulled back into a tight bun and her features looked like a woman's twenty years her junior. Fran had been his father's advisor. She'd been there when he and Beth were kids, and she'd shepherded him in the early days after his father's death. So far, she'd never steered him wrong.

Don't forget what she did to me, said Beth's childish voice from within his head. A lump caught in his throat as he glanced back down at Earth. Beth was only a figment of his imagination now. The scene of her death came back to him and he pushed it away.

With a set jaw and erect posture, Nigel turned and went over to the sideboard behind his desk. He poured himself two-thumbs widths worth of bourbon into a crystal tumbler before slumping down into his chair. Putting his feet up on his desk, he leaned back and took a sip.

"You know my plans are bigger than that," he said in a casual tone. "The endgame has been foretold. I'm going to make it happen, but…" He paused for dramatic effect. "I don't have all the necessary pieces."

Fran turned and raised an eyebrow.

"I need the cube back." Nigel locked eyes with Fran.

Maintaining his gaze, she returned to the chair facing his desk. She sat on the edge of the leather seat and crossed her legs.

"I have a plan," she said. "On their last comms window, the colony on Thesan requested proposals to mine the indium on their world."

Nigel gulped down the dregs of his bourbon. "That indium

327

would have lined our coffers nicely, but I'm over it now." He stood and poured himself another glass remaining facing away from Fran.

You can't trust her, said Beth in his head. He looked at the decanter of amber liquid and refused to respond—he couldn't trust his sister either. In the reflections of the cut-crystal he thought he saw his big sister's face. She always appeared as a child, but then she'd been a child when she died—no was murdered.

Nigel turned and leaned against the wall. Fran continued to sit primly, waiting for his response. She didn't even fidget with her hands, instead she kept them stationary, one on top of the other on her lap. Beth's worry about trusting Fran echoed in his head.

Sipping his drink, he continued to stare at his long-term advisor. She was the only one he had dared share his cube induced visions with. The only one who knew the extent of what he intended to do. And, the only one in as deep as he.

"Fine. Tell me your plan," he said.

"Winning the mining contract is our way into the colony," she said in a school teacher's tone. "Without raising suspicions."

"Of course they'll be suspicious and they're not going to fall for letting in any of our contractors, especially now that they've added former insurgents to their ranks." He raised the hand holding his glass and extended a finger towards Fran. "Remember, they now have that teenage hacker—you know, the one with a colour instead of a name."

"I'm not suggesting we use an existing front." Fran stood and placed a holographic cube on his desk. She activated it and an image of a mining ship appeared. "This is the *Ankh*, registered on the New Egypt Space Station. It's currently mining minerals on Jupiter's moons—and it has a long history of independent operations."

"So?"

"It's captain has a gambling problem and is in over his head in debt. Plus, the ship has already scheduled a major retrofit in the dockyards of its home port," she said putting both hands on his desk, either side of the projection. The glowing blue lines of the holographic ship added a pale glow to her face.

"You want to buy the ship and use it to apply for the mining contract?" Nigel took another sip of his liquor. "As I told you, they're going to be suspicious of all the applicants. How are we going to evade their scrutiny?"

"I've got that part sorted out," she said turning the image off.

Demand to know the details, said Beth. Ignoring her, he emptied his glass. *You fool!*

"Assuming we get the contract, then what?"

Fran walked around his desk and poured herself a drink from the decanter. Pressing his lips together, but not saying anything, Nigel held up his glass. Fran filled it.

"They have the cube, but it could be hidden anywhere," she said returning to her seat.

Nigel leaned forward. "We'll also need the boy."

"We need someone on the inside," she said. "I have someone in mind, we can contact her on the next comms window."

He took a sip and turned his attention to the view outside windows. "I think you have the beginning of a solid plan."

"Good," she said and stood. "I'll get to work." The sound of her high heels against the stone started to move away.

As Nigel studied the view, motion on the other side of the clear surface caught his attention. He stood and walked over. On the other side of the glass, in the vacuum of space, was a blue butterfly. It fluttered against the window as though it was looking for a way in.

"And Fran," he turned and looked at the woman.

"Yes?" She stopped and turned back towards him.

"I want my revenge on that bug girl," he said.

Fran smiled, for the first time Nigel realized the normally stern woman had dimples. "Keep focused and you'll get your chance."

Thanks for reading!

The next book will be the final instalment of the Settler Chronicles series. How is the colony going to fare when The Conglomerate makes their move? Will Margo and Nigel meet in person?

Please sign up for my newsletter here (http://jeannettebedard.com/) to get news about the next books in the series and some bonus goodies.

If you enjoyed this book, please take a moment to leave a quick review. As an independent author, reader reviews help build awareness for this series.

Acknowledgments

In no particular order I'd like to thank: Christine, Alana, Amy, Corinne, Chris and my Mom for being kind enough to provide feedback on early drafts. To Gavin for biology advice, and giving me time to write.

About the Author

By day I'm a scientist, by night I write science fiction. I have hard drives clogged with ideas and outlines—sometimes they dissolve into ones and zeros, but sometimes they coalesce to form an entire novel. My stories are filled with action and adventure where something always blows up, usually in the first fifty pages.

You can connect with me here: http://jeannettebedard.com/